FATHER OF
THE MAN

FATHER OF
THE MAN

A NOVEL

STEPHEN BENATAR

Copyright © 1993 by Stephen Benatar

Cover design by Gabriela Sahagun

ISBN: 978-1-5040-0789-4

Distributed by Open Road Distribution
345 Hudson Street
New York, NY 10014
www.openroadmedia.com

FATHER OF THE MAN

THE MAN

A NOVEL

STEPHEN BENATAR

Copyright © 1993 by Stephen Benatar

Cover design by Gabriela Sahagun

ISBN: 978-1-5040-0789-4

Distributed by Open Road Distribution
345 Hudson Street
New York, NY 10014
www.openroadmedia.com

For the late Dr Howard Gotlieb
of the Howard Gotlieb Archival Research Center
at Boston University, Massachusetts—
in memory of all his kindness, generosity,
and encouragement.

FATHER OF
THE MAN

PART I

Father of the Man

1

The shop had been there, near the British Museum, since 1867. On the outside it still advertised, in painted lettering at the top of each window, such wares as swordsticks and dagger canes and tropical sunshades. The present day was more prosaic. Mrs Whittaker-Payne had bought only a folding black umbrella.

Roger held the door open.

"As usual, such lovely service," she said. She was white-haired and patrician. Her gloved hand bunched arthritically round the silver crook of a rosewood stick. Her voice was resonant with a belief in herself and everything she stood for. "I shall see you in a month or so," she told him, "when I return to buy Christmas presents."

He felt tempted not to mention it. "In fact, madam, I'm leaving at the end of next week."

At first she didn't hear.

"Why? You struck me as being so happy in your work."

"I am. But some time ago we had to move to Nottingham."

She stared at him. "You can't possibly mean that you travel down from Nottingham each day?"

He nodded.

"Are you married?"

"No. I'm living with my parents."

"Then surely you could rent yourself a room or flat in town?"

"I did for a bit but . . ." He paused. "I really didn't like it."

"How old are you, young man?"

"Twenty-four."

"Well, I suppose you know what suits you best. In my day, young men of twenty-four no longer lived with their parents. I wish you luck, of course. I wish you every success." For a few seconds he watched her walk haltingly towards the traffic lights; her chauffeur, he knew, was parked around the corner. He'd wondered if he ought to escort her. Instead, though, he slowly closed the door and turned to where Rose was sitting, watching him sardonically. Mrs Whittaker-Payne had been their only customer for at least a quarter of an hour.

"Mrs Whittaker-Payne-in-the-Bum," remarked Rose. "Mr Roger Mild. Funny how people's names sometimes fit. Made me feel quite sick to see you sucking up to her!"

Rose was round-faced with a short haircut: bleached streaks amongst the natural brown. She looked neat in white blouse and black skirt yet had a tendency to dumpiness which a dress might better have disguised. Roger often thought her sharp-tongued but there were times when she could be unexpectedly generous.

"Why's she a pain in the bum?" He sat down next to her, on one of the upright cane-seated chairs. These were mainly intended for the customers but in the afternoon if trade were slack the assistants were permitted to use them. "And I wasn't sucking up to her," he added.

"Here! That's enough of that language if you please!" Running the length of the shop was a gallery from which the manager, seated at his desk, could survey nearly everything that went on. Thus had the founder of the firm kept himself informed of how business was progressing and been instantly aware of when the more distinguished of his customers set foot across the threshold: Mr Gladstone, maybe—Lord Shaftesbury—Sir Arthur Sullivan. Thus did Mr Alan Cavendish also keep himself *au courrant*. "Pain in the bum! Sucking up! I can't believe I'm hearing such low-class expressions from the staff of this establishment!" Mr Cavendish rose to his feet and glared. "I thought

I always made it abundantly clear: those were the prerogative of the management."

"Yes, you tell him, Mr Cavendish. Did you hear him just now? All but holding out his hand for the tip he was!"

"And so might I have been . . . if I'd considered it would work." Mr Cavendish was approaching fifty; tall—not quite so tall as Roger—pleasant-looking and bald. Like each of his male assistants he wore a suit. "It's plain you're going to miss him when he's gone," he said to Rose. He rubbed his forehead a little. "Anyway, I suppose it's nice that somebody is," he added mournfully.

2

On Sunday afternoon Roger's father invited him for a walk in the park to exercise Polly, their young cocker spaniel. But Roger, who was ensconced in one of the fireside chairs in the small dining room, flipping through a magazine and chatting with his mum, answered apologetically. He said there were things he needed to get on with. Ephraim Mild called him, lightly, a rotten so-and-so but otherwise concealed his disappointment. Collecting a handful of nuts in case he saw some squirrels, and shoving it into a pocket of his duffel coat, he left the house with a fairly jaunty "See you!" and an animated bit of conversation with the dog. He was feeling vulnerable; on the verge, he feared, of a depression, the first in about three months. Vulnerable, because he was jealous of his wife and hurt by the indifference of his children; also by the indifference of his wife—or by what he now perceived as such.

Two facts, closely related, had been edging him towards the pit. Last Friday his daughter, who lived with her boyfriend in Brussels, had returned there after a short holiday at home. On departure (Ephraim had cancelled an appointment at the office to be sure of getting to the station in time) his wife had received a warm hug and a kiss—"I'm really going to miss you, Mum!"—but he'd been given only a bright smile and a wave and when he'd moved forward with a *Hey, what about me?* had gained merely an impatient *Oh, Dad!* and a meaningless brush on the cheek.

He couldn't understand it: there hadn't been any conflict—not unless you put under that heading his insufficiently suppressed agitation at a call to Brussels lasting practically two hours. And admittedly Abigail had often been undemonstrative towards him when she'd been younger, but he'd supposed she had got over that by now; admittedly, too, she could on this occasion have been a shade preoccupied with guarding her luggage and her seat. Yet this hadn't drained the warmth out of her parting from Jean. "I'm really going to miss you, Mum!"

And then, yesterday morning, following so closely on this initial blow (and you could see how self-pitying was the word 'blow', how quick he was to assume the role of someone wronged)—okay, then, following so closely on this initial *occurrence*, there had come a news-filled letter from Oscar. Oscar, three years younger than Abigail and two years younger than Roger, was cycling through India at the present, sensibly making the most of his time between college and career to see as much of the world as he could. What had started as a bicycle tour round Europe with a friend—and already Ephraim had felt envious enough of this—had changed character in Budapest when the pair of them had been told, by young Australians, of an irresistibly cheap method of travelling into Asia and beyond. Perhaps the letter had been written with a wineglass at the writer's side, although the flowery, humorous language was anyway typical of Oscar; as indeed would have been the wineglass.

" . . . But you do all know, of course, that my love and prayers are ever with you. Particularly, I must say, with my beloved mother, who inevitably receives a large portion of my thoughts here in Calcutta . . . Abby, my sweet. Are you still home in the bosom of your loving family? Did you somehow forget to answer my little jot, which I hope reached you in Brussels? . . . Rodge, old pal. Fares well the world of commerce? Do you still sell brollies to the rich and famous and make merry conversation with hardy travellers from across the globe? . . . Father, my 'Great Man'. How is office life? I know how well you've managed to dodge and weave under the veil of your own overdrafts but will you be quite so astute with someone's account that's actually in the black? 'You've still got a little nest egg? Why come to me? Go home and be happy!' Write and let me hear of all the bankruptcies and people jumping out of penthouse windows . . . And darling Mother. Still holding the family together? The linchpin and the cornerstone? Blessed, sweet and unappreciated?" . . . and so on and so on, for this had come very close to the beginning—and might even have hinted at homesickness if any of the rest of it had. But no. Altogether it gave rise to little concern and was a source of much entertainment, enlightenment and speculation.

The 'Great Man', incidentally, referred to a three-year-old encounter of Ephraim's on an afternoon of sightseeing in Rome, where he had spent two penurious and abortive weeks looking for employment. At the Coliseum he had shared both an umbrella and an interesting conversation with a middle-aged Austrian advising on a nearby engineering project. Georg, who lived in Vienna, still corresponded with him roughly twice a year and last June he and his wife had given Oscar and Rick several days of lavish hospitality—during which, apparently, the alcohol had flowed and during which, apparently, Georg had spoken of Ephraim as being a great man.

"He spoke to me with clear emotion in his eyes, explaining the difficulty of talking of a father to his son, yet managing to emphasize your 'greatness'. 'I think your father is a . . . *great* man (this 'great' did not merely have the tones of 'fab' or 'brill' but of 'a leader of men' and 'newfound Messiah'). 'He has great . . . how should I say . . . insight. He sees through the surface.' I hope he didn't take my wild laughter in the wrong way."

How Georg had ever formed this opinion of him was as big a mystery to Ephraim as to everybody else; 'imperfect grasp of English!' was the predictable consensus. Ephraim remembered only that they had spent six hours together in the rain ("All the ingredients for a fine romance," wrote Oscar), that he had felt debilitated from a lack of food and that he had spoken of his dreams and disappointments. Georg had spoken about *his* ambitions too, the principle one being to become an interpreter, and since, despite the occasional, charming wobble—

"Dear Ephraim, you cannot imagine, or maybe you can, how a nice day it became after I received your letter. I read it in the tramway, standing amidst a lot of people and surely they got some radiation of friendlyness that escaped the envelope . . . "—since, despite the occasional charming wobble, this was a dream which Georg had realized, perhaps he then had proved to be the greater man. One thing, however, was certain. Ephraim had warmed enormously to Georg since learning of this radiation in the tramway or, with any luck, inside the tram itself, and had found it unaccustomedly easy to sit down and write a long letter to Vienna thanking him for his hospitality to Oscar. He really ought to nurture Georg, he had thought yesterday, somewhat listlessly, on having him brought back to mind. But at the same time he felt he wouldn't ever again have the energy, or inclination, to nurture anyone; the bottom line, he believed at present, was that people were only truly concerned about themselves . . . a reflection, maybe, more upon his own egotistical state. He could remind himself that people had died under interrogation rather than imperil the lives of others; he could remind himself of this but at the moment couldn't feel it. Nobody, other than a mother or a lover, genuinely cared deeply about anybody else: that should be the motto in this year's Christmas cracker. The only unqualified constancy came from the likes of Polly.

He found it helped a bit to walk with Polly in the park.

This afternoon, though, he unfortunately saw no squirrels. But as always when he walked this way he lingered by the pond where the ducks and geese kept up their usual clamour; and stood for several minutes gazing at the birds in their cages opposite—he hoped that they were happy—the budgerigars with their powder-puff blues or yellows, the pheasants and parrots equally beautiful in their brilliant, multi-coloured plumage, the ordinary domestic hens which he perhaps liked best of all, reminding him as they did of a childhood holiday near Lincoln, when with such seriousness and wonder he'd picked his way into the centre of the coop, scattering the grain, and been allowed inside the henhouse to collect the eggs. These were mostly brown and mud-smeared, with a feather or a wisp of straw sticking to them—sometimes, even, a spot of blood—and he could still remember the distinctive smell of it all, occasionally catch it sharply, borne in on a double-edged wave of nostalgia, during those frequent moments that he loved to spend here by the cages in the Arboretum. When they'd first moved to Nottingham, indeed, he had briefly hoped they might themselves be able to keep a few hens in the back garden—and Jean would have liked that too—but it was impractical, had gone the way, she remarked bitterly, of all their other little fantasies (a smallholding in France had figured amongst these). Had said it ironically, maybe, rather than bitterly.

After a while he left the park and let Polly off the lead again, in the cemetery across the road. He moved slowly, without his usual springiness of step—a man of middling height, quite nicely built, who had once, many years before, won medals for his dancing and a cup for his jiu-jitsu. You would hardly have looked at him twice, except perhaps for his eyes, which were blue and somewhat unexpected below his darkish—now receding—hair. People said of his face that it was open and good-natured; but what the hell was that supposed to mean? Open? Was it, for instance, the face of a man who would be expected to enjoy a walk through the cemetery as much as a walk through the Arboretum? Normally he found a graveyard salutary—especially when, as this, it was a place of trees and winding paths and had the prospect of a distant spire.

Yet today he found no solace. Today all the inscriptions which said in loving memory of this beloved wife or that lamented husband—mother, father, whatever—struck a merely mocking note. Today for possibly the first time in his life he could scarcely bear to contemplate them.

Take Abby, now.

Ephraim thought that Abby would never lament him, cry for him, as much as she had lamented, cried for, a friend, a fellow undergraduate, who had six years ago hanged himself.

And Roger? Well, about Roger . . . Ephraim even now admitted that he couldn't be quite sure. About Roger he would simply have to reserve judgment.

Oscar, though. Oscar was easy. Like Abby. Oscar was unlikely to mourn him as he had mourned Rick's dad—again this had happened six years before—Rick's dad, whom he had hardly known; mourned him pale-faced, almost silent, for two whole days, maybe three. At the time Ephraim had put it down to a sense of shock (no, it was Jean who had formulated this): shock that the tanned, athletic forty-three-year-old, with the boisterous sense of humour and the particularly loud laugh, who had reportedly collapsed in the middle of a nearby court whilst clawing grotesquely at the net, could in fact just as easily have been his own, Oscar's, dad. "You see, there but for the grace of God," said Jean, soberly, to a forty-six-year-old Ephraim, "there but for the grace of God, my love, go you."

But that had been then—then, when he'd had a fairly decent job and the money had been coming in with unwavering regularity.

Now he truly believed that Jean would never cry for him as much as she had cried last winter for her cat.

Oh, well. Who cared? He said it aloud. "Who cares?" Not just once but several times. Shouted it. "Who cares?"

A snatch of tune ran through his head. "I care for nobody . . . no, not I . . . and nobody cares for me."

It made him think not so much of *The Miller of Dee* as of an old black-and-white film he'd seen on television—and long before that, but he could scarcely remember it, at the Classic in Baker Street. The one with the Cornish Rhapsody and Margaret Lockwood; made sometime during the war.

Love Story. From the days when he had wept and been romantic . . . when he had actually believed in the possibility of a happy ending, even for the very messiest of situations and against the most unlikely odds. He had always wanted (well, perhaps this was a legacy from his parents, who certainly didn't have one, anyhow not together) . . . he had always wanted a love story.

3

"Heigh-ho," said Roger, "I suppose I'd better shift." He had to catch a
bus to the railway station. "Otherwise Dad will be back and I could
just as well have gone with him and Polly." He'd meant to get it over
with quickly, this chore of seeing to his ticket, and then return in time
to do some studying before tea. Once tea was over, it would be television, bath-time, bed. He had to be up in the morning by half-past-five.

"Anyway, it's good to see you take life easy," said his mother. She
too was relaxing: working on the embroidery pattern she'd bought two
years before in London. "I mean, doing nothing, not even watching
the wretched box." (By this time he'd cast aside the Sunday supple-
ment.) She herself watched television—quite a lot, indeed—but she
felt irritated by the fact. For her, it symbolized vicarious living, empa-
thy with those residing in trouble spots as well as anywhere else, whilst
Ephraim chiefly wanted to watch old movies, which he regarded as
a much-needed form of escape. Well, Ephraim would, wouldn't he?
"Take a leaf out of Oscar's book," she now counselled Roger, smilingly.

"No, thank you."

Jean looked up. Decided not to comment. It was the ant-and-
the-grasshopper syndrome. When she'd been fifteen or so Somerset

Maugham had been her favourite author. The trouble was that she liked—no, loved—both ants and grasshoppers. Loved them equally, though the first could be priggish, obstinate and far too serious, whilst the second could be infuriating, wildly irresponsible, leave an emptied saucepan standing on a burning hotplate, allow the bathwater to overflow.

Ironically, though, each had the wrong appearance to match up with his own half of the metaphor. The ant was long and scrawny; the grasshopper was squat. The ant didn't care much about clothes but could easily have been stylish. The grasshopper, when in England, subscribed to the *Gentlemen's Quarterly* but failed to attain the casual elegance he saw therein and struggled so to emulate. Roger took after his granddad—Jean's father—not only in height but in his regular and clean-cut features; his hair was thick and lightly waved, dark brown, possessed a natural sheen. Oscar's was dry, mouse-coloured, kinky. Furthermore, Oscar's nose had been broken at football, then badly set. Nor were his teeth as white and even as his brother's. But what he did have was his *smile*. His smile and his charm and his sex appeal. Jean had often told him this and she didn't care if that wasn't the sort of thing you were supposed to say to your own son. She wanted her children to be confident.

In fact, Abby and Oscar *were* confident; nowadays she had few fears for either of them. In the latter's own words he was 'a bouncer-back upon the tennis court of life'. The same was true of Abby. And the game they played was one which they'd both most likely win; plus, there was almost sure to be good money in it. Yet regarding Roger she felt less certain. Far less so. For one thing, he was too sensitive. His siblings were sensitive as well—she couldn't have loved them so dearly if they weren't—but they hadn't the same vulnerability (Oscar called it softness), they wore a protective covering which their brother seemed to lack. Roger carried Abby's and Oscar's qualities to extremes. He was completely reliable, more so than they, perhaps more considerate too, more attached to concepts of justice and integrity—this time Oscar called it stuffy, yet did so with unmistakable affection—indeed, Roger was everything that from some viewpoints was the most admirable; but it wasn't necessarily the world's viewpoint, and these days, for Jean, it was sometimes the world's viewpoint which mattered most. Roger was a plodder. A plodder could be held up in school as an example, but a plodder wasn't dashing, didn't gamble, and didn't, not usually, end up rich. Not poor either, maybe, but not rich-rich, let's-go-for-a-first-class-meal sort of rich, let's drive to London for the weekend, let's fly off to the Bahamas or the Caribbean. Plodders didn't get the fun out of life that life should have on offer.

Nor unfailingly, of course, did non-plodders. Look at herself. Look at Ephraim.

No, don't. Don't look at either of them; the spectacle would prove too disheartening for the observer, too shaming for the observed. Yet once—the pair of them—oh, such high hopes as they had had, such plans, such conversations: midnight conversations; lights-out and holding-hands-in-bed conversations, one o'clock, two o'clock, three. Not invariably sinful hopes, either, requiring the bended knee to Mammon—what about that smallholding in the Dordogne they had so frequently discussed?—she thought they could have made a go of that. A secondhand camper or estate car? . . . now they didn't have *any* sort of car and, anyway, Ephraim still couldn't drive, neither of them could, nor had they taken lessons. (Both Abby and Oscar, however, had passed on their first attempts.) Theirs was the only family she knew that didn't have a car. She had to drag the shopping back from Tesco's in a bus. She'd used to catch a taxi home but in recent weeks even a taxi—although the journey cost well under two pounds, they didn't live that far from the Victoria Centre—even this was out of the question. (And if she ever went to Sainsbury's, which actually she preferred, there was a far longer walk to the bus stop.) Oh, damn it. Damn it all. She wanted so much better for her children.

Suddenly she stood up. "Darling, how about a cup of tea before you go? I'll put the kettle on." It was comfortable, sitting here before the gas fire with Roger; she didn't want the moment to end too quickly.

As she ran the tap she allowed herself a bleak, unwitnessed smile. She herself at one time could have been described as a bouncer-back upon the tennis court of life . . . before twenty-six years of marriage had worn out the soles on her Reeboks. Had broken the strings on her racket. Had, into the bargain, made her overweight.

Too bad that she, like Oscar, hadn't taken after her father, that she'd inherited the waistline problems and relative lack of inches on her mother's side of the family.

But she'd also inherited the prettiness of her mother, and on good days, in a good light, the prettiness, much of it, remained. Chestnut hair was now reinvigorated from a sachet but on the increasingly rare occasions when she could afford to have it cut or when, as Ephraim's Great-Aunt Julia had been wont to say, it looked as if it were her birthday, she could still draw a glance or two in the street . . . unless, that is, she was with Abby, who seemed to have inherited the best from everyone, the willowy figure, the regular features, the smile, the sex appeal, the auburn hair—the only thing she had obviously missed out on was Ephraim's blue eyes. Well, Jean didn't begrudge her one iota of that admiration. Just so long, dear God, as she always made the most of what opportunities it might present and didn't get entangled with weak men. If a man was weak, it probably didn't compensate if basically he were lovable. And most certainly it didn't as you grew older, had less energy, fewer illusions, a greater need of protection.

She remembered whilst waiting for the kettle that she hadn't yet looked today at the paperback which Oscar had given her on her last birthday, along with the chocolates and the wine and the flowers, and which she kept propped against the microwave. "Listen to this, darling," she called. Then she came to stand in the archway between the two rooms—there wasn't a door—holding the book at some distance from her eyes. "It's exactly twenty-one years since Jackie Kennedy married Onassis. There was a marriage settlement. If she left him in the first five years she'd get twelve million pounds; *pounds*, not dollars; and if he left her he'd pay six million for every year the marriage had survived. What do you think of that?"

"Not very much. What do you?"

"No, not very much, either." Even as she said it she recognized that maybe she wasn't being consistent. But naturally there was a difference between avarice and ambition; between fighting for alimony that was astronomical and fighting for your rightful place among the stars. "Oh, listen. This was the birth date in 1780 of a man called Thomas Horne. Apparently he spent a whole seventeen years counting every word and letter in the Bible. Concluded there were three-quarters of a million words—well, give or take—and three-and-a-half million letters."

Roger bit his lip. "He evidently imagined he was doing something useful. Poor fellow. Seventeen years! I wonder if he woke up every morning and felt excitement about the day that lay ahead?"

The kettle began to boil. Jean returned the bulky volume to its place. "Anyway, thank you, Oscar, for today's addition to our little store of learning. Bless you, my sweetheart, wherever you may happen to be at this moment and whatever you may happen to be doing."

"Amen," said Roger. Even with a friend, he knew he would never have dared to emulate his brother's behaviour.

To be so far from home! To have so little money! To be able to speak only English and a smattering of French!

He sometimes resented Oscar but he wished he had a portion of his courage.

Blu-tacked to the fridge was a picture of the Ganges: not surprisingly, Oscar sent more postcards than letters, though not even a great many of *those*. The Ganges! Well, at any rate, thought Jean, last July she and Ephraim had bought themselves a time-share flat in Spain. They had borrowed heavily but it was worth it. *Mi Jardin* didn't appeal to her that much—oh, of course it would be interesting to have a look at it just once—yet the joy of the thing was its incorporated system of exchange which meant that, in theory, they would now have the option of travelling almost anywhere, even to places like the banks of the Ganges, or Japan or Canada or South America. It was like a throwing open of the world's portals when she had begun to believe them closed to her forever. A time-share apartment meant, *in theory* (if they could only raise the cash), the almost unheard-of luxury of going on holiday each year, because a good part of it would already have been paid for and Ephraim couldn't bear to throw away his money—although in fact there was an arrangement whereby you could let the apartment and not lose anything, a kind of escape clause, but she didn't think Ephraim had absorbed this yet and she certainly saw no need to point it out to him.

Escape clause . . . when a time-share in itself symbolized the happiest escape route anybody could imagine? Adventure! A broadening of horizons! Unending source of wondrous anticipation and of wondrous conjecture! Before this, she had often lain awake torturing herself with the thought of all the faraway places she would never get to see; for some nights back in July, however, she had been kept awake by sheer excitement at the prospect of the countless enticing paths which now led off from the prison.

She poured their cups of tea and brought them through. "Like a rock cake?" she asked. "I think there should be one left."

"No, thanks."

"Yes, do. If not, your father will only get it. And you're the one who's still a growing lad."

But again he shook his head. He took a reflective sip.

"There's nothing wrong between you and Dad, is there?"

She shrugged. "Oh, well," she said. "You know your father. We often have our moments."

At first it seemed as if she might clarify these statements. But she went on: "No, no, of course there isn't. What even made you ask?"

She rose from her chair and went to add some more milk.

4

There were three people ahead of him in the queue at the ticket office. The first was a soldier who was having trouble with his rail warrant; the clerk was needing to explain the same few points over and over again, his patience waning visibly at each repetition. The clerk was a young man with a ponytail and one earring, both of which assorted oddly with his collar, tie, tweed jacket. While Roger waited—there was also a male dwarf in front of him and a fat teenage mother, with a black eye and a baby—he idly looked around the vast booking hall at things which he had never noticed before: particularly at some decorative pillars high up on the walls with, between them, porthole windows encircled by stone wreathes and, beneath them, squares of green and brown marble. None of this was especially interesting but it annoyed Roger that in a year of coming and going he hadn't once been aware of it. He was also annoyed by the obtuseness of the soldier; by the unchecked mucus running from the baby's nose; by the minutes ticking past without apparent progress. His annoyance deepened. What was really beginning to get to him was the economy of having only one ticket window open, when the price of the annual fare to London had now risen to roughly three-and-a-half thousand pounds—when, because of this, he was having to give up his job and didn't know what the heck he was going to do about a new one—when even trying to work out the alternatives had the power to make him speedily loose-bowelled. And in the face of all this they had only one ticket window open. You'd suppose for the prices they charged they might offer you a bit of service.

No. That was unfair, he thought. After all, it was a Sunday afternoon; such complicated business over a rail warrant was possibly quite rare. Nor was British Rail responsible for his general lack of awareness. Nor for the baby's mucus. Not even for that wretched sinking feeling which grew daily more weighty in the pit of his stomach.

Well, not *wholly* responsible, anyway . . . he managed a tight grin.

But for the moment he felt as though it were.

The dwarf, in red lumberjacket and shiny black sneakers, who could barely reach the round portion in the window through which you were supposed to speak—and, momentarily, Roger felt guilty and ungrateful: how could he ever have supposed his own life to be difficult?—the dwarf was quickly seen to. So was the young mother, who looked strained, desperate, ground down, beaten. And where, he'd wondered, was *she* going, in what kind of room, amidst what degree of comfort, would she finally find some sort of refuge—and, likewise, what chance of any healthy, innocent childhood could ever exist for her baby? But what might he himself do about it; how could he possibly interfere? Potentially insult her by offering money? For he couldn't offer her anything else, not even very much of that. He could—and did—say a silent prayer, but the fact he had only belatedly thought of it showed he didn't basically have a lot of trust in the power of prayer.

And then, pretty soon getting back to his own problems (of course!), he knew it didn't really help, at least not for very long, his trying to concentrate on others who were worse off than himself; you merely had to think of Cardboard City or of all those thousands who spent the night in shop doorways, often in temperatures that must be freezing, even inside a sleeping bag . . . He often imagined how he would feel if he were homeless. By God, it had been bad enough during the time he'd lived in a bed-sitting-room, in Hampstead. That had been in the first year after his parents removed to Nottingham. The room had been small but it had been adequate—bed, wardrobe, table, wooden chair—and, no, he had not been cold. But he hadn't managed to make any friends and he'd hated having to return to London early every Sunday evening; had invariably been close to tears, the complete and utter milksop. He was a Cancer, a crab, just like his mother: a home-lover, not happy when he hadn't got the things—or, rather, the people; things didn't matter to him much—the people round him that he loved. He was a little boy. He was twenty-four years old and yet a little boy. When Mrs Whittaker-Payne had asked him on Friday why on earth he commuted he had felt ashamed, as though the truth were immediately self-evident: *Because I miss my mummy and daddy.*

At the moment, however, even if he were a little boy he was an angry little boy. He'd spent over fifteen minutes in the queue and not simply had it seemed longer, far longer, but if he didn't throw off his present bad mood he would probably waste more of his time when he got home. And he had no right to be in a bad mood. So much for trying to enter into the trials of the pair who'd been immediately in front of him! So much for asking God to shower his blessings down on *them* and to instil in himself a profound and lasting gratitude! (And *at once Lord*, he had meant, *at once!* In both cases.) Besides, he had no right to be in a bad mood, not even on other grounds; the delay hadn't been the clerk's fault.

And now, as he walked up to the window, he reminded himself of this.

"I want to inquire about my season ticket," he said. "I'm afraid it expired yesterday. Would it be possible, please . . . I mean, I think it is possible . . . to extend it by six days? By the six days I lost when you were all on strike this year."

The clerk replied: "Those six days will be added to your new season ticket, sir." He was perfectly polite but he sounded bored; bored yet impatient. It was nearly as though he'd yawned or as though he'd looked over Roger's shoulder and already said, "Next, please." Making up for lost time. There were a couple more in line he could have been saying it to.

"But I don't want a new season ticket," said Roger. "I only need those six days."

"No season ticket, no extension. But you can put in for a refund."
The young man rubbed the lobe that had no earring.

To Roger this sounded like a typically bureaucratic way of saying
the same thing. "Okay. I'd like to do that, please."

"Six pounds a day," said the clerk.

"Excuse me? I don't quite follow. What's six pounds a day?"

"The amount of the refund."

"No, I'm sorry, I've explained myself badly. I've got to go to London
just another six times, then I'm finished. So in a way, yes, I do need a
new season ticket, but only one that's going to see me through this
coming week. Therefore all I need to ask you for—in place of an extension—is a six-day pass, starting from tomorrow."

"Fine," said the clerk. "Ninety pounds fifty, then." He seemed to be
waiting for Roger to hand over that amount of money.

Roger simulated laughter. "No, don't forget this is a refund!"

"Yes. A refund of six pounds a day. Making thirty-six pounds in all.
Which means your weekly season will now cost you . . . " he hesitated
" . . . only fifty-four pounds fifty."

"So the fare is roughly thirteen pounds a day," said Roger, after a
rapid calculation, "and you're offering me back six?"

"If you want to look at it like that."

"Do you think that's fair?"

"Nothing to do with me."

No, of course it wasn't, but surely the man could have shown some
glimmer of sympathy. They were approximately the same age. Yet,
instead, his patience seemed as strained as it must have been when
dealing with the soldier. "Sunday bloody Sunday!" he might say, when
he was next in a position to unwind. "*What* an afternoon I've had! You
wouldn't believe it!" And for a moment Roger simply stared. Then he
turned away, without another word. He didn't know what more to say
and definitely 'thank you' wasn't going to be an option.

He sat down limply on one of the wooden benches nearby. He felt
numb.

After about five minutes, however, he went down to the station
manager's office, which was situated between platforms four and five.
It was red-bricked, had an entrance on either platform—though one

21

said Private—and small, opaque windows through which a stack of empty cartons could be seen, a clipboard propped against the glass, and a couple of rubber plants. He knocked, then entered without hearing a response. The room was far from spacious. There were white walls; an old bicycle leaning against one of them; polystyrene tiles on the ceiling. In the centre of the place stood a desk that had a litter of paperwork scattered over its glass top. Two middle-aged officials had clearly been chatting companionably: one sitting behind the desk, the other with his bottom perched on a corner of it, tearing with his teeth at a thumb cuticle. They looked at Roger in a friendly and inquiring manner. When he explained that he wanted to speak to the station master, the one with the cuticle rose and said he ought to be getting back to his work anyway. Roger had to move over, to make room for the passage of a fairly striking girth. The official nodded amiably.

The one who was left wasn't in uniform. He wore a brown suit. Brown tie. He was a slight man; had a long narrow face and a long narrow nose. Gingery hair surrounded a bald pate which reflected the light—there was an illuminated square, glass-covered, amidst the polystyrene. Still seated, he prompted Roger to disclose his problem.

"I didn't realize," answered Roger, "there was going to be a problem. Otherwise, you see, I wouldn't have left it so late. I'm sorry about that."

In fact, it had all seemed so simple and straightforward. The neatness of the six days owing and the six days required . . . Roger had viewed this almost as a sign that everything was *meant*.

He told the man, less succinctly than he'd hoped to, exactly what the trouble was.

"And if you can't extend my ticket I was wondering if I couldn't . . . you know . . . have a . . . whether you couldn't just give me some kind of a pass." He shrugged, and again gave an apologetic smile.

"Wish I could," said the station master. "But even if something like that were possible—which I doubt—I'd still have to get authorization from our area office at Derby." He pursed his lips slightly and looked at the two plants on the windowsill as if speculating on whether or not they needed water.

"Excuse me, then, but . . . but couldn't you give them a ring?"

"What, on a Sunday? No, no, they don't work weekends." The very idea that anyone should think they did appeared to fill him with wonder and amusement and even a touch of pity. Now his glance travelled towards the bicycle. Roger imagined an ironical lift to the eyebrow: perhaps he was envisaging low handlebars and seeing himself bowling along country lanes on this bright October afternoon instead of sitting in a poky office poring over paperwork.

"So what do I do tomorrow?"

"I'm afraid you'll have to pay."

"But I haven't any money."

"Borrow some." There could have been the hint of a question mark but certainly no more than a hint. Perhaps absentmindedly, he had picked up a pencil and was now rolling it beneath his right palm, back and forth across a small uncluttered space of desk. A poor substitute for freewheeling down an autumn hillside—maybe with your wife and children. The interview had not contained the friendliness it promised. Nor any feeling of genuine goodwill.

"I don't know if I can."

"Better stay home, then. You haven't got much choice."

Rather than catch a bus back Roger decided to walk. When he opened the front door the smell of baking bread came out to him. His mother was chopping vegetables for a soup; Polly sat begging for pieces of potato peel. "Darling, you wouldn't like to feed her, would you? Get her out from under my feet?"

By this time Roger had grown calmer. He collected the dog's bowl and took the tin-opener from the drawer. "Where's Dad?"

"I think he must have gone upstairs. I think he must be lying down." Jean's tone was suddenly so neutral, so audibly neutral, that in fact it wasn't neutral at all.

"Oh dear."

"Yes. Oh dear, indeed." But she made a visibly conscious effort not to elaborate on the point. "Were things all right at the station?"

"What makes you think they wouldn't be?"

"Nothing whatever. Just an unconsidered turn of phrase, you poor pedantic boy." She threw a carrot in the bin, as having grown too rubbery even to make soup. Then, possibly alerted by something in the tone of his response, she repeated her question. "Were they?"

"No. Not really."

"Why? What happened?" Her vegetable knife stopped slicing and she turned to face him with automatic concern.

As he spooned out the dog food and Polly scrabbled excitedly at his trouser leg, her tail lashing frantically, he reported as faithfully as he could the substance of what had been said. "But as I walked home I got more and more bolshie. Even if I have to pay for only one day's ticket, that's over forty quid. And it's so unfair. When they took my money they engaged to give me three-hundred-and-sixty-five days of travel. Consecutive travel." Roger had rehearsed that phrase.

"I know, love, I know. But it's no good getting all het up over it. I still have a spot of emergency cash left in the building society. I'll write you out a cheque."

"Yet it *isn't* fair, Mum. I shouldn't just give in to it. 'If we can keep you as a customer we'll certainly pay you back the days we owe! If not—sorry, mate—just thirty-six pounds, not a penny more!' That's effectively what they said to me."

Jean touched his forearm sympathetically, then turned back to her preparation of the vegetables. "Darling, you never seem to learn. All your life you've complained that something or other isn't fair; but what have you ever been able to do about it? The world *isn't* fair—sooner or later we all have to become resigned to that. So why not follow the man's advice: just stay at home tomorrow? We'll go to the cinema . . . and afterwards have coffee and cake; we can pretend we're on a date!" At the moment Jean worked only three days a week, in an antiques shop, although she was thinking, regretfully, that she would soon have to look for something better-paid. She laughed; there was a note of excitement in her laughter. "Have we *ever* been to the pictures together, without anyone else in tow?"

But Roger refused to be drawn. He watched Polly, who was by now pushing her bowl right across the kitchen, pushing it with tongue reluctant to acknowledge there was no more left. "And then what happens on Tuesday?"

"*Indiana Jones,*" persisted his mother, "you said you wanted to see it. Oh, darling, do say yes! And I'll be the one to speak to Mr Cavendish, to tell him you're not well."

"*Anything—so long as you never lie!* That's what you used to say."

"Oh, Roger, don't be such a . . . "

"What?"

"And apart from anything else, my pet, think how embarrassing you'd find it." However, she didn't expatiate on what 'it' was. "You—who won't even wear a bright tie in case it draws attention to you. You—who always wear a belt *and* braces."

"What in God's name has that to do with anything?" Yet he didn't wait for an answer. "And, anyway, when do I complain so much about everything being unfair?"

"Don't say you don't even realize you do it. I thought you knew yourself better than that."

"No. Tell me. When do I do it?"

"It's not important," said Jean.

"But I want to know."

She sighed. The excitement had gone out of her. "It's only over small things. Like when Oscar's had one of those little strokes of luck he always does seem to be having. Don't you remember when you said to me, 'How is it that Oscar keeps finding things—like that Rolex wristwatch which nobody ever claimed—or discovers money in his account which was clearly put there by mistake but just as clearly nobody ever missed? How is it that every time, whatever happens, he comes up smelling of roses?'"

"And you said he was born under a lucky star, that's simply the kind of person he is."

Jean was wiping her hands down her flowered apron. "Anyhow, will you come to see *Indiana Jones* with me?"

He shook his head. "Sorry. No. I can't."

"Then I'll go to write you that cheque." Her voice had taken on something of the expressionless tone in which she had spoken about his father.

"No, Mum. I don't want one."

"All I'll do is sign it. You'll fill in the rest. You'd better take my card;

for heaven's sake don't lose it." This last bit was intended to be humorous.

"But I don't want them, neither the cheque nor the card."

"Don't be naïve, Roger—please. I'll leave them both on the sideboard. You've got long enough to consider it. I can't do with two difficult men in this house at the same time."

Roger shook his head again. His mouth was set in a stubborn line. She had sometimes told him he had all the stubbornness of his father.

"Because if you get a police conviction and completely ruin your prospects don't think you can just run back to us to fix it. Oh, and by the way, the money's a gift, not a loan. We'll manage somehow; your father needn't know." She indicated vaguely the vegetable rack beside her; on Saturday mornings, in the market, she always stocked up on plenty of vegetables. "The only way I want you to repay me is by not making a mess of your life because of some adolescent idea about the way things ought to be. That might have been all right for Sunday school in the reign of Queen Victoria but after ten years of Margaret Thatcher I can tell you it absolutely *isn't!*" There was a tremor in her voice. He was suddenly afraid that she was going to cry. She walked rapidly past him.

There was a further question he had meant to ask but now realized he couldn't. If it had been Oscar and not me . . . would your advice have been the same? Or do you think that he, born under his lucky star and able to talk his way out of practically anything, might *still* have come up smelling of roses?

Though he wondered whether Oscar, caught in such a situation, would also have declined her proffered means of escape.

One thing sure, however: his fears, when he next saw her, proved well-founded; it was clear she had been crying. Him? His father? She didn't refer to it or to what had caused it but Roger naturally felt responsible. He knew this would have sounded corny but he really thought she must be among the best of mothers in the world.

His father, too, remained very quiet.

Yet somehow they all got through their supper, without anyone tempestuously leaving before it was over.

* * *

He didn't sleep well. Supposing I'd been an American at the time of Vietnam, he thought. Or old enough to be called up during the war? Supposing I'd been a dissident Chinese student only a few months back? Not much comparison, really: on British Rail no tanks nor bombs nor bullets. No napalm. Not even all that many sticks and stones.

And words can never hurt me.

He'd been awake before his alarm rang. About an hour later, on the train, he opened his briefcase and took out a packet of the sandwiches his mother had prepared the night before: every morning he found two such packets in the fridge, carefully foil-wrapped; also a banana, washed apple and some other piece of fruit. Occasionally a bar of chocolate. He'd considered waiting for his breakfast until the conductor had come—or more accurately, of course, gone—but that mightn't be for ages. He wasn't hungry, in fact to eat would be an effort, yet he didn't feel that *after* would be any easier than *before*. And by then, too, people would be more aware of him. Besides, he had to try to take his mind off things.

For this reason also, while he was getting through the first half of a sandwich, and beginning, against all expectation, to realize it was doing him good, he opened his ring binder; studied the printed sheet that lay immediately inside. It was the Advanced Level paper in History, 1399-1714, set for the previous summer. As a painstaking method of revision Roger was slowly working his way through it; he himself would be sitting the examination next year. It was even possible some of the same questions could resurface.

He'd already passed his 'A' level in Literature and his 'A' level in Geography. When History was added to these, his way would then be clear to go to university, like Abby and Oscar. For a long time now Roger had been half-regretting his decision to leave school at sixteen. He'd been stupid and obstinate—yes, his mother had been angry with him then as well; it had been only his dad who had backed him up— but he had never had much of an academic bent, nor been all that keen on mixing with his peers, and it had somehow seemed more important to begin to earn a living, help out at home, get an early start. Degrees no longer appeared a certain passport to an interesting career.

But he had stayed with the bank for only three-and-a-half years. He had never expected breathtaking adventure—no. Yet nor had he been prepared for the sheer, corrosive boredom of it.

By contrast, he had really enjoyed the umbrella shop. Despite the daily dusting and other small elements of drudgery, he had felt liberated. And because the business was still family-owned he had felt, too, an appreciated and individual part of it.

For shop work, moreover, it was outstandingly well-paid. He had been looked after and he had done his best to be of value. He had believed he had a future there.

And now—this! If the business had been doing well, Mr Cavendish had said, he'd somehow have found the three-and-a-half thousand pounds . . . with no one but the firm's accountant being aware of it. Yet the last two summers had been unusually dry, the rates were about to be increased, if the increase were dramatic the shop might even have to close. And Roger hadn't saved the wherewithal out of his wages; was amazed he hadn't so much as thought about it. Also, he couldn't work out where all his money had gone. Of course, there was what he paid his mother, plus a few pounds a week to Scottish Widows—a friend of Uncle Nathan's had fixed him up in that—and there was a standing order to Oxfam, too, for he had followed Abby's example; from the age of eleven or twelve she had always given to charities. But otherwise . . . well, it had just gone. He had spent it on bits and pieces round the house: some curtains, a carpet, a wardrobe: and on taking weekly driving lessons in the hope that he'd become the first member of his family to drive. But he'd already taken his test three times and although he was good (his instructor told him he was near-perfect, apart from his tendency to be overcautious) he kept on failing in confidence whenever the examiner got in. He had parked in front of somebody's driveway, had mounted the kerb whilst reversing, had even, incredibly, messed up a hill-start. Crazy things like that.

Yet when faced with only a written exam he was fine; and he was glad that he now had these 'A' levels to concentrate on—in some ways it was almost lucky he hadn't taken them at school—if simply to show there were things he could actually succeed at. University still didn't appeal to him but he'd suddenly needed to prove, even long before the driving tests, that if he didn't go there it was simply because he'd chosen not to. Also, in a vague, unformulated way, he'd viewed it as a kind of present to his mum. Added to which, he'd never had a proper hobby. His studying had been a godsend during his year in that bed-sitter. It had been yet more of a godsend, maybe, during these past twelve months of Intercity travel.

He wasn't going through the questions in the History paper in sequence and unfortunately he had finished over the weekend the one he'd spent the whole of last week answering. Which meant he was having to start an entirely new piece of work this morning; and at the moment he was finding it hard not merely to make a choice but even to understand the meaning of the question.

Discuss the view that the ambitions of Henry V in France left a task for his successors that was too great for the resources of the English Crown.

His sandwiches today were cream cheese with sultanas and stem ginger; and, more conventionally, Cheddar with cucumber and pickle. He'd told his mother more than once she ought to write a recipe book on the making of sandwiches. Even though money was tight her invention seemed practically unflagging; repetitions rarely occurred within a fortnight and, anyway, were seldom unwelcome. Each day she provided two kinds: a round of each for his breakfast and a round of each for his lunch.

How far was English cultural development in the later Tudor and early Stuart period both Court-led and Court-inspired?

He just sat staring through the window, not really noticing the taste of cream cheese or ginger or pickle, nor the golds and russets of the countryside, the blue sky, the brightness of the grass—yet possibly deriving benefits from each of them—and thought of all the different ways in which he might have saved money and how different his situation at this present instant would then have been. His own resources, or lack of them, temporarily took precedence over the resources of the English Crown, or lack of them, either in the later Tudor period or at any other time. Considerations of English cultural development were similarly delayed.

Therefore, when the conductor came, it was a total anticlimax.

"Tickets, please. Thank you, sir. Thank you, sir. Thank you, madam." His approach seemed agonizingly slow.

Roger held out the little plastic wallet that contained his out-of-date ticket. The conductor gave it only the briefest of glances.

"Thank you, sir." He moved on down the carriage.

5

Despite his depression, Ephraim—whilst shaving on that Monday morning; and at least he could bring himself to shave, unlike other occasions on which even getting out of bed had seemed practically beyond him—Ephraim now found himself humming a song which must have been popular at the beginning of the Fifties. He could pinpoint it like that because he could recollect singing it to his mother in the kitchen of their flat in Marylebone: his hitting home the punchline and her pretence of being aggrieved at such a display of sauciness. Indeed it was only the finish he could properly recall.

> "Dearie, life was cheery
>   In the good old days gone by . . . "

And—ah, yes—shock, horror!

> "If you remember, say you remember,
>   Then, dearie, you're much older than I . . . "

Surely he couldn't have been much more than thirteen when this type of humour would still have appealed to him. He might have said surely he couldn't have been much more than thirteen when he would still have sung to her. But he knew this wasn't so. They'd often had spot-the-tune competitions until he was maybe in his twenties and even now he could see his mother's look of concentration when trying to identify the song being hummed to her or trying to recapture the tune of something she was hoping might then confound *him*. And he could see the little table at which they'd generally been sitting, the little table with the American oilcloth on it and the flimsy flap nearly always extended, and over their heads the shelf containing all the jars and breakfast cereals in daily use: the Nell Gwyn marmalade, the extract of malt, the barley kernels, grape-nuts or post-toasties.

Suddenly he had such a vivid picture of the whole kitchen: the dresser with the willow-pattern china, the wooden draining board, soft and scuffed between the worn-down ridges, the window with its view of other war-neglected chimneys, roofs and windows. He saw the tiny shaky-legged fridge, dating back to sometime in the Thirties, the equally insubstantial cooker set into a recess, the bottle of Bev on the mantle above this, along with the Mazawattee, the matches, the candles, the cookbooks—suggestions for wartime dishes from Countess Morphy or from Betty Brand of the *Sunday Graphic*—and right in one corner, hidden by the books, his mother's totally indispensible Lixen, aka Elixir of Senna. Ephraim smiled; his smile was wistful rather than amused. Because the room was easy to warm with just a one-barred electric fire, they often sat there in the evenings, he doing his homework, she also sitting at the table, typically in her black-and-white checked housecoat and reading the latest Philip Gibbs or Frances Parkinson Keyes, smoking her Senior Service, making frequent cups of tea and equally frequent inquiries into the progress of his work. These last were seldom nagging; almost invariably sympathetic and encouraging, or congratulatory. She thought he had such a brilliant future; the word 'loser', had she known it, would never, not even remotely, have entered her head. When Ephraim looked back on these times, his mother's companionship seemed almost inseparable from her approval. Indeed, as he razored the lather off his chin (it was impossible to believe this could be essentially the same chin which he'd had in 1945, on that sunny July afternoon when he'd first walked into the empty echoing flat three floors above MacFisheries, the flat which to this day he could still think of instinctively, before any other place, as home), as he razored off the lather he saw a slow tear forming in the corner of one eye, and then another instantly brimming beneath the other lid. He hadn't always found his mother fault-free—far from it—but he now, fleetingly, had an unexpected vision of the moment of his own death: saw her waiting to greet him at the end of that dark tunnel, saw her again looking young and very pretty, all the later lines of sadness and abandonment erased, as she stepped light-footedly towards him, half-dancing, to the tune of *Dearie, do you remember* . . . ; she, too, in her youth had won several medals on the dance floor.

Abruptly, Ephraim wiped the remnants of foam from his face. "I miss you, Mum," he said. He also wiped away, a bit impatiently, the large yet unspilt tears.

"I miss you, Mona," he said.

"I miss you, Joan."

He could easily have added several others to the list.

Downstairs, there was a letter from the bank. He and Jean had a joint account but he was the one who had to deal with all the correspondence. Six months ago she had told him flat that she wanted no more to do with money matters; that was to be his department. Their financial situation only got her down, she said, she already had more than her share of worry over such things.

"Dear Mr and Mrs Mild,

"We are concerned that you are using your Connect Card when there are insufficient funds available in your account to meet them (sic). In the circumstances you leave us with little alternative than to formerly (sic) request that you return your card to us forthwith. Your failure to take this line of action will result in a caution being placed on the card which will cause you embarrassment when you come to use the card in the future. (Sick.) A prepaid envelope is provided for your use. Please cut the card in two before posting.

"Yours sincerely."

Nobody had signed it.

There was a second item of mail. This was a Notice of Proceedings, " . . . to effect the recovery of total amount owing—£4,275—which sum is due to Swan International . . . " They had hoped to buy a share in a flat on the Costa Brava.

The timing, once again, was laughable.

And on any other morning of the past three months he could possibly have laughed. For the past three months—since a week before he'd started at Columbia—he had sworn that, from now on, he would be not only depression-free but positive and cheerful and thankful; and for those past three months, more or less, he had managed it. Had maybe been a little manic to begin with, but that was all right; actually it was great; caused the aridness of the few preceding days to seem nearly worthwhile. Yet disappointingly—as had happened on every single occasion—his whole new secret formula for life, which he was so sure that this time would nourish him for ever and ever, soon became too tiring to maintain, lost its potency after barely a week. Its aftermath, admittedly, was a relatively long period of stability: long enough, anyway, to make him believe he had finally outgrown the malady. But this morning—yesterday afternoon—such optimism had again proved premature . . . 'from now on' a hurtful joke, a mockery. 'From now on' there was nothing.

Nothing.

Quite certainly little in the way of laughter.

And when he arrived at the office things speedily grew worse, simply on account of this very absence of laughter.

Columbia Life Assurance was located near the Lace Market; it was good to have the tower of St Mary's parish church so plainly visible from where he sat. It was a spacious, well-appointed office. You might quarrel with the pillar-box red of the window frames and skirting boards, but nearly everything else was either white or grey, and the effect was pleasing.

Fifteen desks and fifteen telephones; thirty swivelling chairs; a computer and a fax machine. A typewriter. A great brass bell to clang whenever a new customer had been secured.

His development manager was already seated and about to make a call.

"Eff, good morning!" he said. "Nice to see you. *And* almost punctual, for a change! Be even nicer, though, if you could put a smile on that mournful old face."

Ephraim was able to turn his back whilst taking off his gabardine and hanging it on a coatstand. "I think it may be sometime," he muttered, not actually intending to be heard, "before *that's* likely to happen."

"Oh dear. Do I get the feeling your own weekend can't have been as entirely fabulous as mine?"

Barney Watson was twenty-seven. He had been with Columbia since he was eighteen and reputedly now earned more than thirty thousand a year. At first Ephraim had thought he might make a good husband for Abby: warm, dynamic, good-looking—in an Italian sort of way—by no means unintelligent. Plus, his suits and shoes, even his shirts, were handmade; his cufflinks were of gold . . . Oscar'd have approved. But that had been before Barney had started to irritate him; irritate him by his insistence on certain selling procedures and telephone scripts ("The trouble with you, Ephraim: you can't ever be told!"), by his repetition of eager platitudes and favourite catchphrases, by his constant promotion of books like *How to Win Friends and Influence People*, by his unvarying style of response when asked how he was: *Brilliant, Fantastic, Never Felt Better*: above all by his physical arrogance, shown in the way he moved and the way he boasted about his weight-training, even about his body hair. "Oh, I've got a great big penis!" was also one of his catchphrases. What had been forgivable—even endearing—during their short-lived honeymoon period now appeared considerably less so: indeed, now appeared more like the mannerisms of a complete dickhead . . . to employ an epithet for which Barney himself seemed to show a predilection. It was a pity that such initial liking should have turned, for both of them, into disillusion.

Twice more within the next fifteen minutes was Ephraim exhorted to get rid of his frown and replace it with something that told the world he was glad to be a part of it.

It happened for the fourth time shortly afterwards. They were in the training room, which opened out of the main office, a room where such things as application forms and promotional literature were kept, along with the television set—used chiefly for the screening of inspirational videos—and the photo-copier; and Barney and half a dozen of Ephraim's fellow workers were supposed to be holding a meeting there to do with target-setting and prospect-finding and appointment-making: in other words, the usual load of bullshit; Ephraim's own terminology had deteriorated—or grown robust—since his arrival at Columbia. Barney suddenly said: "And talking of goals, my own most pressing goal at the moment is to bring back the smile to Eff's face." Everyone turned to look at Ephraim and in that instant he felt a searing burst of body heat rush to the surface.

"Oh, for God's sake! Can't you shut up about my smile! I happen to have personal problems. Okay? Whether I choose to smile or not has nothing to do with you!"

There was silence. Barney rose to his feet.

"I think the rest of you had better leave. Ephraim and I should maybe have a talk."

Ephraim, however, stood up too. "No, thank you. There's nothing I want to talk about. My problems aren't the business of this office."

"It isn't your problems we need to discuss. It's your appearance. And your attitude."

By now the others were starting to file past. Ephraim pushed in front of one and headed for the door.

"You—get back here! I forbid you to leave!"

Ephraim left. He walked over to his desk, sat down and picked up the telephone receiver. He had a prospect he meant to call.

But he hadn't had time to press the seven necessary digits before Barney was standing over him, leaning forward, his own face close to Ephraim's. "Get back in that room! Do you hear? Get back in that room before I count to ten!"

Ephraim remained silent; looking towards the window.

"This second! This very second! Get your bottom off that chair and back through that door! *Now!*"

Ephraim slowly swivelled round to face him. Until this moment he had never seen anybody literally shake with anger. He had thought it was just a metaphor.

"Put down that phone at once or I'll pull it off the wall and shove it up your arse!"

Ephraim said sullenly: "Then go ahead and do it." As an ex-teacher he recognized the foolishness of making threats you couldn't fulfil.

Barney merely stood and stared at him. Gradually he straightened up. "We *shall* talk," he said. "Before this day is out! And when we do we shall talk about a lot more than just a smile."

Then, after a pause, he turned and stalked off. Before long, Ephraim heard him making loud and jovial conversation in another part of the office. The volume wasn't especially significant, Barney often spoke as though he were conferring Maundy alms in letting everybody listen to his *bons mots*. But there were two schools of thought, reflected Ephraim, sourly. If you wanted to, you could describe such a comeback as being admirable.

On the other hand you could say it was pathetic.

At lunchtime he walked around the churchyard of St Mary's. Did he do it, he wondered, simply to torment himself? There was one particular inscription which he had looked at very often.

"If anyone ever fulfilled the Christian duties of husband, parent and friend, it was Alexander Gordon Donaldson. Late of Kirkcudbrightshire. He died at Nottingham on the 30th of August 1824, aged 33 years.

"As a testimony of her esteem for his memory and of her deep regret for her loss, this monument was erected by his mourning and afflicted widow Sophia Donaldson.

"The memory of the just is blessed."

Ephraim probably knew it by heart.

Far from having any talk before the day was out, they didn't exchange a single word; even avoided looking at one another to the extent that Ephraim became aware of eyestrain—the same which he experienced when he and Jean were being mutually aloof. (Eyestrain at home; eyestrain now at work.) Fortunately, though, he had to spend the latter part of the afternoon out of the office: had a pair of potential clients to interview. *Potential*, however, was the key word. The first was Wendy Cooper, who had ticked the 'yes' box on the questionnaire she'd filled in when Ephraim had been manning a stand at Texas—"Would you like more information about the services Columbia has to offer?"—thinking no doubt she'd then have a better chance of winning the prize draw, a luxury hamper worth upward of fifty pounds. But she had twice failed to turn up for an appointment at the office, although on both occasions Ephraim had confirmed it just an hour or so beforehand. Wendy now turned out to be a single parent living in a squalid maisonette, its back entrance boarded up by rotting planks—heaven help her, Ephraim had thought at first it was the front entrance. Her child was a stolid two-year-old: Amber Jade: at present repeatedly clambering over and tumbling off the possibly sperm-stained sofa, and wearing only a grubby vest that exposed an unsavoury, brown-streaked bottom. Sometimes she stumbled across to scrutinize Ephraim more closely, unsmiling, unblinking—"For heaven's sake, Amber Jade, just show the world you're glad to be a part of it!"—her fat little hands implanted stickily on the knees of Ephraim's best dark suit, *only* dark suit . . . he was petrified she might be wanting him to take her on his lap and that the mother would dispassionately expect him to comply. But Amber Jade at least displayed some curiosity. Wendy on the other hand was not simply husband-less and unmadeup and uncombed . . . she seemed apathetic. She was also unemployed. Nor had she much prospect of finding employment, perhaps didn't even want it; my God, he sounded like a Tory—or like Abby and Oscar when they were trying to wind him up! She was so evidently unable to afford even the smallest savings or protection plan that Ephraim didn't bother to fill in the fact-finding sheet. He reasoned she wouldn't know about fact-finding sheets, therefore wouldn't feel herself slighted. But she did ask—twice—when the results of the prize draw were due to be announced; and Ephraim determined secretly that if the draw could possibly be rigged then he would truly do his damnedest. In fact merely being with Wendy and her stolid, smeary-bummed daughter made him suddenly more positive. Sod everything, he thought. Sod Barney, sod the bank, sod Swan International. Come to that—why not?—sod Oscar and Abby too. Even Jean? (But domestic troubles would soon drop into place. He could already feel it happening.) And sod Shane as well—yes, that, most definitely. Shane worked at Kentucky Fried Chicken and was supposed to be doing business with him today, i.e. handing him a cheque. But Shane, who had told him that this time there was really no need to reconfirm—yes, honest to God, cross my heart!—and who had seemed like a decent, serious lad the one time Ephraim had actually managed to run him to earth; Shane, of course, had changed onto a different shift and had forgotten—forgotten?—to let Ephraim know. "Tell him, then, I'll telephone on Thursday," he said to the woman who had gone to check the duty roster. He smiled at her and tried to keep his disappointment, his *anxiety*, from appearing obvious. Was the boy actually serious or did he just not have the bottle to say no? It was demoralizing, demeaning, to have to pursue and pander to these types of people. Generic term . . . all those who proved themselves so unreliable: the ones who surprised you as much as the ones who didn't: the middle-aged school teachers or borough engineers or community workers; the woman who had sounded so very pleasant on the telephone, advising him assiduously on which bus to take, or rather which *combination* of buses, and where to change from one onto the other, and yet, scarcely ninety minutes after that, had just refused to open the front door, although he'd rung and knocked viciously for a full half-hour—well, at any rate knocked viciously, you couldn't be all that vicious with chimes which merely informed you repeatedly that there was no place like home—refused to open, pretending she wasn't in, although a young male neighbour, drily sympathetic, had assured Ephraim that they were there all right, her and her hubby, you could tell it for certain by the two flash cars parked in the driveway—and when Ephraim had seen *those* how his hopes had risen!—but not to take any of it too personal, mate: it happens all the time; in some way it must give 'em both a buzz.

So, then . . . Nothing from Wendy and nothing from Shane. But he almost didn't care. Despite these letdowns he was returning to his house feeling a lot more cheerful than when he had walked out of it some nine hours earlier.

Jean, however, didn't come to greet him and when they did say hello her voice lacked any suggestion of warmth. Before he could tell her he was sorry for his behaviour, he was discovering that perhaps he wasn't so sorry for it after all—and indeed was already starting to behave that way again.

At first he struggled against this. He could accept that Jean's spirits should have been affected by his own; depression was contagious. What he couldn't accept was that, when one of the children's friends rang up, she should sound as lively and as ready to laugh as ever. People always marvelled at how wonderful Jean was: what a wife for any man to have; nothing ever seemed to get her down. And when towards nine o'clock Roger returned home you should have heard her wanting to learn about his day. Had there been any interesting customers, good sales, gossipy conversations, where had he strolled at lunchtime, where had he eaten his sandwiches, had it been sunny enough to sit out? In other words, virtually every last detail except for the changeless monotony of his two railway journeys—at least they were spared that.

But you wouldn't have recognized her as the same person. Ephraim felt excluded.

6

Jean had gone to see the Harrison Ford film on her own, mainly to demonstrate that she wasn't, nor ever would be, dependent upon anyone else. She didn't enjoy it much. She would have done better opting for the costume museum, or the display of china at the castle. She and Ephraim had lived in Nottingham for two years now but *still* they hadn't been to either of these things. It was useless waiting for other people. If only she'd had some close woman friend, someone she could wander round the Lace Hall with, or the inside of an old church, without having to worry lest the experience might have been undertaken only out of kindness or a sense of obligation. With Ephraim, it was even difficult to get him to sit down in front of the foreign films she occasionally taped, and then most keenly looked forward to, without her suspecting that in all likelihood he'd very soon be dozing ("No, I swear I'm enjoying it, I've missed hardly anything, it's been a busy day!"), when he always managed to stay alert throughout the most escapist rubbish, Bette Davis, Joan Crawford, Alice Faye, *their* films were sacrosanct. Oh, sometimes it was fun to watch rubbish—she admitted that, willingly—but if your whole diet was composed of nothing else . . . Nor would Roger have been the right person with whom to watch these more serious films, even if, most mornings, he hadn't had to get up so very early. Abby was the only one who genuinely shared an enthusiasm for Satyajit Ray or Kurosawa or even—heaven help us—Ingmar Bergman. And it would have been wrong somehow to watch a video in daytime, would certainly have lessened her enjoyment in it . . . although her puritanical upbringing plainly didn't dictate against an afternoon spent in the cinema!

Besides, in another way it had been a mistake to see *Indiana Jones and the Last Crusade*. Harrison Ford was one of the few contemporary stars she found attractive and this, she had learned, could be unsettling. Strolling home afterwards (since, although the walk itself was tedious, it was a pleasant late-afternoon and she was in no hurry to get back . . . if Roger had been with her they'd have gone to a café but this wasn't the kind of extravagance she felt she could indulge in on her own), strolling home afterwards she glanced discreetly at the men she passed, to see if any amongst them looked at all interesting, sexually. None of them did, not a single one . . . which, indeed, could suddenly feel a little worrying. She had used to enjoy making love, it had once been important to her, you often heard that women of her age still enjoyed it. Yet here *she* was, for God's sake, being physically stirred only by film stars . . . So was it any surprise it had grown to be one of Ephraim's major complaints that it was always him who needed to initiate things in bed?

But all the same there were several good reasons for this.

A, when she was worried sick about money she couldn't feel romantic. *His* word.

B, unless he romanced her first, with dinner out and candlelight and wine—or even dinner at home if she hadn't had to be the one to plan it, shop for it, cook it—she couldn't feel romantic.

C, unless she thought that this time he might vary his repertoire a little, come up with something slightly more inventive . . .

And, D, how when these days there was no guarantee he could maintain his erection for more than a few minutes or get it back once it had gone, how could he really expect her . . . etc, etc, etc? She didn't feel that Harrison Ford, who was only about five years younger, or Paul Newman for that matter, the one other star she could think of who had the power to quicken her pulse and was perhaps a dozen years older, she didn't feel that he (or they) would be having any trouble with his (or their) erections.

Oh... At least she could give a wry half-smile, in full acknowledgment of the absurdity of this. How could she possibly know about the sex lives of either Harrison Ford or Paul Newman? Confusing reality with illusion! Just watch it, kid. It was bad enough to have one person in the family who already did too much of that. Far too much of that.

But it wasn't Ephraim who concerned her right now; she had neither the time nor the mental energy any longer to worry about Ephraim. She looked at her watch.

It was nearly half-past-five. In only a few minutes Roger would be setting out for St Pancras.

Jean had thought of him as soon as she awoke that morning and again while she was breakfasting and having her bath; had thought of him and prayed for him. She did the same thing now as she walked up Woodborough Road.

"Please, Lord, be with him, as I ask you to be with my entire family, but especially at this moment with Roger..."

Yet when he came home she wouldn't want to hear about any of his problems with regard to travel; she had definitely made that clear. She simply couldn't face having to take all of that on board as well as everything else—which wasn't precisely because she disapproved; fundamentally she didn't; how could she?—it was only because she felt so tired, so very, very tired, and because at present she found it hard enough to keep *herself* from drowning, let alone anybody else. The idea of Roger actually going out of his way to invite in trouble seemed so... seemed so... well, *unnecessary.*

Yes, that was it. These days she felt so tired. Bone tired. She remembered how her mother, dead at the age of forty-five, seven years younger than *she* now was (which was the sort of thing that frequently gave you a start, "Dear God, I'm at least as old as Mum was, when...!")—she remembered how her mother had told her once about the exhaustion experienced by everyone who'd undergone the Blitz. "Except for those times when your adrenalin was racing you mostly couldn't think how

you were ever going to carry on, how you were ever going to keep performing all those dreary little everyday tasks which drained all your
energies and seemed not just boring but so wholly unimportant!"

Jean didn't know how people had survived. She herself, of course,
had none of the excuse of the concentrated bombing, the V1s and V2s,
the wailing sirens, the constant removals to the air-raid shelters, the
night after night of broken sleep, the night after night of *no* sleep—but
she sometimes felt, too, that she had little of the mutual support, the
sustaining sympathy, which must have done so very much to help. At
least people hadn't been alone. She felt guilty about thinking this, as
if she were downplaying the ordeals which city-dwellers in particular
must have gone through, whilst upgrading her own very trivial experiences, which anyone who'd been bombed out would happily have
exchanged with her, without hesitation. And yet, however her problems might have seemed fifty years earlier, in 1989 they weren't perhaps so utterly trivial.

For instance . . . moving house. Where, after all, did moving
house figure on the stress ratings? Wasn't it only a short way down
from bereavement? And recently, lying awake worrying about what
interesting variations on lentils and the like she could possibly come
up with—and other such inspirational nighttime topics—she had for
some reason started counting how many times she and Ephraim had
moved house during the course of their marriage. A dozen! Twelve
times in twenty-six years. Admittedly, the first few, before the children had been born, had been merely from one furnished room to
another, but even so, nevertheless . . . And on every single occasion,
the lion's share of packing and unpacking and arranging things and
finding things had inevitably fallen to her. And because they had
nearly always moved in an attempt to get out of debt, this had naturally meant choosing somewhere cheaper, where, nearly every time
as well, they'd experienced all the upsets of having central heating
installed, and/or a damp course put in, with plaster dust then lying
like a skin upon everything, and maybe dry rot needing to be treated
too—with the smell that so invariably got on her chest, brought on her
asthma—and probably the wiring having to be renewed as well and
God knew what else. Not to mention the hideous carpets and wallpa-

pers by which they'd been confronted on virtually every occasion . . .
One terraced house, in Gillingham, in Kent, had had a *bar* in the front
parlour and almost a jungle in the bathroom: plastic birds and animals
perched on trellis over Chinese-style wallpaper, in basically black and
pink and gold surroundings. They had kept the jungle, as a curiosity so
staggering it practically cried out—screeched, squawked, roared—to
plead the cause of conservation.

And nearly every time also, although they'd always made a profit
on the house they'd left—if nothing to the profit which they could have
made on at least a couple of occasions had they been provided with a
crystal ball and sufficient staying power—the new removal had solved
nothing: Ephraim's eagerly embraced appointments to jobs as unre-
lated as the advertising business, hotel porterage, the management of
a seaside rep, a place in Baker Street that taught ballroom dancing, a
place in Colchester that taught the martial arts, all these had eventually fizzled out, from their initial heady promise of amazing prospects, to their ultimate very grudging provision of an income that just
couldn't meet the bills. The other kind of teaching was the only job he'd
ever had which managed to keep their account in the black; but his
being a schoolteacher—he had been trained in secondary education—
had culminated in a minor nervous breakdown (which was hardly to
be wondered at: some of the classroom incidents he'd described were
clearly the work of incipient criminals) and she much preferred, even
to financial doldrums, a bubbly, singing, optimistic husband to one
who was morose, hopeless and sometimes close to tears.

No. The only time when a sustained high income and sustained
high spirits had actually coincided had been during the three years
they'd spent in Bordeaux, where Ephraim had been teaching English
to adults at the university. This had been a happy period, with a fine
standard of living and a number of exceptionally good friends who
had constantly entertained them, given them conducted tours of the
whole south-west and had them to stay, repeatedly, at their second
homes in the country or in the mountains or by the sea. They too had
entertained, of course—"*d'une façon tout-à-fait anglaise et même dans
la tradition de sa Majesté la Reine, ça c'est sûr*" (Xavier)—and had felt
they'd at last discovered a real niche for themselves, as well as a newly

decorated flat, right in the centre of the city, which they'd been able to get at a miraculously low rent.

And she'd even had friends with whom she could go shopping, go out to lunch, go to the hairdressers, to a fashion show—anything; a sudden phone call, "Jean, let's play truant, there's a new film!"—and apart from not being able to express her thoughts in French as quickly as she would have liked, especially when any discussion had turned to politics or philosophy or religion, about all of which she unfailingly had plenty to say, apart from this fairly slight language problem it had all been as good as, realistically, one could ever wish life to be.

So *why*, oh why on earth, should she and Ephraim ever have decided to return to England?

Mainly because Abigail was ready to start her secondary education and they'd worried that, remaining in Bordeaux, the children would never feel wholly French nor yet wholly English.

Partly because they'd begun to miss certain members of their family and a few British friends and, more foolishly perhaps, things like secondhand bookshops and pubs and London theatre; to miss the very ambience of home.

But even the question of the children's education, although it had seemed of key importance at the time, now appeared practically irrelevant. They'd most likely have done just as well under the French system.

However, upon their praying about it one night, Ephraim and she, an answer had turned up the very next morning: a letter which Oscar's godfather had carried around for weeks before he'd remembered to post it, a letter in which he said he'd been sent to a new parish with a large rectory, where, should they ever want to move back to England, there'd be room for them to stay for as long as they liked, whilst reviewing their options. Patently, literally, an answer to prayer.

She remembered the farewell party they had given two nights before they left Bordeaux. There'd been nearly forty guests, all of them good friends whom they were really going to miss. A cousin of Ephraim's, a naturalized Frenchwoman, who'd journeyed down from Paris expressly, said it was extraordinary how many pleasant and interesting people they had come to know, and be befriended by, in such a comparatively short period—had said it must have had a lot to do with their own easy charm and attractiveness.

And although they absolutely could *not*, in effect, have ignored Bruce's letter, from then on life had contracted and deteriorated—not for the children maybe, two of whom had made excellent progress in England, but certainly for Ephraim and herself. And now again, about a decade further on, when they had been in Nottingham for only two years and hadn't yet got round even to putting white paint over all the walls (what decorating had been done was chiefly due to Roger—although Abby, with enviable flair, had turned her bedroom into something highly attractive and would no doubt have helped with the rest of the house if she hadn't reluctantly gone to a party where she'd happened to meet Paul-Michel) . . . now again, a mere two years later—yet after all, Jean supposed, two years was really pretty average—Ephraim was already thinking they might have made a mistake in coming here and was pondering the possibility of a return to London. Could she stand it? Could she stand it, especially now that he had gone into one of his depressions, probably the signal for a whole new series of ups and downs covering many weeks during which she'd have to fight so hard just to prevent herself from being submerged? When they'd first come to Nottingham—and, yes, as usual they'd sold their previous home, this time on the outskirts of Cambridge, at something of a profit—Ephraim had wondered about going back into permanent teaching; but had found out that he couldn't face it. So at the start he'd taken on supply work, and managed to effect a switch to primary education, which was unquestionably more bearable, but there hadn't been enough teachers going sick, particularly at the beginning of each term, and he didn't get paid at all during the holidays, so again the few funds which they'd built up as a result of moving to a cheaper part of the country had all but evaporated when he'd seen the advertisement in the local evening paper which turned out to have been placed there by Columbia.

Although exceeding the stipulated age, he'd been granted an interview, had liked the young man interviewing him and been greatly enthused by Barney's picture of the fortunes to be made out of life assurance. Even Jean had thought, for once, that this could be the answer to their troubles: in fact Ephraim was a good husband, she felt there was little wrong with him that financial security, in tandem with a job which he enjoyed, wouldn't put right. And everyone needed to provide for his future—didn't she and Ephraim know this better than most?—and certainly he could always speak persuasively about something he believed in. Indeed, it was during this period, before his training finally began, that they'd been tempted into signing for the time-share, which even now, although they'd dishonestly given teaching as still being his profession and a steady salary as still providing their monthly income, she couldn't genuinely regret, so long as Ephraim was somehow managing to keep stalling the repayments. It had seemed a symbol of their belief that at long last they would be getting their affairs into order; attaining the kind of comfort which people of their age and abilities, in this society, had almost a *right* to expect. She didn't ask for wealth. Her wants appeared simple: a chance to see something of the world before she grew too old (apart from their three years in France she had done pitifully little travelling: one all-too-brief holiday in Sweden when she was barely twenty); an attractive home that didn't need to be luxurious, just pleasant, civilized; a garden, which again didn't have to be enormous, all she demanded was that it shouldn't be covered in thick concrete, as this one was—yes, a garden in which she could put a birdbath and a wooden bench, grow a few flowers and vegetables and maybe a little fruit for bottling or for turning into jams and chutneys which might, ultimately, fill a whole shelf in the pantry. Polished floors and polished furniture smelling of beeswax; books lining the walls; records; sunlight and lots of flowers—preferably those which she had picked from her own garden. All fairly modest things . . . plus an occasional outing to the theatre and to a good but unpretentious restaurant, sometimes to a country pub for Sunday lunch . . . surely none of this was really too much to ask? Such aims were hardly sinful.

But whether it was too much to ask or not, it still *appeared* so, and she was now in danger, she often thought, of becoming that very type of person she had sworn she'd never be: shrewish and embittered. (And outsiders always saw her as so bouncy, such an unfailing source of joie de vivre. Ha—if only they *knew*!) And if she had so little control over her development of personality, how much less would she have over that other dark fear which for no good reason—after all, *everybody* forgot things, *everybody* was subject to the occasional mental block—had lately come to haunt her: the recurring dread of Alzheimer's and the attendant worry that the children wouldn't then, as she would wish, just find a sympathetic home to place her in but instead feel duty-bound to let her turn into a burden; the memory of what she had once been—and what she had once been might then be all there was—gradually becoming layered and tainted and insidiously distorted.

The home would have to be a National Health one, of course; and she thought in terms of the children rather than of Ephraim because to be truthful she didn't think that Ephraim, for all his good intentions and intermittent buoyancy, would ever be able to cope. Almost certainly he would sink into a permanent depression—and one, moreover, that could possibly end in suicide.

Or was she perhaps misjudging him?

But obviously she hoped she'd never have to put him to the test. For, apart from all of that, at such terrifying times as these she became almost panic-stricken, desperate. She was only fifty-two. There was so much in life she still needed to experience and explore. She wanted a long and productive voyage in front of her. She felt that, as yet, she had hardly even begun.

7

Roger arrived at St Pancras at six. As usual he bought a *Standard*—
in the evenings he normally felt too tired to study—and glanced at
the headlines while waiting to be allowed onto the platform. Tonight
the train was actually in and being serviced and people were queuing
sedately at the barrier; but sometimes, when the train arrived only
a few minutes before departure, there was a rush, a seizing of seats,
which owed more to the law of the jungle than to the love of fair play
allegedly dear to an English heart. Even now, with twenty-five minutes
to go, there were already those who'd decided not to queue and with
elaborately innocent air were taking up strategic positions all ready for
the off. Roger as always glared with resentment, and as always wished
he had the nerve to address them. But these feelings never did anything but agitate him and to what purpose? So, again as always, he did
his best to focus on his paper.

It was odd. There'd been a Summit debate in Kuala Lumpur and
one of the first things he saw was that an 'astonished and appalled'
Mrs Thatcher had been accused by Canada of flouting the British tradition for fair play. After signing a unanimous Commonwealth declaration which called for the tightening of sanctions on South Africa,

Mrs Thatcher had apparently pushed out a separate British statement with a completely different line. "I am astounded that anyone should object."

The rest of the news on the front page was about an escalation in the pay dispute of the London Ambulance Service—police vans converted into makeshift ambulances had been called out for the first time—and about Christian Lacroix looking East for inspiration in his ready-to-wear collection shown yesterday in Paris.

But this evening it was growing especially difficult for Roger to concentrate and it didn't require smart-suited businessmen angling to jump the queue to produce agitation in him. In fact, tonight, such a distraction was vaguely welcome. Even the report on page two of a peaceful protest on board an early morning InterCity train into King's Cross, staged by passengers 'from as far afield as Grantham and Peterborough', didn't fully occupy him. (These passengers had warned that fare rises directed at long-distance commuters would force people to sell their homes or leave their jobs. BR's response was blunt: "We did not encourage them to move to the North.")

He folded the newspaper, moved around restlessly within a small circumference, took out a Yorkie. But having broken a piece off he decided he didn't want it. What he did want was a pee. Yet he'd had one just before he left the shop and the weather wasn't cold, his bladder wasn't weak. It was nonsense. He would be glad to have this whole sorry affair out of the way. He would be glad to be at home, sitting in front of a hot dinner. He would be gladder still to be burrowing under the bedclothes in his cosy sloping-ceilinged room right at the top of the house. Yes. *This* at the moment represented the true peak of his ambitions. He'd always known he was a high-flyer.

He loved that room. In it he was surrounded by all the most treasured acquisitions of his youth and childhood—amongst them, even, some battered old cuddlies who sat together in a corner, gazing soppily, and a yet older pine chest with many metal reinforcements, like a tuck box out of *Tom Brown's Schooldays*, that bore his neatly arranged collection of vintage and veteran cars. Chests or boxes of any sort, particularly those which locked, had a perennial fascination for him, and there were several to point to as evidence of this. Also picked up from junk shops were such miscellanea as coins, a ship in a bottle, some tobacco and biscuit tins, stone ginger-beer receptacles and a splendid globe with tiny but colourful illustrations of things like kangaroos, the Taj Mahal, Mount Everest, Red Indians, the Empire State Building—it dated from the time when that had still been the tallest edifice in America—and a variety of bright postcards from all around the world that almost mosaically decorated an entire wall. On another wall, behind his bed, there hung a movie poster his dad had given him: *It's a Wonderful Life*: showing James Stewart lifting up Donna Reed and exchanging a look of adoration. They also had that film on video and at least once a year he and his dad watched it together, side by side on the sofa, each with a tumbler of whisky nearby and a plate of snacks which they'd ritualistically taken time and thought over preparing . . . they did one for his mum, too, but on this night she usually drank her whisky and ate her snacks while sitting up in bed reading a book. He liked that poster: it reminded him of certain priorities and aspirations, although he wouldn't have confessed this to anyone he didn't fully trust, including his brother and sister, both of whom would probably have ribbed him every time they saw it.

It had once been Abby's room and she admitted it was something she still missed: its shape, its character, its atmosphere. Its window . . . not quite a dormer but flush with the sloping roof, and opening so wide you could stick your head out and obtain a panoramic view of distant hills, as well as gardens, trees and houses. It was the nicest room he'd ever had; perhaps the best thing about their having come to Nottingham. He had screwed a porcelain nameplate on the door—with fittingly twee bluebells in one corner and primroses diagonally across from these—and every night, in a way (and this he wouldn't have confessed even to somebody he *thoroughly* trusted; he was aware how wimpish it sounded, practically abnormal, in a man who wasn't yet twenty-five), every night he actually looked forward to going to bed, because of the peaceful and inviting nature of this room. The half-hour that he kept his lamp on after settling back against the pillows, which were themselves against the wall—for his mattress lay directly on the floor—was quite possibly his favourite time of day. What on earth would he be like when he was old?

Yes, what would he be like when he was old? As a matter of fact, only the other evening, during one of his permutations of route from Bloomsbury to St Pancras, he had seen an old lady sitting at her first-floor window above a bakery in Lamb's Conduit Street, had just happened to glance up and meet her eye—he remembered the geraniums on her sill and the glimpse of something red in the shadows beyond her (could it have been a dressing gown hanging from its hook on the back of her front door?)—and they had smiled at one another, that was all. And it was silly, he knew, but this trifling incident had provided him with such a disproportionate glow of pleasure that as a consequence he had gone that way again tonight . . . although disappointingly she hadn't been in evidence and the window had been closed. The point was, however, that he'd reflected last week about the time when he himself would be old, and about the fact that if he were then on his own he might wish for something similar, where he could sit by the window and watch life going on in the street below; have his bed tucked into an alcove, a gas fire that looked as if it burnt real coals, all his cherished bits and pieces close at hand, a wall lined with his favourite books, an affectionate cat to keep him company . . . it sounded so comfortable, a haven, such a fine and private place in which to spend whatever time remained.

When he was old . . . he grinned . . . just twelve months or so in the future, it sounded like, or possibly right now, or maybe even last year. Or conceivably he'd been born old? On his tombstone they could write: *Home at last! Half of him was here from the beginning.*

Well, anyhow, at least he could smile about it. Surely that was something in his favour. Even smile about it tonight, here at St Pancras. So who knew but they might add a mitigating footnote: "He *was* able to laugh at himself, even if some people, mother included, often considered him a pompous ass."

(Yet he didn't believe his father thought of him like that—although why in fact he should believe this he didn't know. Simply a feeling. Sometimes he felt he talked more freely to his father, which was odd really, considering how unalike they appeared to be . . . Oscar always seemed to have more in common with their old man.)

This meditation on tombstones didn't strike him as at all macabre. Indeed, he recollected one particular stroll he had taken with his dad and Polly on a Sunday afternoon at the beginning of the month. "Instead of the park, Rodge, let's wander round the Lace Market! It'll make a change for Polly; give her a whole new range of smells. Remind her of her scruffy London past and her disreputable salad days!" They'd gone as far as St Mary's, where Dad had shown him, inside the church, the moving inscription to Lieutenant James Still, RN, and in the graveyard the monument commemorating Alexander Gordon Donaldson. "In years to come," he'd asked, with his blue eyes sparkling, "what would you choose to have written about you on just such a monument as this?"

"I don't know. It doesn't worry me."

"Then perhaps it should. You see, I'm asking you about your priorities, what you'd like to be remembered for. Apart from being my son."

"Apart from being your son? What else is there? Disreputable salad days, maybe." He didn't know why he'd said that. Just one of those silly things one did say. He didn't at all regret having no memories of a misspent youth.

But at least he'd been given the chance to acquire them. One man who'd grown strangely important to him had scarcely been allowed that. Lieutenant James Still had died in his twenty-second year . . . 'a victim to the ravages of the Yellow Fever, on board His Majesty's ship, The Pheasant, while stationed off Sierra Leone, on the 12th of October 1821. That he possessed the best feelings of the heart was manifested in his unwearied watchfulness over those whose aid he was in sickness. That he was endued with the spirit of Enterprise was proved by the testimony of those who had witnessed his skill, and admired his gallantry. That he was characterized by suavity of temper and prepossessing manners was apparent from that regard, excited in every breast, which held him forth as an Ornament of Social Life . . . ' Roger had thought a good deal about this inscription, speculated long—and no doubt inaccurately—on the reality which lay behind it; and because at some point he'd idly mentioned that one day he might go to make a copy, his father had beaten him to it, handed him a typewritten card shortly afterwards and clearly been gratified by the surprise it had occasioned—it was such small things as this Roger hoped he wouldn't forget when his father was no longer around. In the meantime James Still, however romanticized, had come to be more than an ideal to him. He had come to be a friend. Not only was Roger now a stiff-kneed spectator from a window in Lamb's Conduit Street, he was also a little boy in short trousers communing with a make-believe companion! Oh, Lord! But the thought of that old lady who, having once given him a warm and kindly smile, would presumably have done the same tonight if she had seen him passing, coupled with the thought of the young man who had died off Sierra Leone a hundred and sixty-eight years ago ("to the very day," his dad had said, as he'd given him the card, "I'd thought that might appeal to you"), of Lieutenant James Still now standing here beside him at St Pancras, was unreasoningly a spring, as soon as the notion had occurred to him, of flooding reassurance. He felt glad to be related to watchfulness and gallantry and the best feelings of the heart—however tenuous or crazy the connection.

The queue started to move.

It was only ten-past-six; another twenty minutes till departure. He found a window seat in a non-smoking compartment facing the way they'd be going, placed his raincoat and neatly furled umbrella in the rack above his head, his briefcase and paper on the table in front of him, and hoped to heaven the other three with whom he'd most likely be sharing would prove sympathetic types; preferably, he thought, women. He retrieved his Yorkie bar and this time ate about half—his mother was always speaking about blood-sugar levels, usually his father's—before deciding he couldn't manage the rest of it. He turned to the back page of the paper ('England sack Auckland Commonwealth Games athlete—"I was a silly boy," he says after visit to a sex club') and the quick crossword. Two women came and after several seconds' worth of glancing round, sat down opposite him, and he wondered if their hesitation had been due to the fact they'd been hoping to see people whom they knew or to something quite different. Possibly they didn't like the look of him? Or possibly it was just that they preferred to face forward. Before the first had fully eased along the seat he said: "If you'd rather not have your backs to the engine, I don't mind changing." This offer might have been practically spontaneous but he knew it wasn't unselfish. He wanted to show the world he was a good guy. How could the heartless authorities single out for persecution Mr Wholesome, Mr Nice? But the ruse failed dismally, certainly as regards the pair it had been practiced on—perhaps other passengers, across the aisle, had heard and been impressed. Both women looked at him more as if he were Mr Here-I-Am-Girls-Must-Be-Your-Lucky-Day. The one still standing shook her platinum-blonde head. "No, you're quite all right," she said. The other, whose bottom was by now midway across the seat, didn't bother even to reply.

He looked down at the crossword, already felt he was about to blush. Furthermore, none of the first few clues seemed remotely solvable. Suddenly, not only did he want to pee: he wanted to shit.

Again, though, he put this down to nerves.

One of the young women, the one by the window, took out an emery board; started to file her scarlet-painted nails. Usually this would have pissed him off, the continual rasping sound, the differences in speed, the pauses, new beginnings—above all, maybe, the idea that this was something which people ought to do in private; if he'd been trying to write an essay the scrapings would have speedily grown strident, he'd have visualized powdery nail settling imperceptibly like flurries of fine dust, and if it chanced that he'd just eaten, his tightened stomach muscles would unfailingly have produced indigestion. Travelling on British Rail had taught him as nothing else had ever done the extent of his neuroses. Previously, he had never dreamed how fidgety the fare-paying public could become; never stopped to consider the potential foot-swinging, finger-tapping, head-scratching, throat-clearing—the list could probably be extended to cover, in an average-sized hand, at least one side of an A4 sheet out of his own writing-pad; and at spot number one on that list, without argument—yes, this would undoubtedly have taken first prize—the nose-picking. The nose-picking. He realized that in most cases this was merely a nervous mannerism, but the number of apparently respectable, professional, middle-class men—for some reason it was nearly always the men—who just couldn't leave their noses alone and who would as often as not, following their stealthy or thoroughly unconcealed excavations, revolve the ball of their thumb against the tip of their index finger was, to use the Prime Minister's front-page vocabulary, 'astounding', 'astonishing', 'appalling'. Roger sometimes felt as if he were travelling on a sea of snot; in need of fresh air; in need of his bath; in need of a psychiatrist.

But tonight neither the nail-scraper nor her companion, who every few minutes was playing with her hair, pushing it back and prodding it and smoothing it, had any power to disturb him. Or perhaps the two of them simply cancelled one another out—irritations were more bearable when they came at you in pairs, or even droves; on occasion you had no option but to smile, life was so ridiculous. Yet at times, too, its absurdity could arouse not wan amusement but deepest self-contempt: the person sitting next to you could search for bogies unremittingly, or cough, or sniff, or swing their hair, hiccup, whatever—then your eye might slip from the crossword, as had happened only last week, to where the stop press informed you of a seven-year-old boy who'd been left paralyzed and almost blind as the result of an operation blunder. Dear God.

He slowly put away his biro; leant back and closed his eyes; half-listened to a conversation about the women's respective offices and about a new boss who was proving unreasonably petty on the subject of personal phone calls and the timekeeping of his staff. "Suppose he feels he's got to thrown his weight around. The plonker." The woman giving herself a manicure kept moving her legs and knocking against his shins or shoes.

Ten minutes later a man of roughly his father's age took the seat beside him, raised the lid of his black attaché case and withdrew a double foolscap page of squared paper, the inside spread covered with figures and columns and coloured underlinings. He was quite possibly an accountant; even looked like Roger's stereotypical idea of one: a thin-lipped, sharp-angled kind of face, short hair carefully parted and combed flat, with every plastered strand attesting to the individual passage of the comb. He wore pince-nez. Roger had hoped for someone who looked less correct.

The train began to move.

Incredibly, despite everything, he must have dozed. When he opened his eyes the women had miniature bottles of gin in front of them and tonic water and plastic beakers containing lumps of ice. The emery board lay on the table. He blinked bemusedly, then lifted his arm until the cuff edged back. They had been travelling for almost half an hour.

The conductor came into their carriage before the train reached Wellingborough: first stop on this evening journey. He too was a man of about his father's age, similarly blue-eyed, though not as strikingly so, but somewhat taller and heftier. There was a strawberry mark covering the whole of one cheek—faint, however, and by no means seriously disfiguring. Roger held out his plastic folder.

Waited.

"Thank you, sir." The man's eyes flickered away from the card; after a moment came back to it. Roger's reaction was unexpected. He felt a measure of relief.

"Yes . . . I know." Even his voice sounded calm. Now that the encounter was actually underway his heart-rate slowed. "My ticket expired on Saturday."

The official looked at him an instant while he assessed the situation. "Then it's no good to you, is it?" His tone wasn't indignant or threatening. It was merely businesslike.

In a low voice Roger explained why he thought the man's statement inaccurate. On the whole, because of the number of times he'd rehearsed what he wanted to say, his argument cohered. This defied the fact that the two blondes were openly attentive. Their heads swivelled impartially. Roger's nextdoor neighbour kept his eyes lowered. Other passengers within earshot also showed undisguised interest or evidence of tact.

"I see," said the conductor, finally. "What happened, then, this morning?"

"The fellow didn't notice." Roger had never been to public school but had the mildly uneasy sensation he was being a sneak—just as this morning, in fact, he'd had a similarly uneasy sensation, albeit one swiftly suppressed, that although he wasn't behaving dishonestly in not holding a valid ticket he was perhaps behaving *dishonourably* in not drawing the man's attention to it. He hoped he wouldn't get him into trouble.

"Then you were very lucky. But tonight, I'm afraid, I'll have to charge you the full single fare." He flipped open a pad which had an elastic band holding the used portion.

"I haven't any money."

"In that case a cheque will do."

"I haven't got a chequebook." He added: "I haven't any credit cards, either."

The conductor gave a sigh. "Very well. I'll tell you what we'll do." The blondes looked at him expectantly. "Tonight I'll make you out a free ticket for Nottingham. I'll have to take that defunct card off you but I can't do any fairer than that, now, can I?"

"Which means I'll have to get on the train tomorrow without a card?" He didn't know why he had turned it into a question.

"No, I warn you. That would be foolish, sir. Extremely foolish."

"What else can I do?"

"And in fact," continued the conductor, "I'd strongly advise against it. If I see you on this train tomorrow night travelling without a ticket you won't find me nearly so lenient." He finished writing out the free one, tore it off and handed it to Roger. He stood there waiting for the card. There was a moment's silence.

Sheepishly, Roger took it from its folder and passed it over.

"But the thing is . . . " He tried to retrieve some little dignity. The conductor began to look impatient.

"Yes?"

"I don't want to be difficult or anything. But . . . Well, I reckon you will see me on this train tomorrow night; there's no other way I can get home."

"In that case, sir, the police will be seeing you as well. Not a very pleasant experience, not one I'd really recommend. Also, it would involve a fair amount of delay. I don't imagine that would win you a lot of popularity among your fellow commuters." With which he turned away—quite sharply. "All tickets, please. Everybody have their tickets ready, please."

The train was slowing down for its approach to Wellingborough. Roger's neighbour started putting his things back in his case. "Why don't you contact Melanie Phillips at the *Guardian*?" he said. "If there's an arrest in the offing it's possible they'd want to send a reporter along. Might make good copy for them."

"Yes. Thanks. I will." The words were surprised out of him, due solely to politeness. He didn't suppose for one second that he'd follow such advice.

But with so many people at this moment getting up from their seats, reaching for their overcoats and hurriedly shrugging their way into them, gathering together books and papers and Walkmans, it was difficult to tell what had been the overall reaction—and therefore doubly morale-boosting to have received this sign of solidarity from the perhaps not-so-stereotypical accountant, if that's indeed what he was. Roger said a grateful goodnight and wondered if there might be any chance of sitting next to him tomorrow.

Authorization from Derby? Worryingly, the conductor had paid scant attention to any such possibility, and now, when Roger returned to the station manager's office, he not only found it closed, with no voucher for him pinned to either of its doors—which, anyway, he would hardly have expected—*or* left at the ticket office . . . although prior to the conductor's words he had felt confident he would collect it there; almost as dismayingly, he was told that in the morning the manager certainly wouldn't have arrived until Roger's train was well on its way to London.

Indirectly, as he was leaving the sitting room and heading for his bath, his mother made a speech acknowledging his problems. (Sadly his father appeared not to know about the situation and was still feeling depressed; it didn't seem a good moment to tell him. Damn. He'd normally have been supportive. The timing was all wrong. How could he have thought, even fleetingly, that the whole thing could be *meant*?) She said, "Darling, remember a mother always loves you, no matter how foolishly—or quixotically—you behave. I hope you'll have a good day tomorrow. I hope you'll like your sandwiches." This last bit made him think she'd probably gone out of her way—things being as they were—to get him something special.

8

Tuesday. Ephraim awoke from a dream in which he had been surfing in Southern California, hang-gliding in the Lake District and planning excitedly around an outdoor table with Jean and the children; he couldn't remember for what they'd been planning but it was clearly something they'd all been feeling pretty good about . . . he awoke from this dimly recollected aura of sunshine, affection and peace, to the abrupt and plummeting awareness that nobody loved him and that life wasn't worth the living. Also, it was raining.

As usual he brought Jean her tea and cereal in bed; she didn't have to open up the shop till ten and he was supposed to be in the office by half-past-nine. ("I thought I was classed as self-employed," he'd grumbled once, upon a somewhat late arrival. "Well, I've discovered something: I'm an easygoing boss." But all being self-employed meant at Columbia was that you weren't given any salary and that your National Insurance contributions didn't get paid for you. He'd thought of photocopying the definition of self-employed from the Shorter Oxford Dictionary, getting it blown up and tacked to the wall above his desk, in place of all the gilt-framed certificates and photographs of handshaking or boozy backslapping at the annual sales convention 'held in exotic locations around the world' that some of his more established colleagues, the sporters of tiepins, 'enamel and silver and gold pins which become studded with diamonds and other gemstones as a recognition of your achievements', considered the main essential of office décor. But in the end he just couldn't be bothered.) Yet today again, instead of her customary cheerful greeting as he set down the tray and poured out her initial cup of tea, she only thanked him stiffly and they spoke no more than was necessary to observe minimal courtesies and maintain a feeble pretence that they were still communicating.

Around nine o'clock, in the very few minutes he had this morning between walking the dog and leaving for work, and as he was too roughly towelling her dry—poor Polly standing quite as patiently as ever—the telephone rang. He heard a faint feminine voice telling him, and it took several seconds to adjust to its accent, that there was a call for Mrs Mild from her son in Calcutta and would she please be prepared to accept the charges?

Inwardly Ephraim cursed. He had no desire whatever to speak to Oscar at the moment and only wished that the call had come through two minutes later, even though Jean probably wouldn't have heard it ring—indeed, partly because of that. But he didn't go to the foot of the stairs and shout: by the time she arrived he could imagine those charges racing towards a positive frenzy of ticks and whirs and revolutions. This was the fourth time Oscar had rung—"Just wanted to say a big hello to my folks and tell them how my heart is pining!"—but such endearing messages would have meant more to Ephraim if they hadn't always come collect and at the most expensive time of day. Added to which—no, thoroughly superseding which—he felt resentful that it was *Mrs* Mild who unmistakably had been the person asked for.

"Yes, yes, we'll pay for it. This is his father. Please put him through."

"Hello, Pop. How's my pop?" Oscar's voice sounded amazingly loud and clear, especially after the soft incomprehensibility of the operator. He might have been speaking from somewhere just a mile away. Ephraim would have preferred it if he had.

"Worried about the cost of our next phone bill, my son." But he struggled to keep his tone light—and truly believed he had managed it. He felt relief. It would now get easier. "How are things in our late lamented empire?"

"Actually, not too good. That's why I'm phoning. Is Mum there?"

"What's the matter, Oz? Mum's in bed." Despite the abbreviation, his answer had been sharper. Well, you could ascribe that—and with some legitimacy—to concern about the boy's wellbeing. He also realized he might have given the impression that Jean was unwell; if so, let it stand.

"I've had my wallet stolen," said Oscar.

"Oh, Christ." Oscar was frequently having things stolen—or in any case mislaying them—because he was too forgetful, too trusting, too careless. Recent claims on their insurance had included a newish bicycle, which they'd had to pretend had been padlocked when taken, and an equally valuable camera. This wasn't to count such sundries as a suede jacket, three Walkmans, a sweater, a pair of swimming trunks and even two long-playing records still in the carrier bag from HMV, for all of which Ephraim had refused to seek reparation, but each of them gone missing within the past couple of years. (On the other hand, Oscar was continually finding things, as well: five- and ten-pound notes, coins, a pair of good sunglasses; most importantly, a Rolex wristwatch, unclaimed after the statutory month it had needed to be left at the police station, but then, barely another month later— almost incredibly—lost again.) "Was all your money in it?" asked Ephraim.

"Yes. *And* traveller's cheques. *And* credit cards."

"Oh, Oscar, I don't believe this! Don't say you kept them all together?"

"Listen. Can I just speak to Mum?"

"No, you can't just speak to Mum. Does this mean you've been left without a thing?"

"Yes."

A pause. A voice cried out in Ephraim: "For God's sake . . . only connect! Only connect!" Maybe he hadn't ever let the bathwater run over, or the bottom burn out of a saucepan, but he too in his time had been known to be casual about certain articles of clothing . . . although never about money. Perhaps in their different ways they were both

63

adventurers, daredevils, possessing all the plusses and minuses that being such things entailed. "Only connect!" cried out this voice.

"Some students I've fallen in with," said Oscar, "have managed to lend me a bit."

"What about Rick? And, thank God, at least the living is cheap."

"Don't be stupid! It's not the living that matters. I haven't got any way of getting home."

Don't be stupid! Ephraim bit his lip and dug his fingernails into the palm of his free hand. Why did this have to be happening now? Only a few weeks back, during his manic period, he could have coped brilliantly with such a crisis, might even have welcomed it, seen it as a test, as something that would inevitably—and forever—reestablish their closeness. (When had that closeness slipped away? Why had it? How?) "Pop," Oscar would have said, in years to come, "do you remember the scrape I got myself into in India? And how calmly and effectively you rescued me! Never one word of recrimination! Did anybody ever have a dad like you?" But already it was too late, it was blemished, his exasperation manifest, irretrievable. *No, you can't just speak to Mum.*

"And didn't you receive my last letter? Rick and I split up six weeks ago."

Ephraim remembered it now: information tossed off in a single sentence and driven from his mind by one that closely followed it, involving love and prayers and the particular way in which these and all his thoughts had been apportioned . . . "Have you still got your passport?" he asked. Yet that was merely something to say, to cover the fact he'd failed to pay due regard to a casual remark—*ostensibly* casual—masking a matter of concern. (But why the fuck hadn't Jean made more of it?)

"Yes, Dad, I've still got my passport. I've never kept my passport in my wallet. Do passports even fit in wallets? One day let's carry out a survey."

But then this air of strained tolerance abruptly turned into something else. There was a sudden break in Oscar's voice that quivered audibly along five thousand miles of telephone line. "Don't you understand? *I haven't got any way of getting home!* I don't know what to do." In the space of only a few seconds, Ephraim saw the little boy who used to grip his hand so tightly whenever they had to pass a large dog or a bearded old man; who at the age of four—standing, straining, with both arms fully stretched—had stopped a tall and badly balanced cupboard from falling on a baby cousin; and who more than anything had nearly always borne him extremely good company. He saw the two of them moving like quarries along an empty moonlit street, arms linked, glances swinging from side to side—"Lions and tigers and bears, oh my, lions and tigers and bears, oh my!"; he saw them, with Roger, skipping down a hilly path winding amongst trees, himself in the centre and holding his sons' hands: "We're busy doing nothing, working the whole day through, trying to find lots of things not to do . . ." He saw them playing *Little House on the Prairie*. ("Paw, I surely appreciate how you can spit tobacco juice further than any other man in Kansas; I feel plum tuckered out with only thinking how much you and Maw jus' love me and with hoping she'll be waiting for us with some of those li'l old corncakes covered in molasses; shucks, I sometimes figure I must be the luckiest critter that ever was born, because the good Lord's been so kind in giving me a maw and paw like you . . ." He could carry on in this way for hours.) It was like what happens to somebody drowning, supposedly. Ephraim saw the youth who had provided a bottle of champagne for each of his parents' last four wedding anniversaries; who once—eight years ago?—when he, Ephraim, hadn't known where to find the money to renew their television licence, had simply disappeared and paid for it himself, out of the fund he'd been amassing from his paper round to buy a music centre. (And how completely out of character for *Oscar* ever to have saved!) He remembered how bereft the boy had been at the death of Rick's father. Those drowning seconds had made him feel ashamed.

"Well, look, Oz, somehow we'll get the cash. How much do you think you're going to need?"

"I want to come home. Enough to fly me home."

Fifteen thousand, four hundred and ninety rupees. Divide that by thirty-five. Nearly four hundred and fifty pounds. Dear God.

"Anyhow, don't worry. Truly. We'll manage something."

But only two weeks ago he'd tried in vain to raise some money for the mortgage . . . no, *re*mortgage, this time they daren't get too much in arrears, he was frightened by the thought of repossession. He had realized, of course, that the bank wouldn't help but he'd been disappointed by the few friends and relatives—some of Jean's, too, though none of this was known to her—whom he'd then determined to approach. Yet today it would be different: no longer a matter of just the mortgage but now of a twenty-two-year-old boy practically destitute in a strange place literally thousands of miles from home. (But thank God for those students; thank God, thank God for those students.)

"Phone back tomorrow," he said. "I'll let you know what I've arranged." A sudden thought occurred to him. "There's none of your friends I could try to borrow from?" After all, the lad had been to Oxford.

"No!" All the vehemence voiced in one syllable suggested that Oscar, who subscribed to *The Gentlemen's Quarterly* and had his street cred to consider, would rather have starved in foreign lands than be exposed to such embarrassment.

"All right. It was only an idea."

"May I speak to Mum now?"

"Yes, I'll go to call her. And keep your pecker up. Remember Meursault."

This was a longstanding joke between them: Oscar had often compared himself to Camus' hero in regard to the fact that nothing fazed him; he was cool to the nth degree. (In an early letter from India, for instance: "You may have noticed a certain vagueness in our plans. In Budapest, unfortunately, we weren't able to buy any sort of practical guide to Asia, so we've been catapulted onto this continent without much sound idea of whys or whats or hows or wherefores. Walk the tightrope, Pop! Live on the edge! Meursault would quake with approval.")

About to shout for Jean, Ephraim changed his mind. He returned to the telephone. "No, Oz, speak to her tomorrow—not now. She'd only be thrown into a panic. You wouldn't want that."

"Okay. Do what you can, then. Thanks. Well done, Dad. And when you do reveal all, just give her my love. Tell her I'm fine."

His son's spirit might be reviving but still, Ephraim thought churlishly—and was aware of being churlish—it was Jean who received the love and 'Dad' was not changed back to 'Pop'. "Right . . . well, I'll give her your love but you'd better give *me* your credit card numbers," he answered drily.

Oscar told him where to find them—also the numbers of his traveller's cheques (what organization!)—and reiterated his gratitude. But when Ephraim replaced the receiver he realized that although the greater part of him felt thankful, after all, that the phone had rung just when it did, the other part felt thoroughly hard-done-by. As well as thoroughly worried.

The trouble was, the more hurt you showed you were, the less affection you received.

It was a vicious circle.

Yet what was the good of recognizing this, if you knew you couldn't break free?

He picked up the towel and finished drying Polly. She, too, seemed a little worried. But he stood stroking her after he'd done, and then she tentatively wagged her tail.

Walking down Woodborough Road in the fine rain, this long and boring road that was dreary even when the sun shone, he first worried about Oz and how on earth he was going to raise the money for him. But then a van passed advertizing Delia's Gourmet Meals Delivered To Your Door and he was unexpectedly distracted. Delia was the name Jean had chosen for the heroine of a series of bedtime stories about fifteen years earlier. Jean and Ephraim had taken turns telling their stories but Ephraim always read his out of books; and on the nights when Delia's adventures were related he had sat on one of the children's beds listening just as eagerly as they did. "Jeannie, you really ought to write these stories down. Remember what we always said!" It was what they had said for the first time that evening they went to see *Pickwick* at the Saville Theatre, in 1964, the evening he had asked her to marry him. (He hadn't realized when he booked the tickets that she didn't care that much for musicals. But he thought she had enjoyed this one.) He remembered her telling him over supper, after they'd been talking for a bit about Dickens, that one of the things she had always wanted was to be a writer. But until then, it seemed, she'd received little but discouragement . . . all the way down from the nuns who had never praised you for anything, perhaps on the grounds that praise would make you prideful; from them to her stepmother, who, unpermitted, had read the opening pages of an exercise book which Jean had thought safely hidden in a drawer; on to a boyfriend who had considered novels were a waste of time, politics and sociology were all that mattered; finally to the girls in the office where she'd first worked, to whom she'd made the mistake of reading out a love poem she had stayed up half the night composing. She had laughed as she told him. It was her own fault; she should have known they'd only tease her, make facetious comments. But the net result was that she'd lost her confidence, become inhibited, far too critical of anything she did write.

All this, however, she had said with such humour that he had loved her for it. It was he who'd felt the bitterness—against unbending nuns and prying stepmothers; earnest radicals and giggling office girls—"a curse on all their tribe!" . . . he had drunk a toast to that. And this great surge of sympathy, and love, was what had suddenly confirmed him in his purpose to propose. "Sweetheart, you'll get your confidence back! I promise! You're interested in everyone, curious about everything, you express yourself so vigorously. You'll always have plenty of encouragement from *me*. I'd be so very proud." And he'd had visions—they both had—of Jean's making up for all those wasted years and of her having her own small study, inviolable to everyone, except on invitation. Preferably it would lead out to a garden or at least be overlooking one.

But despite such visions the years had swiftly passed, bringing children, removals, money worries. No study, no desk, and only a secondhand portable typewriter, whose keys had soon begun to jump. And there were times now, after a quarter of a century of removals and money worries, times when—especially if he were depressed—he couldn't be sure he hadn't killed off most of the affection she had once felt for him; and whatever Shakespeare might say about love not being love that alters when it alteration finds . . . (Had he also written: Hunger looks in the window, love flies out the door. Well, if he hadn't, that gave someone else a break.) She had recently said—during a row when he had asked her: what do you really *want* from life?—"I'll tell you what I want! I want a mother. I want a wife. I want a hero out of Georgette Heyer. I want to be *nurtured!*" And he was none of these things; he never would be. He suddenly had such a longing for his own mother, for his childhood, for a time when he had been loved and secure and had never had to worry about how to pay the mortgage or how to cope with failure—well, never at least with any failure that was comparable to the kind he now faced, because Jean couldn't live even the simple sort of life for which she so despairingly hankered.

Despite the narrowness of the pavement, his own umbrella hadn't collided with anyone else's; nor at the bottom of the hill, where at this hour the traffic was always busy, had he caused any kind of accident. He had turned, correctly, into Huntingdon Street.

But here his automatic pilot developed some malfunction: at his subsequent crossing point, a motorist had to brake.

"Jesus Christ! What the fuck—?"

"I'm sorry. I'm very sorry." Ephraim stood alongside the driver's window. He managed a conciliatory smile.

"Suppose I'd gone into a skid—what then? Suppose the car behind me couldn't stop?"

Ephraim drew in a bit, allowing those other cars, which fortunately hadn't been any nearer, to move out round him. For some reason he closed his umbrella, as if wet hair and face might emphasize his penitence. "Yes. I'm sorry." He couldn't think what else to say.

"You tired of living, then?" The fellow seemed relentless.

"Possibly."

It all happened at a great speed. Suddenly the man was out of his car, with one large hand grasping the collar of Ephraim's raincoat. "Right, so it's a joke, is it?" He was probably *en route* to a building site. He wore torn jeans and scuffed boots and his grey jumper could now be seen to be cement-smeared.

It was also inevitable he should be about three inches taller than Ephraim. Let alone some twenty years younger.

Ephraim thought: All right, let him take a swing, I don't care. He had a fleeting image of that cup he'd won all those many years ago—saw it sitting on the mantelpiece in one of their former houses. In London it had got relegated to a cupboard. Here, he believed, it was still in one of the packing boxes.

"No, it isn't a joke. And I've said I'm sorry. And, anyhow, I don't see why cars should always be given preference over pedestrians."

As a general maxim this might have been perfectly valid but he realized that in the present context it didn't quite fit.

"Because they're fucking well bigger than you are."

The same as I am, mate.

"Is that a proper reason?" asked Ephraim.

The man stood staring at him. Both hands were now gripping his collar and their faces very close. There was a brief hiatus, comical as well as threatening. Ephraim noticed the uneven trimming of the man's moustache.

Then, with a shove, he was released.

"No, you're not worth bothering about. Prick. Go and kill yourself somewhere else. And this time make a decent job of it."

"I wouldn't mind," Ephraim told him—or told the departing end of his car. "I wouldn't mind, you bastard. I honestly wouldn't."

In fact, at times, it sounded quite appealing.

9

"Fairy tales can come true,
 It can happen to you,
 When you're young at heart . . . "

Henry Maynard, who was one of the part-time staff at the umbrella shop in Bloomsbury, had, surprisingly, a rather pleasant singing voice.

"For as rich as you are
 It's much better by far
 To be young at heart . . . "

He was apt, however, to show it off a good deal when he was down in the basement of the shop. The basement was where the new umbrellas were made and the old ones got repaired—ditto the walking sticks; where the stock was stored and the parcels prepared for post; where elastic bands were sewed on—and rosettes—as well, of course, as covers; where the staff, at their appointed times, could make themselves a hot drink and sit with their newspaper and sandwiches, or possibly their pot noodles.

"You can go to extremes
  With impossible schemes,
  You can laugh when your dreams
  Fall apart at the seams . . . "

The public was never allowed in the basement other than in highly exceptional circumstances—and this depended somewhat on the mood of the manager. Journalists, an art student, representatives of the National Theatre researching a production, photographers, even a small party of schoolchildren working on a project, all these had been permitted down to it within the past twelve months, and Norman, who was close to retirement, and Joe, his West Indian assistant, had patiently explained and illustrated (and cunningly propelled the children towards a cache of Mars Bars left by Mr Cavendish); but during that same period the only people to receive such treatment *without* a prior understanding were a couple from Atlanta—and not just because they had given the shop a lot of business through the mail, nor yet because it had been their long-cherished aim to see the surroundings in which their umbrellas were made and to shake hands with the craftsmen mainly responsible, but much more because, indeed *entirely* because, they had declared it their intention to start a fan club which would celebrate the history of the company . . . Mr Cavendish envisaged no vast financial gain arising from such an enterprise but he had a weakness for engaging eccentricities; it was for this image of a *fan club* that he had broken his rule.

Roger, to a small extent, quite often broke it. He did so for anybody elderly, pregnant or distressed who asked him for the toilet—or, more frequently, the bathroom. ("If you must appoint yourself the patron saint of bladders and bowels," Alan Cavendish had said, "although it is not my intention, you understand, to encourage the use of either of those words in this establishment, nor either of those functions they are unhappily associated with, then you must warn these geriatrics before any of them attempt the descent that it will be pointless their trying to sue us if they fall"—the narrow, twisting staircase was certainly a structure which had to be negotiated with care—"and you must go ahead of them so that if they *do* fall it's you they fall upon.

And if they *do* fall," he had added, with a certain gloomy relish, "I hope they're heavy. Very heavy indeed.") Roger didn't actually enjoy conducting customers to the lavatory. The lavatory itself was always spotlessly clean but the room in which it was housed looked almost prehistoric, while the passageway outside the door could easily have led into the catacombs; it made all too feasible the story of the ghost—albeit a benevolent ghost—supposed to haunt the premises. With a mention of Uncle Henry, indeed, during the brief journey to the lavatory, did Roger seek to distract from the bare brick walls and from the impression, perhaps more than the reality, of dust and filth and cobwebs.

Uncle Henry's namesake had no connection to the family. Henry Maynard had been taken on partly because of the bias Mr Cavendish felt in favour of things eccentric; his belief that people who were characters blended well with the whole anachronistic flavour of the place. Though even Mr Cavendish admitted that—in this *one* instance—he might conceivably have made a mistake.

Henry was a man of about sixty, balding, portly, always smartly dressed. His blue pinstripes looked as though he pressed them every night; he wore a fresh buttonhole daily—picked by his loving and obviously green-fingered wife from the boxes on their Neasdon balcony—and his black shoes were never once unshone: if the weather was in any way inclement he brought them in a carrier bag. But the self-importance of the man, thought Roger; the sheer stupidity of him! And this intolerance was clearly mutual. Almost from Henry's first week at work he had been making snide remarks about Roger—Mr Cavendish had privately told Roger to ignore them, they could only be a form of jealousy. If Roger committed any sort of infringement, if for instance he was a few minutes late returning from his lunch or from a tea-break, Henry would remark on it in a loud voice; ostensibly to be humorous or even comradely, in reality to make sure that the manager, up at his desk in the gallery, was fully aware of the fact.

There were three incidents concerning Henry that had particularly remained with Roger, out of a host of similar occurrences. When Alan Cavendish's wife had made one of her rare visits to the shop and Henry had been introduced to her he had said afterwards to Mr Cavendish:

"*Very* charming, *very* pretty; as a matter of fact she reminded me a great deal of my own dear wife; and, do you know, the moment that she opened her mouth I could tell she was a lady." (Mr Cavendish had written it down immediately, in case he should have forgotten any of it by the time he arrived home that evening.) Secondly, when a customer, who had been holding what was plainly an extremely sophisticated camera, had asked if it would be all right to take some pictures of the shop, Henry—who fancied himself a photographer—had answered, "Certainly, madam. If you'll let me finish helping this gentleman I'll be glad to come and show you how to do it." And thirdly—but this wasn't the sort of thing that made you want to hide, pretend you weren't associated in any way with such a person; this was just pathetic—when another part-timer had casually remarked about himself that one day he might like to write a book, Henry had nodded very wisely and declared, "As a matter of fact one of my best friends is a very famous writer. He lives on the same floor that we do and coincidentally I happened to travel down in the lift with him this very morning." It was only natural, of course, that Henry should have been asked what this man's name was; surely it would have been very strange indeed, discourteous, unkind, if no one had inquired. There was a pause. Unaccountably, Henry looked uncomfortable, a little shifty. "Well, the next time I see him," he had said at last, "I must remember to find out."

Another thing which was pathetic was that he'd been telling everybody for weeks that tomorrow was his birthday and inquiring from all of them, even from Roger, what kind of cakes they liked the best. It was not the custom in the shop for people to bring cakes on their birthday or even to announce that in fact it was their birthday. Henry had been going round with a list on which there were such headings as Almond horseshoes (chocolate-tipped), Danish pastries (apricot, apple, raisin), poppy seed cakes (delicious), rum truffles (a bit on the stodgy side but my beautiful and darling wife enjoys them) and had stood patiently with pencil poised, purse-lipped, looking over the tops of his glasses and nodding importantly at each slow but well-considered response . . . This morning, while Henry was downstairs, Roger wanted to know if Mr Cavendish—or anybody else—was buying him a present. "Then oughtn't we to organize a small collection?"

"Oh, for goodness sake!" exclaimed Mr Cavendish, from on high. "No precedents, if you please! Just think where it could all end. We might even have to give Rose a birthday present—and she has many more birthdays ahead of her than I do. Would you call that fair?"

"Not even a card?" asked Roger.

"I'll buy him a toilet roll!" said Rose. "Well, what I mean is—I'll tear him off a couple of sheets, anyhow."

For once, the manager didn't appear to disapprove of such a sentiment. Roger felt surprised. Mr Cavendish was one of the most generous people he'd ever encountered and Rose herself was far from mean.

Equally, sent downstairs a short time later, he felt as surprised as he always did by Henry's easy way with a song . . . although today he was also vaguely disconcerted. 'Young at Heart' had always been a favourite of his father's and Roger didn't like to hear it coming from Henry—who now sat contentedly on a stool in the stockroom counting rubber ferrules and sorting them carefully into their correct sizes. It was all right for Frank Sinatra to sing his father's song; it was far from all right for Henry Maynard. Roger, who had been dispatched to fetch more hazel and cherrywood knobs for the baskets by the entrance, was very seldom dilatory about taking stuff up to the shop—but on this occasion he really did get a move on.

Nevertheless, he was still saddened to recall that he was in his final week—and grateful for the sanctuary he found between train journeys, even in the company of such as Henry Maynard. Not that this morning's journey, in fact, had been particularly awful: all he'd had to do was to give the conductor, or ticket collector, or inspector, he didn't know the right designation, a brief rundown of the situation, followed by his name and address; and no one had appeared especially interested; unusually, it hadn't been a very full compartment. He'd had two sandwiches packed with shrimps and mayonnaise—with a warning note to be sure to eat them for his breakfast and not risk saving them for lunch—plus a carton of fruit yoghurt; and he'd managed to make a good start on (what had been his final choice) *Assess the contribution of the Cecil family to Elizabethan government.* But all the same it didn't make the prospect of this evening's encounter any less nerve-racking. He felt very much tempted to catch a later train but considered that somehow this wouldn't quite be playing the game. (*Game*?) If, as occasionally happened, he had a last-minute customer who kept him late, well then, that would be splendidly providential; but whenever it looked as though he were going to be delayed, Mr Cavendish—supposing that for some reason he hadn't already left—was practically certain to say, "You go off, Roger, you've got your train to catch; I'll attend to this gentleman." *Very* occasionally Mr Cavendish had said to him, "Look, since we're quiet and since I happen to be in a good mood—which, as you know, doesn't occur all that often—I think you may as well slip away and catch an earlier train. Why shouldn't your parents be made to suffer for a change?" And that too would be terrific. But not to be expected, let alone actually asked for.

He hadn't informed his manager of what was going on. To satisfy the demands of British Rail, Mr Cavendish would instantly have taken the money out of the till, or out of his pocket, and Roger didn't want that—he genuinely did not want that. He wasn't quite clear why this should be.

Whatever it was, though, the same complicated motive must have kept him from phoning the stationmaster at Nottingham. Pure cussedness was definitely a part of it, he knew, but surely it couldn't be the sole ingredient.

At any rate, Directory Inquiries were still able to be of service. At twelve o'clock he rang the *Guardian*.

The telephone was in a cubbyhole between the staircase and the counter and only an eavesdropper could have overheard much of what was said on it.

"Is there any chance, please, of my being able to speak to . . . to Ms Melanie Phillips, please?"

Apparently, there was every chance. Ms Phillips showed herself to be both accessible and sympathetic.

"I can well understand," she said, "how it's come to be this big an issue for you. But I'm afraid that from our point of view it sounds like small potatoes. I am sorry. And I certainly wish you lots of luck . . . "

In truth, he hadn't expected anything else—hadn't even known he

was going to make the call until about two in the morning. Nevertheless, he felt disappointed.

Small potatoes. He knew what she meant, of course, but still had
something of a struggle not to let it rankle. The phrase itself, as much
as what it stood for.

At lunchtime, hoping to cast off his disgruntlement, he went out.
The rain had stopped; sporadically a weak sun was shining and he'd
been thinking he might get some reading done—preferably, around
the subject of the Cecils.

However, instead of his crossing New Oxford Street and heading
for the benches outside the British Museum—or if those weren't dry
enough the ones a little way within—some instinct made him turn
to the left and round the corner into Shaftesbury Avenue. Not long
since he had last done this: a week, maybe two, it could scarcely have
been more. But in any case he was surprised to discover—barely a few
yards from the last of their own windows, the one displaying riding
crops and swagger sticks—that something new had taken the place
of the expected travel agent's. This was a shop selling greetings cards
and wrapping paper, handmade chocolates and reproductions of old
photos. At the moment it had no customers and seemed to be staffed
by only one person.

Roger nodded to her and then wandered over to the rack of birthday
cards, where he was relieved to find an interesting selection. And nearly
straightaway he saw the perfect card for Henry: a man and woman and
three small children having a picnic in a field where the grass was studded
with daisies and splashed with poppies and where from the other side of
a low stone wall a couple of cows looked on in somnolent curiosity. But
the main thing was, the adults were clearly the grandparents . . . and one
of Henry's few redeeming features in Roger's eyes was the pride he took
in his grandchildren. Practically every week he would bring in a new
wallet of photographs, pictures not quite so technically accomplished
as he always implied they were—and, most especially when the subject
was grandchildren, he even appeared to forget he didn't much care for
Roger and would include him as eagerly as he did everybody else in his
stately yet chuckling monologues. Henry's son, his only child, had two
little boys and a girl, and here, on the card, there were two little boys

and a girl. "Do you believe in divine guidance?" Roger asked the young woman, without taking thought, and then began to blush, because she would no doubt think him a religious freak.

She smiled. "There's no wording in that one, I'm afraid. Is that all right?"

"Fine. By the time I've got everyone to write their names in it . . . " It was a pound and twenty pence. While waiting for his change he said, "You've a nice selection."

"Yes. Maybe a bit overpriced. I suppose I shouldn't say that."

Happily, his blush had been sidetracked. "You obviously aren't the owner. I hope for his sake—or for hers—that things have been a little busier than they are right now."

"Not much. But I'm told it will take time before people get to know we're here. It was only yesterday we opened."

"Oh, I'm sorry. I should have realized. You see, I work in the umbrella shop on the corner."

"Is that right? Well, *you* must have had a busy morning. I mean, after all that rain."

"So-so. It wasn't anything like enough. I think it packed up around eleven."

Otherwise, of course, Henry wouldn't have been banished to the basement; there'd have been little chance to refer to either birthdays *or* toilet rolls. Not to mention small potatoes. Nor would Mr Cavendish have chosen this particular time to have the baskets by the door replenished.

(So at least they must have been selling *something*—too bad it hadn't been sufficient to save him from losing his job.)

"And for ages now it's generally been very quiet. We had a fairly dry summer."

He wished he could think of something more interesting. Oscar wouldn't have stood there and spoken of the weather. She was a pretty girl—well, not exactly pretty but she had a nice face and he enjoyed its expressiveness. Her blonde hair was wavy and well-cut and reminded him of hair you saw in the commercials; he bet it would bounce as she walked. He bet too that if you were able to get close enough it would smell pleasantly of shampoo.

"It must be fun to work there," she said. "It looks so Dickensian. I've often meant to come in but—well, I don't know—it also looks a little . . . "

"Intimidating? As if you can't just walk around but will immediately be pounced on by some toffee-nosed salesman?"

She nodded.

He held up the birthday card, now inside its paper bag. "This chap might pounce on you!" No, that wasn't fair. Besides, Henry was too ponderous to pounce. "But all you'd say is—please back off, my good man! Please take a running jump!" Ah, that was better; a little better. (She also had nice teeth, he noticed.)

"But wouldn't the shop fall down if a customer said that?"

"Not if she did so politely."

"I can see I'll have to practice. 'My good man, please back off, please take a running jump!' Was that all right?"

"Absolutely. *You* don't need to practice. To the manner born."

"Thank you."

There was a slight pause.

Roger said: "It's one of the oldest shops in London. We've been there since 1867. Before that it was a dairy. On the floor there are still some of its blue tiles."

"Gracious."

"But they've had to be covered up, for reasons of safety."

"Shame."

"I used to say to people: imagine what it would have been like in those days. Nothing but green fields connecting the villages of Marylebone and Holborn. Customers enjoyed that—especially the Americans. Then someone pointed out, quite kindly, that all of this was nonsense. Far from being green fields—and, anyway, what other colour *could* they have been?—it was actually one big notorious slum."

She laughed.

"Poetic licence. I hope you said it *should* have been like that."

He shook his head. "I felt a charlie. I stuttered and was tongue-tied."

"You should have said: I'm sorry but we don't serve killjoys. And, besides, those fields could just as easily have been *brown*—after they'd been ploughed—or white, when they were covered in snow. That fellow sounds despicable."

"No, he wasn't; like I say . . . "

He realized he was treating her remark too seriously. Another pause. But this time not an awkward one.

"So now all I can talk about is Lord Curzon and Mr Gladstone and Bonar Law. But I still cheat occasionally. I throw in Henry Irving, although really there's nothing to suggest he was ever a customer."

"Why do you choose him, then?"

"Because I heard that on his deathbed he said it was a pity to be leaving life just when he was beginning to understand it. And I liked that enough to—"

The door opened and a man and woman came in. The man wanted to have a box of chocolates made up for the glamorous redhead clinging to his arm, who, despite the fact he looked about thirty years older than her, was gazing at him as if he were her hero. He wore a camelhair overcoat hanging from his shoulders.

Roger didn't want to leave the shop . . . certainly not with merely a wave and no proper goodbye. ("But that's the way to do it, Rodge. Don't let 'em see you care. Remember, *mon brave*: we walk in the footsteps of the master. *Le grand* Meursault.") For something to do he walked back to look at the greetings cards. He saw one he hadn't noticed earlier: the picture of a tabby cat sitting on a kitchen worktop and surrounded by mushrooms and onions and leaks. The kitchen was as romanticized as the daisy- and poppy-strewn field but the cat itself, with its puzzled, this-must-be-Christmas expression, looked wholly believable. In its mouth was a filched mackerel. Plainly a mackerel. Which made this card as appropriate to his mother as the other had been to Henry. Even more so. Roger well remembered the day when—in her own words—she had "had to chase a mackerel round the kitchen." Round the kitchen, through the dining-room and up the stairs. She had finally landed it, lying on her stomach and following a determined tug-of-war, amongst the fluff and rolled-up posters under Oscar's bed, and had eaten it herself at supper. "I don't mind. It's had a good wash and it was only in the chops of my poor, wicked, disappointed boy—yes, *you*, my little precious," in answer to the frenzied scratchings on the outside of the door, "although you undoubtedly weren't such a little precious at the time. Never mind, baby. If you're good, Mummy will leave you a little bit on the side of her plate and then maybe you'll forgive her." It was abundantly evident that Brindley *had* forgiven her. He still used to follow her everywhere, curl up beside the bath when she was in it, rush to the front door as she returned from work, lie languorously against her pillows as soon as Ephraim was out of bed and had freed both him and Polly from their nightly imprisonment in the dining-room. A more companionable cat it would have been hard to imagine. Hard? No, impossible.

Roger's immediate thought was to buy the card for his mother. His next was to do with having it framed. The one which followed, however, caused him to hesitate. Tears could still come into his mother's eyes even when she saw the Whiskas adverts on TV. Brindley had caught the feline variation of AIDs and had had to be put down. Ten months ago. Which, quite obviously, had entailed a not-very-jolly Christmas. Roger and his father had taken the cat to the vet's the morning after Boxing Day—swollen and perhaps sporadically in pain, the now sedated animal had been kept alive just long enough to have his turkey dinner. When they'd got back to the house they'd found Abby with her arms around her mother, both of them crying. He and his dad had joined in. Oscar had been staying with friends but otherwise he too would certainly have sobbed. Roger's eyes watered now, remembering, although in retrospect that spectacle of the four of them—even the five, Polly had also been patently upset—could well have appeared faintly ludicrous.

He had practically forgotten the young woman. Now she came out from behind the counter and began to tidy some of the postcards on a revolving stand beside him. "What are the odds?" she smiled. "Secretary and married boss?"

"I'm sorry?"

Her tone changed. Her concern was audible. "Are you all right?"

"What? Oh, yes. Fine; I'm fine. Thank you."

Grinningly apologetic, he brushed at the corner of one eye with the knuckle of his index finger.

"I was just remembering something. In fact . . . maybe you could help me?"

"If I can . . . ?"

"My mother had a young cat, the spit-and-image of this one. Well, I mean he was actually the family cat but . . . The thing is, Brindley once stole a mackerel, too."

He explained about the animal's demise—yet even while he did so it occurred to him she had nice legs. Indeed, she had a good figure altogether: slim but curvaceous. The top of her head reached roughly to his shoulder.

She considered for some five or six seconds.

"You know, I once had a cat that was run over," she said, slowly. "I used to cry for her a lot. And I've never wanted another. But I'm very glad now I have some snapshots—even if at first I had to hide them in a drawer."

"How long ago was this?"

"Five years ago last August. So you can see I wasn't still a child. I was nearly seventeen."

"I'm sorry," he said.

"I'm sorry, too. I mean, not only about Scarry, but about your mother's Brindley."

"Scarry?"

"Short for Scaramouche. I was reading Rafael Sabatini when she was given to me."

"I like Sabatini," said Roger. "I've read *Captain Blood*." That wasn't true but at least he'd seen the film, and enjoyed it.

"No, that's one I've never read," she answered. "But I did see the film." Perhaps they'd watched it on the same afternoon. "And after that—for months—I had a crush on Errol Flynn. He was so handsome and so dashing. Well, perhaps it wasn't *months* but it felt as though it were. I told myself that I could never love another."

It was strange in a way, he thought: I've known you for only minutes and yet that, too, could feel like months.

"I don't know why I never read the book," she said. "It would have seemed the natural thing to do."

"Anyhow," he replied, after a moment, "I think your advice seems good. Yes. Thank you. I'll have this one as well."

"That makes it sound as if I've been a clever saleswoman. I only wish I didn't have to charge."

He hotly disclaimed.

"But what I *can* do," she added, as they went back to the counter, "is offer you a chocolate. They're fantastically expensive but I've been told to eat as many as I like—on the principle, I think, that if I make a big enough pig of myself . . . Here," she said, "this one's got a continental filling and is definitely one of my favourites." She picked it up in a pair of silver tongs and held it out to him. "And this one . . . ," she began, when he had taken it. But he only raised his hand and laughed.

"No, no! Thank you. Just this." He bit the chocolate in half and pronounced it delicious—and in all likelihood it was. "What's your name?" he asked.

"Jenny. Jenny Maddox."

"Mine's Roger. Roger Mild." He was half-prompted to shake hands but, instead, only passed across the money for the second card.

When he left the shop he felt great. In the end, ironically, all he did was give a wave, because an old man had come in, inquiring for Camerer Cuss—"Jewellers, you know, antique clocks and watches; up until the First World War all the apprentices slept in hammocks!" But now he didn't care in the least about the offhandedness of his farewell. He ate the rest of the chocolate, still without really tasting it, and then broke into a run—ran down Shaftesbury Avenue—for no other reason than that he wanted to. And if there'd been any tree branches for him to leap up and touch he thought he would have leapt up and touched them . . . and furthermore looked graceful doing it. He believed that for once he was moving like an athlete instead of merely lolloping; and even if this were pure illusion—which probably it was—he didn't give a toss. He'd had a brainwave just prior to the arrival of the old man and had realized he should act on it before his courage went. It was like receiving inspirations at two or three in the morning. A few hours later—well, it wasn't exactly that you mistrusted them—it was simply that by then sobriety had come back and sobriety was generally synonymous with loss of nerve.

But he *had* telephoned Melanie Phillips, for all the good that had done him. Anyway, he felt pleased he hadn't chickened out.

He was still running when he reached Charing Cross Road. He dashed to the other side of it, untypically defiant of the traffic, and ran into Foyle's, dodging exuberantly amongst its customers—exuberantly, also apologetically. First to the fiction hardback department and then the paperback.

Yet neither of the harassed assistants had even heard of *Captain Blood* or Rafael Sabatini, although the second, apparently under the impression Roger was after a book about Japanese wartime atrocities, offered him something called *The Camp on Blood Island*.

At Waterstone's, though, a computer having been consulted, he learned there was nothing of Sabatini's still in print.

All the same, he checked stubbornly along the shelves. The little miracle he'd hoped might happen—he was a firm believer in a personal God, possessed a half-belief in guardian angels; and, incidentally, wasn't it about time for his father to suggest another viewing of their film?—well, that small miracle didn't take place. *Oh, but come on. I know you can do it.*

Back across the road—in Books Etc—he carried out the same search. This time, he found a dusty Pan edition of *The Sea Hawk*, with some of its pages creased. That sent him, darting in between the traffic again, to Collet's: the possibility of old stock. He then pursued a zigzag course as far as Cambridge Circus. Here it suddenly occurred to him he was a fool: the places to look would obviously be the ones specializing in *secondhand* stock. When you were giving a present to a person you'd only just met you automatically thought in terms of something new but in this case an unashamedly secondhand copy would almost certainly have more character—and suppose he were to find a 1930's edition? That would be all right. *Eh, God?*

Eventually he came to a green-painted bookshop, seemingly nameless, which occupied a corner site near Leicester Square. Inside, it had a pleasantly musty atmosphere, narrow aisles, stepladders, well-spoken people who smiled and said "Excuse me," a man in charge who sounded both erudite and interested. When Roger found the shelf which represented the start of the S section, *Captain Blood* was the first book he saw on it.

Not a 1930's edition. The blue binding looked quite cheap; there wasn't a dust jacket at all, let alone the one he'd been imagining: boldly, even gaudily, suggestive of piracy in the Caribbean—California-style—and of gay swashbuckling gallantry. This was a copy published in 1973, by Hutchinson. But it was only one-pound-fifty: cheaper and in much better condition than the paperback he'd just seen: and it *was*, essentially, the book that he'd been looking for. At least he remembered to offer up his thanks. He rushed back to the shop where Jenny Maddox worked.

The moment before going in he paused to wipe his face and blow his nose. He hoped she'd be dealing with a customer, so he'd be able to leave the paper bag on the counter and not have to furnish any explanation.

But she wasn't—again there was no one else in the shop—and he had to place it directly in her hand: "Only something quite dopy! " She looked from him to the bag in smiling mystification and he'd already got back to the door by the time she'd taken out the book.

She stared at the title on its spine.

"I . . . " She opened it up; flicked aimlessly through its pages. "I don't know what to say. I really don't know what to say."

"I just happened to see it. Seemed like providence. Divine guidance!"

He trusted she'd realize this was humorous. Or at least—he quickly amended that—so far as she herself need be concerned. Once more, he had to wipe his forehead, was still having trouble with his breathing.

"Must go. They'll be wondering where I've got to."

And indeed as he entered his place of work, which was also at the moment devoid of anyone other than staff, he saw Henry, who'd been sitting sideways on one of the cane-seated chairs and staring intently out of the window, above the various kinds of seatsticks, instantly swivel back towards the door and purse his lips and shake his head and tap his wristwatch and look expressively towards the gallery.

"Is something the matter, Henry?" Alan Cavendish remained seated and could not be seen behind his wooden barrier. "Or are you perhaps rehearsing for the birthday dance you're going to have to entertain us with tomorrow? I imagine you've been told about it: a tradition of the firm which dates back to our beloved founder. There's no way we can break with it."

Henry took this in good part. "Ah, that's a fine joke," he laughed. "I must say, that's a *very* fine joke!" He chortled at it for maybe half a minute—he would return to it several times during the course of the afternoon—and then, without leaving his chair, allowed his feet to execute a fleeting form of soft-shoe shuffle.

And to accompany himself he hummed—but at least he didn't sing—the first few bars of 'Young at Heart.'

Roger was about to go downstairs, to put his bag containing the two cards, together with his lunch and study materials, into the cupboard where he always left his coat and umbrella if he'd brought them, when he heard himself addressed.

"Oh, good afternoon, Mr Mild! How very nice of you to join us! We thought you might be attending the dentist's—or else the funeral of some favourite grandmother—and simply forgotten to mention it."

"It was actually the dentist's funeral and my favourite grandmother asked me to cleverly avoid telling you. You see, it wasn't very nice, the thing he died of. She thought any *truly* elegant establishment would much prefer to stay in ignorance."

Even Henry gave a smile. Even Rose appeared amused.

"Did you hear that, Mr Cavendish? Isn't he a cheeky bugger! Honest! I didn't know he had it in him!"

Inadvertently, she had risked taking over from Roger in front of the firing squad. But possibly the manager had been too appalled to notice.

"Do you realize that not only did you take most of the day off but, on top of that, you actually split an infinitive?"

Roger laughed and, guessing he could now go, descended to the basement. He felt pleased with himself—and not purely on a single count. *Honest! I didn't know he had it in him!* Good old Rose! He would remember that tonight, when heading for St Pancras. A form of recognition which maybe most of his life he had subconsciously desired. *I didn't know he had it in him!*

Also, of course, it was scarcely ninety minutes ago that he had first seen Jenny Maddox. But he had never met anybody like her and already he could tell it was a turning point. He may not have read Sabatini (although he would! he would!) yet he had more than once read of people who—immediately after meeting their future spouse— had brazenly declared, "*That* is the person I am going to marry!" Well, he himself could prove as brazen as any of them! Why not? Why not? Jenny Maddox was going to be so *completely* the person he needed.

10

Since he was so late already Ephraim decided he might as well be hanged for a Doulton figurine as for a phone call from Calcutta. *Royal* Doulton. *Two* figurines. One was a wistful-looking Columbine with diamond-patterned skirt and sleeves—yellow, blue, black, green, white and purple—and bodice cut extremely low, both front and back, edged by a broad white frill repeated at the wrists; she stood on a black base, wore black shoes, green stockings and a black tricorn—but beneath the hat her grey hair made her face too old (a little like Billie Burke playing the Good Fairy, Glinda, when really she was past it) despite the peachy smoothness of her neck and upper chest. The other was more chocolate-boxy, ginger-curled, and had a Cupid's bow that could have roused the jealousy even of Ann Blyth: pink riding habit, and plumes that tumbled to one shoulder from her hat; pale blue underside to the brim of that hat; white Puritan collar, black gloves, black riding crop. Turn her arse-over-tip, you saw she was identified as "Maureen", whereas the first was merely Harlequinade, without inverted commas, and apart from being less sentimental carried the distinctive mark of its potter and was almost certainly older and more valuable.

Not that Ephraim was considering selling. They were a part of his childhood, good companions at either end of the mantelpiece in his mother's bedroom (fireplace boarded up), and he could remember at an early age running his finger over each of them ("Darling, you'll hold it *very* carefully, won't you?") whilst sitting at her curtained dressing table on the matching stool—the same brocade that hung in the bay window—and being especially susceptible to the prettiness of Maureen; holding her *very* carefully in front of the triple mirror on the glass-topped dressing table . . . before which mirror, many years later, on occasions when he was alone in the flat, he could recall sometimes standing naked and using the silver-backed hand glass and opened wardrobe door to assist him in his narcissism: of course with an erection: and the mortified anxiety of having once to scrub, with dampened flannel and remorseful vow, at the linoleum-framed beige carpet; could recall the repeated inspections—and the ultimate relief when nothing was noticed, no far-fetched, squash-spilling assertions necessary.

No, nothing would ever induce him to sell either of these figurines; he had so little of his mother's; just those and one of her dancing medals and her beautiful Persian lamb coat which Jean unfortunately could never wear—"Unless I had a placard on my back: 'I swear, it belonged to my mother-in-law; what would you have me do?'" But merely *pawning* them . . . that surely was allowable. In fact, National Home Loans, Solihull, West Midlands, might well regard it as advisable. At the moment he wasn't too worried about the bank; didn't give a sod about Swan International; all he cared about was staving off the bailiffs—and the repossessors. Well, anyway, that's all he had cared about when he'd first looked in the Yellow Pages, but now there was Oscar to consider—Air India top priority. The directory listed no more than three pawnbrokers: only one in central Nottingham: Carlton Street, which led down into Goosegate.

He didn't know quite what he had expected . . . yes, actually he did: some backstreet moneylender's straight out of a black-and-white late-Forties second feature, with a fleshy, stubble-jowled Semitic dealer (and Ephraim, who had been born Jewish and could still recite the Shema, well at least its first part, as easily as the Lord's Prayer, was permitted—wasn't he?—frankly to acknowledge *that* bit without needing to feel racist); in short, a stereotypical fence, complete with eyeshade and eyeglass and a shirt maybe gaping clammily above the waistband.

But Messrs William Taylor & Co, though established in 1854, had perhaps never been to the movies. They had the three brass balls, it's true, yet there was nothing else that seemed right. Despite a tacky picture in the window—of a watermill whose wheel was represented by a shoddy and gaudily bright clock—they looked like any other respectable jeweller's, with welcome symbols on the door from Visa and American Express and Diners Club International; it was all a very long way, thought Ephraim, from ill-lit alleys and running footsteps and Edgar Lustgarten and *The Shop at Sly Corner*. Inside, there were carpet tiles, cuckoo clocks, closed-circuit television and a fresh-faced young fellow in a neat suit.

"I'd like to talk to you, please," said Ephraim, "in your *pawnbroking* capacity." He began this way because, notwithstanding the brass balls and the Yellow Pages, he still half-wondered if he could be making a mistake. And besides the measure of quaintness in his manner of expression there was even a measure of challenge. He wanted to indicate that he found the situation amusing—and completely free of stigma.

"Yes, sir." The assistant was encouraging.

Ephraim explained. " . . . And I believe one of them at least might be worth six or seven hundred. Could I raise a thousand on the two?"

"I'm sorry, sir. We only deal in gold."

The shop door opened and in came a sinister-looking black, very tall, with beaded shoulder-length hair. Both hands were in the pockets of his trench coat. He pushed the door to with his foot.

"Only in gold? But . . . " Ephraim glanced about him. "But you seem to sell everything. Cut glass—pictures—rings—pearl necklaces . . . " It was a fact, however, that he couldn't see any porcelain. "Lumps of amethyst, masses of wristwatches . . . " He wished the black would at least turn and look the other way. "A couple of bone china figurines would surely fit in nicely. Besides, I'm not talking about selling them. It's just their value that's in question."

"But you see, sir, we wouldn't be able to judge their value. We're not experts in bone china."

Ephraim felt like a man who'd come for interview and was being turned down for the job. "Perhaps you'd first like to serve this gentleman?" he said, mainly to give himself time to think of reasons why he shouldn't be turned down.

"That's all right, man. I'm in no hurry. Just take your time."

Damn him.

"But if I went and fetched them, later on today, and left them here for a few hours, couldn't you have them independently assessed, by people who *are* experts?"

The assistant said: "I'm sorry. But, no, we don't do that." He produced a regretful little smile and really did sound as if he were unhappy about it.

"Why not?" Ephraim asked.

"Yes, man, why not?" The fellow wasn't behind him any longer but alongside.

"I don't know, sir. It's our policy."

"May I speak to your manager?"

"The manager's away this week." (*I trust in thee, O Lord; my times are in thy hand.* Psalm 31: 14-15.) "And neither of my colleagues"—he indicated a mirrored door to his right—"could be of much assistance to you. Yet anyhow . . . " He shrugged. "I think I can guess what the manager would say."

"Piss off?" suggested the newcomer.

But this time it was Ephraim who ignored him. Ephraim, fighting for his loved ones. Fighting for Oscar. Fighting for Jean.

"Then here—what about this?" He wrenched the bracelet off his wrist. The bracelet was made only of base metal and of stainless steel and he suspected that the watch itself was much the same, although it certainly had the appearance of gold. "Here's something you'd be qualified to judge."

And at least it was a Seiko. Quartz. And the time it gave was always accurate even if its date-keeping wasn't: for the day—and in shining vermilion, what's more—it still provided SUN.

He had forgotten it had once belonged to Liz.

"Sir, I'm afraid that unless it's a Rolex or a Patek-Philippe a second-hand watch has scarcely any value. But there's another pawnbroker, you know, at Beeston. Mrs Barks. She might easily be interested in figurines."

"There's also one at Radford, man. Though the two guys I saw there—I don't know as they'd know a whole lot about any bone china. I don't know as they'd know a whole lot about any Crown Jewels either come to that, even if they arrived there with a note on them saying Signed by me—personal—with love and thanks—the Queen."

Ephraim laughed and restored his undervalued watch to its rightful place on his wrist; he had now remembered it had once belonged to Liz. He appreciated their companion's consistently lighter note. It supplied him with an unexpected lead.

"Well, then, all I've got to offer is myself. People always say I'm worth my weight in gold." (Oh, yeah? *Really?*)

"A pound an ounce, sir," declared the assistant. (And there were so many who merely stared at you when you attempted that facetious kind of pleasantry.)

"Up on the scales, man!"

Ephraim, for a moment, felt such gratitude that it was almost love. He could have hugged the pair of them and when he left the shop—though having, instead, only shaken their hands—he was still smiling. (If I can't be anything else in life I may as well settle for being a character. A star. "Dad, you're a star," Abby had used to say, when he'd done something a bit special, like, for instance, taking up the children's breakfasts in bed and giving them croissants or *chocolatines*, or peanuts or Maltesers, in an attempt both to surprise them and to vary their diets a little. "Dad, you really are a star!" Oscar had been apt to imitate her, or else gently to tease her, most memorably when he'd broken his arm in the school playground and for weeks Ephraim had sat next to him after supper, writing out the homework he dictated, or copying up the geography and history notes he'd been obliged to borrow.) Now, walking away from the jeweller's, he thought it was a shame about the cash—but communication was also very necessary. As he turned towards the Lace Market it struck him that his depression seemed to have lifted again; he actually felt good. Yet such was often the way of it. Here one minute—gone the next—dependent on responses.

When he got to the office it was nearly half-past-ten—but still not as late as he'd thought, he was glad he'd kept his watch. Barney was on the telephone. The question of whether or not they were again on speaking terms, therefore, remained to some degree in abeyance, although Barney was observant and certainly hadn't looked up or given any kind of wave. All the rest greeted him in normal fashion: "Hi, Eff!", "How you doing, matey?", "Morning, lad."

As he settled at his desk he listened to the conversation of his boss.

"I swear to you she's only known the guy for four months. And she always wanted a big wedding: marquee—orchestra—all the trimmings . . . No, she really meant it; why would she try to bullshit *me*? . . . Well, having lived with her for five-and-a-half years I'd say that, yes, I knew her *fairly* well . . . And now to have done it in a registry office! Poor kid! Can't help feeling sorry for her. Bet she'll be regretting it by Crimbo—probably before! Still. I suppose there'll always be some things you have to find out for yourself; no one can teach you. But I never dreamed she'd come to this. Poor deluded kid."

Barney picked up a second phone that stood beside the first. Apparently it was some woman from the Technical Department, at Head Office. "Sorry, darling. I'm on the other line. Phone me back in two." Ephraim picked up his own receiver and rang his brother Nathan, who was likewise at his Head Office in London.

Nathan and Angie had been on holiday at the culmination of the mortgage crisis. (Which wasn't to say that it was over, or anything like over, but Ephraim had felt too dispirited to ring them yesterday. *Hi! How was Turkey? Look, I need to borrow several hundred quid.*)

"Hello, Nathe. Only me . . . wanting to find out if you and Angie had a good time."

But hadn't he just warned himself about that?

"Then I wish you could have wanted to find out while I was at home and not at work," replied his brother. For some reason, if he hadn't been the one to initiate the call, Nathan was seldom at his best on the telephone; not with his family. It didn't necessarily mean this was a bad moment.

"Oh, you know me!" said Ephraim. "Why run up my own bill when I can run up the company's?"

"Besides, didn't you get our postcard?" (Christ Almighty! Letter or card—who else was going to ask him that today?) "Must have told you then that we were having a good time. May even have said: wish you were here! Lying through our teeth, of course." The gruffness was alleviated by a glimmer of enjoyment at his own wit. "Mind you, I sup-pose we might have had a giggle. How's the girl?"

Invariably—on the telephone—the 'girl' was Jean. "Do you happen to mean my wife?"

"Yes, that's the one. Is there any other I should know of?"

"Jean's fine. She's fine." *Like flowers are at their cheapest in the run-up to Mother's Day.* "Angie?"

"That one's *my* wife. How is she?—well, I don't know; never bother to ask." Ephraim thought that in fact he might have picked a reason-ably good moment. He imagined Nathan sitting there in his smart lawyer's office, considerably larger than himself, in height as well as girth, nearly six years older and looking a good deal more, at home a blazer-and-tie-and-flannels man, never a jumper and jeans, at the very least a crisply pressed shirt and silk cravat. Hair always short, brilliantined, well-brushed. Margaret Thatcher's staunchest supporter (these days, possibly, a hint of self-parody whilst claiming this). The pair of them—Nathan and he—had practically nothing in common other than memories of boarding school in North Wales, the High Street flat, shared apprehensions when taken to meet their father's future wife, things like that. Nathan had often been good to him: given him extra pocket money when he'd first started earning, treated him to the cinema, come to spend weekends at Cannock and Wolverhampton when Ephraim was doing his National Service in the RAF (only six months: a wangled medical discharge—wangled but real: he'd always had depressions, albeit more typically referred to as sulks). Later memories included the giggling fit they'd caught from one another at the altar—*Ephraim's* wedding, although it could have happened just as easily at Nathan's—with Jean eventually succumbing too; and a whole lot closer to the present-day, merely the previous year indeed, the pleasant weekend they'd spent together at Portmeirion, wifeless, in order to attend the annual reunion of Old Boys (but Matron had only recently managed to trace them—well, to trace Nathan). And hadn't everyone become so rich, such pillars of society! But still it had been fun, and might have been nearly as much so for himself as for Nathan, except for his discovery that the boy he had regarded for nearly half a century as being his best friend at the time, even, in a way, his best friend ever—the possibility of his presence there and of all that this might lead to having been the clinching factor in his decision to attend—that this boy had neither the smallest recollection of *him* nor any of the lovingly remembered escapades which Ephraim had more and more halfheartedly described, adventures shared by just the two of them . . . until in the end Ephraim had been forced to smile and turn away: "I'll simply have to strike you, then, off the list of my best friends!" Some list! They had avoided each other for the rest of the evening and Ephraim wondered now if unacceptable disappointment was what he'd been afraid of when he kept postponing his attempts— or, at best, made excited efforts lacking in persistence—to track down this symbol of the perfect friendship. But it was always as well to know where you stood; you couldn't go through life clinging to sentimental illusion (and he was *glad* John Leyton now sported a paunch and a florid network of capillaries). And during the course of the dinner he'd had at least one worthwhile memory restored to him: how Nathan had taken him—probably at the request of Miss Kean—into his own bed in the Senior Dormitory on the night their mother had gone back to London, gone back to the Ministry of Food and to her poorly heated room in Mrs Hilling's house in Abbey Road, following a brief half-term visit (during which they'd been to *The Demi-Paradise* in Porth-madog; possibly the first film he had ever seen), and he hadn't been able to stop crying, hadn't even wanted to be shown the apple she had left him or read the book which she had slipped, last thing, beneath his pillow. Therefore, despite their differences, his and Nathan's, differences of attitude and character and circumstance, there was still a lot to bind them . . . well, at least on Ephraim's side there was; he hoped that Nathan felt the same—but then of course Nathan had always been the giver, him the taker. So how could you be sure?

Still, think about the past. Forget the brusqueness of the present.

"All right, let's suppose Angie is also fine," said Ephraim. "In that case, the only one who isn't quite so good at the moment is Oscar."

"Why? What's the matter with him? Pregnant or something?"
Ephraim told him.

"And to be truthful that's really why I phoned. You're my last hope."

"Who else have you tried?"

"Everyone. Half the population of Nottingham. Even the ones who are already out to sue. Like the bank, for example." What a liar he was! (Anyway, in regard to the first part of that statement.) And how could lying possibly equate—he remembered that inscription he had copied out—with the best feelings of the heart? While he'd been writing those words, he had paused and thought he must do everything he could to be able to lay claim to them himself. One day.

But that was before he'd grown depressed again.

Yet lying worked. Nathan laughed. Miraculously—he laughed.

"How would you pay us back then?"

"I wouldn't. Oscar would."

"Where's *he* going to get the money?"

"He'll get a job as soon as he returns. And a well-paid one: at any rate an Oxbridge degree still counts for something. Even now." He wasn't quite certain that it did (anyhow, not Oscar's disappointing two-two) but then neither of Nathan's children had been to *any* university, let alone to Oxford. So there had to be a little that he, Ephraim, had managed to get right; perhaps he couldn't on *every* count be called a loser; even if he had to give some of the credit—most of the credit— all of the credit?—to the 'girl'.

But at least he'd had the good sense, or the discrimination, or the sheer luck, to choose the right girl.

Or had been guided towards doing so. He very much hoped that this had been the case.

"And will he pay the interest?" As so often with Nathan—even after more than fifty years—Ephraim wasn't wholly sure if he was joking.

"Yes. Naturally. Of course. He would expect to."

"Well, I'll have to ask Angie. She's the moneylender." Like Ephraim— like indeed practically everybody else in the family—Nathan had married 'out'. Their own mother was just about the only one who hadn't; and look what had become of that! Angie was a theatre sister. "Every- thing *I* earn," added Nathan, "goes on insurances and things."

Ephraim didn't believe this. He knew that a rough translation would have been: *You've sprung this on me and I'll have to think.*

"Listen. He's no more than a boy—he's just a boy, Nathan."

But he wasn't really worried any more: he knew that even if it were truly a matter of conferring with Angie she would immediately be a lot more sympathetic than Nathan; or at least than Nathan sounded. (Bless you . . . you mothers of the world.)

"Okay. You can spare the sob stuff. Where do you want me to send the money—supposing we can rake it up? To your place?"

"No. No. I'll find out details. Ring you back."

"Haven't you a fax machine at that crummy dive of yours?"

"Yes, certainly we have." A touch of proprietorial pride in that: classy sort of office in which to be allowed to set up your own business; pay your own National Insurance contribution. (Not that he actually had, of course.)

"Talking of which. Have you made any money at it yet?"

"Spasmodically. In fact I did quite well my first month."

"How much?"

"About eight hundred."

Nathan laughed.

"Well, if you think *that's* funny, you'd simply double up at what I made last month."

"Try me."

"Nothing at all." Ephraim's financial adventurings had always been something of a joking matter between Nathan and himself. "What's more, I bet you thought I was exaggerating when I said the bank was going to sue."

"Weren't you?"

"And the building society probably about to foreclose?"

Nathan had evidently thought he *was* exaggerating but that Ephraim's version bore a close enough resemblance to the truth to be practically believable. It was this combination of sailing close to the wind and displaying chronic insouciance that seemed to appeal to Nathan. His laughter was starting to recur with every answer that his brother gave.

"And this month?"

"Looks like being the same."

Or perhaps Nathan realized there was no real exaggeration and was merely being more honest than most: people might not always laugh, or even want to laugh, at the cockups of others, but there was no doubt that the uprooted tree in your neighbour's garden made you feel better about the snapped hollyhocks in yours. Nathan was at least receiving some reward for services rendered—for services about to be rendered. He actually admitted as much, without dissemblance.

"I must say that talking to you can sometimes brighten up even the bloody sort of morning *I'm* having. And it sounds as though your son is all set to follow in your footsteps . . . so if for any reason you yourself weren't here, there'd always be somebody to maintain the family tradition and provide us with reminders of what might have been. If Angie were at home I'd be tempted to ring her right now to pass on the entertainment. Just the same, you can fax me rather than disturb my work a second time. What does Thingummy—you know—that girl of yours—what does Jean have to say about all this?"

Ephraim had listened with mixed feelings to this relatively long speech. He didn't object in the slightest to his brother's family choosing to see *him* as a buffoon but he didn't want them casting Oscar in the same role. He didn't want Oscar at fifty-two to find himself in any situation analogous to his own. And yet, simultaneously, perhaps he did—deep down—but this was not the kind of thing that you could ever confess to; not if you were the natural sort of father who, on one level, wished wholeheartedly for his children's success in as many spheres as possible that were compatible with decency.

Also, he didn't understand this affectation of never being able to remember Jean's name. Nathan like Jean. So did Angie. (So did absolutely everyone, heaven help him.)

(And heaven be praised for it, as well.)

Still. At the moment, of course, he couldn't afford to take issue.

"What does Jean have to say about it? Well, she doesn't know yet about Oscar but if I were to tell you *fully* about the rest of it you'd soon feel sorry you had asked. Basically she says we keep on repeating the same mistakes, not just ourselves but everyone—that subconsciously I must have chosen to live as I do—and so what the fuck do I intend to do about it? I paraphrase."

"Okay, I'm beginning to feel sorry already; and I think I've got a client." Nathan supplied him with his fax number. "And if I don't get back to you today you'll know that we did in fact manage to come up with the five hundred. Under extreme pressure. Not to mention blackmail. And we'd better be getting a bloody good Christmas present this year . . . " He said a quick goodbye and rang off.

After this Ephraim phoned the Indian High Commission and the Bank of India and the Foreign Office. He was starting to see there were advantages to having fallen out with Barney: despite the latter's impassioned threat—"We *shall* talk!"—obviously the time for parley hadn't yet arrived, however overdue, not even in regard to this protracted series of Ephraim's plainly personal and (as must with every justification be suspected) long-distance phone calls. Ephraim should have asked Oscar for his number in Calcutta while he was about it.

Well, perhaps he should give Abby a bell in Belgium (Columbia-speke). That would at least have been something; but unhappily his inconsiderate daughter was bound to be at work.

In any case, within an hour of reaching the office, he had the Oscar situation sorted out, even down to reporting the theft of the traveller's cheques and the credit cards; and he was feeling satisfied with his performance. Nathan's bank would send cash to the Foreign Office by special messenger; the British Consulate in Calcutta would be instructed to release an equivalent sum to Oscar.

Ephraim had discarded some options and picked up on others. Everyone had been wonderful but he still considered his own part in it no negligible achievement. Perhaps, after all, he couldn't be so *very* much of a loser.

The word 'achievement' always reminded him of Neville—who had many years ago been married to Joan, and more latterly to Liz. He had died some eighteen months previously, at the age of seventy-eight. "Old boy, I have achieved *nothing!*" he would often say. "For a gifted man . . . I have achieved *nothing!*" It wasn't true—not of Neville. But Ephraim suddenly had an intimation of his own approaching end and a desolate awareness of his being afraid to face it.

11

Tonight it was especially important he should get an inside seat. If any-one unauthorized was going to try to pull him off the train he wanted there to be as much of a barricade as possible. But maybe, too, it was as much of a psychological thing: the feeling of finding refuge in a corner, of being protected on all flanks.

He wondered if by any chance the accountant from yesterday might sit beside him. Often it seemed to happen that way: you saw somebody two or three times in quick succession and then not again for several months—if, indeed, ever.

But he got neither the accountant nor the girls. The seats across from him were taken by men in dark suits, one in his mid-thirties, the other ten years older. They chatted desultorily about the September trade figures, which showed a £1.64 billion deficit, and about the pros and cons of TV cameras being introduced into the House of Com-mons. Then they settled to their newspapers and there was only inter-mittent comment as something in particular struck one of them. The seat next to Roger was taken by a student as gangling as himself—they could have been brothers—with a personal stereo and a thick textbook concerning the geological timescale and rock formation and suchlike.

Roger felt God had been kind to him; and no doubt because it had been such a very good day generally, believed He might continue to be.

Perhaps, even, it wouldn't be last night's conductor on this train. Rosters got changed, didn't they? People bluffed. (His dad said he was coming to think you couldn't take anybody's word for anything these days.) Was it really too much to hope?

He discovered that it was.

"And so you *still* haven't got a ticket? Well, I warned you, didn't I? Last night I told you what would happen."

The two men lowered their newspapers. The student removed his earphones.

"Yes, you did." Roger noticed the faded blueness of his eyes again almost more than he did the strawberry mark.

"I don't get you. This means the police will have to be called out to meet the train at Leicester and all these people will find themselves inconvenienced by a delay of maybe half an hour or more. Have you thought of that?"

"I'm sorry."

The man stood there and gave a sigh—really a deep one. Then he shook his head and shrugged. It took at least fifteen seconds; possibly even thirty. Eventually he moved off. All without a further word.

Yet almost at once he turned back. "And you're definitely saying you don't intend to pay the single fare to Nottingham tonight?"

"I don't have the money."

He departed again. "Well, what's all that about?" asked the older of the two men. Roger had guessed that he'd be sympathetic as soon as he'd heard him reading something from his newspaper: "The Prime Minister made clear that she was totally unconcerned that she had been outnumbered by forty-eight to one on the dominating issue of South Africa. 'If it's one against forty-eight, I feel very sorry for the forty-eight,' she remarked." The man had grinned. "Well, so do I. And that's what worries me. I used to believe I had a natural affinity for the underdog."

The other man had answered: "Seems to me you've just displayed it." Despite their city suits and their veneer of belonging to the Establishment, Roger had surmised that he was blest to have them.

He related what had happened. He spoke principally to the two men but didn't exclude the student.

"Well, I think we should get up a petition for him—fast," declared the younger . . . what . . . actuary, stockbroker?

"But haven't they covered themselves? Somewhere in the small print? I'm sure, Greg, there'll be a line to the effect that they aren't responsible for any days lost owing to strike action."

"Yes, could be. Yet the fact that they're willing to extend a season ticket suggests they must consider themselves liable."

The older one nodded. "In any case, whatever the situation legally, you'd suppose that morally and for the sake of good relations they wouldn't want to push it."

Roger said: "Yes, that's what I was hoping. Wouldn't it put them in a bad light having the police come on board to arrest me?" He added, because he found himself in such supportive company and derived a measure of courage from it, something that would have surprised him only two days previously. "And I definitely won't go out to meet them on the platform."

"Would you resist arrest?" asked the student.

"Oh, no. No. But what I mean is . . . if anyone who wasn't a policeman . . . tried . . . tried to pull me off the train . . . "

The younger man—the one called Greg—was sucking, or gently biting at, the pad of one thumb. "Looks like you'll become a test case."

This statement, too, in its way, was mildly intoxicating. Between the three of them they managed to distract his thoughts as far as Leicester, since, although the two men soon returned to their newspapers (each of them from time to time throwing up some new comment on Roger's predicament; or merely repeating an old one), the student began a conversation which was by far the pleasantest Roger had ever had with a stranger on a train journey. It was ironic that it should take this kind of incident to promote it, and a coincidence it should occur on the same day that he'd met Jenny. He felt astonished when people started getting up and donning their outdoor things.

Greg, who was sitting directly opposite Roger, had the ball of his thumb between his teeth once more. He removed it abruptly. "I can see two policemen talking to our friend on the platform."

Roger said, "Well, this is it then, isn't it?"

Nothing happened. The time and the suspense stretched themselves out: a full five minutes of buttock muscles clenching, bladder-control feeling chancy, feet unable to remain still. Finally it was the student who put an end to this. When he spoke his voice was scarcely louder than a whisper.

"Isn't the train moving?"

Greg said: "Yes . . . yes, I think it is. My God, it certainly is." He smiled his relief at Roger. "Looks like you've been granted a reprieve."

His companion also looked more than merely pleased. "Well," he said. "Well." He wiped his forehead on the handkerchief from his breast pocket and laughed. "Another day, another dollar. In this case another mighty battle won."

"Or anyhow a skirmish," suggested Roger.

"Battle—skirmish—rout . . . who cares? All I know is: it cries out to be celebrated. What will you lads have to drink?"

It could have grown into a party. The sad thing was that the party had to be curtailed. Roger needed to change at Loughborough.

An even sadder thing was that neither of the men was a regular traveller. Far from being stockbrokers or actuaries they were ear-nose-and-throat specialists who'd been attending a day's conference in town. And equally as disappointing, it was a one-off for the student, too. On the other hand this was hardly a time for sadness. Although he'd had to finish his gin in a hurry Roger shook hands with all three of them. In the entire course of his life he would probably never set eyes again on either Greg or . . . Anthony . . . or James; but at any rate they had been there for him this evening, just as the accountant, who was possibly an undertaker, had been there for him last night. If it weren't for this bol-shiness of British Rail he wouldn't have got to know any of them, even thus briefly, and he felt in that case he would definitely have missed out. So, standing on the platform at Loughborough, it came to him suddenly that he was *glad* this dispute had arisen. It might be just a question of ships that passed in the night but the more ships he could at least wave to—if they were friendly and well-meaning craft—then the more varied and worthwhile, surely, would be his own voyage. It was a dictum worthy of his father.

His only regret at the moment was that he hadn't asked for phone numbers. It threatened to be a big regret, one which might nag at him indefinitely, and he couldn't think why he had not done it.

In the end he had to ascribe it to conditioning. His mother's influence rather than his dad's. Could you ever break away from your conditioning?

He had meant to get some mileage out of Henry's choice of song; out of the purchase of his birthday card. He had meant to tell his parents a little about his lunch-hour encounter. (He wondered if she had started reading yet—or was perhaps reading at this very minute—*Captain Blood*; he wanted her to enjoy it nearly as much as though he'd written it himself.) And if his dad were feeling better, and the chance arrived to speak to him on his own, he'd been hoping at last to share his major preoccupation of the week; or joint-major one . . . now that he'd met Jenny. He would have told him not simply about the bad things but about all the camaraderie as well, his aim being not to worry him but just to find another sympathetic ear, another bit of backup; damn it, it felt *unnatural* not to be talking in his own home about something so terribly important to him.

But almost as soon as he had washed his hands and sat down to table his mother exclaimed, "Ah, darling—such exciting news! We heard today from Oscar. He should be home by the weekend." And even if she again sounded a little cool as she added, "I didn't learn about it till tonight; your father sorted the whole thing out with Uncle Nathan, which was very kind of him . . . ," her vivacity quickly returned when she cried, "Oh, shall we throw a party? What a shame your sister's timing was so poor! I wonder if she'd consider coming back, though, for a killing of the fatted calf . . . well, at least we can ring her and find out. Paul-Michel might like it, too—he gets on very well with Oscar."

The fatted calf! Although he naturally did his best to sound pleased Roger thought the metaphor more fitting than she realized. In fact he *exactly* understood how the Prodigal Son's poor boring older brother must have felt. Already he could imagine the grins and the whoops and the hugs, and the interminable tales of exoticism and adventure, and the photographs, and the buccaneering suntan, and the demands for everyone's attention and for masses of home-cooked food. Oh God! That miserable bloody pickpocket five thousand miles away! Whatever age he was, this rotten sodding thief, wherever he'd been born, the fact that the date of his parents' coupling should have stirred up such emotions in the stomach of a complete bastard in Nottingham on the 24th of October 1989—such emotions that he could barely lift his fork to try to eat his dinner—was . . . it was . . . "I'm sorry but I don't feel hungry," he said. "I think I'll go upstairs."

He saw his mother's expression yet felt he couldn't do anything about it. He hoped she'd put it down to overtiredness. But one of the best days of his life had unexpectedly turned sour and he had nothing save his own fantastically mean nature to blame it on. Maybe it *was* overtiredness and by morning he'd have regained a truer and nicer perspective. In the meantime, he thought, as he lay despondently in his bath, he was pleased no opportunity had arisen to tell his father about his own unexotic adventures which, comparatively, could be viewed only as very small potatoes. Very small potatoes indeed. He decided he would keep that tale to himself—possibly for ever, certainly until it was all finished with (unless, of course, he had to spend the night in a police cell). It was *his* tale; he suddenly didn't want anyone—not even his dad—taking it over . . . sorting it out. He could manage on his own.

At home he was still a child; one of the children; and perhaps parents never fully realized that their children had grown up.

The next morning there were some half-dozen guards manning the appropriate barrier at St Pancras, making sure they saw—and scrutinized—the ticket of every passenger who had travelled on the 6.30 InterCity from Nottingham. Roger shuffled forward in the midst of an increasingly cross and indignant crowd. At the start, this crowd must have taken up a full fifteen yards of platform and people were continually calling out for information. They weren't getting any, however— the officials remained stolidly uncommunicative and the only person with the relevant knowledge didn't feel sufficiently bold to share it. Yet though he was understandably apprehensive, perhaps he wasn't any more so than at certain points during the past couple of days, and again he felt gratified at the resources he was discovering in himself. "I think I must be the one you want," he announced, fairly calmly, on reaching the barrier.

The man he had addressed produced an ID card, which Roger scarcely glanced at. While the rest of the passengers off his train were released with a whoosh that was less aural than visual Roger was marched away across the concourse between two of the officials. Aware of people staring at him, of their even turning to stare at him, he wasn't as perturbed by this as he might have expected. He found he could meet their gaze quite easily, without blushing and without bravado. His father, he guessed, would have grinned and feigned indifference. Oscar would have done so, too, while his mother would undoubtedly have kept her eyes lowered. Roger couldn't tell about Abby; he believed she might have shown sardonic composure and looked pretty damn good in the process. He suddenly had a vision of Henry being frogmarched through the station; saw vividly his air of pained and pompous perplexity—it was a picture which honestly made him smile. He thought, as well: I'm looking forward to my Danish pastry filled with cream cheese—good old Henry!—and I must remember to get Nick to sign that card. I wonder when I'll next see Jenny? It was such reflections as these that occupied his mind during their minute-long progress through the surge of rush-hour commuters. It occurred to him—as indeed it had occurred to him last night, in the company of James and Anthony and Greg—that God most assuredly *did* temper the wind.

He was taken to a large bare room in which a number of railwaymen were standing drinking tea and chatting. There was a solidly old-fashioned sink in one corner and there were girlie pictures on the walls. He remained between his escorts at the further end of the room while they wordlessly waited for someone. The dozen or so railwaymen glanced at him incuriously and proceeded with their conversations.

The man who came in was tall and thin. He looked a little like Norman Tebbit and this again gave Roger grounds for mild amusement; he wondered if he might be told to get on his bike and simply leave home a bit earlier.

106

His escorts moved away.

The man said: "I'm the Revenue Protection Manager." Roger thought he must try to remember that. "I'm acquainted with your case. You have the right to remain silent but I must warn you that anything you do say may be taken down and used in evidence. Has it been pointed out to you that travelling without a valid ticket is a prosecutable offence?"

"Yes," said Roger.

"So you actually knew that by being on the train this morning without a valid ticket you were contravening the law?"

"Yes."

"Then why didn't you buy one?"

"Because I believe you owe me further travel. Besides, I haven't any money."

"What you're saying, then, is that if you'd had the money you'd have paid for your ticket?"

"No."

Irrelevantly, or maybe not, it suddenly struck Roger that, tall though the man was, he was still having to look up to him. It was the first time he could recall ever regarding his height as an advantage (indeed he had more often thought of it as a drawback—as making him conspicuous and at the cinema, for instance, even antisocial—and on account of this, despite his parents' nagging, he had always been inclined to stoop) but now he straightened himself, to an extent that he felt the slight resistance in his shoulders, which were unaccustomed to being squared. He hoped that the movement were imperceptible; but what did it matter if it weren't?

He was perhaps three inches taller than his questioner.

"But you can't really pretend you don't have any money. Why are you leaving your job if you don't have any money?"

At first Roger thought that the man couldn't have heard what he had said; but in the next instant he saw his grandmother, his father's mother, laughingly wagging her finger at him when he had been—what?—about five years old. "None so deaf, my lad, as those who will not hear!" (He associated many such finger-wagging maxims with his grandmother, whom he wished he had managed to see more of. And he could have done: she hadn't died till he was seventeen.) Now he realized a few things simultaneously: that the railwaymen in the room had all stopped talking; that this Revenue Protection Manager obviously *was* better acquainted with the case than some of his questions might have indicated; and that if Gran's maxim upon deafness were right, then this automatically added a certain strength to his own position.

"I'm leaving my job because there's no way I can afford three-and-a-quarter thousand pounds to buy a new ticket."

He had slightly raised his voice. Whatever their feelings of loyalty he believed there couldn't be a single man present—other than possibly the one in front of him—who wouldn't sympathize with his explanation.

"But your ticket expired last Saturday. You should have left your job last Saturday."

"My boss and I had taken into account the six extra days you owed me."

"No. I'm sorry. We don't owe you anything."

"But doesn't that seem a bit inconsistent? I was told if I'd bought a new season ticket there'd have been no problem adding on those missing days." *Thank you, Greg.*

The man didn't answer. There was a pause: no, something that seemed far longer than a conversational pause: and, although he felt its awkwardness, Roger was determined not to fill it. He thought: Perhaps I ought to begin visiting a gym. If extra height can give you an advantage, think what extra breadth could also do for you. He imagined Norman Tebbit in confrontation with Arnold Schwartzenegger. Roger would hate to be like Arnold Schwartzenegger. But there was always, of course, a happy medium.

"You could leave your job today instead of Saturday."

"No. It would mean letting everybody down. It would also mean my losing three or four days' salary."

"Well, suit yourself. But if you're on that train tomorrow morning you know you'll be arrested?"

Coming from someone of such standing the threat carried authority. It had carried authority before but might now have stood in danger of being dulled by repetition.

"Yes."

"And will you be on that train tomorrow morning?"

"Yes."

"I see. Well, as I say, that's up to you. You've been informed about the possibility of a refund, haven't you?"

"Six pounds a day."

"No, I haven't mentioned any figure. I haven't worked it out. But in court I shall say I offered you a refund. You're totally clear on that point? I want to be absolutely fair."

"Then perhaps you'd like to work it out now?" suggested Roger. "I can wait a while. I'm not in any hurry."

"Excuse me?"

Roger was aware he could have sounded impudent. "I just meant I don't have to be at the shop until nine. And anyway, if necessary, I can always say I was delayed by my journey . . . that I was unavoidably detained."

Not the least hint of an answering smile—and he didn't look to see if anyone else might have appreciated his small attempt at humour. Had he perhaps made things a little worse? Could such a tongue-in-cheek remark be taken down and used in evidence?

"No, I certainly can't work out a figure while we're standing here."

"I'm sorry."

"But I hope you won't deny I've offered you a refund?"

"Of six pounds a day."

"That's not correct. I haven't named a figure."

"It's the only figure which anyone *has* named."

There was another, but this time much shorter, pause. "Why not simply go to the Complaints Department, Mr Mild? After all, that's the reason we have a complaints department."

The production of his name was almost as disconcerting as the phrase *in court*. In their different ways they were equally insidious.

"I didn't even realize you had a complaints department. I suppose I should have done. Could they settle it, then, by this evening?"

"No, they could not settle it, then, by this evening." The man was clearly getting riled.

"Well, in that case . . . ?"

The Revenue Protection Manager looked at his watch.

"So for the rest of the week I would advise you to stay at home," he declared, crisply. "Because if you try to come back to London in the same way tomorrow it won't be just us, it will be the police that you'll find waiting for you. Understood?"

He would have liked to say: *I'd be a numbskull if it wasn't, after the number of times it's been repeated! Yeah, life gets tedious, doan it?*

"Yes," he said. "Understood."

Nick Barratt was shortish and solid and although he was only in his early fifties—the same age as Roger's father—the little hair he had remaining was not simply grey, it was almost white. Rose taunted him about his need to lose weight (which was one point you might have thought Rose would keep quiet on) but he responded genially to these jibes, even though he didn't much care for Rose and even though he could be quick-tempered and oversensitive about other, apparently less hurtful digs. Roger got on well with him and was apt to confide things he didn't talk about to anybody else at work except—normally—to Mr Cavendish. Nick had led an interesting existence and it was he who'd made the comment about writing that had prompted Henry's claim to friendship with a famous author. While Nick was signing Henry's card in the basement, Roger gave him an update on the train situation. His mention of it on Monday had been an error because he hadn't taken into account Nick's habitual pessimism and he spoke of it today only because Nick had asked about developments. (But on Monday Roger had simply felt the need to unburden himself to *someone*.)

Nick paused in his search for something original to put on Henry's card, to say to Roger in a discouraging tone (and this from the man who'd crossed rope bridges over yawning chasms in South America, opened a marriage bureau in Chester, taken up the study of Arabic only a couple of years ago with a view to obtaining a degree in it): "No, I think it's extremely dangerous, what you're doing. I think you're tempting providence—not to talk of prosecution and prison! I feel at the very least you ought to tell Mr Cavendish."

"No. Absolutely not. He just wouldn't understand. Any more than you do."

"He probably thinks you keep arriving late because it's your last week and you've lost interest."

"I wasn't late yesterday. Hardly late today. And on Monday some sheep really had got onto the line. Nothing to do with me."

"And tomorrow?"

Roger shrugged. "Buck up with that card. He's already been here half an hour. He'll be dishing out the cakes at any moment. I think we should have bought him a present."

In fact he was toying with the idea—and this wasn't merely self-interest—of slipping out to buy a pound of handmade chocolates from nextdoor.

Actually his motive wasn't at all one of self-interest. What largely prevented him was the thought that Jenny might believe he was chasing her.

Another deterrent was the knowledge that if he were indeed to buy such chocolates his parents were more the ones who ought to have them . . . except that his mother was currently on a diet; and, besides which, there was this niggling fear that if Oscar were coming home it might be Oscar who would end up getting most of them. Also, there was his awareness of how much better spent—probably—those several pounds would be if he simply divided them amongst the people of both sexes and all ages who absolutely every night, while he was on his way to St Pancras, asked him whether he had any change. (One night recently he had been accosted four times, although the average was only half of that.) Not of course that if he didn't spend the money on Henry he would this evening give away more than a fraction of it but even so . . .

Milk Tray was possibly the answer.

And surely Mr Cavendish knew him well enough by now to realize it wasn't at all because he was leaving that it might appear he was taking liberties.

"I will say one thing, though," volunteered Nick, as he handed back the card. "Whatever the rights or wrongs of all this, you've got more guts than I have. I couldn't do what you're doing. I don't know many people who could."

12

If it wasn't raining Jean usually walked to work. She did this partly for the exercise and partly for economy but also because she enjoyed it: her route lay mainly among trees and brought both interest and perspective. They lived near the reservoir and from here the view over the city—with its tumble of houses and chimneys, skyscrapers and spires, its backdrop of blue-tinted hills—almost never failed to please her. The path eventually led down to a busy road but from this it wasn't far to the Arboretum, and even setting aside the splendour of trees and flowers and shrubs—not to mention sightings of such things as squirrels, robins, blackbirds, magpies—just the skill with which the gardeners planted out the seedlings made her envy them their occupation; could there be many jobs so satisfying? (Since a spacious garden of her own now looked less and less likely, the only thing she thought could equal this in kind was a lovingly detailed model railway or doll's house—and doll's house she did in fact possess, an expensive one, double-gabled, half-timbered, which Ephraim had given her ten years before . . . but although she had built up a small collection of furnishings, had worked out biographies for the two elderly people who lived in it—enjoying frequent visits from their grandchildren, naturally!—had even bought the wiring with which to electrify the house, still she'd never found the time, or the energy, or the money, still after all these years, to do more than plan it and re-plan it in her head, most often during wakeful nights; it was like her wish to write, just another source of embittering frustration.) And then, leaving the Arboretum, you crossed to the cemetery. This also was beautiful: two pathways winding through it unobtrusively, leading you gently out of the hollow—so far your walk had been entirely downhill—but soon beginning to rise more steeply. Here the turf was less smooth and the only growing flowers were the wild ones which clustered under trees or along banks: a woodland atmosphere in spite of gravestones. If she hadn't disliked so much the notion of being buried she would have considered this as good a spot as any in which to be laid to rest, prefer- ably somewhere sheltered and close to one of the paths.

Laid to rest . . .

She was only fifty-two, three months younger than Ephraim . . . although already she was seven years older than her mother; a thought which wasn't merely terrifying—heredity?—it was totally incredible. Yet, despite this, those three tranquil syllables appealed to her so powerfully that recently she had come to under- stand how old people could claim the prospect of death no longer worried them, indeed was positively reassuring, something to wel- come. And that, too, was scary: that at a comparatively early age, with at least another quarter of a century absolutely vital to her—and even then only sufficient if every day was used, lived to its uttermost—she had actually begun to empathize with such a claim.

Apart from anything else, what percentage had she yet seen of this intriguing world she lived in? A little of France, a little of Germany, a tiny bit of Scandinavia; shamefully, just an equally small proportion of Britain. And she had always wanted so very much to travel (even—in the days of being a dreamer—to explore: one of her childhood hero- ines had been Mary Kingsley, who had fought off crocodiles with an umbrella: although Jean the explorer, forty years ago, had been still more scared of spiders than she was today). Oh, but how she envied Oscar all his travels—and not merely these current ones, either; he and his friends had been taking holidays abroad for several years now . . . And, oh, how she envied Abby, who had spent ten months in America au pairing, followed by a further three in Rome with a girlfriend whose aunt had an apartment there—Abby, who was now living, and would be doing so for as long as it suited her, with a forceful up-and-coming young executive in Brussels, from where she could at any time hop in a car, get on a train, cross so many frontiers . . . simply breathe and expand. (And their stay-at-home mother was thirty years older than this globetrotting son, twenty-seven than this gallivanting daughter!) And she envied them not the fact of being young but the fact of having been born at a time when it had become usual for students to swan off with backpacks and sleeping bags and send home little but the odd postcard: going on to Florence . . . or Venice . . . or Athens . . . or Krakatoa . . . or Alice Springs . . . Mum, could you please extend insurance: the world, instead of only Europe? . . .

Well, anyhow.

The reservoir—the Arboretum—cemetery. This was the route that Jean generally followed to reach Canning Circus and the small antique shop where she worked.

It was possible, the police said later, that the man had been lying in wait for her.

It happened shortly after she entered the Arboretum. A hundred yards inside the park the path ran under a tunnel. She'd never liked this tunnel. It was only short and wasn't particularly dark; it provided support for the road above and a frame for the vista which lay ahead. And yet it possessed an aura that made her quicken her step and hold on more tightly to the wicker shopping bag which contained her reading matter for the day, writing materials (ha!), bread and fruit for lunch, her purse and cosmetics and keys and all the usual paraphernalia. Especially did her grip tighten when—as today—there was nobody in sight: no gardeners, no dog-walkers, no students on their way to college. She was seldom unaware of this tautening of her fingers, however automatic. Once, in the Nouvelles Galeries in Bordeaux, at the checkout from the food department, she had discovered that her wallet, with more than five hundred francs in it, had been snitched from her shoulder bag. At first she just couldn't absorb the truth of it, even though she should have been alerted, had of course been alerted, by the opened zipper, the obtruding hankie. But when the truth could no longer be evaded she had started to shake—and couldn't stop shaking. The strength of this reaction was perplexing. Admittedly the loss had been of a fairly large sum—she had just come from the bank—yet could that really justify a state of shock? The thought of some thief's fingers touching her belongings, or the sight of the week's provisions jostling one another on the belt, in supermarket limbo, naturally hadn't assisted, but nevertheless it was all so . . . all so . . .

Feeble.

Everyone was very kind. Along with the money, she had lost her French and must have seemed half-witted but the woman next in line put a weathered arm about her, and those trying to press forward behind this bulky black-garbed barrier condoled vociferously with Jean and vilified all pickpockets. The cashier left her seat and began packing the groceries into carrier bags—including, with understanding shrugs, the items Jean had already stowed at the bottom of her shopping trolley—so that there'd be no need for her to search them out again; and the manager of the department, summoned by his staff, finally took a gratefully smiling but still visibly trembling Jean into his office for a small cup of black coffee, slightly sweetened, into which a generous dollop of brandy had been poured. This helped considerably; and leaving her shopping trolley in his office she'd turned in the opposite direction to home and weaving dexterously among the crowds half-run along the rest of the rue St Catherine (she'd still been in her thirties then; it was only a kilometre from the store to the Place de la Victoire; and the threat of an asthma attack at the checkout had been averted, thank God, by her Ventoline inhaler—contaminated or not). When she'd got to the Faculty of Medicine, in which the English Department was housed, she'd obtained easy access to Ephraim, in private, and had blurted out the whole occurrence whilst sobbing in his arms. After that there was a full recovery: she'd apologized repeatedly, and even laughingly, for making such an idiot of herself—"I don't see that you did," said Ephraim, "but in any case why do you think you would need to apologize?"—had washed her face, told him he was very sweet ("I can't believe you realize just how good you are! Please promise you'll never stop loving me, no matter how silly I become!" "Okay," he'd answered, "if you promise you'll never stop loving me!"), had returned to the bank, where luckily, although they weren't exactly flush, Ephraim's salary for last term had recently been paid in, then gone back to the Nouvelles Galeries and expressed her appreciation in gratifyingly coherent French, with a lot of sincerity and some not very good jokes which had all been warmly responded to. So in the end it had been an episode to regard as something by no means entirely bad; even as one she might almost have been sorry to pass up.

But it had formed her only known close contact with a criminal; and even then she hadn't seen him.

Now—in the Arboretum—again she neither heard nor saw. Her mind had been full of her recent conversation with Oscar; unusually she hadn't even realized she had reached the tunnel.

At the last moment, however, she must have caught some warning sound or movement because she whirled round and encountered this . . . this thing . . . practically beside her; and its hands were coming not for any bag but straight towards her throat. It seemed less like a man than like some half-human monster from a horror film; its teeth were bared and as their eyes met it even started snarling.

But she acted from instinct. She brought her basket up—swung it with all her strength—full into the creature's groin.

The impact not simply stopped him but sent him reeling back, still grimacing but in a different way, no longer snarling but gasping, whimpering, hands covering his crotch.

He was bent double now but she felt no compunction for the pain she had inflicted. She moved towards him and possibly planned on inflicting more. Certainly she brandished her basket. Certainly her words reverberated—like bullets—off the brickwork. "Bastard! Pig! Wimp! Shit! Pathetic, inadequate, undersized prick!" The belligerence unleashed was greater than any aggression she had ever shown, except perhaps once, when during the worst of her rows with her violent, jealous, radical boyfriend, she had gone for him with a carving knife— thank heaven he had turned in time! Now, not only did she advance on her would-be assailant—who far from looking like a monster was in fact merely insignificant, not a lot taller than she was, a little man, twenty, twenty-five, sallow, pockmarked, mangy. She lunged for his dirty parka when he began to run away.

She was going to chase after him, too; she was still so enraged she might well have caught him—his run was little better than a fast hobble—but what prevented her, bathetically, was the thought of being so late in opening up the shop (Oscar had already lost her fifteen minutes); so she stood and watched him get away and pursued him purely with her taunts . . . where are those snarls, you snivelling wimp, why don't you show me your teeth again? . . . although when, at the top of the low embankment by the road, he turned to look back she shook her fist at him contemptuously.

And she wasn't shaking; she wasn't shaking in the least. Her asthma wasn't bothering her. She felt almost jubilant as she proceeded on her way—still furious, yes, but raised up by her fury, proud, vengeful. Now that that piece of scum had disappeared there was again nobody in sight; possibly, from start to finish, the whole thing had taken no more than three minutes: the fullest three minutes she had ever known? But she strode out confidently, swinging her basket, glad of the thick biography of Lord Byron that Ephraim had recently surprised her with (for no good reason, he had said, other than that he loved her, had been overcome by one of his wild fits of extravagance, and knew how much she wanted the book—blast, though, why had she needed to remember that?). She didn't see anyone, although she kept looking behind her, until she was nearly as far as the bandstand—and then the old gentleman with a carnation in his buttonhole, whom she quite often met, lifted his hat with a flourish and wished her his customary robust good morning; and a little further on, admiring the rockery, the poor old fellow in his cloth cap and woollen scarf—yet why 'poor'? he always seemed content—waved his walking stick at her and called over to ask where her cocker spaniel named Polly was.

"At home, I'm afraid. She has to spend today cooped up at home. I don't think that she'll like it very much!"

He nodded, smiled at her happily. "Where's your cocker spaniel named Polly, then?"

She didn't abate her walking pace and with a farewell lift of her hand was quickly out of earshot. Both she and Ephraim were getting to understand his speech much better these days; sometimes they saw him here, sometimes near the path leading down from the reservoir, thoughtfully inspecting a tuft of grass with the tip of his walking stick or peering over a fence at the blossoms on an elderberry; and at first he had caused them perplexity, especially when remarking without preamble on the sharpness of the creases in his new trousers or the fact that his dad had used to collect matchboxes or that his mum knew a girl who made marrow jam. To begin with Ephraim had been the more skilled interpreter but nowadays the old man chiefly inquired into the whereabouts of their cocker spaniel named Polly or—depending on the circumstances—might say, "That's your cocker spaniel named Polly!", and was clearly much pleased that he could so easily recall both her breed and her name.

At the pond—miniature lake?—and by the bird cages (a plaque in one of these commemorated 'Cocky, sulphur-crested cockatoo, died 1968, aged 114') there was a father showing his little boy the nearly luminous green plumage around the head and breast of one of the ducks. There were also a couple of gardeners leaning on their forks and smilingly listening to the driver of a lorry who sat above them in his cab. Everything as normal. But what was even more reassuring: she saw, on the other side of the water, a young man in communion with a goose . . . putting his arm about its neck—laying his cheek on top of its head—just chatting to it, dreamily. He was frequently there, this man; she had never spoken to him but self-evidently he was nice: thirtyish, not at all odd-looking, well-built, rather handsome; apparently always recognized at once by his friend the goose. Sometimes Jean quite wished somebody would chat to her like that. It reminded her of Brindley and made her want to cry.

It wasn't until she reached the shop—striding out through the cemetery as she had stridden through the Arboretum, not because of lateness but because of unaccustomed energy—that she began to have a reaction that was altogether different. This time she didn't shake precisely but several violent shivers racked her within half a dozen minutes. She saw his hands zero in towards her throat and for the first time she thought: what if I hadn't had my basket, or that heavy book inside it, or the time or the space in which to swing it, or the instinct which had made me do it? Supposing I hadn't turned would he have encircled my neck and throat from behind? And once his hands had found their target would she have had the strength to dislodge them? She imagined herself gasping for air—unable to breathe, worse than the worst kind of asthma attack, as bad as her nightmare vision of the potholer with shoulders wedged between the rocks—and saw her hands flailing against him with decreasing power; lived through the agony of straining to gulp for oxygen now being denied.

It was then that she needed her inhaler—Ventide these days, not Ventoline—and to grasp at the edges of her desk while telling herself not to panic, to take slow steady breaths, it's going to be all right. Gradually she was able to look about her at the cluttered interior of the shop and think about a man maybe pouring out his innermost emotions to a goose but it was only as she did so that she realized there were tears running down her cheeks and dripping onto the stockbook. She blew her nose and she telephoned the police. As she gave them her account it sounded practically unreal—melodramatic—a hysteric overreaction to a student prank. When they told her there'd be somebody round immediately she wanted to say no, no, please don't bother, I'm sure it isn't worth it.

Before they arrived, or before any potential customer should come in—quite often, however, she might see nobody until lunchtime—she splashed cold water on her eyes; reapplied her makeup. She felt better for this and could even smile, tentatively, at her reflection in the cracked glass. She knew she'd had to report the incident. Later in the week, they'd said, perhaps this evening, she'd have to go across to the station and look through some photographs; which was a nuisance. She also knew she would never again, or at any rate not for a long time, be able to walk through the Arboretum, or the cemetery, on her own—one of the few remaining pleasures in her life and he had spoilt it. (No, it wouldn't be a nuisance: nail the bastard.) And he wasn't the only one she was angry with. She was also angry at Ephraim. She felt she didn't know him any longer; recently they hadn't seemed to talk. (Perhaps they never had—perhaps it was only their shared interest in the children which had given the illusion that they used to speak about more than just the things you could discuss with strangers at a party.) So there operated a kind of force field which made it impossible for her to reach out now and dial his number: Help—please come to me—this is an emergency.

I need you.

13

"Do men have to pee right in the centre of the bowl?"

Joan had continued to pop in often after the breakup of her marriage to Neville and it was when she was living with her new husband in a luxury block in Weymouth Street, literally round the corner, that one evening she had put this question to Ephraim, apropos of being awoken every night by the man upstairs emptying his bladder. "Imagine! Of all the things in this world, I'm slowly being driven mad by a three o'clock piddle!" Ephraim sometimes thought of it these days when he himself was urinating and stirring up a froth. (Another thing he sometimes thought of was the way he'd used to create pictures in the water: cloud formations, animals, trees, the design of the newspaper advertisements for *The Wicked Lady* where half the advert had been shaded, presumably to indicate duality.) "Does it make a man feel more . . . more masculine or something?" They'd all laughed about it, the three of them, drinking tea in the lounge, with the great brown wireless on a nest of tables in the corner, and the elegant escritoire in the bay window, and the still life of dusky, bloom-laden fruit on the wall above the imitation-coal electric fire. His mother had suggested that Joan should knock on her bedroom ceiling with a broom handle. "That might encourage him to do it more discreetly! Or write him a letter; you could make it anonymous." They'd had a lot of fun deciding how to word it. Ephraim had said, "Why not send Emil up to speak to him, or go yourself and speak to his wife?", and still today he considered he'd got it right, but their laughter had grown quite manic while they rehearsed the variety of conversations it would be possible to have with one or the other of them . . . Ephraim thought of it on Wednesday morning, in the john at work, and was still half-smiling as he shook his penis, put it back inside his trousers, pulled the zip.

His first distinct memory of Joan had, paradoxically, nothing in it of Joan. It was of an incident that had happened on the staircase in the days when the High Street had still had something of a village character (the small open greengrocer's, with the shutter rolled down at night, where Mrs Brown saved him and his mum his first-ever bananas—slightly disappointing after all he'd been led to expect of them; the Ridgeway, occupying a large site on the corner of Devonshire Street, where waitresses like the ones you got in cinema restaurants brought you toasted teacakes or salads or, once eggs were available again, poached eggs on toast; Gaylor & Pope's, the haberdashery store that had those overhead tracks along which ran brown balls containing your change, after the assistant had dispatched your money, rocket-like, up a hissing chute) . . . still something of a village character, despite the side-street slums and also the bombsites, covered in rosebay willowherb, to front and rear of the flats.

The staircase was of bare stone, light grey, the colour of cement. Dingy. Its walls were just as bare; the white distemper flaking, grimy. There were four flats in the building, one on each floor, except at ground level, where there was only access to the basement and the dustbin area and space to keep his brother's bike—which later had been passed on to him—solid, black, and rusty. On every half-landing was a grimy sash window that looked out on the backs of other tenements; and on every full landing was a green front door—and a push button encased in brown Bakelite to operate the lights. The lights lasted solely for a minute and went out with a loud click. Of course, during the day you never needed them, unless the sky was exceptionally overcast. In the daytime it naturally grew lighter between the third floor and the fourth. It also grew more cluttered: an upturned trunk and empty suitcases in the corner opposite their own front door (the third), tea-chests and cartons covered by a large blue-gingham cloth—or sometimes green-gingham—outside Neville and Joan's, overhead.

Joan was the one person who lent an air of luxury to the staircase; and that, not because of her draped gingham but because of her perfume. Ephraim couldn't think how she had managed it. You always knew when she had recently come in or gone out . . . even in 1945 or '6. And he was sure it wasn't cheap or sickly; that wouldn't have been at all in character. She was at that time the most glamorous woman he had ever encountered. (Still rated amongst them.) Red fingernails weren't, he supposed, unknown to him; but blue- or green-shadowed eyelids were.

One afternoon he met her on the staircase—or so he thought. It was that twilight time of day when the place was at its gloomiest and yet for some reason (she had a shopping bag in each hand) they'd neither of them bothered with the lights. He was no more than eight-and-a-half but ghosts had never been a thing to worry him. At that point Joan and Neville had only just moved in, and, despite Neville's being Ephraim's first cousin once removed, they were still comparative strangers to him. Ephraim had seen Joan perhaps two or three times previously—that's what his mother said—but his recollection of their meetings remained hazy.

However, she seemed slightly different now—he realized that—as regards her makeup and her dress, her lack of scent and lack of laughter (or at least the lack of welcome in her smile). But the change that really shocked him was her heavy built-up shoe and calipers.

"Oh, crumbs!" he exclaimed. "Oh, crikey! Whatever's happened to your leg?"

There was a moment of stunned silence.

"I think you are a very rude and nasty little boy!" Joan's sister eventually remarked.

And she continued on up, pushing brusquely past him and leaving him to stare, cringing heartsick in the corner by a window.

For a long time—maybe several months—he couldn't really quite believe this was her sister: that the faces of two women who weren't twins could look so very much alike that it was possible to do what he had done. For those several months he even half-believed in a sort of Jekyll-and-Hyde scenario: a Joan who wore high heels and perfume and was friendly and vivacious; a Joan whose club foot and set, unsmiling features expressed the darker side of her personality—with this one, if he met her in the street or on the stairs, he merely touched his cap and hurried on. Awkward. Baffled. Ashamed.

Humiliated.

Angry.

This incident ranked in embarrassment next to one which had taken place in Wales a couple of years earlier, involving the headmaster, who at the time had seemed so old to Ephraim, old and thin and unapproachable, but who in fact could have been only in his mid-thirties (and if you heard him spelling out his name over the telephone to some poor silly operator—silly, because even Ephraim at six knew how to spell it—it would make you want to giggle: "S for Stuart, T for Tuart, U for Uart . . . "). Mr Stuart had taken some children on what had seemed a long nature-walk, through damp sweet-smelling woods filled with rhododendron, down to the rocks and sandy winding tracks and creek and estuary, and during their return Ephraim, who'd been too diffident to mention his extremely urgent need, had shat in his short trousers; and the headmaster, noticing his slow distressful progress and no doubt ascribing it to tiredness, had suddenly scooped him up and sat him on his shoulders, uttering a merry whoop as he did so. Mr Stuart, though, must soon have realized what had happened. Yet he didn't say anything about it to Ephraim and, when they had reached the school, merely set him down to scurry off to Matron . . .

And that excruciating little episode (yet it was mainly the tact which he remembered now) matched another, when he had been travelling up in the train, accompanied by Nathan, to that farm holiday near Lincoln, and there'd been an airman sitting just across from him, not yet demobbed, who'd been entertaining them with noughts and crosses and I Spy and by sketching aeroplanes and helicopters and parachutists; and Ephraim, who had been leaning forward so as to see better, and who had invariably suffered from travel sickness—yet supposedly on this occasion had had no warning of what was imminent—suddenly spewed up into the airman's lap . . .

How one thing led on to another . . . all while Ephraim unhurriedly washed his hands at Columbia. One Christmas Day at the flat—surely it must have been in '45?—there'd been another airman, only this time an American, and Ephraim could remember the two of them lying on their stomachs on the floor in the lounge playing a game of . . . "Checkers? It's not called checkers! It's called draughts!" and during the course of the afternoon his falling in love with the man. He never saw him again but he thought about him for weeks: cast him as father, brother, friend. It was like a little later when he fell in love first with Laurence Olivier, after seeing a revival of *Lady Hamilton*, and then with Gregory Peck (*Gentlemen's Agreement*), and dreamt about having each of them, too, as a father and about performing heroic exploits that would save their lives or their reputations or their careers or *something* . . . but generally their lives . . . Laurence Olivier had died some three or four months ago but Gregory Peck was still flourishing, had just made a film called *Old Gringo* which Jean was keen to see . . . Ephraim would have loved to know the story of that Christmas airman, whose name he had forgotten. He hoped he'd led a happy life. He wondered if, once in a blue moon, he ever thought of that little English boy who had lain next to him on the carpet and gazed at him with growing veneration, despite his earlier note of pained incredulity. "*Checkers?*"

Joan had always been good to him. For even the simplest shopping errand she would give him a shilling—when his pocket money had been just threepence a week—and, once, when he brought a duckling home from Regent's Park because it had strayed from its mother, it was she who looked after it overnight, found a box and padding and tried to feed it, she and not Nan, who was a little frightened of birds, who accompanied him back to the park the following morning to look for a duck who might adopt this wandering homeless chick amongst its own progeny. (They discovered one who, whilst waddling across the grass, looked back at the line of her offspring as though she might be counting, but then entered the water with all the ducklings fanning out behind her and to Ephraim's huge relief seemed finally unflummoxed by the increase to her retinue.) Neville, years later—long after Joan was dead, of cancer, and when he himself had reached his late seventies—used to say that she'd been hard and mercenary and selfish and that the breakdown of their marriage had been absolutely her fault; but Neville by then, with a failed acting career behind him, followed by a failed writing career, followed by thirty years of merely selling handmade chocolates, had been a cynical and disappointed man; and Ephraim heard that even in his youth he'd had a budding persecution complex. But by then also he'd had eight years of singlehandedly nursing Liz, whom he'd married when they were both approaching fifty: Liz, who could more justifiably, it seemed to Ephraim, have been described as hard, although he thought that she'd become much nicer, gentler, after she'd contracted Alzheimer's. (Once, looking up at a jumbo jet flying out of the clouds, she had argued sweetly, "No, Nev, you must be wrong! How could anyone ever fit inside something so *tiny*?") Neville had refused to put her in a nursing home, had cleaned her, cleaned up after her, with such exemplary patience and humour and undiminished fondness—still, even when she was completely gaga, dreaming up new ways to try to stimulate her, "my poor old hopelessly bewildered darling"—while remaining lively company for other people, well-informed, amusing, challenging, generally tipsy, full of exciting plans, an excellent cook and generous host (although he took offence easily, suspected everybody's motives, bemoaned their shallowness—and did this to their faces—felt that the family had never given him its full support) . . . so that in a way, despite such paranoia, you could almost think that this had been his one unqualified success, looking after Liz, for surely few husbands could have coped with it so admirably. (And, atrociously, there were moments when Ephraim nearly envied him the chance.) *A ministering angel, he . . .* Even in his seventies he had still looked a little like an angel, a paunchy angel, with his round good-natured face, although the plummy voice and the throaty laughter, and the *dear boy* that larded his conversation, tied him forever to the theatre; but when Ephraim had first known him his golden curls and his good looks and typically jocular expression had given him very much the air of a raffish cherub. Perhaps it was an attribute of angels, however: he had by and large been excessively happy-go-lucky: my dear child, heaven will provide. To Joan it had seemed that she was the one doing the providing—she was assistant to an art director in the film business—added to which, Neville was far more often away on tour than he was ever at home (Ephraim had seen him, though, at the Metropolitan in Edgware Road . . . *Worm's Eye View* . . . dancing on a table spread for tea and sticking his bare foot into a plateful of jelly). With only a little more luck the providing aspect might so easily have been taken care of: he sold a script to Hollywood, about a vampire named Lilith, but it was never filmed and he received only two hundred pounds for it. He had a play put on in Shaftesbury Avenue; yet *All the Year Round*, drawing on his experiences of the family, ran for just two nights and although it was subsequently produced on television this didn't help a great deal at the bank. He had a comedy tried out at Kew—Ephraim could remember finding it extremely funny—but it was a week that coincided with the sort of pea-souper in which conductors had to walk in front of their buses carrying a lantern, and none of the hoped-for impresarios turned up. (One person who saw it, however, *To Christabel*, was Robertson Hare, that stalwart of the Aldwych farces, and he liked it so much he asked Neville to write a play especially for him. This could have been the making of Neville, theatrically, and along with that the salvation of his marriage, but frustratingly for all concerned he just couldn't come up with anything) . . . In the middle Fifties, when he had started living apart from Joan, he had had to be rushed into hospital to have his stomach pumped out; but ever afterwards denied, apparently, that his overdose had been anything but accidental.

Something else that might have saved the marriage was the survival of their son, stillborn. They would undoubtedly have made devoted parents . . . although Neville, with his persecution complex, might finally have grown a bit demanding, a bit possessive, who could say . . . ? As an old man he'd certainly have adored—spoilt—been adored by—the grandchildren he'd have wanted to have staying with him, constantly. Between them, they'd have given smashing birthday parties; Neville would have been the conjuror, the magician, always with one further item to produce out of his wondrous sleeve . . .

So, childless, Joan had rescued Ephraim's waifs-and-strays and taken him on treats and, borrowing his bicycle for *The White Unicorn*, had made sure he not only got paid for it but paid for it extremely well (and that was the film, too, for which his beloved Norwegian aunt had prepared table-loads of *smorgasbord*; but then the sequence containing them had been cut); and carried his autograph book to and from the studios and on at least three evenings a week regaled him and Nan with fascinating firsthand anecdotes—he particularly remembered one about a display of temperament by Marlene Dietrich, during the making of *No Highway*—and generally made him feel . . . what? . . . grown-up, important, a *somebody*. He could recall the impression he'd had of standing out from the crowd; he could recall carrying himself extra straight and being self-consciously charming and debonair—and no doubt a very great pain in the arse. Especially when seen not in the company of just a pretty woman (after all, his mother was a *very* pretty woman) but in the company of a strikingly glamorous one . . . then had he walked tall.

It was good to have people turn to notice you.

In fact, it had been one of the major disappointments of his life when he had finally realized he'd stopped growing at five foot nine inches. In his late teens and again in his middle twenties he had experimented, uncomfortably, with platform shoes. It was a source of occasional reassurance, however—even now—that Alan Ladd had been a heartthrob; and Ephraim sometimes reminded himself he would practically have *towered* over Alan Ladd—by a full four inches.

His beloved Norwegian aunt . . . She came from Trondheim, from a handsome and well-to-do family of skiers and skaters. He could recall being surprised, on the rare occasions she'd gone back to Norway, that she could ever have brought herself to return to England—away from the fjords and the islands and the mountains and the pine forests; Amersham-on-the-Hill, even forty years ago, must have seemed a very poor substitute. And at this moment Ephraim recollected how he'd been there once, in Amersham, sunning himself in a deckchair in the garden at *Wildflowers*—yes, he must have been about twelve—when she'd returned from her shopping in a state of perturbation because she'd somehow lost a pound note and because, not being able to do without it, she would later have to tell his uncle. (Ephraim had gone to walk along Sycamore Road, on both sides, with his eyes scarcely leaving the ground . . . but to no avail . . . and if he himself had had a pound he would have lied to her; but she wouldn't even accept his three-and-ninepence-ha'penny—"You can pay me back," he'd cried, "you can pay me back!", though that wasn't at all what he had wanted—yet anything less than fifteen shillings simply wouldn't do.) And part of the sadness here was that Uncle Jack, who had always flared up over the silliest and most trivial of occurrences—although, equally, he'd usually calmed down again very fast—had been essentially a decent and kindhearted man; just not the right kind of husband for any woman who wasn't a lot more placid than Mona. Ephraim had gone to stay with them a lot. Mona had once said to him, in her charmingly accented English, "Perhaps one of the reasons you and I have such a soft spot for one another: we both came into the family at the same time." He remembered how he had tasted real coffee for the first time in her kitchen—coffee black and rich and aromatic, out of a chunky Scandinavian mug—and *Geitost*, goat's-milk cheese, slightly sweet, eaten in slices even thinner than a wafer and scraped off the main khaki-coloured lump with a special implement—and pistachio ice-cream—and homemade raspberry jam . . . these things had seldom tasted quite so good again. And she had taught him to say, "Tusen takk for maten," and had many times taken him to the Regent, although only once allowed *him* to take *her* ("It doesn't in the least matter who actually pays, we're still out, you and I, on a really enjoyable date!") to see such films as *Born Yesterday* and *Copper Canyon* and *Run for the Sun* . . . *The Happiest Days of Your Life*.

Mona had died of a brain tumour, in her middle fifties.

In those days everyone had taken him on treats. These treats mainly involved visits to the cinema. Sometimes to the theatre. His mother—well, with Nan it didn't really come into the category of treat, mothers were expected to do that kind of thing—nearly every Sunday when they weren't due to have tea, or lunch and tea, with Gran, at Marlborough Mansions, his mother took him to the first performance at the Classic (and now he had only to hear 'The Skater's Waltz' by Waldteufel to be instantly back in that four-to-four-thirty rosy dusk which was snug and slightly scented—boring, too—but full of plea-surable anticipation, the promise of new worlds to come, new dreams, new revelations: the nourishment you needed to get you through the drudgery of school, the ropes you couldn't climb, vaulting horse you couldn't clear, neuroses you found difficult to cope with, even before you knew of such a word). Gran, too, had often taken him to the cin-ema—as had another first cousin to Nan, Maggie, a dozen years his senior, in her case to the cinema and then always to a meal; and Great-Aunt Madge had also made 'assignations', bringing large packets of sandwiches to many cheery lunchtime performances. Aunt Madge, effervescent, disrespectful, had often been at Sunday tea as well; Gran and her sisters were very close and several of them had congregated in West Hampstead—Madge, for instance, the mother of Neville, lived right across the road, would drop in nearly every day; whether she did or not, would spend at least an hour on the phone with Gran (all the sisters shared everything: gossip, hats, dressmakers, even prescribed medicines: would beguile many a happy minute rooting through each other's bathroom cabinets to see if there was anything they might enjoy a speedy sample of). Sunday teatimes were a focal point for the entire family, being noisy and chaotic, full of laughter and good food and unity, although they also had their *longueurs*: their sometimes forced, almost frenetic, high spirits: their irritations, emptiness. One of Nan's younger brothers was usually there, with his wife and small children (he had married late); sometimes both her younger broth-ers; and sometimes Jack and Mona came from Amersham, for lunch as well as tea. Often there was good conversation in place of simple noise: Gran was interested in metaphysics, attended Rudolf Steiner lectures and—as she said of herself—could have been the cleverest woman she knew, taken her seat in parliament, reformed the whole world . . . if only she'd had an education. In her youth she'd been a tearing beauty ("Full many a flower is born to blush unseen," she'd sigh, "and waste its sweetness near the Finchley Road!") and at seventy—eighty—eighty-five—this was still readily apparent; but she claimed now she would have chosen university over almost anything: "I could have been another Nancy Astor . . . or Vera Brittain . . . or Isobel Barnet . . . instead of just a supremely stylish charming Jewish

matriarch." Stylish—charming—and benignly domineering; she liked
to be consulted, to be kept informed, to influence her children's lives.
But right, okay, Ephraim knew only that she'd been wonderfully kind
and well-intentioned and full of energy; had really put herself out to
love her neighbour in a way that he, Ephraim, hadn't done now for
years, not since his idealistic twenties; and that he'd been immensely
fond of her, basking in her generosity and wit and warm approval.
(Normally, that was, her warm approval: it was true, you had to toe
the line.) Some of his most fondly cherished moments were of Sunday
evenings, when the rest of the family had departed, just the three of
them still sitting at that solid refectory table, Gran at its head, he and
his mother often holding hands—even when he was eighteen, twenty,
twenty-two—contentedly watching Perry Mason, or Rowan and Mar-
tin, or Doctors Finlay and Cameron. (Mary, the German au pair, after
she'd seen to all the clearing up, would have gone to her bedroom to
write letters or listen to her records or read the magazines her parents
sent her.) An evening of good viewing—particularly he remembered a
series called *The Defenders*, a father-and-son courtroom duo—would
always leave him with a bubbly glow of wellbeing, God's in his heaven,
all's right with the world.

But all wasn't right with the world any longer. The last time he had
seen his grandmother, in the nursing home, her jaw had been slack
and there'd been dribble running down her chin . . . of course she
hadn't known him. The last time he had seen his mother had been a
week before her heart attack on her way to the lavatory, when his sister-
in-law had found her, this once-so-pretty woman, lying face-down on
the lino, in a spreading pool of urine, in a seeping pool of shit. The
last time he had seen Joan was when she'd had a breast removed and
laughing a little too gaily had cried, "Well, life or beauty? I think I've
been sentenced to life!" And the last time he'd seen Mona she had said
privately to Nan, "No, they may not have let on yet, but just the same
I'll bet you she *is* pregnant." (Jean.) "Oh, and what wouldn't I give to be
in her shoes, young and pregnant and having such a husband! . . . You
know, I'm not too sure I'll be able to go through *another* twenty-five
years with Jack . . . "

And the last time he'd seen Neville, Neville had said, "Oh, my dear boy, when you think of all I *might* have achieved . . . and then of what I actually delivered. The trouble is, I had so little encouragement. If Joan had only been a bit supportive! But Joan, as you know, never had a single moment for anybody other than herself . . . "

Madge too, like Gran, had sunk into senility—although, in her case, it had been a gentle going down; *she* hadn't suffered any stroke.

So, of the treaters, only Maggie survived (and Nathan) . . . and the man whom Maggie had loved had finally married somebody else; and he'd done it—as he'd even confessed to her, possibly believing this might somehow make things better—solely because of the other woman's money.

And the last time he'd seen Jean, merely an hour or so before, she had given one of her increasingly typical sighs. "Oh dear, just another tedious day, I suppose; another non-day in which nothing will be accomplished, apart from our growing older and drawing that much closer to death. Heigh-ho. If I only thought there could sometimes be a little variety in my life! Some excitement! Something vaguely memorable for more than just a day or two." She smiled: her twisted, brave, self-sacrificing smile.

"Oh, don't whine," he'd said—though only *sotto voce*—as he had descended the stairs and walked out of the house. "I'm damned if I know what *you've* got to be so miserable about! Damned," he'd repeated—shouting it—whilst slamming the front door.

14

He arrived at St Pancras a little late this evening. The train was already in. There were no guards at the barrier but there were three sauntering separately along the platform. He didn't believe that they would bother him, yet he still felt like a fugitive, a latter-day Richard Hannay. (This thought faintly pleased him; at one time Richard Hannay had been a hero of his.) With a mixture of boldness and stealth, therefore—not looking to see if any of the guards had spotted him—he made swiftly for the door closest to him. It was the First-Class end of the train. Still feeling furtive he hurried through the interior, fearful as he crossed from one compartment to another, passing doorways, that from the platform supple arms might suddenly reach out for him—the ghostly remnants of a dream he'd had the night before. As always this week, he searched for a seat in the most crowded section, a window seat where somebody would screen him, fence him in, and until he'd found one—settled into it—he didn't feel properly safe from these double-jointed, elongating arms, sinuous and surrealistic pursuers.

But it was surprising all the same how you got used to things.

For the third night in succession it was the conductor with the strawberry mark.

"It's all right," Roger told him. "I saw the Revenue Protection Manager this morning and he says that if I'm travelling illegally tomorrow the police will meet me at St Pancras."

"He said that, did he? But what about tonight?"

"He left it vague about tonight."

"Well, you can't expect to travel free again. I gave you a free ticket on Monday."

"I know you did."

"No one could have been more amiable than me."

"You've all been amiable. I wouldn't deny that for a moment."

"You wouldn't? I just don't get you."

"So you said last night—and the previous night, as well. I don't get why you don't get me."

"Do you realize that last night the police were waiting for you at Leicester? They must have missed you."

"Last night I changed at Loughborough. Sometimes I change at Leicester; sometimes I change at Loughborough."

"And tonight? Where will you be changing tonight?"

"I don't know. You see, it all depends upon my mood."

When they were approaching Leicester the conductor returned, busily, businesslike. "I've arranged for the police to be waiting for us here at Leicester."

"Sorry to be a nuisance. But I've decided tonight to change at Loughborough."

"Right. Then I'll have them there at Loughborough."

But he didn't have them there at Loughborough; or perhaps it was just that the police didn't wish to be had there at Loughborough. It seemed less like cloak-and-dagger now, despite the bare, windswept platform, the chill drizzle slanting across the station lamps, the shiny pools of light at your feet, the feeling of film noir; less like cloak-and-dagger, more like cat-and-mouse. But still a kind of game, maybe. You *played* at cat-and-mouse. And, incredibly, it had occurred to Roger this evening that although he didn't look forward to them he was practically *enjoying* these confrontations whilst they were in progress; that he no longer felt so shy before an audience (some way from this, indeed, he actually welcomed the presence of one); and that even with threats of the police being bandied about so publicly he no longer felt any great embarrassment. He was changing. At St Pancras, it was true, he'd averted his head and slouched into himself as he was getting on the train, but now he remembered to square his shoulders again, as he had done on several occasions during the course of the day. He liked the thought of change.

Nonetheless, it came as a relief not to find any policemen standing on the almost empty platform; and he walked right down to the end of it—wanting to put whatever distance he could between himself and their still-possible arrival. Acting on the same instinct he found he was keeping well to the back of it, as though a mere wire fence overlooking a car park could furnish him with cover.

Yet when he understood what he was doing he quickly moved away from the perimeter. The next thing, he thought, half in humour, half disgust, the next step in degradation, will be to hide out in the Gents.

Even so, he was glad when out of the greyness of the rain and mist the local train could eventually be heard, seen taking shape; glad there should still have been no scream of tyres upon the asphalt.

And as the comparatively short conveyance pulled in, a smiling black face looked out from the window of one of the carriages.

This, too, could tie in with the image of film noir.

"Hope you've got a ticket tonight!" The conductor was youthful-looking yet there was a sprinkling of grey in both the frizzy sideburns.

"No! Sorry!" Roger returned the grin, shut and shook his umbrella, stepped aboard the train.

Like the platform, there was hardly anyone on it—not, certainly, in this half.

"I better pretend I didn't notice you was here."

"Won't you get into trouble for that?" Roger asked. "I ought at least to write down my name again. Oughtn't I?"

"Well, I don't know."

"That would show them you'd done something—as much as you were able."

"The problem is, you see, last night I didn't make out no report."

For a minute or two they considered this companionably.

"But you can say you knew the conductor on the InterCity would be doing that," suggested Roger, finally, "and that you didn't realize two reports were needed on the same subject."

"That's right. And anyhow, what might happen is, you'd get charged twice over, for both nights. And that wouldn't be fair, would it? I can't see how anyone could say as that was fair."

"Thank you for being so nice about it."

"Well, you're very welcome, I'm sure."

But that, for the moment, was where the niceness ran out. The following morning, when Roger got to the station at nearly half-past-six, the conductor who'd been on the London-bound train the previous day was standing vigil by the guard's van. Twenty-four hours earlier he had sounded easygoing ("Travelling without a ticket, sir? Eh, we can't have that, you know") but of course it was his signal which must have set those half-dozen officials waiting at the barrier; and today he no longer sounded in the least easygoing.

"That's him!"

This, to the much younger, shorter man who stood close to him and who was squat, pug-nosed and could be seen—because he happened to be scratching his head when Roger first noticed him, with his cap pushed over to one side—to have a corn-coloured crew cut.

"Yes, that's him!"

In just a second the cap was back in place and the wearer of it was now standing close to Roger.

"You, sir. Do you have a ticket to travel on this train?"

"No, I don't."

"In that case—off the station!" He grabbed Roger's upper arm; hard.

Roger tried to shake him off. "It's okay, you know: the police are going to be waiting for me at St Pancras."

"Well, they won't find you then, will they?" The ignominy of this was that he was such a *little* man and yet he was propelling Roger so easily along the platform; not that Roger was putting up any resistance, except for his attempt to get back his arm. "It may come as a surprise to you but we have ideas in this country about people who set out to break the law."

"We also have ideas in this country about principles of justice."

"And you can talk about those all you like—after you end up in court!"

"And how will I end up in court, unless the police arrest me?"

"You can sue British Rail. But right now you're getting off this station! Come on—off this station!"

Up the steps he pushed him; through the booking hall. When they reached the open automatic doors he administered a final shrug of no little violence.

"And I wouldn't show your face round here again—not if you know what's good for you!"

Roger felt like saying, "One day, when you're big enough, you might grow up to be a bouncer." But he saw three elderly ladies looking at him in perplexity; and since they were different from everyone else who'd been staring, in that their perplexity quickly gave way to a small smile of sympathy, he restrained himself. It wouldn't, moreover, have been a particularly bright idea.

He thought afterwards that he should have asked these women for their names.

But by then they had crossed the booking hall and were probably on one of the platforms.

Roger caught a bus to Beeston.

There was no chance, of course, of catching up with the train he had just missed but he didn't want to do that anyway. The bus journey lasted twenty-five minutes. The station at Beeston had the air of a country one from days gone by, yet Beeston was still a part of Nottingham. He could hardly believe the authorities wouldn't have anticipated this move of his—after all, it seemed so obvious—therefore again it was *The Thirty-Nine Steps* syndrome as he walked through the entrance and over and down towards the London side: heart hammering, raincoat collar pulled up, eyes looking mainly at the ground. (So where were those bravely squared shoulders *now*, that upheld head, that noble chin?) Unfortunately there weren't many people on the platform—no way to mingle with a crowd—so he sat on a green bench and simply stared at his briefcase, which he'd placed across his lap. When the next InterCity arrived he was back on his feet but supposedly studying a couple of posters as it slowed to a halt . . . although this again, he realized, was merely an ostrich tactic; he viewed his height once more as a distinct disadvantage. The moment the train had stopped—and not glancing in either direction for heads that might be leaning watchfully out of windows, or for the guard with whistle and flag who might even now be bearing down on him—he hurried to a nearby open door at which a woman was disembarking, with packages and two children. Roger's hadn't been a good decision. Although he helped the woman with a suitcase, and with one of the little girls, the ten seconds he had to stand waiting at the door appeared to him interminable.

But as had happened in London last night, once he was actually on board the train, he felt relatively secure.

Secure . . . with a conductor soon to walk along it? Secure . . . with the Law about to meet him at the other end?

The conductor this morning was one he hadn't seen before. The other three passengers at Roger's table held out their tickets without pausing in their conversation. Roger smiled somewhat wearily at the man, preparatory to launching yet again into his explanation—was there any ticket inspector on this line who still didn't know of it?—but unexpectedly the conductor simply smiled back, nodded and moved on, evidently under the impression he must have looked at Roger's ticket earlier.

Roger was about to call him back.

Checked himself.

The barrier at St Pancras was totally unguarded.

He just walked through it and away.

Yet he was over an hour late for work. He'd telephoned before leaving the station—spoken to Rose ("Oh, you're going to catch it, mister, if there's any justice left in this world *you're* going to catch it!")—but after he'd deposited his mack, umbrella and briefcase in the basement he went back to the ground floor, looked up at the gallery and said, "Mr Cavendish, may I have a word with you?"

"I think perhaps you better had. Pray step up into my office, if you'd be so kind. As a matter of fact I, too, was about to seek the favour of an interview."

Roger climbed the aged, ladder-like wooden stairs—"the steep-and-narrow," Mr Cavendish called them, "for those amongst us who have difficulty in going straight"—and worked his way along the cramped balcony until he reached his manager's desk. On the wall there were many framed cartoons dating back to the time of Rowlandson and Jonas Hanway, and among the items which had to be negotiated during his progress was another large desk, over which Dickensian clerks had no doubt crouched whilst perching on their high stools and attesting by the industrious scratching of their quills to the propinquity of the founder; a cupboard full of receipt books which, though still in use, were so venerable they gave the Temple Bar telephone exchange; and a rack of horn-handled crooks for shepherds, of whom there weren't a great many left in the vicinity. There was also, lying on the floor, a long carton containing swordsticks (the most magnificent of these boasting a dragon's head carved, lacily, out of ivory) and an ordinary-seeming black umbrella which likewise concealed a blade, far less impressive but still extremely lethal; these were just for show, on request, since a new law had belatedly prohibited their sale, although the price of the dragon stick, nearly fifteen hundred pounds, had in itself proved quite restrictive—Roger, as so often, caught his ankle on the box. He gave a grimace and saw Rose, who was standing looking up at him expectantly, snigger in partial sympathy. "Yeah, I've done that, as well; it really hurts, don't it?"

When Mr Cavendish spoke to Roger, however, he made no attempt to modulate his voice. "They say little pitchers have large ears; but I don't think they can have seen what's happening to Rose's. Have *you* noticed how her ears have grown since she started to work here—that is, if we can speak of it as work? I'm sure they didn't make me think of Babar when she first came for interview."

"Oh, go on with you, Mr Cavendish. You're just saying that. You know I never try to listen."

"In that case, Rose, I shudder to imagine where we'd be if you really put some effort into it." He sent her down to the ladies' end of the shop, to open up each umbrella on two of the racks and give it a thorough dusting. She protested volubly . . . but went.

"Now then, Mr Mild. What did you wish to see me about? Being presented with a good alarm clock as your leaving gift?"

The use of surname only further underlined the fact his boss was in a waggish and indulgent mood. He certainly didn't appear to believe that Roger had lost interest since the previous Monday. The auspices were favourable.

"No," he said. "I'm having trouble with British Rail."

Mr Cavendish replied: "And you think that makes you special? Please don't try to brag. Do you know how long it took me to get home last night?" Home was merely Watford.

Roger listened, expressed sympathy—but was rebuked: "I don't want sympathy; I want outrage; unqualified outrage!"—and then, hoping for a little of this himself, started to narrate his own story.

Mr Cavendish became less droll.

"Oh, for heaven's sake! Why didn't you tell me? I could have given you the money."

"That's exactly why I didn't."

"Now I feel angry. As you know, I was prepared to make allowances when I thought your lack of punctuality was due to signal failures and the like—"

"I never told you that. Except on Monday. When it was."

"But if you're held up tomorrow and the weather's bad . . . People who are keen on principles seldom seem to mind how much they inconvenience anyone around them."

"I don't think that's quite fair." There was a trace of sulkiness in Roger's tone.

"Which is another thing. I don't care very much for this streak of arrogance that I've begun to see in you lately. And no future employer is going to care very much for it, either."

"Why is it arrogant to stand up for your rights?"

"I get the feeling you may almost be enjoying yourself. So I wonder if you're doing it entirely for the proper reasons . . . " He paused. "Anyway. Listen. I'm giving you the money. No travelling any more without a ticket. How much will you need?"

"I don't want it."

"Why not? What good do you think you're doing? For you or anybody else?"

Roger shrugged.

"I warn you," said his manager. "If you use that phrase again—'not fair'—I shall probably want to clobber you."

And my mother would fully sympathize. (No, but she wouldn't really, not at heart, any more than Mr Cavendish himself really meant it.) "If I gave up now it would seem as though they'd beaten me. And talk about anticlimax . . . all that wasted effort . . . wasted emotion . . . Besides which. I'm sorry but I genuinely think that it's important."

"Important? Speak to the ghosts of the six people who died in yesterday's fireball on the motorway; or of all those blacks hacked to pieces in last night's township massacre; or of the latest policeman who's just been shot in Northern Ireland. Then speak to his wife and three young children who saw it happen. And afterwards tell me how very important you still believe your own little problem can possibly be."

"I know. I know. Do you honestly suppose I'm not aware of all of that?"

He turned his back in surly irritation; but—after he'd taken only three steps—returned. "Well, tell me how much they'd say it mattered, all those ghosts and people, even if I did arrive late tomorrow and it did happen to be raining."

"Oh, go away!" said Mr Cavendish.

Roger went. Providentially, as he arrived at street level, several Americans came through the door and he was able to lead them to look at some of the more expensive merchandise and make a good sale. It took nearly an hour of encouragement and helpfulness—fairly ostentatious helpfulness, Roger knew—that had as much to do with recommending plays and places: even a good fish-and-chip restaurant: as it did with any discussion of walking sticks or umbrellas. When he finally showed these customers out, he was feeling a good deal more satisfied with his morning. Also, it was time for coffee.

"Would you step up here again for a moment, please."

He sighed. "Oh, Lord—is it really necessary?"

He truly hadn't meant to respond in this way. Mr Cavendish could well be right about detecting arrogance. But he remembered his mother had once told him, "You're like me: you can't say boo to a goose!", and if recently he had been learning to say boo to a few geese wasn't that all to the good? Surely not arrogance. Yet answering back might indeed be a sign of arrogance.

"Thank you, you don't have to address me as Lord. I can see why many would want to but I don't insist on it . . . not yet."

Clearly Mr Cavendish had recovered from his anger. Roger again went up the awkward staircase.

"Following our little altercation of half an hour ago . . . "

"More like an hour."

"I purposely offered you that opportunity. I realized that in your new persona you would want to contradict me. I thought we'd get it out of the way quickly and without its doing enormous damage."

Roger smiled—guardedly.

"It's lucky," continued his boss, "that one of us always keeps a cool head and is *never* prone to moodiness in any shape or form. However . . . Earlier you were so full of why you wanted to see me that you forgot to ask why *I* wanted to see *you*."

"I thought it was about the same thing."

"I see: yet *another* of your mistakes . . . I take it nothing's changed since yesterday? You're not fixed up with any job yet?"

"No."

"In that case if the business pays your travel expenses for the next two months would you consider staying on? You'd be doing us a favour. Christmas is obviously one of our busiest times and—believe it or not—I'm having difficulty in finding a replacement worthy of you. Also it's not really the best period to be training anybody."

Roger said: "Yes—of course. I'd be happy to stay on."

"Good—and we'd be happy to have you. (Well, naturally I can't speak for Rose, or Henry, or Norman, or Joe . . .) I only wish there were some way we could afford to pay your fare indefinitely. If we'd had a better couple of years and we didn't have that accursed new business rate hanging over us . . . "

Roger hastened to assure him that he understood. "But thank you, anyway. Thanks for the thought." He felt convinced Mr Cavendish had meant it—if only because he had said it so many times before and because he was invariably so generous. When he'd heard it was the anniversary of Roger's parents, for instance, he'd bought a bottle of champagne to be taken home to them. "Special instructions, however. None for you." (That had made two bottles for them, that year, with Oscar's.) He gave expensive Christmas presents—as well as an extra week's wages. He had supplied more than one Mild with a free umbrella. On the occasion when Oscar had dropped in to see his brother and confessed that he'd never owned a brolly Mr Cavendish had told him to pick one out: "Anything that takes your eye, so long as it's the cheapest we have and is irredeemably shopsoiled." Oscar had replied: "That's very sweet of you but I'll tell you what's really taken my eye—and in a week or two, when I'm a bit richer, I'm going to come back in and buy it . . . " The umbrella in question had originated in Milan, had a cover and case richly patterned in gold paisley and cost nearly fifty pounds. Oscar of course, who at the start had been pointed towards the twelve-pound range of plain black, by the finish had so charmed Mr Cavendish—and everyone else (except for Roger)—that he ended up in possession of the gold paisley. "Really? You don't mean it. I can't believe it. You're an angel." If anyone other than Oscar had addressed Alan Cavendish as an angel after an acquaintance of barely twenty minutes it would have sounded thoroughly over-the-top. It *was* over-the-top. But Oscar could get away with such effusiveness; even Rose had stated, "I wouldn't mind marrying your brother, if it didn't mean I'd find myself lumbered with *you*, as my brother-in-law!"; and it certainly hadn't prevented Mr Cavendish from meting out the same generosity to Abby when she too came—umbrella-less on a rainy day—to visit her brother at his place of work. Admittedly she didn't do quite so well, but admittedly her manner was more restrained than Oscar's (her restraint still had a lot of charm) and her aspirations considerably less lofty. Even Jean had been sent home a smart umbrella—plus a bottle of wine—on Roger letting slip it was her birthday. The bottles of wine, indeed, were fairly frequent; their only motivation one of whim . . . Roger, without warning, would find a carrier bag in the cupboard where he kept his things. And when, during the train strike, he'd had to spend six nights at a B and B near the shop, he had been taken only to excellent restaurants for his dinner, as well as being supplied with an absurd allowance for his lunches (whilst being forbidden "even *once* more!" to speak of his giving back the change. Afterwards, Roger had bought him a box set of James Cagney films, in a bid to express his gratitude). So he now had no doubt at all that Mr Cavendish would have paid for his annual rail ticket if he could possibly have managed it.

"Anyway, today's the twenty-sixth. How neat, how fortuitous! Two monthly seasons will take us up to Christmas Eve."

Roger smiled. "And if I buy the first one next Monday, the second will take us almost to the end of December, and I can help out with the stocktaking."

"You're incredibly stubborn—has anybody ever told you? I won't deny, however, that maybe we could do with you at stocktaking. For the present, though, please go to have your coffee. I can't think why you're so determined this morning to run late in absolutely every-thing."

Sitting over his mug of Maxwell House, Roger—despite what he had said today, despite what he had said since Sunday—found himself thinking about being able to buy a new season ticket that very evening. No more hassle; no further fear of conductors or Revenue Protection Managers or police or anything. Sod all the bravado. It sounded very peaceful. He felt tired. And he felt tempted.

That afternoon, Jenny came to see him. He thought the day, which had begun so badly, had really done a U-turn. He was glad he hadn't sought her out. Great that she was the one who—even to this small extent—was demonstrating interest. She looked fantastic. He felt a glow of pride . . . warned himself he mustn't grin like Goofy.

"So this is the renowned emporium where Mr Gladstone and Sir Henry Irving came?" She glanced about with interest—smiling, he thought, a little nervously.

"The one, certainly; the other, not so sure. Remember . . . poetic licence."

"And those are the blue tiles?"

"Yes." He took her over to inspect them. "Cows in the field.

Milkmaids with pails, dropping curtsies, very prettily. Hey, nonny, no . . . and nothing more than a branch of the United Dairies between here and the next little village—sparkling, gurgling stream running down beside its high street." He found, as before, that he could talk to her so easily. She seemed to release in him a heady flow of articulacy.

She laughed; still not, it appeared, quite comfortably. While he wondered how he could make her feel as much at home as he did she tentatively changed the subject.

"I'm really enjoying *Captain Blood*. My parents thought it was so kind of you. And as soon as I'm finished my boyfriend wants to read it."

He managed to say: "That's good. Is your boyfriend into Sabatini?"

She stayed for just a short while. She mentioned her boyfriend three more times. Practically fiancé. Andrew. He wondered if they'd all rehearsed it with her: parents *and* Andrew. ("It was so embarrassing," she might have said. "We'd only spoken for about ten minutes. What *am* I to do? And, no, Andy, not at *all* my type. Honest! You really ought to see him." Whilst he himself . . . he had been feeling wonderful, right there on top of the world.)

"Oy, oy, oy!" said Alan Cavendish as soon as she had gone. "What's a pretty girl like that doing in conversation with a chap like you? Is there something you feel you ought to tell me?"

"No."

He added, because this had sounded too abrupt: "She works in the card shop which opened Monday."

"Old Roger the Dodger!" said Rose. "You got in quick! Bit of an unknown quantity, I'd say, when you really decide on something. Far too good for you, though—isn't she, Mr Cavendish? No, that's only a joke! She looks real nice."

Yet Roger didn't want to hear.

He remembered that final stumbling sentence which he'd ascribed merely to appreciation. *I don't know what to say . . . I really don't know what to say.*

"Though next time she comes," advised Mr Cavendish, "try to speak up a bit if you can. Remember, you do have a certain obligation to the firm. Eh, Rose? Wouldn't you agree?"

But Rose—mindful perhaps of this morning—ventured no reply.

15

Whether it would have happened if he'd been feeling less embittered and more his normal singing, dancing self, he wasn't sure; but he certainly hoped it would have. He thought it more than likely. It was all to do with the prize draw which was due to be held the following day. He suddenly noticed that one of his colleagues, Lucy, who was a gentle and pretty woman in her mid-twenties, one who came from a farming background in Norfolk and whose main goal at the moment was to possess her own horse and take part in gymkhanas, maybe teach riding for a part of every week . . . that Lucy was throwing into the bin a mass of questionnaires which people had filled in when the company had had that recent stand at Texas. Well, not the company exactly. Lucy and Ephraim and two others had paid for the stand themselves—and, of course, for the hamper—manned it the whole week, either individually or in pairs, standing in a very draughty position by the automatic exit doors, inviting everybody as they left the store to take part in a magnificent free prize draw and maybe win that smashing Christmas hamper which you can see displayed on the table there. "Hey, Lucy, what are they?" he asked, pointing to the cards in the green metal bin.

"Oh, just my *no's*, Eff: the ones I've phoned so far who've given me the brush-off." It was the policy at Columbia that even if people ticked the 'no' box, indicating that they didn't want information about the services Columbia had on offer, you still rang anyway and hoped to make them reconsider. Ephraim hated this kind of calling almost more than taking numbers at random out of the Yellow Pages. It seemed to him a violation of good faith and privacy and of the right to choose, even though he could also appreciate the argument that most people were under-insured and you might be violating these principles largely to promote their welfare.

"But you can't do that. They have to go into the draw."

"Eff, these are the no-hopers; the ones you just don't stand a chance of getting any business from." She explained it to him with characteristic good humour, as if it had been owing simply to a fault in her communication skills that Ephraim hadn't understood.

Ephraim answered with equal patience. "Lucy, people kept saying to us, 'Oh, I suppose if I don't tick the right box I haven't any chance of winning that hamper?', and we kept telling them, 'No, it doesn't make any difference; whichever box you tick, all the cards go into the draw.'"

At this point the two others who had been involved with the stand joined in the discussion. All the 'associates'—or 'advisers'—or 'consultants'—who were part of Barney's unit had their desks in the same corner of the office, with Barney himself sitting in a position from which he could easily monitor the activities of each of them; make sure that they were sticking more or less to the requisite, company-approved scripts. Anyone who'd been recruited by the man responsible for the whole branch, a rubicund and hail-fellow-well-met kind of chap named Alf Preston, was then a member of Alf's unit and sat in the part of the office where Alf, not Barney, was the immediate overseer.

Sean, who was also in his mid-twenties and again, like Lucy, unfailingly friendly and helpful, said to Ephraim: "The thing is, matey, that unless one of us is going to get something out of whoever wins the draw it's like cutting off our nose to spite our face . . . " Sean was a big fellow who often went weight-training with Barney and whose own ambition was one day to be the proprietor of a fitness centre himself. (Not that either his or Lucy's aims was acceptable at Columbia as being real goals: 'one day' was far too vague; a proper goal needed to have a definite date set upon it: by the end of this month—by Christmas—by June 30th.) He also had a nose that was, in proportion, as large as the rest of him and in the normal way his use of the cliché he'd just employed would have drawn forth perhaps a minute's worth of badinage. (Ephraim had once told him that Cyrano had one of the most generous and quixotic natures imaginable; but the allusion hadn't been understood by anyone and even the word quixotic had had to be explained.) Today, however, it passed wholly without comment.

"Good God," said Jerzy, who, despite his Polish parents, sounded as British as any of them, had been a coalminer and a publican, and had joined the company at the same time as Ephraim. "I'll be buggered if we're going to include the *no's*. That stand and hamper cost us about seventy quid each and I'm damned if we'll see it just go down the drain!"

Ephraim shrugged. "But the money won't have just gone down the drain, whoever wins the draw. We all derived plenty of leads out of it; you can't deny that."

"I do deny it." Jerzy was balding and burly. He seemed naturally rebellious: 'obstreperous', Ephraim had called him, though again this wasn't a word Jerzy would believe existed until he was shown it in a dictionary—by Barney, as it happened—after which he wrote it down, memorized it, then used it often. He was thirty-eight and had frequently moaned to Ephraim that he resented "being pushed around by these sodding *kids*; what bloody experience of anything do they think *they've* got, they know just fuck-all about life, I could tell them a thing or two!" Although this was a fixation which Ephraim by and large didn't share—for instance, he was thirty years older than his younger son but knew which of them he considered to have the more experience, overall—he was always happy to listen to Jerzy indulging it . . . especially in relation to Barney. Ephraim felt there was a bond between himself and Jerzy that had something to do with their ages, as well as with their having been new boys together. Jerzy had made him the gift of an attractive coffee mug during their first week; given him several lifts since then; had on two occasions lent him a couple of pounds. But right now this bond wasn't very much in evidence as Jerzy added angrily: "You may have got plenty out of it . . . with all your ape-like antics. I'm not so sure about the rest of us."

In fact, Ephraim had obtained many more leads than the other three, since he was quite a showman and, especially when on his own, had been uninhibited about trying to awaken the interest and good-will of potential entrants . . . even to the extent of going down on one knee and wringing his hands like Al Jolson. His colleagues—not only at Columbia but in many of his previous jobs—had often told him that he'd missed his true vocation; and he wished—wished—wished—that he had indeed gone on the stage, been more determined when his grandmother and mother and father (his father had still been acting then as stockbroker to his former wife and mother-in-law, had still sometimes gone to Gran's for dinner) had all highhandedly pooh-poohed any such absurdity. He supposed he simply hadn't wanted it enough to defy so dogmatic a family council; but at seventeen—or at least when *he* was seventeen—you just had so little know-how; he'd been unaware of all those options which he now realized might have been open to him. Besides, when he looked back at himself at seventeen, he felt that he hadn't had much character. (A year later it had been his grandmother who'd been chiefly instrumental in getting him out of the RAF, and two years after that it had been a woman working with him at Harrods, twenty-four to his own twenty, who had made a remark which had remained with him ever since: "I have never met *anyone* with so little personality!" . . . even though he'd suspected that this was at least partly because of her disappointment at his lack of advances when she'd taken him home one day at lunchtime while her husband was at his office in the City.) In any case he felt he would have loved the life of the acting profession and that he might well have made a success of it. "You're right: I *have* missed my true vocation!" And he had frequently beaten his breast or torn at his hair—well, untidied it in simulated anguish—or covered his eyes and pretended to weep. But the simulation, the pretence, at heart, hadn't at all been simulation and pretence.

He said now: "I may have had more than you, but you got leads as well."

Jerzy countered: "Oh, yes, so we all got leads. It's possible we'll do three or four bits of business out of the leads we got—each of us, I mean, okay—but it's also possible we'll get no fucking business out of a single one of them. *Except* . . . you ring up some guy who's shown he's interested and you say to him, 'Look, you've just won the £50 hamper; it'll be easier if you come to the office to collect it but if not I'll be happy to deliver it,' and you really think *he's* not going to do business with you? Like fuck he's not. He wouldn't have the nerve."

"Leastways"—and this was Barney making his long-delayed entrance into the debate—"if he doesn't do business with you, you sure as hell don't possess a grain of talent for this job and should be looking round for something else."

Ephraim swivelled his chair a few degrees to include Barney now (peripherally) as well as the others. "Anyhow, all this is irrelevant. We *said* that it made no difference what people put on the questionnaires."

"Then you shouldn't have. That was your first mistake. Next time you'll know better. Did you all say that?"

"Yes, of course we did," said Ephraim.

"I wasn't asking you," said Barney. It seemed fitting that the first time he'd addressed him directly since Monday it should be to say he hadn't been addressing him.

Sean and Jerzy both denied having said it. Lucy admitted that she might have done. Ephraim looked at her a little sadly. She had been with the company for nine months now and was Barney's star pupil. She was doing much better than Sean, who had been there the same length of time—even though he stuck rigidly to the scripts and brushed up his selling technique just as often as he could find somebody to practice it upon. He was the only one of them who had scored a distinction in the multiple-choice examination at the end of the initial, week-long training course (residential, in a four-star hotel; intensive, interesting, luxurious and free). No one received a licence until he had passed this test in every one of its ten sections.

Ephraim said: "I don't believe either Sean or Jerzy; but what difference does it make? The placard announced a free prize draw and mentioned nothing about it being obligatory to tick the right box."

"Oh, bollocks," said Barney. "That's just splitting hairs and you know it. Do you imagine Norwich Union or Allied Dunbar or *any* of the large insurance companies would give away a valuable prize to somebody who wasn't going to be a client?"

"Yes," said Ephraim. "Why shouldn't I?"

"Then you live in cloud-cuckoo-land and it's no surprise you've got to be past fifty and are *broke*, that you're behind on the mortgage, owe money to the bank—and heaven knows who else—and have practically no insurance. You, a consultant on insurance! An adviser on finances! My God! It would be quite hilarious, if it weren't so damned pathetic."

Ephraim ignored this; it was true and he couldn't think of any satisfactory response. He'd been a fool, of course, to reveal so much of his situation to Barney, but that had been in happier days—last week, maybe—when the two of them had sometimes gossiped together like brothers and he had still believed in his essential ability to pull through; to make something of a life for himself and Jean (or, rather, Jean and himself). "In any case," he said, "I don't care about Norwich Union. I don't care about Allied Dunbar or any of those larger companies. This is the one I'm supposed to be working for and up to now I thought it had integrity. Well, does it have integrity or doesn't it?"

"I can see what Eff means," said Lucy. "I imagine we can all see what he means but—"

"Can we?" asked Jerzy. "No way! Not me!"

"Oh, look, matey," said Sean—and he was talking to Ephraim, not to Jerzy. "In an ideal world . . . ," he began; which was one of Barney's own favourite phrases. Much as he was fond of Sean, Ephraim sometimes thought he was like a sheet of blotting paper. (Much as he was fond of Lucy, come to that, he sometimes thought of her as Little Miss Goody-Goody, always agreeing with everything that Barney said, although both she and Sean had advised him only the day previously, while Barney was at lunch, that there was no law against *thinking* whatever you liked in this office but it was usually a lot wiser to keep most of it to yourself . . . And Lucy had also said—not for the first time—"Eff, I can't believe you're fifty-two. My father's a year younger. He'd never have the courage to take on a whole new career like you've done. I really do admire you for it.") Sean was constantly seeking to inspire him with the platitudes he'd absorbed from the

American paperbacks in circulation round the office: "Listen, matey,"
he would say, "you never have a second chance to make a first impression," or "You know, if there's one thing that failure can't stand, it's persistence," or—a little more surprising, this—"There's nothing good nor
bad but thinking makes it so . . . ," though he always seemed reluctant
to acknowledge plagiarism (which was equally endearing-stroke-
infuriating); he produced these aphorisms as if they'd never been
heard until this very moment, a vaguely puzzled expression in his eyes
which appeared to say: *My goodness, I hadn't thought of that before!
But it's true, isn't it?* And he went on now: "In an ideal world, matey, of
course everyone would like people to act in the way you're describing.
But unfortunately this is far from being an ideal world."

"Crap!" said Ephraim.

"Well, well," said Barney, "so you think this is an ideal world, do
you?"

He didn't bother to answer.

"And speaking of integrity," continued Barney, "I don't see how
you've any right to hold a single view on this whole tedious time-wasting
topic. You haven't even paid for the bloody stand yet. Remember? It
seems to me it's all very fine to go shooting your mouth off . . . "

But Lucy was waving her arm at him and Barney had to stop. This
was really quite satisfying. Lucy had lent Ephraim the money for his
share of the stand, and Jerzy had done the same thing as regards the
hamper. "Eff paid me back," she said.

Barney, disconcerted, looked at Jerzy.

"Yes, me, too." (Reluctant admission.) As Ephraim had told Nathan
on the phone, his *first* month had been reasonably productive, thank
God—thank God—although there'd been a longish wait for pay-
ment and you received only seventy-five percent of your commission
to begin with; didn't see the remainder for a further fifteen months.
(And, anyway, twelve percent of what you earned went automatically
to Barney, twelve percent to Alf Preston, and six percent to the area
manager.) But still . . . thank God. "Though I'm with you about the rest
of it," Jerzy said. "Shooting his bloody mouth off . . . I really don't know
how his wife puts up with it, I don't." Jerzy's good humour was now,
just possibly, beginning to reassert itself but this jocular expression

of it, incipiently jocular, unwittingly assured that Ephraim's satisfaction was short-lived. "And besides, all this airy-fairy stuff about telling them this and telling them that . . . When it boils down to it, how is anybody ever going to *know*?"

"There you have it in a nutshell, matey! There's no way anybody is ever going to know."

"Dear God!" said Ephraim. "How does one even *begin* to communicate with you lot? Whether anybody is ever going to know isn't—just isn't—what I'm talking about here."

Can't you see? What I'm talking about here are the Wendy Coopers of this world. The inadequate mothers of Amber Jade Coopers.

No, not so. What he was really talking about was the Wendy Cooper of this town: the Wendy Cooper who lived in one of a row of council maisonettes with rotting planks nailed across their back entrances, in Radford . . . Excepting *she*, of course, happened to have put her tick in the right box—suddenly he felt confused—did that in any way invalidate his argument? Even *she* had had the spirit to realize that if you weren't sufficiently clued up to express at least a polite interest in what a company had on offer, then why indeed should you suppose you were deserving of a £50 handout? Oh, *hell*.

"Mr Sodding Holier-Than-Thou! Can anyone believe this?" Jerzy appealed directly to Barney. "Jesus Christ, why did we ever have to land ourselves with *him*? 'Ephraim'? You should have known that anyone who had a name like Ephraim was going to be a stuck-up and pretentious little prick!"

"I'll tell you what we'll do," said Barney—who was perhaps exercising considerable restraint in not picking up on this. "Let's get some outside opinion. Vic! Gillian!" He called across the office. *Outside opinion,* thought Ephraim, and was faintly surprised they hadn't come across earlier, the two who'd now been hailed, to find out what was going on; even if they hadn't heard Jerzy's raised voice (and although the office was large it wasn't *that* large) they must surely have been aware of the intensity of the emotions being expressed. They were the only other two around at the moment, apart from Pauline, the secretary. Gillian was slim, middle-aged, with a clipped manner of speech—she came from South Africa—and a practical, kindly approach to things, except that her political views were so rightwing they could sometimes sound almost fascist, which led to confrontations with Jerzy that were now, luckily, becoming increasingly rare, since on both sides the arguments frequently grew very heated ... Jerzy's socialistic principles were aired earnestly and often; far more so than Ephraim's. Vic was a Pakistani who spoke with a trace of Liverpudlian: shortish, athletic, neat, always immensely well-groomed, generally very friendly but—in some way that Ephraim couldn't quite pinpoint—occasionally conveying an impression of shiftiness; Ephraim only knew that he wouldn't trust him to handle any of his own investments ... supposing he should ever have any.

Barney gave them a précis of the situation; it was stated fairly and he brought in no personalities.

Gillian said succinctly: "It's illegal. Every single entry has to go into that draw."

Vic said: "Barney, you just can't be serious. You must have known it was illegal."

"It's got nothing to do with me," said Barney. "I'm simply sitting on the sidelines. It's up to this lot to decide."

"Well, it should have something to do with you," observed Gillian. For the first time Ephraim wondered how much she really liked Barney.

"All I've said is, if we're living in the real world and want to do ourselves a bit of good—without doing anybody else a bit of harm—no one is ever going to be a jot the wiser if we ... if we ... " He gave a shrug.

" ... merely act in a thoroughly dishonest way." It was Ephraim who finished the sentence.

"He's right, you know, Barney. No getting away from it." Vic rubbed his hands and stood there looking smug.

"And not doing anyone a bit of harm," said Ephraim, "might just mean stealing fifty pounds from somebody who could well do with it." It occurred to him he felt no sympathy for the underdog; he was prepared to crow and gang up and go in for the kill in a way that was decidedly unchristian.

"Oh, don't give me that shit," said Barney. "All right, I wash my hands of it. We took it to arbitration and you lot have heard what's been said. Settle it as you like; but for fuck's sake let's get down to some proper work and start making a few phone calls that might bring us in a spot of business for a change."

"Well, I'm fed up to here with the whole thing. Why wait till tomorrow for the draw? Let's get shot of it right now." (Jerzy.)

Lucy retrieved her no-hopers from the bin but these apparently represented just a small percentage of all the cards that had already been jettisoned by Sean and Jerzy and herself. The system was for each of them to number his own cards, write the corresponding number on a tiny piece of paper which was then screwed up and put into an empty biscuit tin, and then ask Pauline to draw the winning pellet. The three others were ready within twenty minutes; it took Ephraim an hour and a quarter to see to all of his.

"Oh, what's the use?" said Jerzy. "We might just as well give him the hamper now and hope whoever gets it chokes to death on the first mouthful. Uninsured."

"No, don't be like that," said Sean. "While there's life there's hope. You never quite know what could be round the corner."

But Jerzy was right, of course. The others each had fewer than seventy contenders; Ephraim had two-hundred-and-fifty-three. (And, oh, how Barney had congratulated him on that Monday morning after their week at Texas! "*Nobody* has ever done as well as this. My God, Eff, you've certainly got the most fantastic future! Was I right—or was I right—to decide on following my instincts and on giving you a chance?" This had been said publicly, in the training room, and endorsed by Alf Preston, with the hands-above-the-head boasting of the boxing champ: the week always started with plaudits or reprimands, with insistence on the necessity of goal-setting, with firm resolves to compete against your own finest performance. Everyone had clapped good-naturedly; and Jerzy, unasked, had even gone back into the outer office and loudly rung the bell.) The winner of the prize was an R. Harrison from West Bridgford, who, on the questionnaire, had signified that he/she had little interest in saving, would react negatively to any suggestion that there were ways in which he/she could be financially much better off, and had given his/her date of birth

(12.5.68) and address, but no telephone number, either for work or home.

"Fuck him," said Jerzy.

"Or her," said Sean, "which, you've got to admit, matey, could at least make it a bit more interesting."

"Please," said Lucy, smiling and holding up one hand. "I don't wish to hear about this."

"So what do you propose to do?" asked Barney, gazing ironically at Ephraim. "Have you looked through the phone book? Have you checked with Directory Inquiries? He, she or it—one supposes—could still quite easily be living with its parents, right?"

"I haven't had much of a chance yet, although I realize it must be all of a minute, or even two, since Pauline drew this name out of the tin."

"I'd have said you'd had weeks in which to try to trace this sexless loser."

"You know how I feel about pestering the ones who didn't want to be pestered."

"And you know how *I* feel about you doing your job in the manner you've been asked to do it." Barney paused; looked darkly handsome, Ephraim thought, in a sleek and threatening, Cosa Nostra way. "If there isn't any phone number—and can you believe it that anyone in these modern times can be without a telephone?"—this was a piece of philosophical inquiry, mystification, not aimed specifically at Ephraim—"you'll have to send off a letter telling them to get in touch with us by Monday; Monday without fail. (And if we haven't heard, everybody, we hold a new draw first thing Tuesday morning.) And oh, by the way, in the letter you say nothing about their having won the prize."

"What, then?"

"You'll ask them to get in touch with us. Nothing more."

"Oh, sure, that's going to fire them up! They'll think it's just another sales pitch. We have to tell them why."

"No. I forbid you to mention it."

It wasn't worth arguing about; and for once Ephraim managed to refrain. He turned away with a look of disbelief which he hoped was as cutting as anything he could have said. He would simply have to go to

West Bridgford himself. Tonight. Something of a nuisance, but since it was the obvious way of getting the better of Barney, totally justified. If no one was at home he could put a note through the letterbox and hope to heaven that R. Harrison and all the members of R. Harrison's household, if any, hadn't gone off on a late-October break. In one way indeed—having no appointments for this evening, because he'd telephoned Kentucky Fried Chicken and heard that Shane wouldn't now be back until the weekend—Ephraim almost welcomed this as a valid excuse for being away from home. (Another valid excuse would have been two or three extra hours of cold calling; but even Jean's present form of politeness was—all things considered—preferable to that.)

"And I should like to see your letter before you get Pauline to type it."

Ephraim didn't answer. He pretended to be sifting through some papers on his desk.

"Did you hear me?"

Lucy said: "Eff. Barney's talking to you."

"Oh?" Ephraim swivelled in his chair. "Great! I didn't think he was going in for that these days." There was a pause. "I'm sorry. I simply wasn't listening, had something more important on my mind. What did he want?"

Barney picked up his phone receiver. Scowled. (*Oh, you sexy brute!* Ephraim felt inclined to say.) Lucy was keen to keep the peace.

"He says he'd like to see your letter before you give it to Pauline," she told Ephraim, gently.

"Why? Doesn't he trust me, then?"

Lucy smiled and returned her attention to her work.

A short time afterwards, Barney went into the training room with a client, slapping the fellow on the back and calling out to Pauline a minute later to bring them in two cups of coffee. The others went on with their telephoning; or, in the case of Sean, with his use of a computer to work out which plan or combination of plans would best suit somebody whom he was going to see that afternoon. Ephraim wished more than ever that he and Jean could have been on good terms. Normally, when they were, he rang her at least once a day, whether she was at home or at the shop. She would have sympathized about the draw;

told him he was right; boosted his morale. She would have sympathized about the row on Monday—though that wouldn't have occurred if they had been in harmony, and, even if it had, she might have wished he had been a lot less confrontational. ("Why do you always have to meet these things head-on? Why do you *always* decline to show a little tact?") But instead he had to keep all of it to himself; and by the time he would be able to tell her—if such a time, he thought dismally, were ever to return—the support she could have given him would no longer seem nearly so important. He felt quite sick with betrayal.

Perhaps he'd have a chance to tell Roger. Roger would certainly be on his side in the matter of the draw, although probably less so with regard to the slanging match: he had learned discretion at his mother's knee, and imbibed her antipathy to making waves. But, in any case, Roger always arrived home so late and had to be in bed so early; it would be difficult to get him on his own. Ephraim had even wondered about ringing the shop but Mr Cavendish apparently frowned upon his staff receiving any personal call unless it was some sort of an emergency ("Help! Help! This *is* an emergency!") since they had just the one telephone. And besides, it would make the whole thing seem too important, because—although it scarcely *could* seem too important—it still needed to be brought up casually, as though it were merely apropos of some other topic that you'd even remembered to *mention* it. Oh, damn! And next week Roger would be around all day. My times are certainly in thy hands, O Lord . . . although, bloody hell, I'm almost beginning to wish they weren't.

No, no, I'm sorry, I don't mean that. You know I don't mean that. But if only you could . . .

What?

Get me out of this mess. Here at work and there at home. Get me out of the mess I appear to have made out of practically everything. And not only in my own life but—over the past two dozen years; or at least a good proportion of them—in Jean's as well. *Please.* By one o'clock, O Lord . . . since, as you know (who better, other than Barney Watson?), a workable goal has to have a time limit. So while we're on the subject, Lord, let's make it half-past-twelve, how about that?

But anyway. Failing all this, on Sunday—if not Saturday night—he could retrospectively garner support from Roger. Possibly even from Jean? That was, if he apologized . . . And he actually reached out for the phone right now; but couldn't quite bring himself to use it.

Yet by Sunday, of course, Oscar would be home and Ephraim wasn't sure how much he was looking forward to his son's return. Oscar would assuredly be partisan, encouraging, full of congratulation; but things didn't seem to cut very deep—although how on earth could you tell whether they cut deep or not?—his mind would soon be on to something else. And hardly any wonder: he'd have so much to talk about, so many photographs to show, so many people to catch up with. (So many telephone calls to make.) Besides, in comparison with all his own great doings a couple of silly squabbles in a Nottingham insurance office could scarcely be expected to carry any vast amount of impact. Perhaps it would be better not even to speak of them to Oscar.

Perhaps it would be better not even to speak of them to Roger. Roger—enthralled and fascinated by his younger brother's exploits— might very well make those same comparisons.

Ditto, Jean.

Ephraim felt his eyes grow wet.

Thank you, God.

At the moment he didn't even know how he was going to face having to listen to the unfolding saga of the traveller's sundrenched odyssey.

He didn't know how he was going to put up with Oscar's exuberant clumping round the house; with tales of his romantic conquests; with heady all-important plans for his future.

That evening, while Roger was having a relatively uneventful journey home ("But what have you done all the other evenings this week?" asked an unfamiliar official; and Roger had answered, "Caught the earlier train—the one to Sheffield which you have to change on"); and while Jean was mixing a cheesecake and thinking up various small ways in which to celebrate Oscar's return—as well as seeing to the supper and making Roger's sandwiches and intermittently trying to raise Abby on the telephone . . . while all this was going on, Ephraim was hunting round West Bridgford for No 5 Stanley Villas, Holloway Road. Not having wanted to draw attention to it at the office, he hadn't consulted his street guide until he was on the bus; and then the light was so poor and the print so small he hadn't been able to read even the index—for a long time he had realized that if he wanted to see things clearly he should really do something about it, but, aware that his eyes were probably his best feature, he had always felt fiercely resistant. Now, in the centre of West Bridgford, he went into a video shop to take advantage of its bright strip lighting. Nodding to the frowsy woman slouching on a stool behind the counter he looked along the shelves of movies and grew distracted by finding several he would like to see again: *Someone To Watch Over Me*, *No Way Out* and—a really old one, this—*The Best Years Of Our Lives*; Gran had taken him to see that in 1946 at the Empire Leicester Square. By the end he'd looked along virtually every shelf in the shop: it was warm in here—outside, it wasn't merely cold, it had begun to spit. Therefore it needed much willpower to turn away from such things as "an unforgettable time in which four adolescents on the brink of manhood learn about friendship, and a lot about growing up" (*Stand By Me*) to the lifeless-sounding street names in his A-Z.

Holloway Road wasn't amongst them.

He asked the woman if she knew it. "Sorry, dear. I've lived round here for thirty years; you'd think I ought to." He noticed that her bleached hair betrayed in abundance its gingery and grey-streaked roots. "Haven't you been able to find what you were after?"

"No—just browsing. You've got a good selection." In fact he'd thought of saying: *No . . . the story of my life!*

"I like musicals myself. *My Fair Lady* now . . . must have seen it more than half a dozen times. My son pulls my leg, though, over that one. Something rotten."

"Sons do. I like musicals as well."

"People say I've got a look of Ginger Rogers about me."

"Mmm. Yes." He stood back; pretended to take seriously this claim. "I think I do see the resemblance."

She laughed, and in a raucous voice suddenly began to sing—he caught the whiff of alcohol. "'I'm in heaven; this is heaven; and the cares that hang about me all the week . . . '"

Still sitting on her stool, she waved her arms and swayed her torso—it was a large one—in undulating accompaniment to a rhythm that was less apparent to him than to her; then much to his relief she stopped.

"I don't suppose I sound like her!"

"It was nice, though."

"Another world," she said. "Another world."

He didn't answer; observed a respectful pause while she lingered in it, in that other world, a moment longer; he felt sorry for her—tried to picture what she'd been like thirty years before. She took a cigarette from a packet on the counter. There was an ashtray containing maybe a dozen stubs of varying lengths, heavily lipsticked.

"So . . . no Holloway Road," he said at last. "Stanley Villas doesn't ring a bell?"

"No." She thought about it; shook her head. "Sorry, dear. You'll have to go on searching." He left her freshly undulating, the smoke rising brokenly across her half-closed eyes.

"'I'm in heaven; this is heaven . . . '"

He did go on searching—until at last he'd had enough. Fruitless. There was no Holloway Road. There was no Stanley Villas. Why should anyone bothering to enter a free prize draw lie about their address? Did it provide them with an alternative to saying no; a chance to retaliate for having been hassled; a comfortable feeling of being in control? Whatever the reason, it had wasted his evening. Worse than that, it had given Barney an excuse to gloat—whether he'd do so openly or not—and to go on feeling superior.

Jerzy and Lucy and Sean wouldn't be all that sorry, either.

And then he stopped—suddenly he stopped—whilst walking along a stretch of broad shiny pavement on which the lights of a Chinese takeaway were garishly reflected.

It needn't have been a waste of time. No. This could turn out to be a golden opportunity. Why hadn't it occurred to him? What R. Harrison had so loftily scorned would beyond doubt, somewhere else, prove most warmly and sincerely welcome.

16

Back to Beeston the following morning: the same train as yesterday. All right, he would be late again—so what? This was Friday, they were nearly at the end of the week, and Monday would mark the beginning of a two-month period, unexpected bonus, when he'd be able to make a whole new start. Lovely feeling. And today—despite the constant pattering against his window every time he'd woken in the night—the forecast was one of sun and mainly settled conditions.

Not so good for business, maybe, but in every other respect—great.

Even the situation with Jenny wasn't so bad as he'd supposed. The mere fact of her having a boyfriend didn't preclude him from seeing her occasionally, popping in for a chat, suggesting lunch . . . or at the very least a coffee after work. Sleep had banished that hurtful statement he'd imagined; he remembered how easy he had felt with her, again believed that she must like him. A boyfriend—even a fiancé, and he wasn't quite that, anyway—wasn't at all the same as a husband. *Many a slip twixt the cup and the lip*; he could see his grandmother again, wagging her finger at him. *All's fair in love and war, my pet.* A shade more questionable, that one, but still.

This morning, as he slowly ate his breakfast, he granted the

Cecils a brief leave of absence and settled down to something different. Yesterday it had occurred to him he should record as much as possible of this week's eventfulness, while the detail remained fresh. For one thing, over roughly a dozen years he'd been thinking about keeping a journal and this seemed a propitious moment to begin (again). In the past his tidy and conventional mind had always insisted upon January 1st but in the past his tidy and conventional mind had always come unstuck, somewhere around the 6th. And for another thing, rather more practically, he told himself that in case he *should* ever end up in court such an account could prove of value to his solicitor.

But he ought to have bought his exercise book in Woolworth's, not the British Museum. Its stiff-covered smartness was intimidating; he felt his jottings needed to be worthy of it. (Yet why? He wasn't his mum. He wasn't hoping to write something with any pretensions to literature. He chewed one of his buttered scones and stared reflectively from the window. Or was he?) At all events, to destroy the pristine quality of the opening page he wrote, "This lunchtime, take cat-and-mackerel to man who frames cartoons for Mr Cavendish." Which would also give him a valid excuse to call on Jenny—as soon as Monday, maybe?—because he thought it a good bet she'd be interested in seeing the finished product.

He hadn't, of course, required any aide-memoire but the strategy worked. He felt liberated to start writing.

"Sunday afternoon. 22.10.89. Nottingham railway station. 'My season ticket expired yesterday. I want it extended please by the six days lost through strike action.'"

Flat. He suddenly remembered the clerk's ponytail and one earring; then the dwarf in the lumberjacket and black sneakers; the mother with her baby; the soldier having problems with his rail warrant. Patently, some of the points he now began to salvage wouldn't be of much use to a solicitor but he himself, unforeseeably, was finding interest in far more than merely plain facts.

So he had written—flowingly—about a dozen lines when the man who had simply smiled at him yesterday, in a mistaken nod of recognition, came along the train this morning.

Usual explanation. Usual provision of name and address. (Less than two days to go and it would all be at an end.) The man moved on.

A bare five minutes later he returned. This time he had company. A tall and suntanned official in his mid-forties, with glasses and a moustache, produced his ID.

"Revenue Protection, sir. I'm afraid you'll have to get off this train at Leicester."

After a moment Roger shook his head. "No. Sorry."

The official stared at him and bit his lip. "So you want all these passengers to be delayed, do you, while we have to fetch the police?"

There was nobody sitting next to Roger but the two men in the seat opposite immediately lowered their papers and made no pretence of not being interested.

They did not look sympathetic.

Nor did those who sat across the aisle.

Time is money, their expressions seemed to say. We all have vitally important meetings to attend. Appointments to keep. Interviews. Lectures. All set up for the stroke of nine. Already they were glancing at their watches.

"Can't you have the police waiting for me at St Pancras? That's what I was promised earlier in the week. No one has to be delayed."

Roger had lowered his voice, partly in the hope it might encourage this stern-looking newcomer to do the same. It didn't, though—not at all. "No, sir. I'm afraid you've got to leave this train at Leicester." Little wonder there were heads craning round curiously, along the whole length of the compartment.

The train, in fact, was already slowing down for Leicester.

"Right. Are you getting off here of your own free will, or do we have to make the police come on board to fetch you?"

"Yes." Roger's throat felt painfully constricted.

"Yes—what?"

"The police."

The Revenue Protection official put out a hand as if to pull him bodily from his seat; but then thought better of it. Instead, he reached up to the rack above Roger's head, took down his raincoat and umbrella, snatched up his briefcase from the table, and walked to the nearest door with them. Roger saw him hurl them on the platform. The train had scarcely stopped; no passengers as yet had boarded through that door. Afterwards he imagined the looks of bewilderment there must have been—almost of alarmed disbelief—as they had to clear a quick pathway for the passage of his belongings. He picked up his biro, returned it to his pocket, placed the exercise book on his lap, along with the greaseproof bag which contained the rest of his breakfast, and remained seated.

He hoped that his briefcase or umbrella might actually have hit someone . . . the type of person who would be bound to lodge a complaint.

The other official, who had stayed at his side, a bit uncertainly, didn't meet his eye. He was bending slightly at the knees, gazing out of the window, apparently looking at something which had caught his interest on the line.

There was a long wait. In truth it was nothing like as long as it might have been—Roger would have expected a full half-hour and it wasn't even a third of that—and yet, because he didn't know when it would end and because he felt acutely uncomfortable throughout, hearing or sensing or imagining the murmur of agitation all about him, it certainly *felt* like half an hour. The Revenue Protection officer was now out of sight—perhaps standing on the platform—but the other man had had to turn away from the window and wander up and down the compartment answering questions about the reason for the holdup. "We're extremely sorry, sir," he was saying, "extremely sorry, madam. It won't take very long. Nothing to worry about. We'll soon be on our way, doing everything we can to make up for lost time." Roger heard him add—when this had failed to satisfy—"The young man has a grievance; it's going to take a bit of sorting out." Roger wished he could have had the bottle, himself, to stand up and apologize. But all he felt able to do was shamefacedly glance from time to time at the people sitting nearest him—and they seemed merely frustrated and impatient; not curious, nor ready to adjudicate. He believed it would have helped if someone had spoken to him, asked non-aggressively for reasons. But he couldn't be the one to start a conversation.

A Mr Smith, the one who'd gone to Washington, might have said, in the drawling tones of James Stewart: "You guys . . . I feel sorry about this. But we can't let City Hall always call the tune, can we?" Immediately he would have smoothed away dissension; won friends and popularity. "At times like these we Ordinary Joes must band together. Because whenever City Hall gives us a raw deal and we don't let out one goshdarned almighty holler what happens? We allow the system to become that little bit more repressive, that little bit more uncaring, that little bit more convinced that it can get away with it. Fellas, it's then we need to reach out for our catapults!"

Unrestrained cheering. A standing ovation. Vows of solidarity. Jefferson Smith would no doubt have been carried aloft in triumph.

The Revenue man returned.

His promptness was something to be thankful for. So was the sight of the policeman he had with him.

Roger, of course, got up as soon as the policeman requested it.

On the platform this tow-haired, plump-cheeked representative of the Law picked up Roger's possessions. He held the umbrella and briefcase—and also exercise book and breakfast—while Roger put on his raincoat and for a second or two brushed unconsciously at a small dark smudge on one sleeve. The train began to pull away. It seemed that everyone was peering out at them . . . and not simply those who were sitting; there was a lengthy line of hands momentarily on seat tops, on tabletops, a lengthy line of hunched-over trunks. Roger turned his head. "You know, we're not unsympathetic to this complaint of yours," remarked the young policeman. *Or to your feelings when you find that you're the object of a peepshow*, he seemed also to be saying. "But there's just no way, unfortunately, that you can travel without a ticket."

Roger relieved him of the rest of his belongings.

"Yet I have to get to London and I haven't enough money." He was putting the food and the book back into his briefcase.

The Revenue Protection officer had apparently disembarked higher up the platform. He joined them in time to overhear what Roger had said.

"Then get somebody to take money into their local station," he advised. "And Leicester will be notified."

Roger shook his head. "No. There isn't anyone."

"Nonsense! There's always someone. In an emergency. If you swallow your pride and forget to be obstinate."

The policeman rubbed the tip of his broad and freckled nose. He said, "Mr Mild, sir. There's nothing we can do."

"You could arrest me."

"Oh, nobody wants that." He said it with a grin, as if Roger had just made a joke.

"*I* do. It's the only way I shall ever get a fair hearing—be able to state my case before those who are impartial. If you don't arrest me I shall simply catch another train later in the day."

"No, sir, I wouldn't do that." The policeman's look remained agreeable but it lost all signs of joviality. "At the moment you're a civil offender. Do as you've threatened and you at once become a criminal offender." He wiped a bit of dirt off Roger's shoulder. "I think we'd better escort you safely off the station, sir."

A few minutes later Roger stood on his own, outside the main entrance, looking about him. Shortly afterwards the Revenue Protection official followed him out.

"Which way's the town centre?" Roger inquired.

"You should have asked that policeman while you had him there. I'm a stranger in this place the same as you are. Had to be on that train specially. Just for you." There was no particular animosity in the man's tone. But there was no particular concern, either.

"How did you know I'd be on that one?"

"We're not daft. We can put two and two together. It's a mistake to underrate us."

"Then perhaps you could tell me what I do now: stranded in Leicester with less than fifty pence in my pocket. I can't go back; I can't go forward. What do I do?"

"Thumb a lift." With that, he turned abruptly and went into a staff office which adjoined the station.

As soon as he'd gone, Roger doubled back through the main entrance.

He went into the buffet on Platform 3. He would have liked a cup of coffee but the state of his finances meant it must be tea.

He sipped this slowly, sitting in a corner, his back to the window and also to the door. There was an announcement on the loudspeaker. It startled him at first—its volume and its unexpectedness—but it was simply to the effect that the next train into Platform 3 would be for London St Pancras.

Up till now he'd felt less nervous than rebellious. As the train drew in, however, his nervousness came back.

Numbers of people got off; numbers got on. Standing inside the doorway of the buffet Roger watched them. He waited until the last possible moment. He heard the guard blow his whistle. Then he made a dash across the platform—in his haste colliding with an elderly man in a bowler who glared after him in annoyance. But the train was already moving; he couldn't do more than call out his apology. At first he was unable to open the door which he had made for; yet somebody helped him from inside; and a minute later he was seated. The train wasn't due to make another stop until it reached St Pancras.

He was now a criminal offender—and felt cross with himself for not having inquired about the actual, practical differences. This omission struck him as being stupid. The trouble was, he thought, that at moments when the adrenalin ceased to run he was simply so very tired.

The conductor came along the compartment asking for tickets from Leicester.

Roger didn't look up from the book in which he was again writing—or pretending to write—and the conductor passed on without a pause.

At St Pancras once more Roger simply walked away.

But it was after ten when he arrived at work.

Mr Cavendish was as little pleased as he had been the day before.

"Damn you," he said. "Damn you. I've offered you the way out. Tomorrow's Saturday. Have I got to give up my day off, just to make sure that the other two won't find themselves short-handed? And you may or may not be interested to know this but heavy showers are forecast for the weekend."

Roger looked at him; came to a decision.

"I can promise you I shan't be late tomorrow."

"How can you promise that?"

"Well, does it matter? If I say—"

"I see at any rate you've taken note of my little homily on arrogance. That's something. So what if not only the entire police force of this country but MI5 and SMERSH are all on your trail by crack of dawn—what then—I can still take my day off and rest secure in your promise?"

Roger smiled.

"Yes. God willing. As long as I get paid today and I'm alive tomorrow I guarantee that I'll be here on time. Even ahead of time."

"Do you feel that you deserve to get paid today?"

"Most certainly."

"And it's all very well to say God willing. But if he's not it's no skin off his nose. He can still have his breakfast brought to him in bed, pick out a long-overdue new sofa in John Lewis's, drive to Chalfont and Latimer for lunch with his in-laws and pop in to see Felicity's Aunt Lizzie on the way back. I mean, whether he happens to be willing or not, as regards the likes of you and me. And if he *doesn't* happen to be so—well, we poor suckers, we're absolutely stuck with it. Aren't we, Rose?"

"You can say that again, Mr Cavendish!"

"You know . . . for once . . . I actually find myself in total agreement with Rose."

17

Usually he listened to Radio 4 when he first got up because he felt that everyone should try to keep abreast of world events, say little prayers, spend a minute or two of concentrated thought on those who were suffering, attempt to picture their conditions, attempt to walk a few steps while wearing their shoes . . . Though what this ever did for anyone other than possibly himself—"Hey, look at me, at heart a decent, *caring* sort of chap!"—he wasn't sure. He had come to feel very ambivalent about the power of prayer: after all, the suffering just went on and on and on; if it wasn't man, then it was nature; and yet the child in him still appealed to the Lord who had got rid of his warts and had appeared to help him in countless small ways, large ones as well, all through his life . . . "How can people live without God?" he had often asked . . . and yet, now, he wasn't sure; or if he was, if deep down inside him he still was, he felt arrogant and shifty and self-centred. What *right* had he to believe in a God who granted prayer? . . . And in any other sort of God he simply wasn't interested.

But this week he didn't listen to Radio 4. Already feeling depressed, he'd rather listen to the disc jockeys on Radio 2 and be reminded to walk on the sunny side of the street and to look for the silver lining whenever clouds appear in the blue. (Though Radio 2, it was often said, drew its audience mainly from the over-fifties—which was another good reason, of course, for not listening to it on any regular basis.) For this week he had a real need to be told about silver linings. About people who love people. And where you see clouds upon the hills you soon will see crowds of daffodils. Yeah! Hallelujah! Amen!

He even danced a little as he put the kettle on—bare feet moving bouncily across cool quarry tiles; Polly sitting in the archway, head cocked, trying so studiously to get to grips with such a code. (This one, in fact, was about only the Deadwood Stage; but whip-crack-away, whip-crack-away, whip-crack-away was in itself a life-enhancing message.)

Yet if Ephraim wanted to be told merely about jolly things he didn't want to be told, immediately after Doris Day, about Renée and Jim. Apparently the disc jockey was reading out the whole of Renée's letter: " . . . and please tell him to take care of himself because I don't know what I'd do without him, and thank him for all the kindness and consideration and sheer fun and all the endless cups of tea he's brought me over the past twenty-six years . . . As a matter of fact, if you play this record between a quarter-past- and half-past-seven, we'll probably be sitting up in bed drinking yet another as we listen! Anyway, please give him all my love."

The disc jockey said: "I will, Renée, I will, and I'll also mention your two lovely daughters, Fiona and Geraldine—hi, girls!—but it seems to me you're in a better position to give it to him yourself! Go on! Don't be shy! Anyhow, here's the song you've asked for—are you listening, Jim, and have a very happy birthday, you wonderful fellow—this song that just about sums it all up: 'There'll never be another you.'"

Ephraim swiftly crossed from the kitchen to the back room and turned off the radio. All that sentimental hogwash was bad enough—a wife with verbal diarrhoea and a disc jockey only too happy to lap it up and regurgitate it undigested; but to have it all commemorated by a record which Jean had once, about ten years ago, bought for *him* . . . well, that was more than flesh and blood could stand. Breathing hard—and aware of the band of heat which had again risen through his body like in the training room at Columbia—Ephraim riffled through their stack of 45s. When he found the disc in question he snapped it across. He did the same thing to another one she'd bought him: 'Nobody does it better.' Both records went into the pedal bin . . . where he knew that, later on, she'd be bound to see them. So much for hypocrisy. So much for sentimental hogwash.

He briefly visualized this very fat couple right now drinking their cups of tea in bed. He imagined them as pudgy and white and beady-eyed; perhaps a little smelly; it fairly made the stomach heave to think about their present smirks—the soft words, the smug caresses.

Sick.

But in a way, he realized, this was quite a turn-up for the book. Even a healthy one. Realistic. Usually when he thought of other couples making love, or being about to make love, he tended to romanticize. They were always young—or at least, if middle-aged, still wholly in their prime—and they always got it right, time after time after time; all other men were perfect lovers and their partners, as well as knowing every art of giving pleasure themselves, inevitably writhed and scratched and bit, and moaned in ecstasy. Where all these perfectly formed people were—perfectly formed for love—he seldom ever wondered . . . although, had he been asked, he wouldn't have said he saw them often on the street.

And all these very suggestive or even very explicit love songs that you heard on the radio nowadays: he had to keep reminding himself that they weren't necessarily records of experience, so much as records of mere wishful thinking. It wasn't the way anybody actually found love. It was only the way they believed they ought to.

Because—let's face it—if you wanted to spend the night inside your lover's arms, heartbeat to heartbeat, and wake up, baby, with the world in your embrace; well, didn't you ever stir during the night, or turn, or get cramps from lying for too long in one position? Didn't you ever get pins and needles, for God's sake, from having your arm lain upon even by an angel?

He switched the radio back on, hoping for an update: "We have just heard that Jim suffered a fatal heart attack and that Renée, unable to wriggle out from under him, not only couldn't reach her cup of tea but unluckily was suffocated. Our warmest condolences go to Fiona and

Geraldine, who very kindly let us know." Ephraim's hope, however, was disappointed, so this morning, as he walked to work, he looked for all those perfect people in Woodborough Road and on Huntingdon Street . . . these days, he was always thinking about sex. Sex, he thought, was unnaturally important to him; which was ironic—well, pathetic—for somebody who wasn't really much good at it. (Because he didn't get enough encouragement, he told himself, encouragement or practice.) And that was why, of course, he was always thinking about sex. Oh, the viciousness of circles!

Indeed, he could scarcely remember when he had last had proper sex. By that he meant sex with someone who was not simply willing to have it, but glad or—ideally—eager. (He had often wished that he could qualify as a Great Lover: a Lothario, Don Juan, Gary Cooper: some fellow who had a reputation both for doing the job well and for having a decent-sized tool, better than decent-sized, to do it with.) But at least if he didn't have a lover—and even if he didn't have the talent, or the equipment—there was still one major advantage to be derived from all of this: it left him free to fantasize. The lover, the tool, the talent could all become phenomenal.

His thoughts were jumbled now. He remembered the night he'd had his first wet dream; or, rather, he remembered the morning after. Luckily he'd been staying with one of his mother's younger brothers at Hastings, where he and his wife ran a workman's caff; Lionel had been able to enlighten his ignorance, assuage his apprehensions. He remembered—though was this before or after?—his first full, unrestrained erection, when his little naked willie had suddenly reared up, disconcertingly weighty against the pale thinness of his unformed body; he and the boy he'd been sharing a room with at the time—again, he'd been away from home—had been getting ready for bed, changing into pyjamas, and they'd both giggled with embarrassment at the sight of this protuberance; yet Ephraim had already secretly felt proud . . . why? . . . what had it then meant to him? And now—what wouldn't he have given now: to be back at the time of his first full-blown erection, his first wet dream?

Once, it had been a cheerful occupation, sex, something to laugh at and treat lightly. Once, he had sometimes used to sing and hum 'The

Galloping Major' during intercourse, and an occasion he now remembered as being fairly typical was that on which he'd put one bare foot around the bedroom door, in the manner of a great tease, and then entered the room stark naked twirling Jean's pink umbrella behind one shoulder and pirouetting like a chorus girl. "Unlucky, unlucky," she had cried, "and totally obscene!" But she had laughed a lot—of course they both had—and if an opened umbrella in the house was regarded as unlucky it had proved so only in the long run; in *those* days, there had been many an evening which had reached its climax with the frenzied, toe-clenching proclamation: *Here comes the galloping major . . .* !

Where had it all gone wrong?

There was no single moment he could bring to mind. No reason why it should have.

But he had hardly developed into the great lover.

He reached the office.

The great lover manqué phoned Mrs Barks, at Beeston.

He explained about his Royal Doulton figurines. Yes, Mrs Barks would certainly be interested. Ephraim inquired about the interest rates on a loan of five hundred pounds. He estimated that he'd be able to pay back such a sum after a period of six months.

Maybe 'hoped' was a slightly more accurate word.

The monthly interest rate was fifteen percent. Seventy-five pounds. Multiply that by six and it came to four hundred and fifty pounds. To redeem the figurines after just six months he would have to pay back almost twice as much as he had borrowed.

Ephraim said goodbye to Mrs Barks.

He bit his lip.

Shortly afterwards Barney came into the office. Ephraim let him settle—after all his buoyant salutations to everybody else and breezy reassurances that he had never felt better in his life: "Oh, fit as a fiddle and ready for love! My God, when aren't I, though? What a lad, *what* a lad!"—and then swivelled slowly to address him.

"Oh, by the way, I called on Mr Harrison last night. I'm going to drop the hamper round this afternoon. He's out of work right now but as soon as he finds another job he'll certainly consider taking out insurance . . . "

He did his very damnedest to sound nonchalant. It was ridiculous but he'd felt his heartbeat accelerating ever since the moment of Barney's arrival; had felt his armpits growing moist. (One of his customary neuroses was the imagined inefficiency of his deodorant; and because he imagined it inefficient, during the course of the day it would speedily become so. But that was only *one* of his customary neuroses. Those others dominant in his life at present had to do with nervous indigestion; with the fear that he was losing his eyesight; that he was losing his hair; would soon need a hip replacement; was acquiring a paunch; was acquiring varicose veins; was acquiring a slack and stringy throat; with the fear that his bottom might be spreading . . . There were others, though, besides these.)

Barney stared at him.

Sean, Jerzy and Lucy also gave him their attention.

"Would you believe it?" asked Jerzy. But he said it with a laugh. He had got over his disappointment of yesterday; it wouldn't be alluded to again.

"Yes. Unfortunately I would." Barney, on his side, spoke without any trace of amusement. "Just too easily I would."

"Fucking unemployed . . . ," murmured Sean, jovially. "Got to hand it to you, matey. Certainly know how to pick 'em!"

"Well, it wasn't your fault, Eff," said Lucy. "Besides, think how it's going to make his Christmas! Barney, we're *glad* that someone unemployed won our prize fifty-pound hamper. Aren't we, guys? Aren't we noble? Aren't we nice?"

Barney gave an exclamation of annoyance. "You lot can laugh about it as much as you like. Me, personally, I think it's pathetic!"

He chewed the end of his pencil and then took a shred of something off his tongue and viewed it with as much disfavour as he viewed the rest of the proceedings.

"Oh, come off it, Barney, it wasn't Eff's fault," said Lucy. "It could have happened to any of us."

"Unemployed . . . ," repeated Sean, chuckling.

"That's what we'll all be soon," confided Jerzy, with bleak humour, "if things go on like this. Oh—but I forgot: we can't get the sack, can we? That's a good thing. I keep forgetting we're each of us our own boss." He said to Ephraim: "So don't worry, lad. You're not accountable to anyone but yourself. And the Missus!" Jerzy, it seemed, frequently had his own share of problems at home.

"Fucking unemployed," said Sean, shaking his head.

The subject dropped.

Soon after lunch Barney went out to see a client, so Ephraim reckoned this would be the right time to deliver the hamper: the fewer acerbic comments he had to put up with on departure, the better. The flaps dovetailed neatly into place but the carton was heavy. Lucy wasn't there. Sean and Jerzy watched him carry it towards the door with expressions of slightly ironic solidarity. Then suddenly, as though he'd been having an inner struggle and wanted to commit himself before the struggle started up again, Jerzy sprang to his feet. He picked up a ring of keys from his desk.

"Come on, lad, I'll give you a lift."

"No, that's good of you, but—but I'm okay, I can manage."

"West Bridgford isn't all that far, not when you've got transport. But if you're having to haul that thing on and off buses it'll be sheer unadulterated bloody murder."

Ephraim began to panic. "Honestly, Jerzy, I appreciate it a lot, I really do, especially in view of everything. You're very kind. But . . . but I'd rather do it myself, in a way . . . It's difficult to put it into words."

"Then don't try. Just shut up. But I can't stand by and watch you rupture yourself for someone who isn't even going to give you any business."

"I have my own reasons."

"So do I. I think maybe some of the things I said yesterday . . . I shouldn't have said them. I want to make amends." Jerzy was holding the door open onto the staircase.

"See you, mateys," said Sean. "Who knows, Eff, he may have gone out and got a job since you spoke to him last night? Stop looking worried. You've got to think positive in this world. Look for the silver lining."

Ephraim and Jerzy walked down the stairs in silence. Already the unwieldy box was beginning to make Ephraim's biceps ache . . . although in fact he was only dimly aware of it. He had other things to compete for his attention. People were often out when they'd said they'd be at home—that in itself wouldn't have been a problem—but in West Bridgford there was no address to drive to. On the other hand, maybe Jerzy hadn't heard the name of the road. Ephraim couldn't remember the names of any roads in West Bridgford but perhaps that wasn't insoluble—"Left here, next on the right, it's that turning over there." He could leave Jerzy sitting in the car and if someone answered the door of whichever house he chose to ring at, Jerzy mightn't be able to hear the conversation. (Though he'd be interested; would probably be leaning out to have a look.) "That was his mum/dad/brother/sister; he'd left a message saying he'd thought about it and didn't want to take the hamper after all; says there's bound to be a catch in it. Poor fucker." But it struck him as being fraught with all possible kinds of foul-up.

What alternative? *Oh, hell, I've just remembered something—what time is it?—he said he might be at his girlfriend's till about four. I think we'd better leave it.*

No, he couldn't do that. It was too unconvincing. And it would only postpone the reckoning; not avert it.

Oh, *God*.

They came to the entrance; went through the glass doors onto the pavement. "You'd better wait here," said Jerzy. During the day he kept his car parked in the Broadmarsh Centre. It was less than a five-minute walk but that didn't take into account lugging a sodding great hamper. He grinned broadly. "See you before you can say 'Fuck Barney!' more than a thousand times."

Jerzy was hardly out of sight before the notion had occurred to Ephraim: *Do a bunk.* All he had to do was turn a corner, mingle with the crowds, he'd be screened within seconds. It was a narrow precinct barred to all but pedestrians. In a minute he'd be well away, totally beyond being found. Jerzy would be furious; hurt, bewildered; perhaps he'd never speak to him in friendship ever again (Ephraim thought about the coffee mug, primrose-coloured with a design of strawberries and green leaves); but it was easier, altogether easier, and Ephraim would then have until tomorrow morning to think up some sort of story. Perhaps he could take in a box of chocolates or a tin of biscuits as a peace-offering.

Because his mind was so preoccupied with thoughts like these, the weight of the carton didn't bother him until he was at the other end of Bridlesmithgate. (By this time Jerzy would probably be arriving back outside the office . . . Ephraim preferred not to think about it; now he actually concentrated on how much his arms were aching.) He turned left towards Market Square and had to lean the box against a wall, wedging it between the wall and his stomach. This hiatus was necessary but profoundly unsettling. Had he reached the point of no return . . . or could he perhaps *still* go back and get there a little before Jerzy? His head moved to face the way he'd come, as if in yearning illustration. No, it was definitely too late; of course it was; there was even some relief in the acknowledgment. His head swung round again.

He couldn't remember what number bus would take him to Radford. He struggled from bus stop to bus stop seeking information—and in the process needed to make way for lots of people whom he'd have thought might make way for him. At last, however, he was on a bus, with the box sitting on the seat beside him. He could scarcely straighten his arms. They shook. This added to the pure awfulness of everything. He had at least expected a little glow of altruism to lighten his afternoon; and while he never liked to feel complacent he was disappointed that he couldn't even tell himself not to feel complacent.

They arrived in Radford by three. He hadn't phoned Wendy Cooper to make sure she'd be there but he supposed that if she wasn't he could wait in a café, with a cup of tea and a newspaper, and try not to think about what they'd be saying at Columbia. Saying at this very moment . . . and then, beyond question, at many others during the afternoon. Even if the topic began to flag it would naturally reinstate itself (and how!) on the return of Barney. Ephraim shuddered—literally. What possible explanation was he going to give? If only he could have spoken to Jean! She would undoubtedly have reproached him for creating the situation; but together, eventually, they would have come up with something. Yet in her present state of mind . . . with this icy force field all around her . . . Though he wondered whether, if an equally awful event had somehow befallen her, she wouldn't have allowed that barrier to be crossed. He recalled the occasion in Bordeaux when she'd had her purse stolen. Of course, neither of them had been depressed at the time, but even so. And if he was right—then, in that one respect at least, he was a better husband than she a wife. More approachable in need. Whatever the depth of his depression.

This didn't comfort him.

He decided, however, that for the present he must attempt to switch off. Give his mind a rest. Perhaps he would buy a paperback in place of a newspaper: a thriller or whodunit: extravagant, of course, but it could turn a bad time into a treat and he really felt that the one thing he needed in his life right now was the opportunity to escape.

Yet surprisingly—and almost disappointingly—Wendy Cooper was at home. She saw him struggling with the box. Her eyes opened wide. "Mine?"

He nodded.

"I was the one what won it?"

"What do you think?"

"Christ! I don't believe it. I never won nothing in my entire life." Throughout the next minute or so it seemed she was half laughing; half crying. He suddenly knew, knew with absolute conviction, that he had done the right thing. It was the best moment he'd had in the whole of the past week; maybe, workwise, in the whole of the past year; certainly, since he had gone to sell for Columbia. "Here, let me help you up the stairs."

"No, that's okay, I can manage." In any case, the stairs would have been too narrow for the two of them but he wanted to show that he was strong. "I've carried it all the way from the centre of town; this last bit isn't going to make much difference."

As if on cue she said: "I bet your arms must ache; you must be ever so fit. It looks real heavy." There was keen anticipatory relish in the last few words. "Honest, I can't believe it."

Upstairs Amber Jade awaited them. This time she wore a dress and plastic pants and a nappy. Ephraim felt relieved.

"We were just going out; I'm ever so glad you caught us. Look, Amber, see what the kind gentleman has brought us: lots of lovely things to eat. If you'd like to put it on the floor," she suggested to Ephraim.

He couldn't have appeared quite so fit as he finally set it down;

he was sorry about that. Again, he could scarcely straighten his arms.

But Wendy Cooper didn't seem to notice.

"Shall I go and make a cuppa?"

Ephraim shook his head. The floor didn't look as though it had known a Hoover for weeks. Maybe months. He could imagine the state of the kitchen and the crockery.

"No, thanks. I've had one. You were just going out."

"Oh, that doesn't matter now." She went down on her hands and knees, started pulling at the solid flaps of the carton. "Come on, Amber, let's see what we got." Amber, who had been staring solemnly at Ephraim, came to stand beside her mother and now stared with equal solemnity at the box. She hooked an arm round one of Ephraim's legs to support her. Ephraim didn't mind, in fact he savoured it. He had a sudden vivid image of Abby at a similar age; she must once have done the same thing. Momentarily his heart longed for the days when Abby might have hooked her arm around his trouser leg, when she might have ridden on his shoulders, tugging at his hair. Later, too, of course, the boys. His eyes filled. My God, he had been happy then. He hoped that he had known it.

It felt like another world, another life. (He remembered the woman in the video shop.) He looked back and the man he saw didn't seem at all like him. Young. Athletic. Full of generosity and thought for others. Taking happiness, and love, and home, more or less for granted—especially, maybe, love. Having no fears for the future . . . other, of course, than the usual financial ones; and those had hardly seemed to matter.

The packing straw was being tossed out on the carpet. He wondered how long it might stay there. Out came the bottles of wine, the tinned ham, the potted meats, the fruit cake, the whole round cheddar cheese, the jars of best preserve, the box of chocolates, packets of biscuits, olive oil, tea, coffee, mixed nuts, raisins, pickle and sardines. Each time she thought she'd come to an end she rummaged and discovered something more.

She opened a bag of crisps, put it into the greedy, grasping hands of Amber Jade. (Trouser leg released.) "There you are, darlin'. Offer one to the gentleman."

Amber Jade scurried off to where she thought she might be out of reach—behind the sofa. Both Ephraim and her mother laughed.

"It's just like Christmas. Except it's not. I can't remember Christmas ever being so good."

"I am glad. I'm very, very glad. It's the right person who won it. It doesn't always work that way."

"I'm ever so grateful. I really am. Ever so grateful."

She hadn't got up off her knees. It seemed apt, he thought. There were times when he still did believe in God.

"Perhaps it's going to bring you luck," he said. "Perhaps from now on things are going to change."

"They could do with it."

"I know they could."

"Hey, shall we have a bit of wine?"

"It's yours. Wine . . . I sometimes get a bit of wine at home . . . it isn't such a . . . " But he didn't want to denigrate her treat. "This is for you to enjoy. All on your own. Every last drop. While you've got your feet up and are watching a good show or movie on the box."

She said: "I just want to let you know I'm grateful."

"You already have."

But from something in her eye—or voice—he knew they were no longer talking about mere words, or even wine.

The abruptness of this realization, the complete unexpectedness of it, allied to the fact that nobody had made him such an offer, unsolicited and without any thought of gain, for an exceedingly long time; allied again to the fact that even at fifty-two he could clearly not be wholly unattractive to a girl of twenty-three (God, younger than his own daughter!) . . . all of this immediately impacted on Ephraim to produce an erection. And, really, she wasn't bad-looking! From where he stood he could see the fullness of her breasts pressing against the thin blue cotton and he now noticed for the first time that she wasn't wearing a bra—indeed, formed the impression that her nipples might be hard.

His erection, he became aware with pleasure, was growing painful.

"You really mean that?" he said.

"Why not? I think you're nice."

181

She stumbled to her feet. He realized it would have been the gallant thing, the charming thing, the Casanova thing, to move forward and give her both his hands to raise her up with easy fluid grace. But he couldn't have moved forward gracefully and his one concern was now to ease the pressure, give himself room, let her see what he could offer, before constriction maybe made it less. As she began unbuttoning her dress, so he threw off his jacket; pulled down his zipper, trousers, pants. She giggled—went and lay down on the sofa. Her nipples were indeed hard.

Even omitting the two most obvious things, it could have been a combination of unfortunate details: the stains on the moquette which might so easily have been the marks of sperm; the grubby hands, unblinking stare, as Amber Jade pulled herself up on the arm at the other end of the sofa, showing no surprise at its unexpected occupancy, her crisps now either finished or scattered over the floor; her mother's unwashed hair and body odours that proximity made obvious; the whole aura of uncleanliness, so pervasive as to be very nearly palpable; the sudden recollection that he had no condom.

Or was it possibly his age? Erections often came, though usually not so solid and imperious as this one—he'd had a longish moment of real pride—and, just as often, soon departed. He experienced the first sensations of slackening, drooping, contraction. Shrivelling. Now he looked merely ridiculous, caught in mid-shuffle, his pants and trousers bunched around his calves.

He saw the gleam of expectation fade out of her eyes.

"I'm sorry," he said.

"It doesn't matter. I was only doing it for you. Don't you fancy me?" she asked.

"No, no, it isn't that. Of course it isn't that. But I'm married, you see, and I've never before been unfaithful."

"Oh."

"So you can imagine how attractive you must be, to make me forget even for one instant . . . "

She looked down at herself, as though trying to imagine.

"Also, it's Amber Jade. I'm not sure how much it might affect her to see her mum making love to a stranger. Or, I mean, to see anyone making love to anyone."

These, of course, had been the two most obvious things. He thought—hoped—they were the points that had neutralized the sad effects of flattery and pride.

He was hastily dressing himself. She got off the sofa and began to do the same. Now, he couldn't wait to get out of there. He felt degraded, dirty, selfish, inadequate. Old. Perhaps no other woman would ever again offer herself to him in that same uncomplicated way. It was a milestone; the last milestone. The visit had been ruined.

The whole thing. The hamper. The spontaneity of her pleasure. His knowledge of the rightness of what he had done. All of it—ruined.

The classy provisions, some lying directly on the carpet, others resting on the straw, now looked completely ordinary. They had lost their specialness, their promise of delight.

"Goodbye," he said. "I wish you luck. You're a nice person."

As he went down the stairs she stood at her front door, with Amber Jade in her arms. "Thank you for coming. Thank you for bringing me the things."

He walked away and wished he'd never come.

A car hooted behind him. Insistently.

It was Barney.

At first he simply slid over to the passenger seat and lowered the window. "Where the fuck have you been? Where the fuck did you vanish with that hamper? Don't try to lie to me. I followed you." Then he decided to slide over again and get out of the car; all his self-help books must have given him the same advice, never to let the other person be in a position to look down on him.

Now he was the one enabled to look down.

And it appeared that of all the places in this whole bloody city in which Barney's client might have earned his living it had to be in Radford; and that of all the minutes out of all the hundreds which existed in the working day, Barney's return had coincided with the moment between Ephraim's getting off the bus and his reaching the turning some fifty yards off down the main road. Was it fate or was it coincidence—and, anyway, who gave a toss? The only thing that counted, it was a further confirmation of the fact you couldn't win. But, if you couldn't win, you might at least brazen it out, your ever-looming defeat. At least this new manifestation had the merit of having overtaken him completely without warning. No need to anticipate, to sweat, to feel his stomach go all loose with apprehension.

Or was there? Barney didn't offer him a lift. "I'm not going to ride back with a total piece of shit. I don't ride with scum. I only ride with people I respect. I'll see you at the office."

They'd had five minutes standing on the pavement. Could even fifty minutes standing in the office supply them with any happier a conclusion?

"It was one of my questionnaires that won," Ephraim had said. "It was one of mine! Pauline picked it out. What difference does it make if I . . . ?"

"Just give it to a friend?" Now it was Barney who had the satisfaction of finishing a somewhat dodgy sentence.

"Come and see her for yourself. You'll soon find out."

"All that shit you gave us! All that bloody well holier-than-thou hypocrisy! I can tell you I'll never forget it. Nor will the others. I hope you've got that fifty pounds; otherwise—I swear it—they're going to tear you limb from limb. And I shan't raise a finger to stop them! In fact I hope you *haven't* got it. Not yet, I mean. Not yet."

"Just come and see her. Please!"

"Shall *I* tell the others what you've done or shall I wait for *you* to let them know? I'll have to think about it."

"In fact, I'd say it's your duty to see her."

"I'll talk to *you* in the office."

As though they hadn't just said all there was to say. As though that was the normal state of affairs: talking to him in the office.

Closing of car door. Even now, Barney was careful not to slam it. The car was a Porsche and he'd only had it for a few weeks.

Well, do you want to hear what *I* hope? I hope you crash on the way back. I hope it puts you into hospital. Gives you something else to think about. For a long time.

And, further, do you want to hear a really good joke? You thought I was just great when I started. Jaunty. Irrepressible. 'A real find!'—that's what you once said. Told everyone you hadn't found work quite so enjoyable in months: the certainty of coming in each day and knowing you'd be made to laugh—and also made to think—by such an entertaining, educated crackpot. And do you know something else that's funny? I'd looked forward equally to being with you . . . maybe, one day, even having you in the family . . .

Ephraim watched the snazzy red car shoot off silently and smoothly and quickly merge into the distance. Merge without mishap.

Well, what were the personal things he'd left at the office? Nothing very much. His briefcase. Mug. Pocket calculator. Briefcase wasn't leather. Nor was there anything in it, so far as he remembered, that really mattered or couldn't be duplicated.

At least he wouldn't have to face Jerzy.

He started to walk home. Better not take the bus. Thank God he hadn't bought a paperback. Unemployed again. The story of my life. Dishonourable discharge. No, that at least was not the story of his life. He'd never been fired from a job nor ever walked out of one on account of any imputation of dishonesty. In the past there'd always been handshakes, smiles, promises to keep in touch. Leaving presents. Lumps in the throat.

There'd never been a situation where he couldn't face the consequences; where he'd had to turn tail and slink away. Like a thief or a traitor.

Supposing he ran into any of them in Nottingham? Not Barney—Barney didn't count any more—but any of the others. Whether next week, or next year, or even the year after that. What on earth would he say?

There'd be nothing for it but to cut them dead.

Or supposing they came to the house?

He had never in the whole course of his life, through shame, through shiftiness, through guilt, had to cut anybody dead. Never. (Nor, apart from during times of depression, pretend that he wasn't at home or be anything but hospitable and welcoming.) Apart from during those times of depression he'd always been quick to smile in fellowship at anyone he passed; head up, shoulders back, a spring to his footstep. He had usually been at his very best in the street: on the lookout for new friends, for admiration, for the potential enrichment of his life.

Especially lately. There wasn't much potential enrichment of one's life within the four demoralizing—sun-excluding—walls of home.

He didn't want to go home. What was there for him at home?

He blinked. Savagely. He would not feel self-pity. (Why not? What was wrong with self-pity? It was reasonable, he felt, in certain sets of circumstances to feel some pity for oneself. Who else ever would?) He had no place to go.

Near the Broadmarsh Shopping Centre, in a rather seedy side street leading to the railway station, there was a sex shop. He had never been in one but he felt scarcely any nervousness as he drew near. What he felt was closer to exhilaration. Abandonment. Recklessness. The kind of feeling that went along with thumbing your nose at the whole wide world and hitching up your pants and making a new start. The window of the place was simply a blank: grey slatted blinds. The glass of the door was painted black. Above it were the words *Private Shop*. Ephraim would have been devastated had this shop been closed; he experienced overwhelming relief as the door yielded to his touch. He was the only customer. A bald young man sat behind the counter reading a tabloid: burly, somewhat dour, yet not discomforting. He hardly looked up; gave merely the curtest of nods. Said they had only the two types of cock ring. Ephraim felt no embarrassment about making the inquiry; he could have been asking for a fountain pen. On the other hand there was a measure of disappointment when he was shown what were his options: one was made of pink plastic, the other was basically a leather strap, a leather strap with two metal rings and two smaller bits of leather to attach them to the main thong. He had hoped for something far more decorative, even beautiful, cloisonné perhaps— like a bracelet—or Chinese and made of ivory and engraved with dragons (as illustrated in *The Joy of Sex*; though obviously he hadn't really hoped for that). But he adjusted, rapidly. Slim though the band of leather was, barely more than the width of a woman's watchstrap, he suddenly remembered that leather was quite macho; began to see it in a different light. Simple—straightforward—tough. No frills; no nonsense; a statement. (Part of that statement: *Up yours, Barney!*) He asked the prices. The plastic one was ten pounds—ten! The leather one was twenty. There was no way he could afford either. It was ridiculous. Sheer exploitation. He would buy himself a woman's watchstrap . . . at least this had provided the idea. Come to that, couldn't he make do with a broad elastic band?

But he didn't want a woman's watchstrap; nor a broad elastic band. He wanted *this*—this proper cock ring, made of leather. He'd set his heart on it.

He tried to haggle.

The shopkeeper was uninterested. Shook his head. Bald, burly— thick. Uncooperative. Take it or leave it.

He had been thinking of four or five pounds, tops. And for something that was a good deal more than just plain plastic. Or even leather. Twenty pounds was nothing more than daylight robbery (to use one of his mother's favourite phrases . . . though never, so far as he was aware, in connection with a cock ring).

He hadn't got twenty pounds on him; he had five. The only place there might have been twenty pounds was in Jean's building society account: her emergency fund. But what he had got on him, it suddenly crossed his mind, was his Barclay's chequebook; also the banker's card which he had certainly not cut in two and posted back in the envelope provided. (He'd felt damned if he was going to do that. Talk about adding insult! It was tantamount to saying: Sorry, bud, but we don't trust you.) In the normal way he wouldn't have liked making out a cheque to a sex shop—paranoiacally, he could imagine that whatever the name of the payee, the eyes of the bank clerk would light up with instant recognition: *Hey, you guys, come look at this!*—but, in these circumstances, what the hell, the cheque was unquestionably going to bounce (hard cheese and yet poetic justice for all these blatant racketeers) and by then, anyway, he wouldn't even be in Nottingham any longer. No job; no money; no marriage; was there anything to keep him? He yearned for a fresh start; he always had done. Jean wouldn't care. She could sell the house. It might take a long time to do so but if it was at least on the market this would surely forestall the threat of repossession—it would, wouldn't it?—and there might be some fifteen or twenty thousand pounds left over to put down on a small flat for herself: a small flat with a bit of garden, or at any rate room for a window box. Roger would help her . . . Roger was a good lad. So if he was ever going to make a fresh start, this was definitely the time to do it. He wrote out the cheque; appended his signature with a flourish.

It was maybe symbolic. Whatever the bastards did to grind him down he would always spring up again.

Cock-a-hoop.

Having pocketed his purchase (it was on a piece of card, with a shallow, clear plastic front) and having asked how long it would be safe to wear it at one time—"For as long as you like, mate," said the young man, certainly not expansive but not unpleasant either—he stopped to look at the covers of some pornographic magazines. The covers were all you could see, since the magazines were wrapped, unopenable. The covers were almost enough. They all showed photographs of well-endowed young men lifting their partners in poses that surely couldn't be maintained throughout sexual intercourse. Or perhaps they could . . . the trouble was, you never knew. In that other realm, the realm of the virile, the imaginative, the suitably partnered—the realm of the perfect—possibly all these energetic postures were practically a matter of routine.

He found the magazines depressing; deflating rather than the opposite. Ephraim was reasonably proud of his physique (he would like to have been taller—and perhaps a bit hairier—but he guessed he was probably stronger than your average man) yet he had never in his life lifted anybody to such heights as a preliminary to a fuck; only his children as a preliminary to a ride, or as part of some boisterous game; and if he were to try it now—say, with Jean—he would no doubt either drop her or they would topple together or he would bring on a hernia. Possibly a combination of all three. (And he could already hear her voice, even if they were by then on speaking terms, let alone on having-sex terms: "Ephraim! What *are* you doing?") What had he missed? Fifty-two years old. What had he missed? Oddly, the only magazine which did give him a hard-on—as distinct to feelings of wistfulness or mild revulsion—was not merely one where the activity looked less strenuous; it was gay; the participants were both male.

And . . . oh, for heaven's sake! . . . the darker of the two looked a bit like Barney.

Despite his detour he arrived home early. Jean wasn't there. She, too, was looking at photographs, albeit not in a sex shop but at the police station. If he'd known this, Ephraim would have been staggered—staggered and hurt and self-reproachful—and would instantly have gone back into town. But he didn't know it and so he went up to the bathroom instead, in order to fit his new appliance, his sexual aid, his symbol of a fresh beginning . . . although without its two clumsy excrescencies, which he had now decided to abandon. There was a little diagram on the piece of card—plus a discreet and mistily romantic photo—but it wouldn't have been hard, perhaps mainly due to *The Joy of Sex*, to see what was required: to pass the leather strip beneath the scrotum and around the base of the penis, mind the hair, draw the strap tight, secure it on the furthest notch he could manage. (He almost had an orgasm, right then and there.) They gave you six notches. It was disheartening but he could use the sixth . . . although, thankfully, only after straining. Yet if it were to be effective it clearly had to be right. (A stud like Gary Cooper could probably have used the third—why not the first?—the fact they provided a first must mean that there were some who didn't need the other five.) He was slightly worried that although, obviously, he gave himself an erection fixing the damn thing, he could still comfortably pull up his boxer shorts half a minute later; he thought the whole point of the contraption was to maintain that erection indefinitely.

But perhaps it was only after ejaculation you could properly test its efficiency. He was vague on the mechanics of it all, yet he remembered the phrase 'stiffening a part-erection following a full orgasm'—something about blocking off the veins of the penis at its roots. It sounded gruesome. But magical. He would have been tempted to masturbate at once if he hadn't wished for the time being to go on savouring in ignorance the possibilities of this wondrous gadget. If it wasn't going to work he didn't want to know. Not yet. He wanted to hang on to his illusions, if that's what they turned out to be, for as long as he could.

Jean came home. She informed him she had spent the past hour at the costume museum—and, yes, found it very interesting, thank you—but he realized two things almost immediately: that, firstly, he couldn't tell her he had lost his job and, secondly, there was still very little chance he'd be able to try out his new acquisition on her tonight. His sense of letdown felt unbearable.

Nevertheless, despite the portents, he judged it to be worth a shot. At half-past-nine she suddenly stood up. "I've had enough of television. I'm off to bed. Tomorrow of all days I don't want to feel tired!"

"Nor me," he answered, "no, nor me. Do you realize that tonight we've got the whole house to ourselves?" He put this question as though it followed on quite naturally and as though he'd only just thought of it.

Then he added a second. "When did *that* last happen?" It was almost equally rhetorical, for he himself perfectly well knew the answer. In the summer, during a rail strike.

"Heaven knows. What difference does it make?"

"I could chase you up and down the stairs. Starkers. Pelt you with peanuts. Every hit scores a penalty."

"No, thank you," said Jean. "Will you take up the water or shall I?"

"Oh, come on, love. We've been gloomy long enough, both of us. Let's snap out of it. We could circle round the fire to music with a jungle beat." Again he meant naked. "Or you could do the dance of the seven veils for me. Me, the Caliph of Baghdad." *Me, Tarzan. You, Jane.*

Before her return he had nipped out to buy a bottle of wine with which to mellow her . . . and paid for it, what's more, with money! But even if it had mellowed her—and, in truth, there wasn't much sign of it—he knew she would never have agreed to this last suggestion: at the best of times she was far more inhibited about nudity than he was, far too conscious of her weight.

"No, thank you," she repeated briskly. "What's got into you tonight?"

"I want to let bygones be bygones! To start all over! As if we were newlyweds—just at the beginning of our glorious dream."

"Interesting choice of word," she remarked.

Hadn't she realized then that it was tongue-in-cheek? "Why? Wouldn't you like to be a newlywed again?"

"Not especially. At all events the circumstances would need to be a whole lot different."

"What about the partner?"

"And in any case that wasn't the word I was referring to. The one I meant was dream."

"I suppose you'd prefer to settle for nightmare?"

"I'd prefer to settle for reality."

"Come on, honeychile. Don't be a spoilsport. Give us a smile."

"Maybe, when I've got something to smile about."

"Enjoy yourself. It's later than you think."

"Yes . . . it must be getting on for ten." The fact that she had made a little joke and that for one whole minute now, possibly two, she'd allowed him to stand there with his arms about her—though, admittedly, without her showing much responsiveness—encouraged him to hope she might be softening.

"How about it, then? Let's do some dirty dancing." (Now there, by all accounts, was a mover. Patrick Swayzee. In the mould of John Travolta. It was a film he'd really like to see. And it occurred to him that he had never used his own talent for dancing as a form of foreplay. Why hadn't he? What *was* the matter with him?)

"Oh, Ephraim, don't be so—" Then she did pull away.

"So what?"

"You can't just switch it on and off like that. Whenever you feel like it. So completely heedless of how anyone else may feel."

"I was only joking," he said.

"Yes—well. You were only joking; I'm only going off to bed. And I'll leave you to turn out the lights."

She stopped for a moment at the door.

"Ephraim? Tomorrow's going to be special, isn't it? Very special. Please remind me why."

In other words, he thought, *you're not going to spoil things, are you, by anger or sullenness, resentment or jealousy?* But he hoped he was big enough not to blame her for sensing some of his underlying feelings and aiming to provide a gentle, non-explicit warning. It was clumsy rather than gentle but he wasn't going to take offence.

He even managed a laugh. "As though you need to be reminded!"

"Oh, it's Oscar, isn't it? Yes, of course."

He stayed downstairs for the next twenty minutes, flicking through the following week's *Radio Times* to see what films they had lined up. (In other words, would he be missing much if he did slip off to London?) He also spent about five minutes crouching in front of Polly's basket, scratching her on the head and underneath her jaw, repeatedly tickling her on the tummy. Whenever he stopped she rolled back into a sitting position to nudge him into more affection. He put his arms about her neck and drew her to him in the kind of hug she didn't normally receive from him; only sometimes from the children. Then he stood up and—not forgetting the water, nor the remainder of the wine, nor the two chilled goblets optimistically prepared—said God bless and went upstairs.

Jean was already in bed, reading.

"You look pretty," he said. He liked her with her hair loose, framing her face, soft against the pillow.

"Thank you."

"As my Aunt Julia used to say . . . you've got a birthday."

"Thank her."

This, again, was faintly promising.

"I bought something today," he said.

"Did you?" But she still kept her eyes fixed upon her book. Tenaciously. "And what was that? I hope it wasn't anything for me." *Because I'm really not in any mood for appreciating presents* was the clearly unspoken rider. *And for having to say thank you.*

"Only indirectly," he replied. "In fact, it's something that will make you laugh." Which wasn't what he meant; not in the slightest. *Something that will turn you on.* That's how he would have put it.

"Oh, yes?"

"I'm wearing it. Watch closely."

Then at last she did look up—though with an air of resignation, even of barely contained impatience. Rather than focus on him, however, her eye was caught by the tray which he'd set down on a table, with the wine on it. "Why've you brought that up?"

"Why do you think?" he said, momentarily diverted from the more important item that he had to show. "Because I'm not taking no for an answer. Because I'm hoping that—like I was pressing for downstairs—we can now celebrate, *properly* celebrate, the end of all depression . . . along with, as we did at supper, tomorrow's triumphal return of our prodigal son!" If she wanted to quibble about any of the words he used, she could certainly question 'triumphal', although he was sure that this was how it would appear. "I thought, too, that we might use it as a love potion." He grinned at her, roguishly.

Or such was his intention.

"Well, none for me," she said. "I've just cleaned my teeth—and I've taken half a sleeping pill. What's this thing I'm meant to be looking at? I thought you mentioned—"

"Ah . . . Abracadabra! Now as I say—watch closely." (She might always change her mind about the wine, he thought.)

He undid the buttons of his shirt, with a provocative glance and a swaying of the hips, as if embarking on a seven-veil exercise himself. Which indeed he was. "Ten pounds to the first contestant who manages to spot it!"

"Ephraim, I'm sleepy," she said. "I want to read my book. Either just tell me or don't."

"And when I say, ladies, the first contestant who manages to spot it, I am *not* referring to the size of my dick. Although, madam, if you thought I was, you might be getting warm. Warmer than you realize."

By this time he had his shirt off—he wore no undervest—and was unfastening his jeans quicker than he'd meant to.

"Any second now, you lovely audience—we're very nearly there!"

But he had forgotten he still had his shoes on. Any pretension to ease and suppleness of movement had to be abandoned. He sat down on the edge of the bed and yanked them off without undoing them. His trousers swiftly followed; were likewise flung to the floor. Socks, too. He stood up in just his boxer shorts.

"Your patience, ladies and gentlemen . . . is about to be rewarded."

He inched down one side of the shorts; then pulled it up again. Jean continued to lie there with her back supported by her pillows and wore the same longsuffering expression.

Now finally he went into his dance. There was satisfaction to be had—even elation and excitement—from improvising below his breath a jazzy accompaniment which his feet could nimbly follow and his body swing in time to. He thought about Swayzee; almost forgot about Jean. When he looked to check on her reaction, she was yawning and glancing at her watch.

He had a hard-on. If this wouldn't do it nothing would. He peeled off his shorts with the fluidity and style (he told himself) which had earlier been missing.

"Tarr-ah!" He gave a showman's flourish, like the master of ceremonies in the centre of the circus ring; and regretted the lack of a top hat he could sweep down to the floor.

But his bow didn't do anything to interfere with the erection. His cock looked enormous—even from above. The leather strap was biting into it and lent an added touch of the machismo he'd originally envisaged.

He didn't know, however, if Jean was going to be impressed or disgusted or amused by it. He remembered the time when he had twirled her pink umbrella, also with a full and—well, depending on your viewpoint—quite obscene erection.

"My God!" she said. "What's that?"

"What I was telling you about. It's called a cock ring."

But even as he said it his cock began to soften.

"It's an erection-maintainer. I should have got one," he remarked, "a very long time ago," putting his hand on the strap as if to straighten it, hoping that the pressure of his fingers would restore the tautness.

"Where on earth did you get it?"

"Sex shop near the station."

"How much?"

"Three pounds."

"You spent three pounds . . . on *that*?"

"It'll be worth it if it works." His cock had shrunk now nearly to its normal size. "Even if it doesn't I still think it's—well, I don't know—I think it's sort of sexy."

"I think it's sort of pathetic."

"Pathetic?" he asked.

"Sad," she explained. "I think it's just so sad."

There was a pause.

"I'm going to brush my teeth," he said.

"I'm going to read my book." She called: "And what's that bottle of wine doing on the table? Where did that bottle of wine come from?"

He didn't take it off—the ring; kept it on as a measure of defiance;

ran down to the floor below, taking the stairs two at a time as he did so, watched his penis swing with the momentum. He peed with it on, stirring up a froth in the water ("Do men really have to pee right in the centre of the bowl?"), cleaned his teeth with it on, and, standing well back from the small mirror above the basin, sucking in his stomach muscles and practising all sorts of supposedly seductive poses and gyrations, brought himself off with it on. The experience was one of almost total joylessness.

As he swilled the semen out of the basin his penis once again contracted. The strap was plainly useless.

He still kept it on, though. To have taken it off would have seemed like the final—but *final*—admission of defeat.

All he needed now was for Jean, with supremely ironic perversity, to reach out for him in bed. "I'm sorry, love. You're right. Please come and fuck me."

Some hope, however.

He spent a largely sleepless night.

In the morning he got up at six—even a little before that. It was unlikely Oscar would arrive for about another twelve hours (unlikely Abby, this weekend, would arrive at all) but he didn't mean to take chances. Besides . . . the sooner he got off, the less time in which to waver; and if he could pack without even waking Jean, then that would obviously be best. One thing he knew at any rate: she wouldn't hear the bath water. From the point of view of cleanliness a bath mightn't be essential—often he would have a quick, over-all wash just standing at the basin—but from the point of view of symbolism it was imperative. Total immersion. Baptism. The only way to set out upon a journey that really mattered; perhaps the last momentous journey of his life.

Perhaps the first?

In the bath he quoted something he had learnt at school.

"'There is a tide in the affairs of men,
  Which, taken at the flood, leads on to fortune;
  Omitted, all the voyage of their life
  Is bound in shallows and in miseries.
  On such a full sea are we now afloat,

And we must take the current when it serves,
Or lose our ventures.'"

The fact that he could remember it so easily, word for word, after forty years, more than forty years—without one single hesitation, nor, so far as he knew, one single mistake—seemed an excellent omen. When the time arrived for him to feel nervous and become less sure that he was doing the right thing (as he was aware would inevitably happen; he was a realist; even now tendrils of lonesomeness and insecurity were beginning to entwine around his gut) he would simply repeat those half-dozen lines quite calmly and think about the classroom in which he'd first stood up and recited them.

Prep school. Lymington Road. West Hampstead.

Where his mother had stood at the front door and rang the bell, in 1945, in time for her appointment with the head. The school had long since been converted into flats but he would go again to gaze at the place on those dull red tiles where his mother had once stood. He felt sure they wouldn't have been changed. The front door, too, would look the same. The house itself would. It would be one of his myriad places of pilgrimage.

He had probably learnt it with ease—that passage from Shakespeare; one of the homeworks you scarcely had to bother with. He'd probably understood it, as well, and shot his hand up to answer all the questions. He'd been looked upon as bright at Warwick House; quite possibly the brightest. Nice-looking. Good-natured. Helpful. Full of fun.

Teacher's pet.

(The way that Mr Dallas, sixty-five-ish, silver-haired, nicotine-fingered, unsteady on his feet—childless—the way he'd used to take him on his lap would these days, of course, be regarded with extreme suspicion, but there had never been the least trace of any funny business . . . Ephraim was sure of that.)

He remembered many things about Warwick House: the fact that he'd always been amongst the top—academically, athletically—a prefect (for the whole of his last year, school captain) but popular with it, courted, looked up to, even literally looked up to, since until he had reached twelve or thirteen he had actually been tall for his age. A hero out of Talbot Baines Reed . . . or perhaps Malcolm Saville; the only time he'd ever won prizes—unless you counted the medals he'd got for his dancing, the cup for his jiu-jitsu, when he was about eighteen. He remembered a story he'd had printed in the school magazine, a story which Mr Dallas had encouraged him, shortly before the end of Ephraim's final term, to send off to the *Evening Standard*. (It had been sent back, with a rejection slip, on the last day of the holiday.) He returned to Lymington Road during his first week at the Grammar—where he was finding it unexpectedly difficult to settle down; and indeed he never particularly shone there, in that far less intimate atmosphere—to discover that Mr Dallas was ill and, for the moment, asleep. When Ephraim went back again, a few days later, the headmaster had died. Mrs Dallas had asked if he'd like to see the body, an invitation he somewhat awkwardly declined but she had perfectly well understood and had told him to pick out a volume from her husband's bookcase, as a memento; he'd chosen *Quentin Durward*. At the end of that Christmas term the school disbanded. For some reason he'd lost touch with all his friends there. Quite frequently in recent years, however, he had thought about putting an advert in the papers or phoning in to some radio show that dealt in such matters, and trying to organize a reunion, the beginning perhaps of an old boys' association. But although the notion had often tempted him he'd somehow kept putting it off.

Of course, it wasn't too late. Maybe now, in this new life of his, he would finally get round to doing something about it.

A time for making resolutions. A fresh set of resolutions.

He got out of his bath and as he dried examined himself in the mirror. He bet that few of the boys from Warwick House would look as good as he did. If he joined a health club and lost half a stone or so he still had the kind of figure that many men his age, or even men a good deal younger, would envy him. (He held his head up. His throat was *not* growing crepey.)

He put on his cock ring.

Just his knowledge of its presence would assuredly give him confidence; would remind him to move gracefully and to hold himself well.

(Walk tall, walk tall, and look the world right in the eye. That's what my mother said to me, when I was just knee-high . . .) He whistled as he shaved. My God, he would walk tall.

Conquer his neuroses. Wage war, do battle. And win.

And even if he didn't . . . then smile cheerfully in defeat. In its own way, perhaps the truest kind of victory.

So—whatever happened—how could he possibly lose?

Every new day was going to mean something.

Hey, look me over. Lend me a ear. Fresh out of clover. Mortgaged up to here.

But don't pass the hat, folks. Don't pass the cup. The only way when you're down and out—the only way is up.

He went back into the bedroom and extracted his clothes in stealth: not just the ones for wearing but for packing too. In quickness and in stealth. (That pleased him.) He planned to be decisive from now on. No shilly-shallying; no weakness; no old-maidishness. He opened and closed drawers, took some things, left others, allowed himself no second thoughts. Jean stirred a little—he stood like in musical statues— but he reckoned that her inner clock had at least another hour to run; maybe two; even on the day her son was coming home. He decided that he had enough time to take Polly for a final walk.

(But he must be careful, even mentally, not to use the word *final*. That made it sound as if he were slamming doors with such vigour they would have to stick. Yet need this be so? And, anyway, what he must concentrate on now was the opening of new doors, not the closing of old.)

Polly seemed surprised at being let out so early—surprised, perhaps, it was with him and not with Roger she should have her first encounter of the day. Surprised but not unhappy.

He took her, as usual, round the reservoir. The lamps were still lit; the sun wouldn't rise for about another hour. He threw her red rubber ring and there was apparently enough light for her to distinguish it each time and come running jubilantly back, dropping it before him with an air of pride. This *couldn't* be the last walk he would ever take her on, the last game he would ever play with her. As he watched her twist and leap and go bounding off, he did so with a fresh determination to live only for the passing moment, to try to hold onto it, string it together with all the other passing moments: a chain of too often unappreciated worth that would wind its way through the rest of his life to such magical effect that if, say, he had only one year of existence left to him, he would live more deeply in just that one year than other men might live in fifty. For instance right now: the expression in Polly's eyes, the swish of her tail, the poised gracefulness of her whole waiting, compact, keyed-up being; the way the ring went sailing through the air, the supple swing of his own body, the feeling of agility and faultless timing and of unleashed strength. There was so much to get out of every single moment; and the days would be jam-packed with single moments! It was purely a matter of practice. He knew that he could do it.

Life begins at fifty-two! On Saturday the twenty-eighth of October at . . . he peered at Liz's watch, dear Liz's watch, he was very glad he hadn't pawned it . . . No, life had actually begun about an hour ago, say at six o'clock, on Saturday the twenty-eighth of October. This marvellous, unique and wholly unrepeatable day. This once-in-all-creation day . . . Life had begun at—

But on second thoughts you couldn't say at six o'clock. He hadn't told himself it was beginning at six o'clock and it was necessary to have been aware of it—right then—at the exact and vital moment; not merely, however happily, in retrospect. There was enough of it . . . time. He needn't regret again the wastage of the past.

Very well, then. It didn't matter. Life began at six-fifty-one and . . . fifteen seconds. Now!

No, he must wait for six-fifty-two. Six-fifty-two precisely. That made it even better. Neater, more appropriate. Add six full years to his present fifty-two. At fifty-eight he would still be a young man. Even at sixty-four he would still be a long way from old: full of bounce and bonhomie and physical attraction. He would deal, indeed, in packages of six. It seemed like a further wonderful and wholly heaven-sent omen.

So . . . six-fifty-two.

Now!

And as one of the first important actions of his new life he decided he would leave a note for Roger. "My dear old Rodge . . . ," he would begin.

He would like to think of something which was matey, wise, inspirational. Memorable. Non-tacky.

"Just a line to say how much I love you and to let you know you've always been one of the best things in my life. Sorry for failures and crossness and mistakes. Good luck with your studies. I hope you'll swiftly find a new job that will be well-paid and bring you lots of satisfaction. But have a short holiday first. Always live for the moment. I shall. Dad."

Or, in fact, would that be a bit naff? The last thing he wanted was to embarrass the lad. On the other hand, a degree of *temporary* embarrassment might not matter, so long as over the years he should derive pleasure from it—comfort?—a knowledge of his father's love. Ephraim hoped he'd keep the note in his wallet and perhaps take it out to reread, reread and pause over, possibly once a month . . . or once every couple of months.

'Pa' instead of 'Dad'?

Cross out the bit about living for the moment? Partly because that was something you had to come to for yourself. But more especially because—and at least he recognized the meanness of this, and recognition of such things was maybe more than half the battle—more especially because . . . Well, it was his own discovery and for the moment he was still a little jealous of it. Roger had almost thirty years before he reached his father's age. Ephraim couldn't give away his secrets until he'd at any rate stolen some kind of march even on his favourite son.

But then, too, he wanted his children to be happy—genuinely wanted this, quite apart from the fact that the happiness of his children, and the happiness they brought into the lives of others, represented the chief vindication of his own existence.

"I really wish I could have measured up to Lieutenant James Still," he would say, in a PS. To endeavour to show he understood; that there were some things he had always understood; shared aims he had always attempted to live up to, even if he'd known better than to try to put them into words. "I think perhaps you'll manage it. No, I feel almost sure you will. If anybody can, it's you."

When he got home he wrote the letter hastily. (Unfortunately Polly had lost her rubber ring and although they'd spent time looking for it their search was fruitless. She came away only against her will, but she would find it, he told her, as good as promised her, upon some later walk.) He wasn't very pleased with it. Inside his head it had sounded almost incomparably better; and he would have liked to make a fair copy but that struck him as false. Better the crossings-out and the few words he had added as an afterthought to make the rhythm of it flow. The spontaneity was vital.

He slipped it in an envelope—annoyingly, he could find only a cheap one, because for stationery he had invariably gone to Woolworth's—and left it on Roger's pillow.

Then he took the Royal Doulton figurines and wrapped each in a teacloth. Packed them among his shirts and socks and underwear . . . and, good, this reminded him also to take a towel; two towels; he had remembered, of course, his sponge bag, shaving things, toothbrush . . . yet still the medium-sized holdall he had so carefully pulled out from under Jean's side of the bed wasn't quite full. He liked that, the idea of that. Dick Whittington, with his bandanna. Not weighed down by possessions. Not weighed down by all the clutter of imprisonment. If he could have managed it he, too, would have preferred just a bundle tied to the end of a stick. Turn again, Dick Whittington—thrice Lord Mayor of London! But in fact this not-very-bulky holdall was (for 1989) almost the same thing. The longing for adventure. The joy of the open road. Mr Toad, as well as Dick Whittington. Where the rainbow ends. The streets paved with gold; the essential decency of life along the river bank. St George and the dragon. He remembered all these things from his early boyhood, this mélange of children's plays and pantomimes . . . and the integral teas at either Buzzard's or Gunter's or a Corner House. With grandmother or great-aunts or mother or cousins: as Dodie Smith had put it, "the family—that dear octopus from whose tentacles we never quite escape." Mona and Joan and Maggie. My God, how he had loved them, all those people who had introduced him to the wonder and entrancement of both stage and screen. The warmth—security—escape. But obviously he hadn't known it then: how enduringly he would love them . . . and how ever more consciously, more wistfully, with time.

201

Such thoughts as these all helped him leave the house without too drastic a lowering of the spirits; he'd realized, anyway, that it was going to be a wrench—in two years there'd been a lot of happy times here, particularly in retrospect. He didn't look about him, then, too lingeringly . . . what was the point? He whistled as he closed the front door; whistled something from *The King and I*. He nodded to the postman three houses down the road but didn't stop to see what mail he might have brought.

He hadn't left a note for Jean.

He wondered if she'd feel concern.

Roger would explain. Not until this evening, of course; but a period of uncertainty might be no bad thing for her, Ephraim considered—although on second thoughts what difference would it make? To her? To anything? Probably, she wouldn't even notice all that much, not on the day that Oscar was returning from his travels. The prodigal son.

He had disappeared before. (Only her husband; not her son.) Once, for a period of about eight hours. He doubted she would worry. More likely, she would simply shrug, resentfully reproach him for the chores he might have done.

The open road. Not so much a question of pootering about along the byways and between the banks and hedgerows as of making your way into the middle of town and down the pedestrian precinct and through the Broadmarsh Centre. The joy of adventure. That for the moment was the business of writing out another cheque; this time, for British Rail. He had seven more cheques left in the book. He thought he could safely go on using them until midway through the following week. What did they do—the banks—in this sort of case, he wondered. How streamlined and how foolproof would be their blacklist of defaulters? Of cheats and swindlers? (He found he didn't quite like those words: cheats, swindlers, defaulters. They didn't fit in with either Dick Whittington or Mr Toad . . . despite the latter's short spell of incarceration. Neither did they fit in with St George; nor even with Paul Gaugin and his notorious escape from domesticity; out of the straitjacket of being the breadwinner, into the paradise of the South Pacific and the freedom to pursue his art and discover love and be bathed in Technicolor . . . albeit only one brief sequence of Technicolor, in a picture called *The Moon and Sixpence*.) Anyway, Ephraim wrote out his cheque. British Rail weren't always all that lovable, or altruistic. Robin Hood, who was Nottingham's most famous son, would undoubtedly have had something to say about British Rail. *And* about Barclay's Bank. He remembered *The Bandit of Sherwood Forest*, starring Cornel Wilde. In 1946 Ephraim had been impressed by a large poster for this film beside a bus stop in the Abbey Road; while it was there, had seen it almost daily on his way to and from West Hampstead. As a boy he had worshipped Cornel Wilde, former Olympic fencing champion, along with Gregory Peck and Laurence Olivier; had wanted him for a brother as much as for a father. And indeed—more than the other two—Cornel Wilde was still one of his romantic heroes.

18

It was half-past-eight on the Saturday morning. Roger was dressed, except for his jacket and tie. He'd had his breakfast: a croissant and brioche, separately wrapped in clingfilm, cold and somewhat solid; a miniature pot of lemon marmalade, a misshapen pat of butter; one sachet of instant coffee, another of white sugar; and two containers of long-life milk, each of which he'd partly spilt in pulling off the foil lids. The plate was cardboard, the knife and teaspoon plastic; incredibly, the cup and saucer were of bone china, rose-patterned. He had an electric kettle in his room, which he'd filled at the washbasin.

The room itself was small—self-coloured maroon carpet, skimpy mauve curtains. It was also gloomy, being situated in the basement, and noisy, because it was next door to some showers and a lavatory and till nearly three o'clock there'd been a party of Australians horsing about in the corridor.

All the same, as a room it had been adequate, and Roger even felt a certain fondness for it. It seemed clean enough and the bed—although too narrow and inevitably too short—was definitely well-sprung, with a couple of firm pillows and a sturdy headboard against which he had sat up very comfortably to watch *I Confess* and to drink the beer and eat the crisps which he'd brought in with him . . . he had felt thoroughly decadent, and sleazy, and liberated.

After the movie he had watched *The Twilight Zone* and then, switching channels, *Crazy Like A Fox*, which wasn't very good, but just because it provided a first-time experience—of viewing television until three in the morning—had given him the simple-minded illusion of living dangerously. He knew it was simple-minded, and probably no more than the predictable consequence of his four cans of bitter, but now, almost six hours later, the mild euphoria persisted. Far from being tired, or from having even the least touch of hangover, he felt refreshed—and capable of bold feats. (Watch out, all you pompous bureaucrats! You don't know who you're tangling with. Superman in a blue suit!) It was as though the short sleep he'd finally managed to get had been shot through with only the happiest of dreams. Today is the start of the rest of your life. *Carpe diem*. Gather ye rosebuds . . .

The Jolly Roger.

Yesterday evening, when he'd first arrived, he'd been pleased that the young Pakistani sitting behind the reception desk—if you could actually call it a reception desk—in the predominantly gold and claret and orange lobby, enlivened by the picture of a naked green woman astride a rearing green horse at sunset, had instantly flashed him a smile of recognition. "Good evening, sir. You were here many times during the days of the rail strike. It is very nice to see you."

"Thank you! And it's very nice to see you, too."

"Maybe this time you are enjoying a holiday?" The young man adjusted—infinitesimally—the volume of *Neighbours*; and assured Roger that, no, it wasn't being spoilt for him in the slightest.

"Wish it was a holiday. But it's just that I have to be sure of getting to the shop on time tomorrow morning. You see, there's only a skeleton staff on Saturdays and sometimes . . . " He hesitated, wondering how to explain himself. For instance, what made tomorrow different to any other Saturday?

"Ah, yes, I understand. Even without strikes, sometimes the British Rail can cause delays."

"That's it, exactly. You've put your finger right on it."

But it was after Roger had printed out his name upon a card that the young man had grinned and pointed to the comic strip in front of him. "Very strange thing," he said. "Look." None too inventively, the pirate ship was called *The Jolly Roger*.

Yet despite his having arrived, as it were, with such impeccable credentials, they hadn't been able to give him the room he had occupied before—a double on the second floor—which had been not only larger but far quieter, although for some reason not having a TV. This one in the basement, however, had proved cheaper; which suited Roger admirably, since now of course it was he who'd be paying and not Mr Cavendish. (Earlier in the year, anyhow, Mr Cavendish had been sufficiently perturbed by the relative cheapness of the terms— "Just because you work in a pigsty, that's no reason why you to have to sleep in one!"—but Roger had assured him, with truth, that the place was fine and the fact it was in a rather dingy side street near St Pancras hadn't worried him at all; had meant, indeed, there was probably much less noise of traffic than in the main thoroughfares. "Well, what about the screams of patrons having their throats slit in the early morning?" "I think they act as an alarm clock." "Oh, yes, I should have thought of that. Of course! Then that all sounds highly satisfactory.")

Now Roger stood before the narrow, gimcrack wardrobe and put on his tie. It was navy blue—pretty sombre—and didn't match his mood at all. But he reflected he hadn't any ties which would really have matched his mood; the half-dozen he had on the rail at home could all be described as tasteful and discreet; or, if you preferred it, he suddenly thought, tasteful and dull. Naturally, Alan Cavendish would never approve of anything gaudy . . . but was there nothing that came between the gaudy and the dull? This tie was the same colour as his braces and virtually the same colour as his suit.

He stared into the mirror thoughtfully. His belt wasn't navy; it wasn't even black, it was dark brown. Slowly he began to unbutton his braces. He held them dangling for a moment over the wastepaper bin. They fell on top of the beer cans and the crisp bags and the wrappers and containers from his breakfast and made a satisfying clunk as they dropped.

He slipped on his jacket; put into his briefcase the toothbrush, tube of paste and deodorant which he had bought last night; took down his raincoat from the hook on the door. (His father had been known to refer to this, approvingly, as his Humphrey Bogart coat and as Roger now tightly belted it and raised the collar—thinking, with a distinct feeling of parody, that he ought to get himself a hat—he could fully appreciate why.) He picked up his neatly rolled umbrella. Just before leaving the room he gave a last look round, but this was purely habit: he knew that his handkerchief and keys and small change were all in his trouser pockets and that there was nothing else he could have left. He hadn't bothered to get himself any shaving tackle, because he had felt it an unnecessary extravagance to buy a spare set—and although, being pretty dark, he now had a very noticeable stubble which rasped as he ran his fingers over it . . . well, Mr Cavendish wasn't going to be in the shop to comment, and even if Rose, like the little tattletale she could undoubtedly be, were to relay the information to him on Monday . . . oh, what the hell, it was, after all, the weekend. He smiled. He might not even wear a tie.

There was no one in the lobby as he took his leave. Which didn't greatly matter: he had paid—as usual—in advance. But he wrote a short note of thanks to the young man who had welcomed him and brought his breakfast; there was a memo pad and biro amidst all the comics and the magazines and clutter. He weighted it down with a pound coin; hesitated—then went back and added a second.

Instead of the rain which Mr Cavendish had said was prophesied, it was at present fairly bright. He stepped out smartly towards the main road, swinging his black umbrella, enjoying the sharp authoritative sound of its metal tip hitting the pavement. Normally he didn't use it as a cane. Nor, for that matter, as a rifle: impulsively, now, he laid it against his shoulder—like a guardsman—but merely for a few self-conscious paces. That too, though, made him feel rakish. He only wished it wasn't black. He would have liked something more like the golden paisley which Mr Cavendish had given Oscar. *Not* the paisley, of course. But a pattern at least equally colourful. (Perhaps he should employ the proprietors of the B and B he'd just left as his technical advisers.) He was sure that Mr Cavendish would let him have it at cost price . . . whatever it was he came to choose.

He crossed Euston Road; turned into Upper Woburn Place, which

STEPHEN BENATAR

led into Southampton Row. One of the shops on his route was a men's outfitters and surprisingly it was already open. He glanced at his watch; then walked in and looked at the racks of ties. There was a silk one which he liked, with thin white stripes crossing the scarlet. It was still a long way from being ostentatious but it wasn't dull; and it would go well with both his blue suit and his grey. He bought it and put it on right then. He slipped his navy into the briefcase. He left his umbrella hanging from the counter. Someone would be glad of it.

As he strode away he wondered if Jenny would approve; felt confident she would.

And then unexpectedly he realized something: that in fact it didn't matter whether Jenny approved or not. Jenny was spoken for. He wasn't going to dance attendance on women who were spoken for. There'd always be plenty more fruit on the tree—unattached, attractive.

Indeed, as if to emphasize this, a pretty girl in T-shirt and jeans just then glanced appraisingly in his direction. Briefly their eyes met and Roger smiled. She smiled back in passing.

Not generally a vain man he stopped before another shop window and surreptitiously surveyed himself; tried to see, as dispassionately as he could, what this young woman would have seen. He straightened his shoulders again, as he had done the other morning at St Pancras. It made a difference. He must try to bear it in mind, this question of his posture, until it became completely a matter of habit for him to stand well. *Walk tall—walk tall and look the world right in the eye . . .* He remembered that he had made a resolution to take some exercise; to get into shape; develop himself—develop himself, that was, within reasonable limits. He wouldn't go mad.

He decided he would look through the Yellow Pages that very morning, find a health club that might suit him, make some inquiries. No time like the present. Again, he could hear his grandmother saying this to him, and it had taken him perhaps fifteen years fully to appreciate it, but now, today, he suddenly saw how right she was. "Okay, Nan. No time like the present!" He turned and looked upwards as he said it—said it out loud—although this was purely force of habit, his looking skyward while he was talking to the dead. "And I bet you thought that I'd forgotten!"

The window in which he'd been looking happened to be an estate agent's. He had hardly been aware of this but the second before he'd moved his eyes away he'd noticed a sign which caused him now to return them. It said simply:

'Flats and bedsitters to let.'

The shop wasn't open yet but no doubt it did open on Saturdays. He resolved to come back to it during his lunch hour.

> "'And I'll be up like a rosebud
> High on the vine;
> Don't thumb your nose, bud,
> Take a tip from mine . . . '"

He didn't even realize he was whistling; let alone what he was whistling; let alone that it was another of his father's very favourite songs.

> "'I'm a little bit short of the elbow room
> And got to get me some;
> So look out, world—
> *Here I come* . . . !'"

It was sad that his grandmother never seemed to have benefitted very much from her own dictums.

He must pass his driving test, it occurred to him, irrelevantly.

Would pass it.

He would like to write a novel, too. The thought was not in fact so new as it sounded.

He had even dreamt something along those lines this morning, shortly before waking. He couldn't remember much of his dream but he knew the book had been called *The Voyage* and had been set aboard His Majesty's Ship, The Pheasant, whilst it was under sail to Sierra Leone in 1821.

He smiled—and shrugged. Well, at least it would do him no harm to pop into the library as soon as he could and see what he might turn up in the way of background material.

Life suddenly appeared so full of possibilities he was frightened that even with, say, another half-century ahead of him he wasn't going to have time to realize merely a small part of them. That was terrifying . . . but it was also exciting. Like mother, like son, he wondered.

The Voyage . . . His own from now on was going to be a pretty damn satisfying one. For instance, just wait until he saw again that little runt who had half-dragged him off Nottingham Station on Thursday morning; because he suddenly hoped—fiercely, longingly—that he would see him again. Whether in court or out of it. Roger had his words down practically verbatim (he now had everybody's words down practically verbatim) and he would take great pleasure in showing that pug-nosed fascist prick that you couldn't get away with being nothing but a thug dressed up in uniform. Right now Roger knew with complete conviction that he was going to be the victor in this petty little squabble with British Rail . . . this fight against the bullies. Whether in court or out of it. City Hall was going to learn conclusively that it had picked upon the wrong fellow.

Outstandingly. Against all the odds. City Hall had picked upon the wrong fellow.

Zip a Dee Do Dah!

He felt he needed a bottle of champagne to break against such gleamingly new-painted bows. In lieu of that, he took out of his briefcase the dark, staid, stuffy tie—and left it decorating one of the potted conifers on the steps of a hotel. It was only a pity he hadn't thought to save his braces, for then he could have ornamented its twin. Christmas streamers in October.

"'So look out, world—*here I come!*'"

This time he realized what it was he was whistling. Then humming. This time he even put the words to it.

19

On the train he thought about Jean. He tried not to but he couldn't help it. Therefore he did his best to concentrate on the things about her which had tended to alienate him; and he remembered a fairly recent outburst.

"I sometimes feel I'm like a mirror," she had cried, "and everybody sees in me only what they want to see. But all the time I'm standing back on the other side of the mirror and wanting to be *me*, not the chameleon I've been cast as!" She had added: "And Lord help me, I collaborate in the casting . . . to the extent that when I'm on the phone my accent even alters depending on who it is I'm talking to. Oscar is forever teasing me about that; so is Abby."

Ephraim had forgotten what had inspired this little *cri de coeur*. Once, he would have felt sympathetic towards it; but now he had seen it only as one of her increasingly frequent and melodramatic bouts of self-pity and had turned away from her impatiently.

It was like when she had cried at him, "I want a mother! I want a hero out of Georgette Heyer! I want to be *nurtured*!" Yes: I—I—I! Why should she think this made her so exceptional? For heaven's sake! He wanted all these things as well.

But on the train he also remembered her saying in Bordeaux—it was on the day she'd had her money stolen from her shoulder bag—"I can't believe you realize just how *good* you are for me!"

This led on to him recollecting other things which at the moment he would have preferred not to.

He dwelt on the way that she'd behaved towards him last night . . . and indeed all week. The way she never said any longer that she loved him; hardly ever these days gave him a spontaneous hug; on the whole, spoke with far less liveliness to him than to the children; seemed to feel for them a much deeper quality of concern. He dwelt on the way she so often put him down. The swingeing irony. The tart response.

Then he thought about the kind of woman he hoped that he was going to meet. (Hoped? Prayed. Truly, if she wasn't waiting for him somewhere . . . then what on earth was to become of him?) Almost certainly a lot younger than he was. But not a modern sort of girl. Not someone who cared too assertively about Women's Lib, always enumerating her rights. Someone who would both look up to him and look after him. (Jean had certainly looked after him.) And love him. Love him. That was the key. You could, if you wanted, regard the concept of true love as being merely sentimental and idealized, but true love, basically, was what everybody hungered for. You had to feel that when you died you would be missed—grievously missed—by someone. He thought of an old lady he had once known; and remembered how she had said that still, after fifteen years of widowhood, there wasn't a single day that went by without her feeling an ache in her heart for her husband; almost, not a single hour.

And what would he give her in return: this woman whom he prayed was waiting for him? So long as she was warmhearted and he found her physically attractive; so long as she wasn't—fundamentally—silly or boring or tiresome; then he knew that all he needed was the assurance of love and he would respond to it in full. For such a woman he would even, perhaps, go back to teaching children . . . and than that (he told himself, with a wry smile) there could surely be no greater evidence of love. He would give her everything of which he'd finally prove capable.

He forgot about her when he reached St Pancras. For the time being. Something awful happened. (Although even that, in retrospect, had its bright side: it reminded him of his grandmother; of how—so she had once told him—she'd been walking along Bond Street with a gentleman whom she hadn't known very well, when suddenly her bloomer elastic had snapped and her knickers had been down around her ankles, underneath her long skirt. With considerable sangfroid— she had wanted him, Ephraim, to appreciate this—she had just stepped out of them and continued on her way . . . "although it hurt me to leave my bloomers decorating Bond Street, because they were such extremely pretty ones; Bond Street wasn't up to them!") Whether the concourse at St Pancras was up to his cock ring, Ephraim didn't pause to consider: on the very tightest notch and it had *still* managed to work its way loose. He couldn't bend to retrieve it: everyone, he was convinced, had immediately identified what it was, and whence it came; and he felt mortified. He half-expected someone to chase after him to ask if it were his; and he didn't feel entirely safe until he was well away from the station and on the other side of Euston Road. (But then he started to wonder whether he shouldn't perhaps go back for it; after all, it had been the symbol of a new life; he didn't like to leave the symbol of a new life lying on the concourse at St Pancras. He wondered how many feet had trampled over it by now.) It was only about fifteen minutes later that he realized a whole cavalcade of magical moments, never to be repeated in the course of his own or anybody else's lifetime, had just passed him by totally unsavoured and without any shred of thankfulness being expressed for them; and it was difficult after that to get back into exactly the right mood for fully enjoying the ones which followed. Yet the mood would return, he assured himself—with determination—the mood would return. But the cock ring wouldn't. And it was simply that he'd had the damned thing for less than twenty hours and it had cost him, therefore, more than a pound for every hour. He couldn't quite believe it. It had cost him *twenty* pounds!

Cost Jean twenty pounds. For the first time it came to him that the bank would expect his wife to honour his debts. After all, it was a joint account, as much her responsibility as his. He didn't understand how he could have failed to consider this.

And in that case . . . so much for his little spending spree over the next few days. Obviously. How could he have been so daft?

Oh, hell.

Oh hell, oh hell, oh *hell*.

But Roger might be able to lend him some? Of course! That was a thought.

He then deliberated whether to call in at the umbrella shop. It wasn't far from here. But he finally decided against it. Firstly, he didn't like the idea of borrowing money from his children, especially if he wasn't sure how soon he'd be able to repay; and secondly, if the shop were busy and private conversation either difficult or impossible, their parting would, at best, be brisk and unsatisfactory . . . and who knew how long before they'd next see one another? (Yes, what *awful* timing: Roger's last day! Ephraim was already missing the presence of his son in London: simply the comfort of knowing that—in an emergency—somebody he loved would be close by.) No . . . much better for the note he'd written at the house, however disappointingly expressed, to take care of his farewells.

Therefore, instead of going to the shop, he went for a cup of coffee.

In a cheerfully bright and bustling cafeteria—full of tourists at even this time on an autumn morning—there remained a vacant table near the window. He felt he needed signs and this seemed a particularly good one: it would be fun to sip his coffee leisurely and to watch the world go by. If the place had been empty this was the very table he'd have chosen. It appeared to have been waiting for him.

He swiftly picked his way across and placed his holdall on one of its two chairs. Then, at the counter, he pushed along his plastic tray in a line of some half-dozen. He hadn't yet eaten, so he selected an iced bun and a small fruit tart with cream: Jean would scarcely begrudge him that little bit of self-pampering, his last splurge, before he went off to find, first, a Job Centre—were the Job Centres open on a Saturday?—and, after that, a pawnbroker. (As soon as he received his initial wage he would buy back whichever figurine he decided to part with; he would also send home a postal order for as much as he could spare.) The woman at the cash register wouldn't accept a cheque, however, not even with his banker's card; not even though he was wearing his suit and raincoat—the things which would have been the bulkiest to pack—and looking at his most respectable. She said they simply couldn't start to make exceptions . . . silly cow. He had just enough money, then, for the coffee; he was forced to forgo both bun and strawberry tart. When he finally got back to his table he found that his holdall had disappeared. Been stolen. His jeans and sneakers; all his changes of clothing; all his toilet articles. He couldn't take it in.

He just couldn't take it in. He dashed round looking on other empty chairs, under other empty tables, although in fact there weren't many. He ran outside; plunged frantically this way, frantically that. Back into the cafeteria. A couple of the customers advised him to go to the police—not that they thought, when questioned, it would do him the least bit of good. Most of the others couldn't speak much English. They did little more than shrug commiseratingly, signify a useless wish to help. (The story of the world.) The woman at the till seemed barely interested: the manager wasn't around right now but, even when he was, there'd be no chance of any compensation—she pointed to a notice about the company, regretfully, not holding itself liable for either theft or loss, just as five minutes ago she had pointed to a notice about the company, regretfully, being unable to accept credit cards or cheques. Nobody, apparently, had seen the culprit. Possibly as much as another five minutes had elapsed before it struck Ephraim that he had also lost Harlequinade and "Maureen".

In a daze he wandered down Southampton Row; he hadn't drunk his coffee, not taken even a solitary sip. He looked at the hand luggage of everyone he saw, head turning almost rhythmically from one side of the road to the other. He peered down all the alleyways and side streets; sometimes branched off along them, entered the network of narrow tributaries, circled confusedly, but always, not even consciously, headed back towards the point he'd started from: he returned to the cafeteria on three occasions, each one separated by at least an hour, practically believing that this time he would find his holdall sitting there—maybe on the chair where he had left it—returned by someone who had either taken it by mistake or else been worked on by his conscience. By God and his conscience. Perhaps the old woman who moved slowly from one table to another with her blank staring eyes and her dampened dishcloth had somnambulistically, and for the sake of tidiness, stowed it away somewhere behind the scenes; and now at long last it had miraculously come to light. "Oh, please, Lord! Yes! Please, Lord!"

The woman on the till frowned more impatiently every time he reappeared.

"There's nothing we can do. I keep telling you, I'm sorry but we just can't help. It's no good your coming back."

However, he did go back, one last time, although no longer practically believing. ("Remember, winners never quit, matey—while quitters never win!") He also went, finally, to the nearest police station. The holdall had not been handed in. He was obliged to give his Nottingham address.

The day was passing. It was now nearly four. He had no further option. He would have to go to see Roger.

Not hurrying—not having the will nor the strength to hurry— he reached New Oxford Street at half-past-four. He had forgotten that on Saturdays the shop closed early. The shutters were across the doors . . . and would now have been so for roughly thirty minutes.

What was he to do?

He felt sick. He needed something to eat. That had to be the first thing.

Feeling sick, he remembered how, in the early days of their marriage, Jean had held his head while he was vomiting out of a train window.

He remembered how, on Snowdon, she had given him her moral support and gentle guidance when, petrified of heights, he had needed to go down on his hands and knees in front of their embarrassed children and numbers of obstructed—though wholly sympathetic—holidaymakers to negotiate a ridge which had had a sheer drop on either side of it.

He remembered these things involuntarily; and with the treacherous prick of tears behind his eyes.

But he couldn't return. There was too much weight of the more recent past that militated against that. He was not—he was *not*—going to return home.

There was nothing for him at home.

He would have to make a go of it on his own.

So there in the street, hesitating, on the broad corner outside the umbrella shop, he took off his wristwatch and gazed at it speculatively. It was the last thing of any value that he had—but, with the figurines now gone, his mother's figurines (Jean had been fond of those, as well), what did this matter? He had to have food; and he had to have a roof over his head.

As always, however, when looking at the watch, he thought fleetingly about Liz—and the incredible way that Neville had taken care of her. "Old boy, I have achieved *nothing*! For a gifted man . . . I have achieved *nothing*!" Well, yes, reflected Ephraim, we can all identify with that. (And for some reason he could identify with it today still more fully than earlier in the week—although earlier in the week he would hardly have believed this possible.) Yet in your own case, Nev, it simply isn't true. I admit that in later life you never appreciated Joan and it was rotten luck you weren't able to come up with the right comedy idea, when that was requested. But in looking after Liz you took both your failure and frustration and laughed at them and turned them into triumph. You redeemed all the waste and all the mismanagement. You *did* achieve.

But those were the thoughts of only half a minute, hardly germane to the present moment in New Oxford Street. And on his way to a supermarket in Drury Lane, which a pleasant young woman in a card shop had directed him to (she had also looked in a classified directory for the whereabouts of nearby pawnbrokers), he stopped in front of a newsagent's board and glanced to see if there were any rooms to let. There were two—if they were still available; but what sent a chill through him, literally, was that each card stipulated a month's rent in advance: in both cases, therefore, a figure of almost three hundred pounds. He had forgotten this question of down payments. Maybe he could find somewhere cheaper; but even if he did there was no way he'd be able to leave a deposit.

As a last resort, of course, he could spend the night out in the park— or in a shop doorway—or pedestrian underpass. (At least it would help him forget about his fear of cancer, heart attacks, stomach ulcers, deteriorating eyesight, receding hairline, encroaching impotence, arthritis . . . et cetera. *Et cetera.*) He had already seen dozens of people settled down for the night in their sleeping bags in shop doorways.

London!

Where the streets were paved with gold!

He hadn't got a sleeping bag, though.

But he could always look for some out-of-the-way bench. At least he had his good thick gabardine.

And tomorrow was another day.

(Early 'fifties. Ex-convict on the run, wanting only to prove his innocence and receive a second chance. Steve Cochran. Ruth Roman. *Tomorrow is Another Day.*)

He had always liked Steve Cochran. Tough. Attractive. Usually cast as a gangster or as some other kind of heavy.

But he had seen him in a film about a reformed drunkard who returns to his wife and kids in 1920s Arkansas (Ann Sheridan as the understandably weary wife struggling to keep the family farm afloat), firmly resolved to make good and to try to atone for past transgressions.

And the way he had eventually won the respect of both his family and the community was the subject of a charming, unpretentious movie, produced by Cochran himself. It had left you with the intended warm glow. Also, it had had a title which could now, belatedly, turn for Ephraim into a symbol of hope. A slogan to encapsulate victory.

"Come next spring," he said aloud, testingly. Though nobody was passing.

He went into the supermarket. His luck was clearly changing; he had half-expected, at this time on a Saturday afternoon, in the West End, to find it closed. And suddenly he found that he had energy. If he could beat all this, why then he could beat anything. Beat the devil himself. Because it was true: a person's character could only properly be forged upon the ashes of his despair. Old Emerson was right.

He felt exhilarated.

The future was going to be okay.

Much better than okay.

"Come next spring," he repeated.

20

That morning Jean had gone shopping. She hadn't taken Polly, because she'd forgotten where they kept the lead and couldn't be bothered to look. In fact she'd almost forgotten Polly herself until she came across her waiting at the front door and looking hopeful and swishing her tail in excitement. Jean thought her own lack of energy and motivation might have been caused by . . . were a delayed reaction to . . . there'd been some kind of incident, a bad one, on Tuesday or Wednesday or Thursday . . . today was Saturday . . . well, if it carried on like this she would have to see a doctor, he'd know what to do. She must have blocked it out; it had clearly been a shock; maybe he'd prescribe a tonic. But in the meantime there were still a couple of things she needed from Tesco's to complete the home-coming meal for Oscar. She assumed that Ephraim would be there for it—supposed he had better be catered for, although she really didn't feel she'd have the patience to put up with him much longer. It was only by the purest chance she had taken clean clothing into Roger's room; had seen the envelope on his pillow; read the note inside. Well, her husband had walked out on her before: ostensibly forever, but, as it had transpired each time, for actually no more than a morning or an afternoon. (And she recalled the first occasion it had happened—twenty years ago—my God, how worried she had been; how wonderfully relieved to see him back!) Now she assumed he would return by lunchtime: looking sheepish and pretending he had gone out merely for a walk. And being overly animated. (God's in his heaven, all's right with the world!) Oh, damn him. Damn him! He wasn't a provider—in no way was he a provider. Not of financial security; not of emotional security; not even of good companionship. Nothing! And as for any sort of sex life . . . ! Well, that was laughable. She suddenly remembered the thing he'd had on his penis the previous night; and that made her want to cry out with—made her want to cry out with—

She wasn't sure with what. Cry out? Disconcertingly, she became aware of where she was. In Woodborough Road. Yet why? And what did she want to cry out for? She felt it had something to do with a note. But after a minute she shook her head and turned back in the direction of home.

A note? She had the vague impression she had torn it up. Now, why had she done that? There were other things that faintly puzzled her. Had she or hadn't she, for instance, also stamped on a Beach Boys record, in retaliation for . . . in retaliation for . . . ? Ephraim had once used to sing her that song, hadn't he? *God only knows what I'd be without you* . . . Meaningless.

The meaningless words whirled maddeningly inside her head.

She smiled, a little bleakly.

God only knows.

Then something very silly happened. For the first time in her life she looked in the wrong street for the house where she lived! Went up the wrong turning: the one which ran parallel to their own but was the one which preceded it!

Well, that was easily done, of course, especially when you were deep in thought. What a fool she was! Really, what a fool! She found the house—*found* the house, indeed!—but feeling suddenly, for some unaccountable reason, so extraordinarily tired, she couldn't be bothered to search for her key . . . she simply put her finger to the bell . . . and kept it there . . .

A dog began to bark. Jean nodded.

Yes, somebody would let her in.

PART II

Hester Berg: A Play

CHARACTERS

HESTER BERG . . . aged 83, 53 and 19.

FLORA DRAPKIN, her daughter . . . aged 49 and 19 . . . the same actress to play HESTER at the age of 19.

TONY DRAPKIN, Hester's grandson . . . also 19 . . . to be played by the same actor as:

HAROLD DRAPKIN, Tony's father, Hester's son-in-law . . . mid-twenties.

ELLEN COTTON, her sister . . . 80.

MAX BERG, her husband . . . in his early forties . . . to be played by the same actor as:

WALTER DAVIS, her lodger . . . in his middle nineties.

MARY, her au pair . . . in her late twenties.

The play is in two acts—takes place, basically, in the summer of 1987; but incorporates flashbacks to 1957 and 1923.

ACT ONE

A Friday afternoon in June, 1987.

Sitting room of a top-floor flat in a mansion block in West Hampstead. Most of the furniture is old—including radiogram. Tea things are laid out on a table set against one wall.

HESTER—aged 83—is arranging flowers; flowers which include at least one red rose. She is slim, elegant, good-looking. She has her back to the door.

After a moment, TONY enters. He is dressed like an average student.

TONY   Hello, Gran.

HESTER   (Slight start before turning, flower in hand) Hello, my darling. I didn't hear you come in.

TONY   (Crossing to kiss her) Don't tell me you're growing deaf in your old age!

HESTER   (Her tone matching his in affection) When I get to my old age there's no knowing what I may tell you. But for the present, Tony, I shall simply tell you this: I had my thoughts on loftier things than doorbells. You're early, aren't you?

TONY   Tutorial cancelled. The bloke's supposed to be ill but I reckon—this week—he wanted to have off *all* of Friday afternoon, instead of merely half.

He starts to wander round the room, communicating—to the audience—the feeling of tension he is doing his utmost to suppress.

TONY   (Cont.) You know one of the things I always like about this flat? That it stays true to the memories of my childhood. The curtains, pictures, ornaments. Even those cracks on the ceiling.

HESTER   Is that your subtle way, Master Anthony Max Drapkin, of telling me it requires doing up? ... If so, you're probably right.

TONY   No, I swear it. I just like the way it never changes.

HESTER   And so do I. We often seem to think alike. No wonder you're so wise.

TONY   Clearly, I was born lucky.

HESTER   (More serious for a moment) Oh, you were, darling! You were! If only I could have had the chances you have! To be at London University. *Any* university ... I tell you, Tony, there'd have been no holding me. I'd have been an even more brilliant woman than the one you see before you now—arranging flowers. (Standing back a little.) And arranging them, I think, not very well.

TONY   They look all right to me.

HESTER Thank you. To recoup your energies, after such fulsome admiration, hadn't you better take a chocolate?

TONY   The cinnamon balls look good.

HESTER Well, only one. I made them for our tea. It would be a shame if you had nothing left to look forward to.

TONY   Oh, I think I could handle it. So in that case may I take two?

HESTER No.

TONY   Okay. Only testing.

HESTER (Finally leaving flowers) Anyhow, they'll have to do. Next time round I'll be a politician. Or a doctor. Or a philosopher. I have no yen to be a florist.

TONY   Next time round I'll be a millionaire.

HESTER It saddens me to find you have no standards.

TONY   So, obviously, we don't always think alike.

HESTER Whose fault is that? And whose misfortune? Though I must admit: if we agreed on absolutely everything life might lose a little of its savour.

A knock on the door. MARY enters.

MARY   (Slight German accent) Excuse me, Mrs Berg. Is it
              time to put the kettle on? It's a quarter past four.

HESTER   Oh, I should think so, Mary. Mrs Drapkin said
              she'd be here by half-past—and she's usually very
              punctual.

MARY   Like you.

HESTER   Yes, like mother like daughter. Not, unfortunately,
              so much like Mr Tony.
TONY   What do you mean? I was extremely punctual.

HESTER   Yes, I know. That's what worries me. The time is
              out of joint.

MARY   I don't understand. Out of joint?

HESTER   Oh . . . all to do with augurs and portents and ghosts
              on battlements!

TONY   Well, now she understands completely.

HESTER   Mary, it's Shakespeare.

TONY   (To MARY) "The time is out of joint; O cursed
              spite, That ever I was born to set it right!"
              Okay? Does that satisfy you?

MARY   (Playful) Oh, yes, Mr Tony! Of course! Augurs . . .
              and portents . . . and ghosts? I don't understand any
              of it.

TONY   (Patient and straight-faced) Augurs were people who watched hens pecking at their grain and then solved everybody's problems for them—advised them whom to marry and whatnot. A bit like agony aunts. Out of joint naturally describes a dislocated bone. And what was the other thing you seemed uncertain of?

MARY   (Loving it) Oh, you're both very cruel to make such fun of me.

HESTER   Mary, 'out of joint' is a phrase difficult to explain—and you probably won't be required to use it very often. Now why don't you just run along to put on that kettle?

MARY   Well, I may or I may not. I'll see if I feel like it.

But she goes—in high good humour—after laughingly wagging her finger.

HESTER   Oh, Tony, Tony, Tony! Why do you do these things to me?

TONY   It was you who started it. You bring them on yourself.

HESTER   What nonsense!

The doorbell rings. HESTER doesn't react.

TONY   That must be Mum.

HESTER   Why? Did the bell go?

TONY   You can hardly hear it at this end of the flat.

HESTER   I must say, I was quite impressed just now. I was thinking that an augur was an omen, not the person who interpreted it. And as for the hens . . . You weren't just making it up, were you? (TONY shakes his head) Where do you learn a thing like that?

TONY   Search me.

HESTER   Wouldn't it be wonderful, to find out something new each day and to be able to retain it?

The door opens. MARY shows in ELLEN COTTON. Like HESTER, ELLEN is slim. But she doesn't quite possess her sense of style.

MARY   It's Miss Cotton, Mrs Berg. Your sister.

ELLEN   Thank you, Mary. I think it's possible she may know who I am by now.(To HESTER and TONY) I'm the only one who sometimes wonders. Don't tell me that it's teatime?

HESTER   (Her manner a degree chilly) Ellen! How nice. Yes, it is, as a matter of fact.

ELLEN   I can't dissemble. When I said don't tell me, I really meant I hoped you would. (To TONY) I'll swear you grow handsomer each day. Since that's the case, I trust I get a kiss? Oh, I'm your great-aunt, by the way—I fear Mary must have forgotten.

TONY   Well, I *was* puzzled. But in that case, yes, you get a kiss. Great-aunts always get kisses.

ELLEN   Oh . . . I only wish it were the truth. Or, at any rate, most of the men here in West Hampstead don't seem to know about it yet. Will you spread the word? Naturally, I mean, just to the attractive ones.

TONY   Yes, of course. (He kisses her)

ELLEN   Were *you* introduced to your grandmother when you got shown in?

TONY   I wasn't shown in. I said I could find my own way. (ELLEN pulls a face) Well, what are you complaining of? You got the preferential treatment.

ELLEN   But only because she thought that—unaided—I most likely shouldn't make it to the end of the corridor. And is it really preferential treatment, having to make small talk to Mary?

HESTER   (Feeling excluded and sounding a little acerbic; to ELLEN) If you really wanted to be in Tony's good books you could have quoted a line or two from *Hamlet*.

ELLEN   The length of your corridor, I could have quoted a scene or two from *Hamlet*. I thought they were Shakespeare's good books.

TONY   And, anyway, when did any of you sisters object to making small talk? With practically anybody?

ELLEN   Oh, I think Hester and I would always have preferred big talk. Much! But, of course, one can't speak for the other four. Though I suspect that even in heaven they're still at their happiest when trying on hats and airing charming banalities.

HESTER   Ellen dear, would you really say that's in the best of taste? It's not even amusing.

233

ELLEN   I suppose a lot of things in this world are neither particularly tasteful or amusing.

HESTER   But we're not called on to add to the sum of them.

ELLEN   No, you're right. And it was certainly patronizing. I take it all back. (To TONY) Isn't your mama here?

HESTER   Expected at any moment. Straight from the hairdresser's.

The doorbell rings.

ELLEN   Well, talk about coincidence!

HESTER   Why? Have *you* just come from the hairdresser's? I was going to say how very nice you looked.

TONY   No, Gran. Mum's arrived—from the sounds of it.
HESTER   Oh, yes, of course. That was the doorbell, wasn't it?

ELLEN   I keep telling you you ought to get a hearing aid.

HESTER   Nonsense. I've no need of a hearing aid.

TONY   Yes—nonsense. Gran was never programmed to lose her faculties.

ELLEN   In that case she must have slipped her creator a little something on the side.

TONY   Wish I'd thought of doing the same. I wonder now if it's too late.
ELLEN   Either that or she may have thrown a tantrum.

HESTER   The two of you are being absurd. And Tony,

darling, do sit down. There's something about you today. You're giving me the fidgets.

TONY   I'm sorry.

He sits; immediately stands again as the door opens and FLORA comes in, saying, "Thank you, Mary." FLORA at forty-nine is still a pretty woman—especially when her face lights up—but most of the time there is a subdued, almost a faded, air about her.

FLORA   Hello, everyone. I'm sorry I'm late, Mother. You shouldn't have waited tea.

HESTER   How nicely he's done your hair!

FLORA   Oh, thank you. I'm so glad you think so; I wasn't really sure. (To TONY) Hello, darling—have you had a good week? (She kisses him) Ellen. This is a pleasant surprise. I don't seem to have seen you in ages.

ELLEN   Oh, I shouldn't be here by rights. I'm gate-crashing. In recent weeks your mother and I have been having one of our little spats.

HESTER   Have we? I didn't realize that. What little spats?

ELLEN   Hester Berg. May God forgive you.

HESTER   (Tolerantly, to FLORA) I ought to warn you, darling. She's behaving rather oddly . . . one of her more outrageous moods. We'll have to pretend she isn't here.

ELLEN   You and the world both.

235

HESTER   (To FLORA) You see what I mean?

FLORA   Oh dear. Poor Ellen.

TONY plays his violin. MARY comes in with the silver teapot and matching jug of hot water, which she sets on an occasional table, next to HESTER—the sugar, milk and slices of lemon are already there, along with cups, saucers, teaspoons; slop basin and strainer. Apart from the cinnamon balls, the tea comprises daintily cut sandwiches, a sponge cake and a plate of biscuits. HESTER pours the tea. MARY passes round the cups—she has brought in an extra one for ELLEN. She also passes round the teaplates, with paper napkins, and the sandwiches. During the scene that follows, TONY will take over from her in seeing that everyone has food.

MARY   (To HESTER) You forgot to ask if anyone wanted lemon.

ELLEN   I think perhaps we're none of us too shy to put our hands up if we did.

MARY   No, but it's a good job Mrs Berg has me here to look after her, that's all I can say.

She is holding the silver sugar bowl—and tongs—for TONY. He takes one lump with the tongs, then two more with his fingers.

HESTER   Has Mr Davis had something, Mary?

MARY   Yes, of course. About half an hour ago. He's probably forgotten it by now.

HESTER   Well, go and see if he'd like anything else. And tell him again that Flora and Tony are here.

ELLEN   And Ellen.

HESTER   (To MARY) Yes, say that Mrs Drapkin and Mr
Tony and Miss Cotton are here, and ask him if he'd
like to come to join us.

MARY   He won't want to.

HESTER   But ask him, anyway. Say that it would give us
much pleasure if he did.

FLORA   (Laughing) Liar! (HESTER silently but smilingly
denies this.)

TONY   (To MARY) And if he says no, tell him I'll come in
later for a chat.

MARY   Yes, Mr Tony. Shall I say you want to hear all
about Henley Regatta as it was before the First
World War, and how little boys used to run
behind the carriages all the way from Victoria to
Cricklewood, so they could maybe get a shilling for
helping with the luggage?

HESTER   Thank you, Mary. That will be all. We'll ring if we
want you. (MARY goes out.)

ELLEN   (To HESTER) How's she been with him recently?
One thing I'll say for her: she certainly makes good
sandwiches.

HESTER   She's been all right with him, on the whole. At least
she hasn't *again* thrown his spare set of teeth out of
the window. His new spare set, I should say.

FLORA   Oh dear, I know it shouldn't, but the thought of it still makes me laugh.

HESTER   (Also laughing a little) Well, I can promise you it wasn't very funny at the time. Although Walter is a lesson to us all. "Oh, my dear girl," he says to me, "what does it matter? A hundred years hence, what will any of it matter?" I'd have got rid of her at once, if it hadn't been for him.

TONY   Yet I suppose anyone can lose their temper—and most of the time she's pretty good with him. Not every au pair would agree to take on a ninety-three-year-old as part of her general duties.

HESTER   But throwing an old man's teeth out of a fifth-floor window! (Despite herself, however, she is still almost laughing; they all are.)

ELLEN   I suppose you could say . . . it's a good thing he wasn't wearing them.

HESTER   And really he couldn't be less trouble. He's always so easy to please. Why, only yesterday I happened to fold over his piece of bread-and-butter—"By Jove," he said, "*sandwiches!*"

FLORA   And actually—no matter how tired you or I may get of hearing the same old stories—Tony always finds them interesting. Don't you, darling?

TONY   (Shrugs) I don't care how often he tells me there were only fields between Swiss Cottage and Golders Green at the turn of the century. It gives me a sense of continuity and connection.

HESTER   (To FLORA) Well, I daresay he'll have plenty of
          scope to go on strengthening his connections this
          evening over supper—and also to make further
          trial of his undoubted saintliness . . . and other such
          inherited characteristics.

FLORA   I only hope it won't be spaghetti again, like last
          week! When Walter got the sneezes I had to hide
          my plate under the table.

She illustrates how voluptuously he sneezes . . . with his hand shaking back and forth in front of his nose, clearly ineffectual.

HESTER   Well, don't think I didn't notice—and don't think I
          didn't feel thoroughly ashamed. I only prayed that
          he wouldn't notice.

FLORA   There were nine sneezes, I counted them. Each
          about five seconds apart. So every time you thought
          it might be safe to . . . And you needn't think I didn't
          see you move your plate over, too.

HESTER   There's a difference between merely edging it
          across a little and actually putting it on your lap.

As before, they are all laughing about it—particularly FLORA. We
get a glimpse of the high-spirited girl she used to be.

HESTER   (Cont.) Ellen dear, you'll stay and have a meal with
          us, won't you?

ELLEN   Is it spaghetti?

TONY   (Suddenly—and not sounding as casual as he might
          have hoped) Oh, Gran, I meant to tell you. I shan't

239

be able to stop for supper this week. I'm meeting somebody at seven.

FLORA What! Oh, Tony! (This is almost a wail—she hurriedly tries to disguise it.) But darling! You always stop for supper on a Friday.
It's . . . tradition.

ELLEN (Sings: just the one word) "Tradition . . . !" Yes, I will stay on, in that case. Thank you, Hester.

TONY (Turning towards her with relief) You mean, Aunt Ellen, you'll stay on now that you know I'm not going to be here? Charming. It always helps to know who your friends are.

ELLEN I hoped I was being subtle. By the standards of this family, I think I probably was.

FLORA (To TONY) If we don't see you on Friday nights, when do we see you?

TONY Oh, Mum, it's only for this evening! Besides, I often see you twice or even three times a week.

HESTER (Tongue-in-cheek; to FLORA) And I imagine—if we really set our minds to it—that just this once we *can* do without him.

TONY I'm sorry I forgot to tell you earlier.

HESTER And who . . . may one be so bold to ask . . . who is it you're meeting?

TONY (Laughs, evasively) Someone.

HESTER   But would it be wrong to suppose this someone
          is a member of the opposite sex?

TONY   No. (Pause) I mean, it wouldn't be wrong.

HESTER   Ah. Then let us take a further small step. Her first
          name doesn't begin with a C by any chance?

TONY   (Puzzled) C?

HESTER nods, sure that his bewilderment is fake.

TONY   (Cont.) No, it doesn't. Who're you thinking of?

HESTER   (To FLORA) Who am I thinking of? No, he can't
          be serious! (To TONY) Now tell me that K, for the
          surname, also means nothing . . . you heartbreaker!

TONY   Oh. Carol Klingman.

HESTER   Carol Klingman, indeed. (Jokily, but not all that
          jokily) The very Carol Klingman who lives in the
          flat right under this. Lives there with her father the
          insurance broker and with her mother the insurance
          broker's wife. The very Carol Klingman, what's
          more, who resembles nothing so much as a fashion
          model—or a princess—or a film star. The very
          Carol Klingman who—

TONY   Who resembles *what*?

FLORA   Darling, you can't deny that she's extremely good-
          looking.

HESTER   Good-looking? Beautiful!

TONY   Always you say that and always I think we must be
              talking about two wholly different people. Aunt
              Ellen, have *you* ever met this model, this film star?
              This Princess Carol Klingman?

ELLEN   Well, with my living right across the road, you'd
              think that I must have. But perhaps I was so
              dazzled I thought I had the sun in my eyes.

HESTER   (To ELLEN) I assure you, she's tall and willowy
              and graceful, and exceedingly distinguished, and
              totally unspoilt—

TONY   —and totally stupid—

HESTER   —and very sweet and unassuming when she talks
              to you—

TONY   —and clearly just as clueless when she doesn't.

HESTER   Please pay no attention to him. They've been out
              together twice and he thinks he knows her. And,
              both times, they've had a really lovely evening—
              her parents told us so. They, by the way, are quite
              as charming as she is, and not simply are they
              extremely well-heeled . . . with Carol being their only
              child . . . they've also intimated, more than once, that
              they could easily imagine worse things than their
              daughter one day becoming a Berg.

TONY   Don't you mean a Drapkin?

HESTER   What? Oh, yes. Well, you mustn't split hairs. I'm
              only thankful that the Klingmans aren't here with
              us right now. For some reason, though apparently
              right-minded in every other way, they seem to

think you possess something called intelligence—
and class—and a really brilliant future. So far, I
haven't disillusioned them. Of course, if you truly
mean to turn your back on such an unrepeatable
opportunity, I shan't feel obliged to.

ELLEN   Perhaps this girl that Tony's meeting tonight has a
          father who's . . . well, let's see . . . a doctor or a banker
          or a lawyer? (To TONY) Tell me something that
          would top a Klingman.

TONY   Hopefully—in this case—an axe.

HESTER   (To FLORA) And there you are. There speaks your
          saint.

FLORA   You were the one who called him a saint.

TONY   Listen, everyone. Can't we just be serious for a
          minute? There's something I want to explain. It's
          about Sandra—this girl whom I'll be seeing
          tonight.

FLORA   My God! He's got himself engaged!

TONY   No. We're not engaged.

FLORA   Well, then, you've got her into trouble.

TONY shakes his head. There's a knock at the door. MARY comes in.

MARY   (To HESTER) Shall you want more hot water?

HESTER   No! (Less sharply) No, thank you, Mary. We have
          everything we need.

MARY   You haven't eaten very much. Is the sponge cake heavy? (To HESTER) You remember—I warned you—I thought the sponge cake would be heavy. (Skittish again) It was all your fault! You told me I should write that letter to my father—so I hurried with the beating of it. Therefore, blame Mrs Berg, everyone. Has everybody finished? Shall I clear away?

HESTER   No. Just leave it all till later.

MARY   Really? Oh, yes. Very well.

TONY   And the sponge cake wasn't heavy.

MARY   Thank you, Mr Tony. But I think I didn't beat it up enough. Next time it will be better.

She goes out.

HESTER   Now. Where were we?

Knock at the door. MARY again, but now she merely puts her head in.

MARY   Oh, I gave Mr Davis your message. He told me to present his compliments to the ladies and to ask them how they did. And he said he would look forward to seeing Mr Tony if it was convenient.

HESTER   Yes. Thank you, Mary.

MARY   But he won't remember it, of course. Bless him.

She gives a benevolent smile—in which she invites them all to share—then finally departs.

HESTER   (Cont.) I hardly know which is more wearisome:

244

when she's being difficult or when she's setting out
to please. Or when she's dropping all the china.
Continue, Tony, if you would. The floor is yours.

TONY   Well, it's nothing very revolutionary. It's just
              that . . .

Pause, while he summons up his courage.

TONY   (Cont.; blurting this out, rather) It's just that we've
              decided to live together. And tonight I'm moving
              my things across.

FLORA   What! (Pause) But we've never heard you even
              mention this girl. How long have you known her?

TONY   Not that long.

FLORA   How long?

TONY   Ten days.

FLORA   My God!

TONY   I've seen a lot of her in those ten days.

FLORA   And nights, no doubt.

HESTER   Flora!

FLORA   Well, that's right, Tony, isn't it?

HESTER   (To TONY) But haven't you given rather short
              notice to the friends you're living with at present?
              Not much time for them to find anybody new.

245

TONY   No, I've already fixed for someone to take my place. *He* was delighted. At least I've made one person's day for him.

ELLEN   And Sandra's too, I should imagine.

TONY   (Wan smile) Yes, I hope so.

FLORA   Hope so?

ELLEN   (Amiably) He's only being modest, you silly girl.

But the audience should get the feeling there was also an element of failing courage.

FLORA   (To TONY) So where will you be living now?

TONY   Sandra has a flat.

FLORA   Her own flat? (Marginally less cold) Or do you mean she shares it with other students?

TONY   No, she's not a student. It's her own.

HESTER What, have her parents bought it for her?

TONY   No, she rents it.

FLORA   Where?

TONY   Just off the Mile End Road.

FLORA   (To HESTER) Of course, you know where that is?

ELLEN   I hear the East End is coming up these days.

Doesn't David Owen have a house there? (TONY nods) Not bad! Having the Owens for your neighbours could carry nearly the same cachet as having the Klingmans.

TONY   Well, this is one of the tattier parts . . . Not that I can see it's relevant.

HESTER   Anyway. This girl has a flat in the East End. She isn't a student. What else can you tell us about her?

FLORA   What's her job?

TONY   She doesn't have one.

HESTER   But her training? What kind of thing is she after?

TONY   She isn't. She's got two young boys to bring up. One who's just four, one who's only nine months.

FLORA   (Pause) My God.

HESTER   You mean—she's divorced?

TONY   Widowed.

HESTER   Widowed? At that age? (Totally sincere) Dear Lord. How dreadful.

FLORA   What age is she?

TONY   Twenty-four.

HESTER   What age was her husband?

TONY   About the same. (Again, getting it over with) He
              committed suicide. Last year. Hanged himself. He
              was into drugs.

Stunned silence.

FLORA   (Without expression) If the father was a drug
              addict . . . that means the children will have it in their
              blood.

The door slowly opens and in comes WALTER DAVIS. He is
bearded, impressive; looks like Edward VII. Sometimes it can be seen
how badly his hands shake.

WALTER   My word. A party. Can anybody come? (Chuckles)
              And do they need to be in their Sunday best and to
              have had their faces washed?

TONY   (Standing, going forward) Hello, Mr Davis-sir. I
              think your face looks washed enough.

WALTER   Hello, Mr Tony-sir. And so does yours—so does
              yours!—I trust you've been inspected behind the
              ears. Good afternoon, ladies. By Jove, what a bevy
              of beauties. Why wasn't I told?

ELLEN   That's a very pretty speech. I think you must have
              rehearsed it.

WALTER   (Chuckles) Yes, isn't it? I probably did. Well, this is
              all extremely pleasant.

HESTER   Walter, darling, I wonder if we could ask you to
              come back in just a little while? We're in the
              midst of a very boring conversation. It wouldn't
              interest you at all.

But WALTER has now caught sight of the sponge and cinnamon balls, etc.

WALTER   My word. Is this a party? (Chuckles) They must have forgotten to send me my invitation. Is someone getting married?

HESTER   Yes, me, darling. (Gets up) Let me put a few of these things on a plate (she does so) although I shouldn't really—you've already had your tea—

WALTER   (Honest bewilderment) No, I haven't.

HESTER   Yes, darling, you have.

WALTER   (With serene good nature) Look here, my child, I'm the one who ought to know whether I've had my tea or not. (With shaking hand, he takes his fob watch from his waistcoat pocket; studies it intently) Yet it certainly does look as though I should have had it; there are grounds for your mistake. (To TONY, chuckling) It never does to contradict a lady. Especially not one who's getting married. Is it my imagination or are brides growing younger and lovelier each year? I wonder who the fortunate gentleman is.

HESTER   You are, darling.

WALTER   (To the rest of the company, as he puts away his watch; marked air of naughtiness) Well, I *have* managed to escape it for ninety years or more. Now that I'm growing up, I suppose it was too much to expect I could go on being so lucky.

HESTER has by this time taken his arm and is vainly trying to lead him to the door.

WALTER (Cont) "But I knaw'd a Quaaker feller as often 'as towd ma this: 'Doant thou marry for munny, but goa wheer munny is!' An' I went wheer munny war: an' thy mother coom to 'and, Wi' lots o' munny laid by, an' a nicetish bit o' land. Maaybe she warn't a beauty:—I niver giv it a thowt—But warn't she as good to cuddle an' kiss as a lass as 'ant nowt?"

TONY and ELLEN clap. WALTER beams.

WALTER (Cont) Yes, 'pon my word, old Tennyson certainly knew a thing or two. (To HESTER) Now then, my child, you mustn't push, you know; it really isn't done—not in the very best of circles. Well, tra-la, ladies and gentleman. It's been an honour and a privilege to meet you all.

TONY I'll come and see you, Mr Davis, in a little while.

WALTER That will be very nice, Mr Tony-sir.

He goes out, holding his plate of goodies. HESTER, at the door, calls, "Mary! Come and take Mr Davis back to his room. And bring his walking stick." Then she closes the door and returns to her chair.

HESTER Sit down again, Tony.

TONY I'd rather not for the moment. Thank you.

ELLEN Really, isn't he the most marvellous man—Walter? It's hard to believe he used to be so wayward in his youth. I find it immensely reassuring: there may yet be hope for the rest of us.

HESTER   He's still extremely obstinate. But yes. One could never wish for a less demanding lodger. However … talking of wayward and obstinate youth … (She looks at TONY, with severe yet tolerant smile.)

TONY   I'm not wayward. Nor obstinate.

HESTER   Well, that remains to be seen.

FLORA   What does 'wayward' mean?

ELLEN   Young people who don't listen to their grandmothers.

TONY   But I do listen. (Smiles) And listen. And listen.

HESTER   No, you don't. Otherwise you'd sit down.

TONY   (Sits) There. You see.

FLORA   (To TONY) This woman. How does she manage? Do her parents support her?

TONY   Mum, she isn't 'this woman'. She's Sandra. But no. She gets the dole. Obviously she has it pretty tough.

We sense more commitment now, less uncertainty.

TONY   (Cont) And, my God, she's had it tough for at least the past five years!

FLORA   What does her father do?

TONY   I don't know. (Pause) He certainly isn't one of the
            professional classes, if that's what you're hoping.

FLORA   (Coldly) So where did you meet her?

TONY   At a disco.

HESTER   At a disco! Oh, this is ridiculous. Ten days ago. At
            a disco.

TONY   What's wrong with discos? Lots of very respectable
            people go to discos.

HESTER   But do they go alone? Women in their twenties?

TONY   Who said she went alone? And what if she did?
            Her nextdoor neighbour suddenly offered to
            babysit and . . . and it was the first time since . . .
            And she decided to get dressed up and have a good
            time. What's so wrong with that? She likes music.
            She likes dancing. She—

FLORA   Who asked who to dance?

TONY   All right, Mum, so she asked me—ever heard of a
            movement called Women's Lib? But the thing is,
            that once we began to talk I realized how nice she
            was. She had this quality. It's difficult to explain. I
            felt drawn to her.

HESTER   You felt sorry for her.

TONY   Not at all. What do you think?—that she instantly
            said, "I'm a widow, my husband was a junkie,
            killed himself, I have two kids." She only started
            telling me that when I was walking her home.

HESTER   And, anyway, I'm not saying you weren't right to
          feel sorry for her. What kind of monster wouldn't?
          All I'm saying is, it's a mistake to let yourself
          become involved. Worse than a mistake. It's
          thoughtless; stupid. You'd be encouraging her to
          grow dependent on you—oh I mean emotionally,
          not financially, she knows you're only a student.
          And then what would happen? When you'd made a
          big difference to her life, perhaps been like a father
          to her children? You'd turn your back on her, let
          her down again, just like she was let down by her
          husband. You can't expect us to approve of any
          situation that could lead to that?

TONY   I don't intend to turn my back on her.

HESTER   Not at the moment. Of course you don't. But
          you'll forgive my mentioning this: I don't think
          you're someone who ever looks too far into the
          future.

FLORA   (To TONY) Don't say you mean to marry her?
          (TONY gives a shrug.)

HESTER   So what do you intend?

TONY   Perhaps only to help her over a bad patch? You
          can't always be looking years and years ahead. You
          have to do what seems right at the moment. If she
          has stability now, then in five or six years' time the
          children will both be at school, she'll have a job,
          she'll be out and about meeting people. And she'll
          have got through that initial period of real isolation
          and hopelessness and—

HESTER   But all this sounds so muddled. I don't understand

it. Are you telling us you love this girl or that
you're just going in for social work?

TONY   I . . . (Hesitates)

HESTER   (To the others) You see?

TONY   I think I do love her. She's nice. She's . . . You'll
            like her. Right now I'm sure you have the wrong
            impression. And the children, too . . . they're great.
            They don't deserve any of this shit that's—I mean
            they don't deserve any of what's happened to them.
            None of them do.

HESTER   Or of what's going to happen to them?

TONY   How can you talk like that? Nobody has a crystal
            ball.

HESTER turns to FLORA, then shrugs and raises her hands.

TONY   (Cont) Besides . . . I like to have people depend on
            me.

HESTER   You're just a boy.

TONY   Yes. You're always saying that. So perhaps it's
            time I grew up and took on a bit of responsibility.

FLORA   Oh, you fool. You say you want to have people
            depend on you. What do you think I've had to do all
            these years but train myself *not* to depend on you?
            (Pause) Never to let you see how much I minded
            when you went out in the evenings! (Pause) Even
            having to make myself encourage you when you
            first spoke about going on holiday without me, and

then, last year, about moving into a house with other students! (Pause) And yet you must know how very lonely I get—how much I hate my own company—how much I dislike being in an empty flat after dark . . . even putting off going to bed because sometimes I get silly and a little scared. (Pause) So, if you want people to depend on you, you should maybe look a little closer to home.

She is by this time having to dab at her eyes and to blow her nose.

FLORA   (Cont) And how do you think it's been for me living for twenty years without a husband or a boyfriend or anyone to take care of me—because your father didn't want a baby and swore he'd walk out if I refused to have you aborted?

TONY   (Embarrassed) I know all that, Mum.

FLORA   No, you don't. How could you? When have I ever told you how much *I* always needed somebody to depend on?

HESTER   Flora, darling, please. You mustn't upset yourself like this. Whether other people knew it or not, I always did, and I respected you for it. *You* looked into the future. *You* knew that to become too dependent on someone who was one day bound to disappear wouldn't be a healthy thing, and you were responsible and mature and courageous in keeping to that decision. I don't know how you managed it.

FLORA   (Bleakly but with a hint of self-mockery) I went to lots of marriage bureaux.

255

HESTER   Of course you did. I haven't forgotten the bravery it required. Nor how beautiful you were—and how incredibly lucky any blind fool of a man should indeed have felt to meet you! But the trouble is you had no money and you had a young son to bring up.

She looks at TONY as she says this, wanting to remind him both of his obligations to his mother and of the folly of taking on another man's family without having the funds to do so.

TONY   I'm sorry, Mum. I really am.

FLORA   Well, I am too, darling. I didn't mean to start on all of that.

HESTER   It's just that your mother and I don't want to see you throw your life away. (Pause) You truly have decided? You truly must go through with it?

TONY   Haven't you yourself always said it's wrong to break your word?

HESTER   As a guiding principle, yes. Though naturally it should depend on the circumstances.

TONY   I don't see how. It's not as though I'd been coerced.

HESTER   Still. Circumstances do vary.

ELLEN   I agree with Tony. When you've raised someone to be honourable you have to accept the consequences. It's a situation sometimes known as being hoist with your own petard.

HESTER   Oh, Ellen, stop being so frivolous; there's nothing to be frivolous about. (Pause) On the other hand, I suppose there's nothing to be so gloomy about, either. (To TONY) Just so long as you won't let it interfere with your studies. Then, in another couple of years, after you've got a good degree and found yourself a decent job—

TONY   I'm leaving university.

This is an interruption which—again—causes a stunned silence.

HESTER   What did you say?

TONY   I'm leaving university.

HESTER   Is that really what you said? I was giving you the benefit of the doubt. I didn't believe you could be so utterly devoid of consideration—or vision—or practicality. So wholly and impossibly puerile. Is that really what you said?

TONY   I've been offered a job at a crisp factory for nearly a hundred pounds a week. (Pause) And I've already seen the sub-dean.

HESTER   Then, of course, you'd better go *back* to see him! How thunderstruck he must have been! How literally struck dumb! (Pause) You'd better tell us what he said.

TONY   In fact he did try to dissuade me. Up to a point.

HESTER   I hope he told you how completely mad you were.

TONY   No. He—

FLORA   Because that's what you are, of course. Completely

and utterly mad! Besotted! A hundred pounds a
week; a job in a crisp factory! (She is now openly
crying.) And if anyone had ever told me . . .
Oh, I can't take any more of this,
I simply can't!

She gets up and rushes out.

HESTER   (Standing) Flora! Flora, darling! (To TONY) Now
see what you've done. That you, of all people—!
And after all those dreams we've had on your
behalf! No, I don't speak about myself—I don't
expect you to have any care for *me*—why should
you? But your mother! I don't think you quite
appreciate—I don't believe you ever did . . . But, as
she said, if she hadn't chosen you—chosen to give
you life—she could still have had a real life of her
own, she could still have had a husband. Yet all
along she's gone without so that *you* wouldn't have
to. How can you repay a debt like that? Certainly
not by thinking only of yourself. Me, me, me:
that's what it's always been in your case, hasn't
it? Hidden behind the sheerest veil of plausibility
and charm. You rely on your sweet phrases and
good looks to carry you through; to make everyone
think how wonderful you are. Well, shall I tell you
what you really are? You're immoral. *Immoral!*
You don't give two hoots whom you harm, so long
as you yourself can sail through life with blithe
inconvenience—and I see no hope for you at all,
not the slightest chance of redemption. For I'll tell
you another thing, shall I? Unless you mend your
ways at once, then I for one shall never wish to see
you again. Never! I hope that's clearly understood.
Connection severed! So I trust that you'll think
about what you're doing—in the light of what I've

just said—think very, very carefully indeed.
(Pause) Now I am going to try to bring a little
comfort to your mother.

And she sweeps out of the room, leaving behind her not merely a
dazed grandson but an almost equally dazed sister.

ELLEN   (Eventually) Well . . . That was a little masterpiece
               of economy.

TONY   (Shakily) No, I shouldn't like to write it on the
               back of a postage stamp.

ELLEN   Of course, the one thing it did economize on—as
               they put it so very quaintly these days—was the
               truth.

TONY   Oh, I don't know. I suppose that has to depend on
               your point of view.

ELLEN   Poor old Tony. You know, you're much too nice
               for your own good.

TONY   (Shakes his head; seems close to tears) *That* isn't
               true at all.

ELLEN   But all you need is the courage of your convictions.
               (Then more positively—clearly hoping to instill
               strength.) And you've certainly got that.

TONY   No. Wrong again. I'm scared stiff.

ELLEN   (Stands; walks about in agitation) Oh, I could
               swear! Most truly I could! What's more, I could
               say a most exceedingly naughty word. (Pause)
               Families!

TONY   Is that your naughty word?

ELLEN   In certain situations there is none naughtier.

TONY   (Avoiding priggishness) I've always been
          extremely fond of my family.

ELLEN   I know you have. I've often observed it—and
          marvelled. My own feelings towards the family
          have always been . . . well, a little more complex.
          (Hollow laugh) I suppose that's what comes of
          being the only plain one amongst six sisters.

TONY   (Meaning it) You aren't plain!

ELLEN   Oh, it's true that by some fluke I may have grown
          better-looking with age. But the trouble is, when I
          was young I never thought of saying to any
          potential beau: why not hang around for half a
          century, I *could* turn into a corker! So what
          happens? One by one you see your sisters marry—
          five times a bridesmaid in your own family alone.
          And you become so eaten up with jealousy and
          longing and resentment. And so sick of being
          patronized. "Oh, Ellie—she's the only one of us
          who has a singing voice. And she's by far the best
          dancer in the family!" Though you can always hear
          the rider trembling on their lips . . . "If only she could
          find a partner!" But all the time you smile. You
          make jokes. You're a good sport. "Oh, Ellie,
          absolutely the right person to have around if you're
          in trouble!" And you take your nephews and nieces
          to the pantomime and out on other treats—

TONY   And your great-nephews, too.

ELLEN   (Now without the bitterness) Yes. And actually you have a lot of fun while doing it. Oh, I shouldn't moan; for all of us down here, life is a vale of tears. (Pause) Do you know what Cary Grant once said— even Cary Grant? He said that his life had been nothing but stomach disturbances and self-concern. I shouldn't be in the least bit pleased by that, and yet . . . It must be my soured and crabby nature. I always liked Cary Grant but I never took to him so completely as when I first read that. And it was only a few months back, yet by that time he was dead. Wouldn't you know?

TONY   And if he hadn't been?

ELLEN   I could have cabled him a kiss.

TONY   (Pause) You called me poor old Tony. I want to call you poor old Ellen. I never knew.

ELLEN   Well, I'm just as glad you didn't. (Smiles, sits down, continues abruptly) And do you realize? I've never had a man. (After a moment lifts a hand) No, I shouldn't have said that. Forgive me. For one thing—what on earth can a person reply? (Lightly) Anyway, perhaps that's why I've survived longer than any of my sisters apart from your grandmother. There's a happy side to all of it.

TONY   What do you think I ought to do? (Pauses) Am I just being stupid, and thoughtless, and obstinate?

ELLEN   (Slowly; as though finally deciding on something) Listen. I'm going to tell you a story. It may prove mildly helpful. Or then, again, it may not. But

think of it simply as one of Aesop's fables. Ellen
Aesop.

TONY looks at her in some surprise.

ELLEN   (Cont) It's something that happened thirty years
ago.

Pause, while they still look at one another. TONY settles back in
his chair, expectantly.

ELLEN   (Cont) It was just after your mother was married;
she was nineteen. Your father wasn't at all the right
person for her—he never could have been. They
were too much alike. He, too, had been dominated
by a forceful mother; he, too, was looking for a
way out. He was twenty-five; had never been away
from home. Always kept very much in thrall;
always to some extent resentful of it. Yes, they
were more like brother and sister than sweethearts:
each weak in the same way, each wanting to show
the world that they were strong. It was a cruel trick
of Fate's to throw two such similar personalities,
spawned by two such similar situations, slap bang
into each other's path—and then make both of
them nice-looking, so that, naturally, they'd feel
attracted. They had known each other only two
weeks before announcing their engagement.
(Pause) Do you mind my talking about your
parents in this way? It is necessary.

TONY   (Shakes his head) And none of it, so far, is new.
It's only what Mum has often said of Dad, and
also what Dad—well, he hasn't come out with it in
so many words but if you put two and two together
—what Dad has often said of Mum. They each see

it in the other; I don't know if they see it in themselves. Apparently, we're an inherently weak family.

ELLEN   I didn't realize you still saw your father.

TONY   Only once a year, at most. Tea at the Ritz—or dinner at Simpson's—or, more and more these days, just a drink at the pub when he's on his way to catch the train . . . the train that bears him back to my wicked stepmother. So, you'll understand, it's strictly duty—on both sides.

ELLEN   Is she very wicked?

TONY   Well, let's just say we don't get on.

ELLEN   And did you ever know your Granny Drapkin?

TONY   Granny Peggy? Oh, yes. I must have been at least eight or nine when she died. Yes, I remember her as very . . . well, forthright. But not at all like Gran. Not the same warmth, nor sense of humour. Nor the same kindness for lame dogs, the same compassion for humanity in general. Perhaps that's a bit unfair: I wasn't really old enough to make those kinds of comparison. (Smiles) All I know is, Granny Peggy cut stingy bits of cake; and never gave me more than 10p whenever I went to see her.

Knock on door. Enter MARY.

MARY   May I clear away now? Oh—where is Mrs Berg?

ELLEN   Probably in her bedroom, Mary. With Mrs Drapkin. Yes, by all means clear away.

TONY   I'll help you.

They quickly stack the plates etcetera onto the large tray MARY
has brought.

MARY   (In chatty, tolerant mood) Oh Lord . . . Mr Davis!
           He's had about six teas. He keeps coming into the
           kitchen and asking is it teatime yet and where is
           Mrs Berg. So the only way I can get him to go
           back to his room is by leading him there myself,
           walking just a foot or two ahead, backwards, with
           a chocolate biscuit in each hand. Poor old
           gentleman. I hope he won't get ill.

ELLEN   In his day, a most excellent dental surgeon—
           renowned for giving hardly any pain. Later on, a
           conscientious magistrate. Widely loved and well
           respected. (Pause) Oh dear. That life can really
           come to this!

MARY   (With feeling) Yes. And all he does is nod off in his
           chair or read the same bit of newspaper over and
           over again. Mrs Berg only buys a newspaper once a
           week. I tell her once a year would be sufficient!
           And when you put on his television he says, "I can
           never understand one word they're saying. Can *you*
           explain what's going on?" I hope they kill me off,
           before I get to his age.

TONY   Drop any more of Gran's china and they probably
           will. You'd better let me take that tray.

MARY   That's very kind of you but I can manage it; I'm
           stronger than I look. (TONY holds door open)
           Thank you, Mr Tony. (She goes. TONY closes
           door)

TONY   (Sits) Right then, Ellen. You were saying?

ELLEN   Right then, Tony. I was saying ... What *was* I
              saying? Ah, yes. At first they hated one another—
              your father and grandmother; couldn't get on at all.
              Or, at any rate, he hated her; must have felt that in
              his attempt to escape one matriarch he'd only ended
              up with two. Because, of course, the marriage, with
              the setting up of their own home down the road in
              Golders Green, a house bought for them by Hester
              and furnished by Mrs Drapkin, their marriage
              didn't—maybe couldn't—break any of the ties. The
              knots if you like were slackened ... although I
              wouldn't even want to bet too much on that. If I'm
              not mistaken, it was dinner with the one on Tuesday
              nights, dinner with the other on Fridays, and
              Sunday lunch alternating between the two: West
              Hampstead this week, Maida Vale the next. Even
              besides that, while Harold was at work, Flora was
              continually popping round to see her mum, most
              likely to expatiate—I shouldn't be surprised!—on
              the various disappointments of her married life.
              Apart from the central one, that is, of still being
              hedged around with apron strings. Which quite
              possibly she didn't even recognize any longer as
              being a disappointment. (Pause) Anyway, my dear
              Tony, I hope that all this adequately sets the scene.
              Do you wish me to continue?

TONY   Of course.

And as soon as he has said this, the lights go down.

In the darkness, the *Pathétique* starts playing on the radiogram. A noticeably different vase of flowers and perhaps two
or three striking cushions should be enough to suggest another

time. It is still summer—still early evening—but now thirty years earlier.

When the lights go up, the room is empty. After a moment HESTER enters, followed by FLORA. They are wearing the fashions of 1957. FLORA, at nineteen, is pretty and youthful and full of fun; but, even so, essentially respectful and compliant.

HESTER   (While entering) How long before Harold comes to pick you up?

FLORA   Half an hour? Depending on the traffic. The curtain rises at seven-thirty.

HESTER   I was listening to Tchaikovsky. Isn't this lovely! (Waves her hands a little, as though conducting)

FLORA   (Shrugs gaily) Oh, you know me: I prefer something a bit less highbrow.

HESTER   Dear God. What did I ever do to deserve such a daughter?

FLORA   (Laughs) Where's Jarvie, by the way?

HESTER   Day off. Would you like a sherry?

FLORA   Perhaps a quick one, before I go and change. I think you'll love my dress. It was madly extravagant. Harry will throw a fit.

HESTER   I look forward to seeing it.

FLORA   (Playfully provocative) The dress—or Harold's fit? (But waits for no reply) Thank you for saying I might have my bath here. Mind you, you could hardly have done otherwise: after all, it was you who told us to install central heating. All the floors up. No hot water. And of course it had to be today, didn't it?—the very first time we've been out together in more than five weeks! Filth inches deep. Men all over the place. (Laughs) Not that in the normal way I'd be complaining about *that*. One of them is rather nice, as it happens. Sleeves rolled right up; shirt unbuttoned down to here; wicked twinkle in his eye.

HESTER   Darling! And you a bride of only four months!

FLORA   Well, Harry hasn't got a wicked twinkle. (Smilingly outrageous) Nor has he got hair upon his chest.

HESTER   Flora, that's enough! I think a little maidenly reserve should be called for. Anyway, I myself never cared for human apes. Smooth-skinned men were always far more to my taste.

FLORA   Besides. I don't feel like a bride.

HESTER   You're not going to say you have regrets?

FLORA   Is that a question, or an order? Besides, you already know I don't find Harry much fun. He's moody and he sulks a lot. I keep telling him that if he loved me he wouldn't be so . . . so undemonstrative . . . and grumpy.

HESTER   And I kept telling *you* that nineteen was too young!

FLORA   You were nineteen.

HESTER   Yes. Yes, I was nineteen. But that was very

different—so please don't make comparisons! The
love which your father and I had for one another
was … was wholly unique. (Much lighter) Anyhow,
my darling—without wishing to be in the least bit
unsympathetic—you were just so determined,
weren't you? To up and leave the nest. Next time,
perhaps, you'll listen to your mother.

FLORA   Gracious! We're just off to a theatre. Not the
divorce court!

HESTER   I'm very pleased to hear it.

The doorbell rings.

FLORA   Could that be him already? (Glances at her watch)
In any case, *I'll* go.

While FLORA is away HESTER crosses to the radiogram and
turns the record over. She listens for a moment with enjoyment.
We hear HAROLD and FLORA approach. HAROLD is dressed in a
smart suit, with well-polished black shoes, white shirt, sober tie. His
hair is much shorter than Tony's. He wears a moustache.

During the next fifteen minutes or so, HESTER will return
to the radiogram at least a couple of times, either to select a new
record or—where appropriate—simply turn one over; the records
don't have to be LPs. Neither she nor HAROLD needs to comment
on the music, other than with—perhaps—a grimace or appre-
ciative nod.

FLORA   (Hardly in the room yet) Yes. The man himself! It
seems there wasn't any traffic.

HAROLD   (Following close behind) An exaggeration. It just
wasn't as bad as it often is. And since I left the

office in extremely good time of course—finding it
wise always to anticipate the worst—

HESTER   Good evening, Harold. (Crosses and gives him a
perfunctory kiss) I must say, I've never known you
be unpunctual for anything. Which I think does you
a lot of credit. And—naturally—your upbringing.

FLORA   (Vivacious again) My goodness! There must be
something in the air. (To HAROLD) Do you
realize what happened? My mother just paid your
mother a compliment.

HESTER   Oh, don't be silly, darling. We're the very best of
friends.

FLORA   Then so were Mr Churchill and Hitler.

HESTER   That's very sweet of you, Flora. But I'd never
have the gall to compare myself to Mr Churchill.
Harold, dear, a sherry? Or perhaps you'd rather
have some whisky?

HAROLD   Whisky, please, Mother-in-Law.

HESTER   Harold, how often do I have to tell you? I just can't
put up with that! *Hester*—or else you don't get so
much as a glass of water.

HAROLD   (Smiles) I know. I'm sorry. I keep forgetting.
Hester.

HESTER   (Cupping a hand to one ear) I didn't hear.

HAROLD   Hester.

HESTER   That's better. (To FLORA) Perhaps we'll train him yet. Punctuality may be the politeness of kings but it's not the full story—not by a long chalk.

FLORA   I'm afraid that the politeness of kings means you're going to have to entertain one another for a bit longer than expected. Can you manage that?

HESTER   Oh dear. I doubt it. What an ordeal. (Splashes soda into the whisky)

HAROLD   (To FLORA) Why? Where are you going?

FLORA   Well, naturally—to bath and change! I told you! I couldn't do it at home.

HAROLD   Why do you need to change? You look perfectly all right to me.

FLORA   I'm certainly not coming to the theatre like this! (To HESTER) How like a man! I could probably have worn my apron or my housecoat and he'd have said, "Oh, no one will notice! Why fuss?"

HAROLD   That isn't true. You know I'd always expect any wife of mine to conform to the very highest of standards. You ought to be flattered I see nothing wrong with what you're wearing at the moment.

FLORA   Oh! 'Any wife of mine'! How many do you plan to have?

HESTER   Now, now, children! Flora, you just run along. Like you say, Harold and I will no doubt manage to entertain one another most *beautifully.*

HAROLD   (Patently angry with his wife) Good God, Flora,
            I'm family. Why should I need entertaining? For
            just ten minutes or so—and I hope it won't be any
            longer than that—I shall be perfectly happy to sit
            and read your mother's *Telegraph*.

HESTER   (To HAROLD) Ah, yes, but I propose to make you
            suffer. A little suffering, I believe, is always good
            for the soul. I'm family too, you see, and I do need
            entertaining. (Hands HAROLD his drink) I think
            that's how you like it.

HAROLD   Thank you.

HESTER   When you're ready for another, you may simply
            help yourself. I always feel the pouring of drinks
            is really the man's job.

HAROLD   Oh, no, I shan't want another. Don't forget I'm
            driving.

FLORA   Right, then. I'll leave you together. I'll be as quick
            as I can.

Her tone has been a little stiff but suddenly we can almost see her
making the effort not to let the evening be spoilt—after all, she has a
new dress and this is the first time they've been out together in five
weeks.

FLORA   (Cont) So try not to miss me too much! (She blows
            them kisses and goes, taking her glass of sherry.
            Then pops her head back round the door) May I
            help myself to bubble bath?

HESTER   You may help yourself to anything.

FLORA'S departure marks a brief hiatus.

HESTER   Well . . . a quarter of an hour, let's say—and that's looking on the bright side. Would you like a sandwich? I imagine you won't be eating until later?

HAROLD   No, thank you, Mother-in-Law. I'm fine.

HESTER   Excuse me?

HAROLD   Hester.

HESTER   That's better. But you're sure—no sandwich? And no *Telegraph*. Oh dear. What shall we ever find to talk about?

HAROLD   I thought the English always talked about the weather.

HESTER   Not us. That would show a dreadful lack of imagination. Let me see now. Do you come here often? (Quickly) I hasten to add that the courteous response will not be, "Yes! Far *too* often!"

HAROLD   About three times a fortnight.

HESTER   Ah. Mmm. Not a bad-sized dance floor?

HAROLD   (Really unpractised at this) No. Actually it almost *would* make a dance floor. A small one. If you moved all the furniture. There's not a bad amount of space.

HESTER   Yes, and the orchestra's not bad, either.

HAROLD   Is it the London Philharmonic?

HESTER   (Surprised) Yes, I believe it is. Do you like it?
           (Pause) Your wife, by the way, dismisses it as
           highbrow.

HAROLD   For Flora, even Cole Porter could be highbrow.

HESTER   And what do *you* think of Tchaikovsky?

HAROLD   Pretty melodies. Makes a pleasant background to
           conversation. The two composers I like best are
           undoubtedly Brahms and Schubert.

HESTER   (Now definitely impressed) Really? I had no idea. I
           suppose we've never discussed music.

HAROLD   One certainly couldn't sit and talk to Brahms or
           Schubert.

HESTER   Now, *that* was a rather grave tactical error.

HAROLD   I'm sorry?

HESTER   You should have said the same about Tchaikovsky.
           Then you'd have had the perfect pretext just to sit
           and listen.

HAROLD   (Pause) As a matter of fact I think I was being a
           little unfair to Tchaikovsky. Well, certainly the
           Pathétique. It expresses something very . . . lonely
           . . . and romantic . . . and striving. I take back
           what I said.

HESTER   Lonely—and romantic—and striving. Yes. Yes . . .
            It's strange that you should feel that way as well. I
            think I might adopt it as my theme tune. (Lightly)
            But it's too late now, you know. You're not allowed
            to backtrack.

HAROLD   (Drily humorous) Blast! All my life I've been much
            too slow on the uptake. Can't we just go back to the
            beginning?

HESTER   Do you mean, five minutes ago or five months ago?

HAROLD   (Embarrassed) Flora says some pretty silly things.
            I suppose because she and my mother don't always
            seem to hit if off she automatically assumes . . .

HESTER   (Not believing this for a moment) Yes, that's more
            than likely what it is. And she sometimes gets
            carried away by sheer animal high spirits—
            exaggerating out of all proportion.

Pause. They listen to the music. They thoughtfully sip their drinks.

HESTER   (Cont) Wouldn't it be wonderful to write a
            symphony or concerto? I'd rather have been a
            composer than practically anything. Oh, how I
            wish that as a child I'd kept up my piano lessons—
            persevered like Ellen.

HAROLD   I never had piano lessons. I wish I'd been made to.

HESTER   Weren't your parents fond of music?

HAROLD   My father may have been. But he was consumptive
            —died when I was only two. So I was brought up by
            just my mother.

HESTER   Oh, you poor boy. That must have been dreadful.
          (Pause) I mean—your father dying.

HAROLD   Yes. People don't always understand what it's like
          to have no father.

HESTER   Never! Not unless they have experienced it
          themselves.

HAROLD   Why, did your own father . . . ?

HESTER   Yes, he died when I was six.

HAROLD   I'm sorry.

HESTER   But then, of course, I had my five sisters. So—awful
          though it was—it must have been a great deal more
          so for an only child. (Pause) Coincidentally, Flora's
          father also died when she was young. (Pause) My
          own beloved Max . . .

HAROLD   I know. Yes. I mean—

HESTER   Of course, my husband was a lot older than me:
          more than twenty years—it didn't seem so much of
          an age gap in those days. But he was never strong
          . . . shell shock, you know, during the First World
          War. And we'd been married for nearly fifteen years
          before Flora came along. Up until then there'd been
          a whole series of miscarriages and . . . And I would
          have liked a larger family but . . . but it simply wasn't
          to be. Yet why should I be boring you with such
          very old history? Perhaps, after all, I ought to go and
          find you that newspaper.

HAROLD   No, no, of course not. Flora's quite a chatterbox but

... But I didn't know you'd been through all of this sort of thing.

HESTER   Flora's just a young girl. She has her head full of dancing and dresses and romantic novels. She ... Harold, there is nobody in this world whom I love more than Flora. But I think it won't come as any surprise to you to learn she isn't exactly the most ... the most ... How can I put it? Well, I always tried to interest her in things. I sent her to the best schools. She was lively and pretty and very popular. But when it came to her studies she had virtually no curiosity, no application. Which mightn't have mattered so much if I'd been lucky and had all the children I wanted—because clearly, if you have six children, there's room for six personality types: the serious and the frivolous, the obedient and the self-willed ... (Laughs) Do you know, I don't believe Flora's ever properly stood up to me? Apart from that one very major exception, which perhaps it's more tactful not to mention right now—although it's unquestionably the sort of exception, I'm afraid, which really does prove the rule. And it isn't precisely that one wants rebellious children ...

HAROLD   Well, hardly.

HESTER   I was never very tractable, you see, and I suppose it's merely that—to some extent—one may want a copy of oneself. What arrogance! In reality, I should probably hate to have any such thing. Would we ever leave off fighting?

HAROLD   (Pause) And, anyway, I can't imagine anything worse than having six children. Why, even to bring *one* new life onto this planet as it is today ...

HESTER   But Flora wants children.

HAROLD   No, she doesn't. Before we got married she was
              well aware of my views on that subject and she
              endorsed them absolutely.

HESTER   Now, haven't I just intimated to you? (Humorously
              but with underlying annoyance) Her will can be
              bent by anyone, the very last person she's spoken
              to, be it her cleaner or even her husband. Besides,
              hasn't it ever occurred to you that I might rather
              like grandchildren?

HAROLD   In a world already so vastly overpopulated? In
              a world that stands on the very brink of self-
              destruction?

HESTER   (Impatiently) Yes, I know all that but are you sure
              you're not just rationalizing? (Tongue-in-cheek)
              Oh, it's a messy business bringing up children. It
              Interferes with your freedoms and your temper. Can
              quite blow away your comfort.

HAROLD   (Apparently unaware of the sarcasm) I thought you
              were the woman who advocated six. Oh, of course!
              In your day you had nannies and parlourmaids and
              things.

HESTER   (Sweetly) And more unselfish natures.

HAROLD   (Without rancour) Nonsense.

HESTER   No, I think people do seem to be growing more and
              more selfish. More materialistic. Naturally, during
              the war it was different, but the war has been over

for twelve years now and we don't seem to have learned very much from it, do we?

HAROLD   I'm only surprised you thought we should.

HESTER   You are a pessimist, aren't you?

HAROLD   In that case, we obviously have much in common.

HESTER   (Surprised) Me? I'm not a pessimist. I'm the biggest optimist the world has ever known.

HAROLD   Certainly the biggest optimist the world has ever known who believes that human nature is fast deteriorating.

HESTER   I wouldn't say that, precisely.

HAROLD   You did say that, precisely.

HESTER   (Slightly confused) Nevertheless, I'm extremely hopeful for the future. I think that men are capable of great things if only they would stop behaving like animals and start behaving like superior beings. (Pause) And I'm thoroughly enjoying this conversation—did you know that? It's not often I get the chance to talk to somebody who *thinks*. In fact—I don't mind telling you—that's always been one of my severest disappointments.

HAROLD   (Clearly flattered but trying to hide it) Aren't there societies you could join? Debating societies?

HESTER   No, no. Everyone wanting to talk rather than—like me—just listen. Everyone wanting to take centre stage. I can't abide that.

HAROLD   Then what about your sisters? They all live very
          close.

HESTER   They do, yes, and they're dear, sweet women, all of
          them, but though I do say it myself I'm the one
          who's inherited the brains of the family—such as
          they are—well, in all fairness, Ellen too, I suppose.
          Yet we were born at the wrong time. To be *your*
          age today . . . oh, what a marvel that would be! But
          to have been born in the Edwardian era, brought up
          by Victorian parents with Victorian ideas, ideas
          about a woman's education and a woman's place in
          society and about marriage and divorce and
          respectability . . . Oh, Harold, how very lucky you
          are! If only I had been a man! A man then or a girl
          now—a girl now wouldn't be so bad, although a
          man still has an easier time of it . . .

HAROLD   Do you really think so? Slogging his life away at
          the office in a job he more often than not . . . detests?

HESTER   (Too preoccupied to have heard) And since I wasn't
          a man myself—nor a woman born in the right
          period—I wanted at least to be able to give birth to
          boys: to *boys*: lusty, grabbing, cast-iron boys. And
          one of my miscarriages didn't happen until early in
          the sixth month and they said it would have been a
          boy. Then how I howled! Not in self-pity but in
          rage. For, oh, how I myself should then have been
          born again—what times, what plans, what lives we
          should have shared . . . Questing! Vital! Triumphant!
          (More soberly) But I'm very glad I didn't have a
          brother. I'd have been so jealous . . . (Suddenly
          aware that she has revealed more than she meant.
          Goes on hurriedly—lightly) If I'd been a boy, I
          would have run away to sea!

HAROLD   (Seizing with some relief upon this) And probably
           you'd have been seasick.

HESTER   Yes, I would. But what a nothing price to pay! Oh,
           the glory of having been a traveller! An explorer!
           An adventurer!

HAROLD   Haven't you travelled?

HESTER   (Scornfully) Indeed I have. To such places as Le
           Touquet and Monte Carlo and Venice—and
           Amsterdam—and, ah yes, Vienna.

HAROLD   And Paris, also? Surely?

HESTER   Yes, I've also been to Paris.

HAROLD   (Pause) I'm sorry.

HESTER   What for?

HAROLD   I don't know. For all of it, I suppose. Or perhaps
           for sounding as though I didn't understand. Or
           something. There've been many times, too, when
           I've wanted to run away.

HESTER   To do what?

HAROLD   That's just it—I never knew. I simply wanted to
           run away.

HESTER   How sad!

HAROLD   Yes.

HESTER   You could have joined the circus. Or is it just a myth that little boys want to run away to join the circus?

HAROLD   I've never liked circuses.

HESTER   Nor have I.

HAROLD   I've only been once. I was scared to watch the aerialists. Felt sorry for the animals—plus, on the whole, found them distinctly boring. And I didn't think the clowns were funny.

HESTER   My own sentiments—all of them.

HAROLD   The only thing that made me laugh was when an elephant . . .

HESTER   Yes?

HAROLD   (Deciding to go ahead) . . . peed over some people in the front row. But that made *everybody* laugh.

HESTER   Except the people in the front row . . . Still, it would have been an experience. Something to boast about. Something to dine out on. "I once got peed on by an elephant." Few people could match that. (They laugh.) Take another drink, my dear.

HAROLD   I'm not sure I should. I already feel quite merry.

HESTER   And it suits you. I must say, it really does suit you. Though, of course, it's not just the alcohol. It's equally . . .

HAROLD   The company. The conversation.

HESTER   Well, thank you, Harold. That's a very nice thing to say.

HAROLD   But true.

HESTER   And totally reciprocated.

HAROLD   Well, just a small one, then. (Goes to help himself) But don't forget I have to drive.

HESTER   You could always take a taxi. And come back later, both of you, to pick up the car and tell me all about your evening.

HAROLD   But are you going to keep me company? Another sherry?

HESTER   Yes, please, darling. (Quickly) Oh, I'm sorry, I wasn't thinking. Mere slip of the tongue. (Pause) And then I shouldn't have drawn attention to it, should I? We could've pretended it hadn't happened.

HAROLD busies himself pouring her sherry. Non-committal smile.

HESTER   (Cont) No—how absurd! Why shouldn't a mother-in-law call her only son-in-law 'darling'? Isn't he one of the family? Indeed, isn't it a mother-in-law's prerogative to be able to flirt a little? Especially, of course, when he's such a very handsome son-in-law. (HAROLD, embarrassed again, hands her her drink) Thank you . . . darling.

HAROLD   That's all right.

HESTER   As a matter of fact I never realized, until this
          evening, that you were actually so handsome.
          Which is possibly just as well. Otherwise I might
          have found myself a fraction jealous of my own
          daughter. (Pause) What it was, I think—you lacked
          the animation. I hadn't seen you animated before.
          (Pause) Indeed, I never realized several things until
          this evening.

HAROLD   (Curious—flattered—and, indeed, something rather
          more) Such as?

HESTER   Such as—let me see, now—you don't like circuses.

HAROLD   Which makes us even. That's something I've also
          found out about you.

HESTER   Ah, but I'm a lot more complex than you are. I
          think I liked them slightly more.

HAROLD   What depth of character!

HESTER   You see, I loved the horses. I was always quite mad
          on horses. And then I have a daughter who . . . well, I
          thought, "When she's old enough we'll have such
          fun, we'll go riding together, she can even have her
          own pony!" And then what happens? The unnatural
          child is scared silly of the poor beasts. Would you
          believe it? It's as much of a myth, perhaps, about
          girls and horses as it is about boys and circuses.
          (Pause) Also, I've discovered that you were always
          wanting to run away but that you had nowhere to
          run to. Now, that was absolutely awful. Lonely,
          lost; romantic, striving. How I would have felt for
          you, how I would have longed to bring you
          comfort—to reach out and clasp that homeless,

questing hand! Also I've discovered ... But no. Now it's your turn. Perhaps I've robbed you of your powers of speech?

HAROLD   You ... you say that you enjoy riding?

HESTER   Riding? It's my very favourite sport.

HAROLD   That's incredible.

HESTER   Don't tell me that you, too ... ?

HAROLD   Oh, yes! *Yes!* How often do you go? *Where* do you go?

HESTER   Well, I haven't been for years. No one to go with. But I used to ride a lot at Radlett and then, too, there's a stable near Moor Park, and—

HAROLD   I haven't ridden for years, either. Hester, sometime couldn't we ride together? Doing things alone is never half so good.

HESTER   Because you've no one to keep you up to scratch, no one to laugh with!

HAROLD   No one to compete with! (They laugh) You've been quite a revelation, too.

HESTER   I have?

HAROLD   Yes, do you know, I didn't even want to come here tonight? I tried to persuade Flora to meet me in the West End. But she insisted ... and it looked as if she might begin to sulk.

HESTER   Flora's always been a little spoilt. That's what
         comes of being so pretty.

HAROLD   Yes . . . How can one be so wrong about people?

HESTER   You're right. I'll never again put my trust in first
         impressions.

HAROLD   Did you know, that was the original title of *Pride
         and Prejudice*?

HESTER   But I would never have expected you to. Not, that
         is, until tonight.

HAROLD   Still waters . . .

HESTER   The strong and silent type.

HAROLD   He who walks alone . . . I'm sounding smug but it's
         true. I don't have many friends. (Suddenly) May I
         pour myself another drink?

HESTER   Harold, do you think you should?

HAROLD   To celebrate friendship.

HESTER   Of course! Then why not? Live dangerously!
         (HAROLD pours more whisky) But you will phone
         for a taxi? (He nods) And you will try not to fall
         asleep in the theatre? That wouldn't be fair on Flora.

HAROLD   Oh, I can tell you—not a faint chance of my falling
         asleep!

Door opens. FLORA comes in, wrapped in bath towel and holding
her sherry glass.

FLORA   Just to let you know I'm on my way. It hasn't been too painful, has it? (Looking from one to the other)

HESTER   We are doing our very utmost to survive.

HAROLD   Lonely, lost and striving.

HESTER   With elephants a somewhat unexpected threat.

FLORA   Elephants? What on earth are the two of you talking about?

HAROLD   Be good, little girl, and I might enlighten you later. But for the moment why don't you just run along and dress? Before we find we've missed not only the overture but most of the first act.

FLORA   All right, darling. But can I have a tiny refill for this? Or—better still—not such a tiny one.

HAROLD   (In a low voice, to FLORA) As the actress said to the bishop.

FLORA   (With anxious glance at HESTER, who is again at the radiogram) Harry! Darling! Shhh!

HESTER   (Turning; wanting to share in the joke) What's that?

FLORA   Nothing, Mummy. Nothing.

HESTER   (Disappointed; even faint hint of resentment) Oh? I thought one of you said something amusing.

HAROLD   I made a very feeble joke. I was just being infantile. Also, it was rude. (He pours the sherry)

FLORA   And not in character. What have you done to him?

HESTER   (All resentment clearing) Ah . . .

FLORA   As a matter of fact I thought I heard the pair of you laughing a short while ago. And more than once. *Was* it you? Or was it the people in the next flat?

HESTER   Oh, it must have been the people in the next flat. Laughter? In here? Unthinkable. I shall complain to the management.

FLORA   (Pleased; puzzled) What *have* you been up to?

HAROLD   Now, then! Just take your drink and run away and get decent. There's a good girl. (She's about to go, still amused and somewhat baffled, when inconsistently he stops her) But first . . . a toast!

FLORA   Oh, nice. What to?

HAROLD   I don't know. To a pleasant evening. And a happy life. To the three of us. (They all raise their glasses) To us! To friendship!

FLORA   To us! To friendship! (Pause) Friendship?

HESTER   To love and friendship. To love! To all of us!

FLORA   Ah, yes. That's better.

The three of them drink solemnly.

The curtain falls on Act One.

ACT TWO

ELLEN and TONY, as before.

ELLEN   And of course it just went on from there. Whoosh!
Your grandmother and your father had fallen in
love. And that evening saw the start of an affair
that would last four years.

TONY   I don't believe it! Gran! My father! For God's sake,
Ellen—she was nearly thirty years older than him.

ELLEN   She was fifty-three. Some women in their fifties can
be more attractive than they've ever been. Look at
Joan Collins.

TONY   Gran was never Joan Collins.

ELLEN   No, she was far classier. And more subtle. I mean,
more subtle than Alexis. But in her own way she
was equally ambitious. She knew what she wanted.

(Stands—and sings) "Whatever Hester wants . . .
Hester gets . . . and little man, little Hester . . . wants
you!" I used to do a fairly decent tango in my day;
but never—that I can remember—with a rose in my
mouth. The things one misses! *Thés dançants*,
before the war. I hear they're coming back . . . I still
had certain aspirations then.

She has plucked a rose out of Hester's flower arrangement; she
now inspects it for thorns—then puts it between her teeth and tangoes
flamboyantly across the room. TONY, also standing, watches. A bit
impatiently. When she has finished, he doesn't clap.

TONY   But my father. He wasn't attracted by older women.
            I can remember he told me that.

ELLEN   (Thrusting the rose back in its vase) Probably made
            rather a point of it, too. His second marriage, by all
            accounts, has turned out fairly well. Isn't she about
            ten years older? I haven't met her.

TONY   (Smiles, reluctantly) All right. You win.

ELLEN   And in psychology-speke, mightn't he even have
            been looking for a new mother? It seems that,
            previously, he hadn't done any too well in that
            department.

TONY   (By now they've sat down) But Ellen. How do
            you know all this? Are you sure that you're not
            simply . . . ?

ELLEN   Making it up? Taking a belated revenge because
            your grandmother and I have never quite . . .

TONY   No, not making it up. Of course not. But . . . but . . .
perhaps allowing your imagination . . . Misconstruing
things . . .

ELLEN   I know all this because I was told.

TONY   Whom by? And whoever it was . . . how could *they*
have known about it any more than you? (Pause;
ELLEN holds his gaze) No, I don't believe it! . . .
Gran?

ELLEN   Gran.

TONY   But why? (Helplessly) When?

ELLEN   When? Fairly near the start. Certainly within the
first few months. Why? Because we'd just had
words and she was putting me in my place. I'd said
my life was arid and she'd told me, in effect, I had
no one to blame but myself. Probably true—but,
still, it wasn't what I wanted to hear. So I shot back
that I couldn't see her own life was any the *less*
arid. And that's when it all came out. With no room
at all for misconstruction. She told me how
wonderful your father's lovemaking was and how it
made her feel young again, and alive, and
unmistakably needed.

TONY   (Pause) But . . . lovemaking? Remember that when
Gran was young 'making love' didn't mean the
same as it does today.

ELLEN says nothing. TONY proceeds, quite tonelessly.

TONY   And anyway. Mum's given me the impression—
more than once, in fact—that my father's

lovemaking was . . . well, quite a long way from being wonderful.

ELLEN   And she's the one whom I'd definitely prefer to believe. All this emphasis on sex nowadays: how it can make the earth move; how you've never known what life is until you've known what love is. Well, who was it who said the position was ridiculous and the pastime overrated?

TONY   I think it was Somerset Maugham. Maybe not the world's *greatest* authority. (Aware that he's been tactless) But he *could*, actually, have got it right.

ELLEN   At all events, not an exponent of one-upmanship—well, not in this case, anyway. (Pause) Of course, one mustn't be too hard upon your gran. She was angry when it all spilled out; otherwise it wouldn't have happened. I'd touched her on the raw.

TONY   Did she ever mention it again?

ELLEN   How do you think I know it lasted four years? The next time it came up was only a day or two later; she rang me to apologize. And if I were really so unhappy with my life, she suggested, couldn't we maybe talk about it—try to find some way of improving matters? You know how she's always setting out to help. Just look at all the blind people she has here to meals; how she's constantly taking one or other of them to the West End, by bus, to make their shopping easier and to treat them to a nice tea. *I* certainly couldn't cope with any of that and I'm three years younger than she is. And you know the way someone only needs to send out

291

some kind of SOS and she'll go to unbelievable
lengths to try to set things right. Without any air of
sacrifice or condescension . . . just with her usual
good humour and an instinctive feel for what's
going to put them at their ease . . . (Pause) Where
was I, before I started on all this?

TONY   Gran rang to apologize.

ELLEN   Oh, yes. Well, I came round here and we chatted
and she gave me all sorts of hopefully useful advice
but . . . Anyway, after we'd done what we could with
my situation, we again got round to the subject of
herself and Harold. What did I feel she ought to do?
Well, my suggestions to her were no more helpful
than hers to me, but by the end of that couple of
hours I found I'd become her confidante - which
wasn't at all what I'd have wanted—and yet I found
it flattering too . . . None of your other great-aunts, so
far as I knew, ever had the least inkling of what was
going on.

TONY   And my mother?

ELLEN   During those four years? Not the shred of an idea.
Well, who would have? Naturally, there must have
been moments when she felt excluded—what with
the horse-riding and the concerts and the various
other things which Hester and Harold had found
they had in common. Not that Hester would ever
have meant to exclude her—not consciously. But
during that time I felt extremely sorry for your
mama. Yet . . . what could I do? And in any case,
even without Hester, that marriage was doomed. In
a way, absurd though this sounds, those were
probably its four best years.

TONY   And why did it finish? The . . . affair.

ELLEN   I think it just sort of fizzled out. They went on
           being good friends—respecting one another. But
           apparently the sexual side of it . . . it simply waned.
           Isn't that what often happens?

TONY   Between a man in his twenties and a woman in her
           fifties? I haven't a clue. (Pause) And so my mother
           never realized?

ELLEN   Oh, yes . . . eventually. Some six years later she found
           out. Don't ask me how. But *that*, you see, was the
           reason for the divorce—not this guff about your
           father demanding an abortion.

TONY   You mean, he didn't want one?
ELLEN   He might have suggested it—halfheartedly. It's true
           he didn't want children. But he certainly wouldn't
           have issued an ultimatum. He had too strong a
           sense of responsibility.

TONY   Sounds like it!

ELLEN   Well, the affair with your grandmother was a *coup
           de foudre*. It caught him off-balance and he felt
           powerless against it. It made him step completely
           out of character. Or, at least, appeared to.

TONY   (Pause) So then my mother cited my grandmother
           as co-respondent? The papers must have had a field
           day.

ELLEN   Certainly they would have had. But she filed only
           for cruelty. Not for adultery.

TONY   Oh, surprise, surprise. Biddable to the end.

ELLEN   Tony, that's unfair! (Pause) For although it *is* true,
              it's only a part of the truth. I'm sure there was also
              consideration for the feelings of others.

TONY   As well as her own.

ELLEN   You mustn't blame your mother for this.

TONY   I know. I know. (Almost a wail) It's just that she
              was so weak!

ELLEN   (Regarding him steadily, yet not commenting on
              this) She changed after she found out. All her *joie de
              vivre* vanished. All her vitality. Not only was it the
              shock—and one can easily imagine just *what* a shock!
              But I think in some way she felt guilty. Exactly as you
              do now—after what has happened here this afternoon.
              And with every bit as little reason.

TONY   No. Thirty years ago *she* wasn't the one who set all
              that business in motion. Whereas this afternoon—

ELLEN   She may have felt she did . . . by being too dull, by
              being too uneducated. Too uninteresting.

HESTER enters: subdued and stony-faced. TONY stands up.

HESTER   (To TONY) We've been talking, your mother and I.
              And we've come to a decision.

TONY   (Cold) Oh, yes?

HESTER   How much is your university grant?

TONY   Why?

HESTER   Would you answer me, please.

TONY   Roughly two thousand a year.

HESTER   And what does your father have to pay towards it?

TONY   About half.

HESTER   Yes, that's what your mother thought. Very well.
            Here's our plan. You can take it or leave it but if
            you decide not to take it you'll be an even greater
            fool than I think you.

ELLEN   (To HESTER) My goodness. What a career you
            could have had in selling.

HESTER   (Ignoring her) You told us you'd been offered a job
            which paid you a hundred pounds per week—five
            thousand a year. Now . . . if you go on at university
            for the next two years I shall give you three
            thousand pounds for each. I can ill afford it and it
            will naturally make a big difference to what I'll be
            able to leave your mother but we are both resigned
            to that. I have already tried to telephone your father.
            Perhaps he can increase his contribution, though I
            haven't the least idea what his reaction to that is
            likely to be—horror and outrage, without the
            slightest doubt! Unhappily he had just that minute
            left his office. Be that as it may, you'll have your
            five thousand a year—so that you can support this
            woman and her two children in a style far richer
            than they've been accustomed to, and at the same
            time fulfil the hopes which your mother and I have
            always placed in you. What do you say?

295

TONY   No.

HESTER   No?

TONY   (Softer tone) Thank you. Obviously I appreciate your generosity—and self-sacrifice—and good intentions. Both of you. But, no, I can't do it.

HESTER   (Ironically) You have your pride?

TONY   Yes—as a matter of fact.

HESTER   And would an extra five hundred a year go any way towards assuaging that?

TONY   No, of course it wouldn't. What do you think I am?

HESTER   An ingrate. And a very deep disappointment to every one of us. But here's what I'll do. Against my better judgment I'll even provide an extra thousand. Which will give you a whole *six* thousand a year. I must warn you, however, that that is my final offer. My very last word on the subject.

TONY   I don't care if you provide an extra ten thousand. Or twenty. No.

HESTER   And can you explain your reasons?

TONY   Yes. It's a matter of principle.

HESTER   What principle?

TONY   I have to make my own way.

HESTER   What, without any degree or qualification? And with nearly four million people out of work?

TONY   Plus, I don't want to feel beholden.

HESTER   You wouldn't need to feel beholden. By the time you're thirty—and with a good degree behind you—you could be earning anything up to twenty thousand a year, twenty-five thousand, possibly even more. Then you could start paying back what we've given you—paying it back to your mother if not to me; we can think of it merely as a loan. But without a degree, you'll be lucky to rise above seven or eight thousand. Ever. And what kind of a life do you suppose you'll be able to lead on that?

TONY   (Pause) Money isn't everything.

HESTER   Oh, what idealistic pap! I've got to sit down. (She sits; TONY doesn't) *You* may think you're very grown up and wise but *I* think you've simply taken up a position, dug in your heels, and aren't man enough to say, "Well, yes, perhaps I've been mistaken. Perhaps I *ought* to be listening to my elders, ought to be grabbing at this lifeline they're holding out to me—a *loan*, after all—it isn't charity!" But your 'pride' won't let you, will it?

TONY   (Moving abruptly towards the door) I'm sorry but I've got to go.

HESTER   You do realize, don't you, that you're not in love with this girl?

TONY   And what do you know of whether I'm in love with her or not?

HESTER   At best it's just infatuation. Infatuation with *her*—infatuation with your own self-image, and noble stance.

TONY   No, it's not like that at all.

HESTER   (Pause; as if genuinely puzzled) Does it mean nothing to you—absolutely nothing: all the dreams and hopes which those who love you have invested in you? Is it so terrible that they only want you to get on, to make a place for yourself in this world, carve out a fulfilling career, since they themselves know what it is to have failed? You see, *I* have no pride, I don't mind telling you my life has been a disappointment—and if you asked your mother I'm sure she would say the same about hers. *We* have made a mess of things: largely, perhaps, because we didn't have the opportunities: though whatever the reason is—whether it's our own fault or simply the fault of circumstance—doesn't in the end make a lot of difference. *You* have the opportunities. This is a golden age. You have the brains (Here HESTER suddenly has her tongue in cheek again) if only you would choose to employ them; you have the personality; you have the grit. Is it so wrong that your mother and I should simply wish to see our own lives haven't been lived completely in vain—that all the waste and error have finally added up to something wonderful . . . in other words, my darling, to *you*? Because—don't you see?—*your* salvation is also our salvation. Is that so horribly selfish an ambition for a mother and grandmother to entertain? Please don't go until we've talked about it further.

TONY is still standing at the door, although his determination has clearly wavered during this last speech.

TONY   I've got to go, anyway. But I'll think over what you've said.

HESTER   Do you promise?

TONY   I promise. In any case, there's nothing I can do till Monday.

HESTER   But when will you let us know? Tomorrow?

TONY   Or Sunday. Sunday at the latest.

HESTER   Try and make it tomorrow. You know we shan't get any rest until we've heard. You're very precious to us. We only want what's best for you, you know that.

TONY   Yes.

HESTER   (Now standing, walking halfway to the door and holding out her arms to him) And, darling, you're not leaving without kissing your silly old granny goodbye? You know that even in the best-regulated circles people have their little . . . disagreements. It's only because they care about each other and feel so dreadfully concerned. You need to look at what's beneath those sometimes, I confess it, ill-considered words, rather than at the unclear, hasty things they express. Even grandmothers aren't altogether perfect.

ELLEN   You surprise me. (This, as TONY returns to kiss HESTER)

HESTER   (Releasing TONY from a somewhat overlong
          embrace) And, as you go, don't forget to look in on
          your mother. She's in my bedroom. I think she may
          still be feeling . . . just a little unhappy.

TONY   I wouldn't have forgotten. And I'll also look in on
          Mr Davis.

HESTER   No, that isn't necessary. Not if you're late.

TONY   Except that I told him I would.

HESTER   Oh, then of course you must.

TONY   Besides, I'd like to. (Goes to kiss ELLEN) Goodbye,
          Aunt Ellen.

ELLEN   Why the return of the 'aunt'? It was Ellen only a
          short while ago.

TONY   I'm sorry. Force of habit. Ellen.

ELLEN   (Lightly) Yes, you mustn't regress. I've greatly
          enjoyed talking to you. Visit me sometimes. I'm
          nearly always at home.

TONY   Yes. Yes, I will.

ELLEN   And when you say you'll do a thing, we all know
          that you mean it.

TONY   I hope so. See you both. (To HESTER) Thank you
          for the tea.

HESTER   God bless you, my darling. I'll be in great suspense
          while awaiting your verdict. Do make it as merciful

as you can. Besides as quick as you can. Don't forget that at my age even a single day can make a difference.

TONY nods; goes out. HESTER sits—sighs—pauses.

HESTER   (Cont; pleasantly) What *were* you both talking about?

ELLEN   Oh, this and that . . . I think, Hester, I may as well be on my way, too.

HESTER   I thought you were staying to supper.

ELLEN   (Patting her stomach) No, I've had enough tea to last me for a week. At home I never bother much with tea . . . unless I've a visitor. In particular a young one. (Gets up)You'll say goodbye to Flora for me? I'm sorry that she's so upset.

HESTER   Thank you. But I'm sure she'll soon be feeling better. *Very* soon, one hopes.

ELLEN doesn't respond to this. They kiss each other on the cheek. HESTER starts to rise.

ELLEN   No, no, don't get up. I'll see myself out.

HESTER   (Sinking back again) Well, if you're sure, dear . . . I can't deny that I'm a little tired.

ELLEN   It's been a tiring afternoon.

HESTER   Yes. But he is only nineteen. It would be surprising if one didn't occasionally have such little contretemps.

ELLEN looks at her a moment—then again takes the rose from the vase, puts it in her mouth and does the same snazzy tango to the door. To the same tune.

HESTER (Amused) What on earth are you doing?

ELLEN (Taking the rose from her mouth) The tango, for heaven's sake! Don't say you didn't recognize it?

She repeats the dance, back across the room, once more replacing the rose in its vase—then back towards the door. Now singing the words.

ELLEN "Whatever Lola wants, Lola gets, and little man, little Lola wants you! Make up your mind to have . . . no regrets; recline yourself, resign yourself; you're through!" Oh, I forgot my handbag. (She goes back to collect it, from the floor beside her chair, then again dances to the door) "I always get what I take aim for—and your heart and soul are what I came for . . . " (Now with Lola's Spanish accent very much accentuated) "You're no exception to the rule. I'm irresistible, you fool—give in! Give in! Give in!" There! Doesn't that remind you of the Café de Paris in the old days? (Leaves, then puts her head back round the door) Just singing for the supper that I never got!

HESTER Ah, is that what it was? I thought you might merely have gone gaga.

ELLEN Oh, I've thought that for years! Perhaps it runs in the family. One of its more appealing characteristics. (Goes)

HESTER suddenly wilts. Is evidently dead beat. But after a short time arouses herself and, with an effort, stands.

HESTER   Must go to see how Flora is. (Heads for the door;
          stops) Or perhaps I'd better wait until he's gone?
          (Sighs) Oh, Tony, Tony, Tony! . . . Still. What can
          you expect? At nineteen? (Stands irresolute,
          thinking about something) At nineteen . . .

She goes and sits; then almost at once rises again; crosses to radiogram, looks for a certain record, puts it on turntable.

HESTER   No, Ellen, this is *not* a tango! (It is Elgar's
          Chanson de Matin. For a while she listens to it
          reflectively) Nineteen . . .

Then she returns to her seat. The lights go down. When they come
up again, most of the stage is in darkness. We can just see HESTER sitting in her armchair on the periphery but she is well outside the pool
of light that illuminates the centre. Here we discover the nineteen-
year-old HESTER, dressed in the style of 1923. She is circling restlessly
around the perimeter of this small space, happy, excited, evoking the
impression of somebody soon to be granted a release.

MAX walks into the pool of light; it is in fact a summerhouse. He's
about forty—not a particularly robust or young-looking forty—but
quietly attractive.

MAX   Ah, Hester, you got here first. (She runs to him;
          they embrace, then draw apart) Stand still a
          moment. Let me look at you. You know, even after
          nearly four weeks, I still can't quite believe it.

HESTER   Tell me again about the ways in which I've changed
          over these past five years.

MAX   No matter how often I tell you, I can't do the
          transformation justice.

HESTER   But try.

MAX   My darling girl, you were fourteen years old. I remember you only as a sweet and serious and appealing child—

HESTER   Sweet? You never said sweet before. I'm not sure I care too much for sweet. Nor serious either, come to that. You might as well tell me I was insipid and dull and have done with it. No, Max, you must do better than this. You have done better than this.

MAX   You're like a child listening to a favourite fairy tale. You can't bear to have even one sentence altered.

HESTER   So, then, why do what I can't bear?

MAX   The trouble is I can't remember how I've phrased it in the past. Was I all right with 'appealing'?

HESTER   Appealing is . . . well, so-so. Bewitching would be better. Striking. Captivating. Irresistible. But I certainly hope I shan't be required *unendingly* to prompt.

MAX   Ah, me. Did I happen to say before . . . ?

HESTER   What?

MAX   . . . that you've become tempestuous!

HESTER   No, you didn't. But don't think you're going to provoke me. At least that isn't dull.

MAX   No, my dearest, there's nothing about you that I
           recall as dull. So will tempestuous find favour?

HESTER   Yes, that's . . . acceptable. At least it's a thousand
           times better than moody—or sulky, Have you
           noticed how Agnes and Ellen are most terrible
           sulkers? But even so. Is appealing and tempestuous
           as much as I'm going to get?

MAX   Oh, not at all.

HESTER   So?

MAX   So heaven help us. What a demanding little minx
           you are. Please don't forget there were six of you—
           and that you were all very much of an age.

HESTER   Upon my word, there's gallantry!

MAX   And truth—which counts for more than gallantry.

HESTER   Well, now. I might agree with you, if there *were*
           any truth in what you said. All right, we were six;
           that much we can let you get away with. But since
           our ages, dear Uncle Max, happened to range from
           fourteen down to eight . . .

MAX   Don't call me that, my dearest girl—please. For one
           thing, it makes me feel so old.

HESTER   Well, we'll see. It depends on whether you can
           remember ever referring to me as unusually
           intelligent. You did once, you know.

MAX   Oh, I remember that exceedingly well.

HESTER   Where?

MAX   How can I say where? I know I've thought it about you so often it's hardly surprising if I'm a bit foggy as to where I actually said it.

HESTER   (Laughs) Well, that at any rate is one you've wriggled out of quite successfully. And if not with truth, at least with gallantry. And resourcefulness. And ingenuity. And invention. In short—I almost admire it.

MAX   Thank you.

HESTER   But it was here, you evil man—here in this summerhouse. We were having a long conversation about the War, just the two of us, and about Mr Asquith and Mr Lloyd-George and you told me you'd never come across any fourteen-year-old *so* intelligent or with such very decided, well-informed views. You said that all my sisters were outshone by me as if they'd been five small candles flickering in the sun.

MAX   Did I say that? Did I use such a cliché?

HESTER   I've never forgotten it.

MAX   (Looking about him) At least I remember how this old summerhouse provided such an excellent trysting place . . . Or, at any rate, if I don't remember it *exactly*, I most certainly ought to. You've reminded me often enough; been so incredibly patient with me.

HESTER   And the reason we never got discovered? (As if wanting, however needlessly, to emphasize her determination in the teeth of a male-dominated society) Because I informed the others the place was full of spiders. Naomi and Agnes became convinced it was a breeding ground for black widows. Probably even dreamed about it.

MAX   Oh, Hester, you didn't? So beautiful and yet so cruel? Besides—Ellen would never have swallowed that. And Ellen . . . Ellen would never have invented such a frightening story.

HESTER   Don't speak to me of Ellen! And don't pull that long and disapproving face—I tell you that I shan't stand for it! The thing is, we didn't want to be disturbed, did we? And short of putting up a sign on the door . . . ? (Pause; now a lot more tender) And do you remember how every time we came in here you would treat me so completely like an adult and talk to me about all manner of things? About books you'd read and plays you'd seen and the sort of life that actors and actresses sometimes led in private— and about King Edward and his mistresses and Jack the Ripper and ladies of easy virtue—

MAX   Oh, Hester, no I'm sure I didn't!

HESTER   Oh, Maximilian, yes I'm sure you did! I don't say that you yourself ever brought these subjects up but when I asked you questions, you never pretended that you hadn't heard. So don't grow old-maidish on me now! Mother would have had a fit if she could have heard some of the answers which you gave—and as for Father, if he'd been alive . . . !

MAX   Your father, yes; there I would agree with you. But your mother wasn't—isn't—in the least straitlaced.

HESTER   Well, admittedly, she might seem different to a brother than to a daughter.

MAX   I suppose that's true. But I still don't think she'd have had a fit at anything she heard me say.

HESTER   (Coyly) What about at anything she saw you do?

MAX   What do you mean?

HESTER   Don't you remember how you used to sit me on your knee?

MAX   Good God, Hester, you make it sound . . . I don't know what . . . like something sordid.

HESTER   Sordid? Oh, it was never that—forgive me if you thought for one moment . . . I'm only teasing, can't you see that? For me it was so far from being sordid . . . It was so lovely to sit on your lap, it was thrilling, it was . . . heaven. Then as now, I used to treasure up my thoughts of it and bring them out whenever I felt wretched. I'd draw such reassurance from them, such energy, such strength . . .

MAX   And, after all, what could have been more natural between any uncle and his niece who were always such very good friends? I also used to push you on the swing, I remember, and run beside you in the paddock, while you cantered round it on your pony—

HESTER   Yes, but you used to push the others too at times and give *them* piggybacks and allow them to come bicycling with us. (Laughs) I used to get so cross.

MAX   (Laughs too) Like I say. A minx.

HESTER   I hope you didn't kiss them!

MAX   Hester! (More softly) What do you think?

HESTER   Ah . . . And I also think you haven't finished telling
           me—or even started telling me—about this grand
           transformation that you found.

MAX   (Impetuously) I'm glad you drew such strength and
           reassurance from all the time we spent together! I
           know that *I* did.

HESTER   (Shaking head) No, that isn't true. How could it
           be? Otherwise you wouldn't have gone away and
           left me for five years. You wouldn't have said
           —(Mimicking)—"Well, there were six of you, you
           see, and you were all very much of an age . . . " So be
           careful . . . Uncle Max. I know you better than you
           think I do.

MAX   (Smiles) And yet I insist—somehow—it is true. In
           part. A sort of mystical truth. I can't explain it.

HESTER   That's most convenient. (Though clearly appeased.)

MAX   Because I was pretty tired when I returned from
           France. Jaded, old, confused. Just like so many of
           the rest of us: the ones, I mean, who were lucky
           enough *to* return. Those moments that I had with
           you—they proved even more important than I
           would have guessed. At the time, they were hugely
           welcome respites from . . . from having to remember;
           which in itself was sufficient blessing. But later—
           all those years in America, while I was trying to get

started there; trying, perhaps, I can't be sure, trying to run away—they came to stand for . . . impressions of innocence, of childlike spontaneity, something pure and incorruptible . . . Does that sound a bit pretentious? I told you I shouldn't be able to explain. But you . . . yes, perhaps you lost your identity as Hester, a little . . . but in that muddled, shell-shocked brain of mine you somehow came to symbolize virtue and simplicity and all those things which were good and well worth clinging onto life for . . . Maybe it isn't very complimentary but—

HESTER   (Holding her finger to his lips) Oh, yes, Max, it's the most complimentary thing you could possibly have said. Like poetry. Truly to stand as the embodiment of such virtue in a war-torn hero's troubled mind . . . Please don't say another word. I'm just afraid you'll spoil it.

MAX   I wasn't such a hero.

HESTER   Oh, yes, you were. I won't hear otherwise! (Strikes a stance, brandishes her rapier) And I'll fight anyone who tries to tell it differently!

MAX   Including me? That's just it. I've never been a natural fighter. I've hated—hated—having to fight. (Sees her fleeting look of disappointment) But I'll tell you one thing that I *am* willing to fight for. Us! Our future. The flouting of convention.

HESTER   The flouting of the law!

MAX   Yes . . . Well . . . Thank God at least that *you're* not too conventional.

HESTER I'd rather be dead first. And thank God that you're my mother's favourite brother. What's more, thank God you're on your way to becoming her richest one also—and will be able to provide not only for us, but for her and the girls as well.

MAX Hester, my dear.

HESTER Why, what's the matter?

MAX It's one thing to be a little unconventional because your situation dictates it. It's another to put things into words *unnecessarily* . . . No, it's the way that you put them into words. You make them sound almost like some kind of commercial transaction. This isn't in the least like that. As I told you just five minutes ago, your mother is a very unusual and exceedingly broad-minded woman and—

HESTER Yes, but how else could I put them into words? Money does make a difference. And I'm not a hypocrite. And never shall be. (Pause) Max, I don't care about money for its own sake. I care about it for the good it can do; for the people whom it enables you to help—whether the lepers and the outcasts of this world, or my own mother and sisters.

MAX I'd be helping your mother and sisters, anyway, whether or not the two of us were marrying.

HESTER Yes, I know. You've a kind heart and a commendable sense of family. But I'm awfully glad that into the bargain you happen to be handsome.

MAX   Thank you.

HESTER   Naomi was telling me she thinks it's terribly
romantic. (Laughs) But she would probably think it
even more so if you were poor!

MAX   (Involuntary; almost stern) Naomi is not your
mother! (Quickly) Even if Katy had been left well-
provided for—which was very far from being the
case—it could never have been easy to bring up
six daughters. As it is, it's almost impossible to
overstate your mother's bravery. Or to realize what
a struggle she must have had over these past
thirteen years. (Pause) And the fact you girls were
largely unaware of it makes such an achievement
all the more remarkable.

HESTER   Yes, poor mother! Poor, poor mother! (With sudden
spurt of laughter) And, apart from anything else,
only imagine having six daughters!

MAX   I don't suppose she'd wish to exchange any one of
them.

HESTER   Maybe not, maybe not. But *I* want boys—boys—
nothing but boys! So do you; did I remember to
mention that?

MAX   I wouldn't mind just one little girl amongst them.
So long, naturally, as she'll be the spit and image of
her mama.

HESTER   When I've presented you with five sons I might
come up with one little girl, as a reward. No, I will;
I truly promise. I'm going to make you such a good
wife. In every way. I shall always look after you

most splendidly . . . in return, of course, for your looking after me! When I'm fifty you'll be over seventy—just think of that—but you'll be the best-looked-after old gentleman anyone ever set eyes on. So wise and good and well-regarded. The world will say, "Those two—since the beginning of time they were surely meant to be with one another!"

MAX   That's very kind but—I'd rather you didn't dwell on them too much, those twenty years. I keep telling myself I'm your cousin, not your uncle. Do you realize that at this time in five weeks we'll be on our way to Austria?

HESTER   Married in Vienna! Naomi's right: it *is* romantic! It's almost like Robert Browning and Elizabeth Barrett.

MAX   But they didn't marry in Vienna.

HESTER   No, but the principle's the same—they, too, had to bundle off in secret. Nor would *they* have been able to send out invitations. However, I don't suppose they had so much in the way of close community; far fewer to close ranks around them and be all nice and Jewish and supportive. Though the Brownings did have the march on us in one respect: they settled in Italy, under blue and sunny skies; we've got to settle in London, amid the chills and swirling fog.

MAX   Ah, but after Vienna did they spend a week in Paris?

HESTER   (Instantly throwing off mock gloom) No, they didn't! Paris! How I've always wanted to see Paris! What a perfect place to spend the last part of your

313

honeymoon. And by the way, Max, just in case you should be worried, I know that I'm the first of my sisters to get married but that doesn't mean I haven't heard all about the facts of life or that—

MAX   Hester!

HESTER   You keep on saying "Hester!"—you're much more prudish than you used to be. I think I'd better warn you: every time you say Hester in that tone I shall wait until we're next in public and very loudly call you Uncle Max. That's a promise. Even when we're registering at the Georges Cinque on honeymoon. Even when we're living in sin in London and taking the children on their Sunday walk. Even on the steps of the synagogue and saying good morning to the rabbi—if we should ever go to any synagogue or say good morning to the rabbi.

MAX   Hester, we shall not be living in sin. We shall have been married in a legal and binding ceremony, we shall have all the proper documents to prove it.

HESTER   But not proper or legal in *this* country, as you well know, my dearest.

MAX   I do so wish you wouldn't interrupt! And as *you* well know, too, that's nothing but a technicality, it—

HESTER   Technicality—oh, fiddlesticks! We may fool the rest of the world, Max, but we're not going to start fooling each other. Our sons will be illegitimate and we shall love them all the more for being so.

MAX   Hester, I have to say it: I don't like you in this mood.

HESTER   Very well. Then go and find somebody else to
         marry! And see if I care!

Then, with a toss of her head, half playful, half genuinely exasper-
ated, she runs out of the summerhouse. The circle of light fades, but
comes up again immediately, over the eighty-three-year-old HESTER,
still seated in her armchair. *Chanson de Matin* will have finished by
this time. YOUNG HESTER and OLD HESTER look at each other for
a moment, sadly.

OLD HESTER   Oh dear. (She starts to cry)

YOUNG HESTER   Yet you deserved your unhappiness. You
                tricked him, didn't you? He was so easy to
                deceive. Shell shock had muddled all his
                memories.

OLD HESTER   It wasn't only for myself—I did it for
                Mama, as well. She had so much to bear.

YOUNG HESTER   Yes. Mama's life became a lot easier.

OLD HESTER   And I was nineteen—quite old enough to
                be married. Ellen, at sixteen, would have
                been far too young.

YOUNG HESTER   Besides, you meant to help her later—as
                well as wickedness, there was a real wish
                for kindness that underlay the act. You
                even told yourself she might be better off.

OLD HESTER   It was too disgusting, the way he used to
                kiss her. Fondle and kiss her. I heard them
                through the door. I peeked in at the
                window.

YOUNG HESTER   But, oh, how it aroused you! You loved his wrists and hands. His eyes were kind and he was handsome but—yes, how you loved his wrists and hands!

OLD HESTER   Well, that excitement quickly died.

YOUNG HESTER   Also, of course, you wished to be the mistress of your own household, to have your own staff. The first of all your sisters to be wed, to have the run of London theatres and expensive restaurants. You imagined a salon—yourself the gracious hostess. Yes, you'd become a source of encouragement and inspiration: to writers, artists, men of wit. (Pause) And your feelings for him *were* real; or at least you persuaded yourself they were, and is there any difference? He was a hero who had been all through the War. He had experience—money; you had exuberance —youth. He would take care of you; and you . . . you would nurse him back to former strength—and enthusiasm—and drive, and make of him the man you thought he had it in him to become. It was a kind of . . . glorious challenge.

OLD HESTER   And I did make him a good wife. I kept my promise. And afterwards—after the first great disappointment, after those early years of disillusion—gradually, so gradually that I scarcely even noticed— I warmed to him again . . . though never in that same way. He was prissy and self-pitying and I felt contempt; but proximity

and shared interests and gratitude and
good intentions—*his* gratitude and *his*
intentions—though mine as well at times—
over the years, these built up a membrane
of affection. I think he never guessed—no,
no one ever did—at my awareness of the
magnitude of my mistake. Continual
awareness. But I had made my own bed
after all; and I lay down on it—to the best
of my ability.

For a moment she covers her face with her hands then suddenly
looks up again, with renewed vigour, at HER YOUNGER SELF.

OLD HESTER   (Cont) But you! At nineteen. With
                  energy. With beauty. With your whole
                  life in front of you. You could have done
                  so much. Cherished each passing day;
                  achieved some little thing, pinpointed
                  some thought, some act, some new
                  experience—salvaged *something* of
                  value, no matter how small, from every
                  one of them, those passing days; written it
                  down, given it substance, saved it from
                  oblivion. Just one good turn a day—and
                  think what your life could have been, and
                  how your passing would be mourned.
                  You didn't know, you didn't see, you
                  were so stupid—I have no patience with
                  you—shoo! Shoo! Just leave me be!

And she waves THE YOUNGER HESTER off, in disgust.

OLD HESTER   (Cont.) Dear God, how long have I got
                  left? My mother lived till eighty-six; her
                  mother was the same. Supposing I still

have a full three years to go? Three more
summers; three more springs. Over a
thousand days. A thousand! That's a
wonderfully long time. A thousand days
could make up for a lot. Used properly,
they could make up for almost
everything. I shall tick them off one by
one and try to treasure every minute of
my time. Only . . . pray God I don't go
senile. Pray God I don't go deaf or lame
or that I don't develop cancer. Don't let
me lose my memory. Let me use these
days to think only about others; let every
one of them contain some shining deed.
Oh, if somehow I could just be *sure* about
those thousand days! (Pause) Dear God.
Help me. Let it all have meant something.

She is clearly invigorated by her prayer. Gets up, walks about the
room, starts to move around it with a certain bounce, a rhythm; finally
follows Ellen's example and breaks into a tango—though without the
rose. She hums the same tune Ellen did; but she doesn't know the
words and makes no attempt to use them.

In the midst of this, FLORA comes in; stands watching in amaze-
ment.

FLORA   (Extremely flat through much of what ensues) You
         seem very happy. Where has Ellen gone?

HESTER   Oh, Ellen went home; she said to say goodbye. Yes,
         darling, I *am* very happy. And so must you be. It's
         all going to be all right.

FLORA   Yes, I've just been talking to Tony. He seems . . .
         well, less sure of himself and of what he's going to do.

HESTER   (Nods) I'm certain Tony is going to be sensible. I
           think he's seen the error of his ways. I've seen the
           error of mine, as well.

FLORA   Meaning what?

HESTER   Meaning we shouldn't try to push him. We should
           try to give him room to breathe.

FLORA   Whether he stays on at college or not I don't want
           him living with that woman.

HESTER   Darling, we have to accept it. She may not be a bad
           girl. Not *la crème de la crème*, of course, but even
           so she may do him some good and he may do her
           some good and her poor little boys as well—we
           mustn't forget *them*. Perhaps we can have them all
           to lunch one Sunday—the Sunday after next,
           maybe—and take them up to the Heath or to the
           zoo and buy them all ice creams. Treats and
           outings; that does everyone some good. I wish he
           hadn't left. I should like to have suggested it.

FLORA   He hasn't. He's gone in to see Walter. But, Mother,
           please. Don't rush things. Let's think about it for a
           while. I'm not even sure if I could bear to meet her
           at the moment.

HESTER   Darling, I understand exactly how you feel. But
           we've got to make the best of it. Otherwise we'll
           only alienate him—which of course is the last
           thing any of us wants.

FLORA   To be honest, right now I don't feel I very much care.

HESTER   Besides. You might like her. Might find she's rather good company. She may be someone to go around the shops with—while Mary and I look after the children. You could take her to the cinema. And Tony said the boys are sweet. It could be almost like having your own grandchildren.

FLORA   Oh, stop it, Mother. Stop it! Don't!

HESTER   Flora, sweetheart, what's the matter? Come and sit down. You're overwrought. Let me get you something to drink. A brandy, perhaps—how would you like a brandy?

FLORA   No, I don't want anything. I'll be all right. (She sits)

HESTER   (Also sits) Why don't you sleep here tonight? Go to bed in your old room. Have a hot-water bottle. A mug of Horlicks. Propped against a comfy mound of pillows. In the morning you can lie in and Mary will bring you breakfast. And the papers. You need a spot of coddling. I don't think you've had nearly enough of it—I don't think you've had any—not for far too long a time.

FLORA   No, of course I must go home. It's only round the corner. And, anyway, I haven't got any of my night things with me.

HESTER   No, darling, I've made up my mind; you know I'm irresistible. And as for your things—we can walk round and collect those later. Or I'm sure we could find you a nightie and a spare toothbrush. You said yourself that you don't like being by yourself in that great empty flat; that you detest your own company —and that sometimes you get frightened.

FLORA   But, Mother, I'm not a child. I mustn't give in to such silly things as that.

HESTER   In fact, I've an even better idea! I don't know why we never thought of it before. You must give up your flat and you must move in here. That's the obvious answer. It will save you a lot of money and it will be lovely for the pair of us. Flora, you can't think what it would mean to have you here again, under this roof. It would be just like old times; it would be just like turning back the clock.

FLORA   (Wistful) Turning back the clock?

HESTER   Wouldn't that be wonderful? And we'll do such things together. *We'll* have outings. Theatres, lunches, concerts. I'll educate you, darling. I'll make you appreciate good music. You'll be forever grateful.

FLORA   Well, I must say—you make it sound quite tempting. I do get very low at times. Ever since Tony left home.

HESTER   I know you do, my pet. Don't think your mummy doesn't know about these things. But that's all done with now. No more loneliness. No more feeling down. (Laughs) I won't allow it, do you hear! I'll even teach you how to tango.

FLORA   (More animated) Oh, have you forgotten that I once won a dancing medal? Anyway, why were you doing the tango?

HESTER   Following in dear Ellen's footsteps. She suddenly got some bee in her bonnet, just before she left.

Here, darling. Together. I haven't danced a proper
tango in about six centuries.

She gets up, almost pulls her daughter to her feet. FLORA at first
resists but then they hold hands and step out solemnly, with some
gusto on HESTER'S part; with readiness to please, rather than real
enjoyment, on FLORA'S. Still to that same tune from *Damn Yankees*—
which HESTER hums alone at first but which FLORA eventually
accompanies her in They don't do very well, however. After a turn or
two they come to a laughing halt.

HESTER   (Cont.) There you are, then—you can teach *me* the
            tango. And the foxtrot. And the bunny hug. And
            then *we'll* go off to the discos and show all these
            silly young things how they ought to be dancing!

FLORA   Well, we'll have to see. I mean, about my moving
            in. I don't want to agree just on impulse.

HESTER   But you will stay here tonight?

FLORA   Yes.

HESTER   And you really find the idea quite tempting?

FLORA   Yes.

HESTER   I promise you—no more spaghetti; I won't permit
            any spaghetti within a mile or so of this house.

FLORA   (Laughs) Flat!

HESTER   (Pause) Exactly. Do you know . . . for a moment just
            then . . . oh how ridiculous . . . I was almost thinking I
            was back at Ashford—you know, the house where
            I grew up. I half-dozed for a few minutes just now.

I was remembering a little bit about the old days. (Pause) Flora, darling?

FLORA   Yes?

HESTER   I want you to forgive me—if ever I've been a less than proper mother to you. No, please don't say anything. I know I've had my failings. If ever I've done things which . . . or said things which . . . I'm sure you know what I'm talking about but even apart from all of that . . . Well, from now on it's going to be so different. I'm going to make it up to you. I've decided that at the very least I shall live for another three years . . . and without losing any of my faculties. Because, you see, Tony told me I wasn't programmed to lose even one of them—and the fact that only this afternoon he should have made such a comment seems to me a truly remarkable sign. Practically a message. So that gives me a good thousand days in which to atone. Probably more but I'm not going to rely on it.

FLORA   Oh, Mother, please. There's nothing you have to atone for. And you'll probably live another *twenty-three* years.

HESTER   I love you, my darling. I love you very much. Did you know that?

FLORA   (Embarrassed) Of course I did. And I love you, too. I'm only sorry that I haven't been more . . .

HESTER   More what, darling?

FLORA   More clever. More witty. More entertaining. I'm under no illusions about the way I am. I'm not

323

surprised that Harold left me. Or that Tony did. I
think I must be very boring company.

HESTER   (Takes her in her arms) No, Flora. I won't have you
talk that way! What an absurdity. Who cares about
being clever? You've always been so sweet and
attentive and . . . Well, tell me this: would I be
asking you to come back to live with me if I found
you such a bore?

FLORA   I suppose not.

HESTER   There you are, then.

FLORA   I wish I could have liked horses.

HESTER   No—no more of this nonsense. (Gives FLORA'S
shoulder an abstracted pat and releases her) Tell me
something. *Was* it just this afternoon that Tony
said that about my faculties? Or was it the last time
he was here? Time goes so fast—sometimes it's
hard to keep track.

FLORA   I . . . I don't know . . . I . . . (With sudden resolution)
Yes, I'm sure it was this afternoon.

HESTER   Dear Tony. He's really such a credit to you. You
should feel very proud.

FLORA   I don't feel anything much at the moment. Proud or
otherwise.

HESTER   You will. Oh, you will. All you need now is a good
night's sleep. And that you're most definitely
going to have. I shall give you one of my Valium.

FLORA   Oh, I don't need—

HESTER   No arguments now. Mother knows best.

FLORA   I feel about eight again.

HESTER   And tomorrow, maybe, you'll feel about eighteen and that will be even better.

FLORA   Will it? All right . . . yes, eighteen . . . if you say so.

HESTER   But, darling—about Tony. I feel sure he's going to be sensible and do the right thing. I know he will, I just feel it in my bones. Yet even if he doesn't we're not going to make a fuss. University or no university. The decision now is his. We've said all we can. If he still chooses to . . . to go his own way . . . well, then we must simply accept it. And wish him well. And not make him feel guilty.

FLORA   He'll simply destroy his life, that's all. And mine. And make the whole thing seem so utterly pointless.

HESTER   What whole thing?

FLORA   Why, the whole business of having children and then planning your life around them.

HESTER   Oh but Flora, my angel, that's an awful thing to say. I'm sure you don't mean it. You don't have children just in order that they'll be successful. You can't live *your* life through theirs—or expect to be a puppet-master who can always pull the strings. They're more than mere extensions.

FLORA   Who's talking about . . . puppet-masters?

TONY comes in.

HESTER   (To TONY) Darling, I thought you'd gone.

TONY   I've been talking to Mr Davis.

HESTER   And I'm sure he must have appreciated it. Dear
Walter. It takes so little to make him happy. The
other afternoon—Mary was out—I gave him a slice
of bread-and-butter for his tea. For some reason I
happened to fold it over before presenting it to him.
"By Jove," he said. "Sandwiches!" I was so moved
I just had to kiss him. "That's very nice," he said,
"whatever have I done to deserve that?" "Walter," I
told him, "you have stumbled upon the secret of
contentment."

TONY   And what did he say?

HESTER   Oh, he chuckled—you know the way he does. "In
that case, Madam, don't think you can worm it out
of me by playing Mata Hari!"

TONY   (Pause) At the moment, Tennyson's still very much
on his mind. He knows quite a lot about him. All
fascinating stuff.

FLORA   Especially if you haven't heard it about a thousand
times before.

TONY   (Indulgently) Oh—you! If he were telling you for
the very first time you still wouldn't be paying
much attention.

FLORA   It's today I live in, not a hundred years ago.

HESTER   A hundred years hence, as he always tells us, none
            of this will make a jot of difference.

FLORA   Yes, that's just the senseless sort of thing he would
            say.

HESTER   (To TONY) Your mother's still a bit upset.
            (Brightly) Well, how about a glass of sherry,
            everyone? I think that's the remedy we all require.
            (To TONY) Though I hope you're remembering to
            keep an eye on the time? We don't want you late
            for your appointment.

TONY   (Glances at watch) No, I'm all right for another few
            minutes.

HESTER   Sherry, then?

TONY   Yes, please.

FLORA   It's a couple of *hours* hence—that's what worries me.

HESTER   Yes, darling; but you must do what you can not to
            let it.

FLORA   Besides, it isn't even true. A hundred years hence it
            will make a vast amount of difference. If Tony gets
            a good job and a good income and mixes with nice
            people, then he'll marry a better class of girl and
            have a better class of child. That child, as well, will
            mix with better types. In a hundred years' time,
            therefore, his great-grandchildren could either be a
            credit to their country or just a drain on its
            resources. Why, with *this* girl he may not even

have children; perhaps she won't want any more.
Of *course* it makes a difference!

TONY (To HESTER; attempting lightness) See what a snob
you've nurtured in your bosom!

FLORA Yes, I may be a snob; but at least I'm honest about
it. I do like nice things and I do like nice people.
And anybody who says they don't is only a
hypocrite.

TONY Don't look at me. I also like nice things and nice people.

FLORA So how many of them do you think you're going to
meet along the Mile End Road?

TONY Yard for yard? Oh, about the same number, I
suppose, that I'd meet around the corner, in West
End Lane.

FLORA Well, I'm sorry, but I beg to differ.

TONY Then, Mum, that's your prerogative and no one
plans to take it from you.

HESTER (To TONY) Darling, in view of your mother's
slightly distressed condition, you couldn't perhaps
give us a tiny hint, could you? About the choice
you're going to make regarding university?

TONY Yes, that's why I came back. But feeling as she does
about the Mile End Road I can't see that either
choice would help to make her happy. I could
become as educated as all get-out and still be
leaving her dissatisfied.

HESTER   (Standing behind FLORA and making urgent gestures for TONY to see; yet managing to keep her tone quite light) Now, Tony, sweetheart. A little understanding, if you please.

TONY   (Impervious to the gestures; voice still full of repressed anger) Understanding of what?

HESTER   (Patiently) Understanding of the fact that others have their needs—not just yourself.

FLORA   Understanding of the fact that I don't give a damn about your education! That I don't want you going to live with some trollop in the East End whose boyfriend killed himself with drugs and whose children will turn out to be exactly like him! That I don't want you mixing in bad company because . . . oh, yes, Tony, you may think I don't know you but I promise you I do! I know how easily you can be influenced by whoever you happen to be around at the time! Live with riffraff . . . you turn into riffraff!

TONY   Then I'd better get out of here pretty quick, hadn't I?

FLORA   Understanding of the fact that I won't have you living with any woman. Not any woman—do you hear?—not even Carol Klingman. You're nineteen, you're a child. Some nineteen-year-olds, perhaps . . . But you—you've always been extremely immature, even at the best of times. A woman of twenty-four would make mincemeat of you, just twist you round her little finger—especially her type of woman. And you do realize, of course, that she's only after the money she thinks you've got—not you, maybe, but your family? I suppose you do at least realize that? Because there's no other reason—no other reason at all—why a woman of her age would ever want to go to bed with a boy like you. Did you think you were a man? No. You're a meal ticket and she's a prostitute!

HESTER   Flora, Flora, stop this, do you hear? You don't know what you're saying. You too, Tony, stop it! Show her that you aren't so young—that you're quite man enough to make allowances. In fact, darling, I think you ought to go. I'll get her to bed; she's going to spend the night here. Why don't you just slip away quietly? Then you can come back tomorrow or the next day—whenever it's convenient.

TONY   I shan't need to. I can give you my decision now.

HESTER   I meant simply, come back to find out how she is. And to give her a chance to say she's sorry. To make your peace with one another.

TONY   Do you realize, when I came in here I was all prepared to do as she wanted—to do as you both wanted? To accept your terms. Sitting there in my usual armchair, talking to Mr Davis, listening to him reminisce just as I've done for roughly the past dozen years . . . I don't know . . . I began to think . . . just listening to him talk about Tennyson . . . But now—

HESTER   I don't want to hear about *but now*! In the first place you're not in the right frame of mind and in the second (Indicating his mother) at present I have more important matters to attend to.

TONY   I shall be leaving college and I don't want any of your money. Nor my father's.

HESTER   I told you that I don't want to hear! We're just not
          listening to you at the moment.

FLORA   (To TONY) And I suppose you *are* going to live
          with her and destroy yourself? Just like that other
          man did?

TONY   Yes, quite probably. And I'll be sleeping with her
          every night, as well. Every night—do you hear?
          You'll recognize me by the bags beneath
          my eyes.

HESTER   I'm not hearing you. I can't hear you. (Trying to
          push TONY to the door; failing; opening it and
          standing at it herself; calling) Mary! Mary! Please
          come and show Mr Anthony out. He's just leaving.
          Please come and show him to the door.

FLORA   (To TONY) You're disgusting. You—are—
          disgusting! And I shan't recognize you by the bags
          beneath your eyes, because I shan't be seeing you
          again. Whenever you come here I shan't be home,
          and you certainly needn't think that I'll ever visit
          you in the Mile End Road—or at your potato crisp
          factory—because I wish to make it plain right now:
          I shan't.

Enter MARY; smilingly oblivious.

MARY   (To HESTER) About a minute ago Mr Davis came
          into the kitchen asking if it was time for tea! And he
          didn't even know that Mr Tony was here—not
          until you called out just now. Poor old fellow. He's
          really very sweet. (To TONY) And he sends you his
          compliments and hopes you're well; and if you
          should happen to have a few minutes left to spare

there's something he'd like to say to you about
some poetry by Mr Tennyson.

She laughs. This interruption has given TONY a moment to cool
down. He just stands there, stricken and deflated, looking about the
room, as if imagining it could be for the last time.

TONY   You know I didn't mean all that.

HESTER   I'm afraid we never seem to know for very long
            what you do mean or what you don't. (To MARY)
            Mr Anthony is just leaving. Will you show him to
            the door, please.

TONY   I said I was sorry, didn't I? What more do you
            want?

HESTER   (Hard) We want to know whether you'll be staying
            on at college. You say you're sorry? Well, let us see
            that. I'm afraid sorry is as sorry does.

FLORA   (Hard) And we want to know whether you'll be
            keeping clear of that prostitute.

TONY shakes his head in disbelief, making his answer to both
these questions abundantly clear.

HESTER   (To MARY) Then will you just do as I ask, please,
            and show my grandson out? No, that's not right.
            From now on I have no grandson. Therefore, will
            you just do as I ask, please, and show this person
            out?

MARY stands at the door, helpless, unhappy, holding it open.
TONY shrugs and walks towards it.

HESTER   (Cont.; to TONY) But, first . . . (TONY pauses) I
          want you to understand this completely. That unless
          you change your mind—on both points—on *both*
          points, mark you—then not only your mother but I
          as well will never wish to set eyes on you ever
          again. *Ever!* And you needn't think to come
          crawling back to us as soon as you find yourself in
          some kind of a fix, because—Mary, do you hear
          this?—this gentleman is never to step foot inside
          this flat again, unless I've first given you express
          permission to admit him.(To TONY) And I suppose
          you realize what that means? Not only will you be
          cut off from your family but also from any kind of
          benefit I have no doubt you hoped to gain when any
          of that family died. Nowhere to call home; nowhere
          to spend Christmas; nowhere to be nursed when you
          are ill . . . You have until Monday to consider this.

TONY looks at FLORA. FLORA says nothing. She and her mother
make a solid front.

HESTER   (Cont.) And it also means—please bear this in mind
          —it also means that you won't be seeing Mr Davis.
          Does that carry a little more weight? Invariably he
          asks, "Is Mr Tony-sir coming for dinner tonight?"
          Every day of the week. Every day of his life.
          Without fail. "Is Mr Tony-sir coming for dinner
          tonight?"

TONY   (Hesitates; ironic) I imagine you won't stop me
          from writing to him?

HESTER   (Shrugs) No, I can't stop you from writing to him.
          And any letter you send him, of course, will be
          faithfully delivered. But any letter you write to us
          will be put back in the box, unopened.

FLORA   Address unknown! So you'll never get it back. You'll never quite know.

TONY   Fine. Well, that suits *me* all right. Goodbye, then.

HESTER   You have until Monday, remember. (TONY doesn't stop in his journey to the door) And while we're about it—remember something else. That obstinacy —and wanting to appear strong, in control, unbeatable—has always been one of the greatest forms of weakness there is. In the end it will destroy you.

TONY   (Pausing only briefly) Goodbye.

HESTER   You realize you'll regret this?

TONY   Yes. I realize that whichever course I take I shall almost certainly regret it.

He goes. MARY closes the door behind them both. FLORA stands looking at the door. Her face suddenly crumples. HESTER goes to her, puts her arms about her, leads her to a chair; FLORA allows herself to be led. HESTER finally pours the sherry.

FLORA   I was just remembering, how he took me out to dinner on my birthday. And this lovely bracelet that he bought. (Holds up her arm to display the bracelet)

HESTER   Don't worry. He'll be back. For all his pathetic show of independence.

She brings FLORA a glass of sherry. Raises her own, in a toast. At first she has to make a real effort to sound positive; but then, admirably fast, begins to find it easier.

HESTER   (Cont.) Yes, happy days, my angel! Oh, Flora, that's right: let's drink to happy days—to over a thousand of them! Happy, happy days! Filled with treats and outings; theatres, concerts; holidays abroad! A little game called *Making up for lost time*! Yes, the lovely little game of making up for lost time ... And how about this, my love, as soon as we can put it into practice? Should we invite them here to lunch one Sunday—say, the Sunday after next—and then take them into Golders Hill Park; either that or up to the Heath or over to the Zoo? (Pause) Can you still, I wonder, be given rides on the backs of animals? As a child, how I used to love going for donkey rides along the sands! In any case we'll buy them ice-creams ... or candy floss if they'd prefer it ... and buckets and spades if they don't already have them ... and take them somewhere very nice for tea, possibly find a little place that overlooks the bay? (Pause) Oh, but there's one thing I definitely do know, my precious—and please don't look so shocked or disbelieving—one thing I shall most definitely be able to promise you. (Pause; raises her sherry glass again, as if to add extra weight to such a heartfelt declaration) I'm going to do everything that lies within my power to make you happy ... so *very* happy, my darling ... *all of you* ... and there's absolutely nothing in this world that's ever going to stop me!

She sips her drink, while pleasurably contemplating the possibilities already busily suggesting themselves—and, slowly, very slowly, the curtain falls.